gathering
the
bones

gathering the bones

Original Stories
from the
World's Masters of Horror

EDITED BY

Dennis Etchison, Ramsey Campbell and Jack Dann

A TOM DOHERTY ASSOCIATES BOOK
New York

GATHERING THE BONES

Copyright © 2003 by Dennis Etchison, Ramsey Campbell and Jack Dann

A Tor Book
Published by Tom Doherty Associates, LLC
175 Fifth Avenue
New York, NY 10010

www.tor.com

Tor® is a registered trademark of Tom Doherty Associates, LLC.

Library of Congress Cataloging-in-Publication Data

Gathering the bones : original stories from the world's masters of horror / edited by
   Dennis Etchison, Ramsey Campbell and Jack Dann.—1st ed.
      p.   cm.
     ISBN 0-765-30179-2
     1. Horror tales, English.   2. Horror tales, American.   I. Dann, Jack.   II. Campbell,
Ramsey, 1946–   III. Etchison, Dennis.

PR1309.H6G38 2003
823'.0873808—dc21

2003042617

First Edition: August 2003

Printed in the United States of America

0 9 8 7 6 5 4 3 2 1

COPYRIGHT ACKNOWLEDGMENTS

Copyright Acknowledgments

This book is dedicated to
Kirby McCauley,
Jenna Felice
and Cherry Wilder

ACKNOWLEDGMENTS

The editors would like to thank the following people for their help and support:

Theresa Anns, Jeremy Byrne, Ginger Clark, Sean Cotcher, Lorne Dann, Tom Doherty, Andrew Enstice, Christine Farmer, Moshe Feder, Linda Funnell, David Hartwell, Patrick Nielsen Hayden, Merrilee Heifetz, James Herd, Barrie Hitchon, Dorothy Lumley, Jennifer Marcus, Sylvia Marson, Shona Martyn, Jim Minz, Rod Morrison, Brian Murray, Maja Nikolic, Richard Parslow, Stephanie Smith, Nick Stathopoulos, Jonathan Strahan, Norman Tilley, Maria Tsiakopoulos, Janeen Webb, John Wilkinson and Kaye Wright.

CONTENTS

Introduction
Dennis Etchison, Ramsey Campbell and Jack Dann   15

The Hanged Man of Oz
Steve Nagy   17

The Bone Ship
Terry Dowling   31

Li'l Miss Ultrasound
Robert Devereaux   42

The Intervention
Kim Newman   59

Blake's Angel
Janeen Webb   77

The Obedient Child
George Clayton Johnson   87

Contents

Sounds Like
Mike O'Driscoll   93

The Wind Sall Blow For Ever Mair
Stephen Dedman   109

"The Mezzotint"
Lisa Tuttle   123

The Lords of Zero
Tony Richards   135

Smoke City
Russell Blackford   146

Moments of Change
Thomas Tessier   162

The Big Green Grin
Gahan Wilson   173

Both And
Gary Fry   178

Love Is a Stone
Simon Brown   194

Memento Mori
Ray Bradbury   203

The Mistress of Marwood Hagg
Sara Douglass   211

The Right Men
Michael Marshall Smith   225

Contents

The Raptures of the Deep
Rosaleen Love
234

Out Late in the Park
Steve Rasnic Tem
240

Bedfordshire
Peter Crowther
246

Mr. Sly Stops for a Cup of Joe
Scott Emerson Bull
270

Finishing School
Cherry Wilder
278

Jennifer's Turn
Fruma Klass
288

Mother's Milk
Adam L. G. Nevill
295

No Man's Land
Chris Lawson and Simon Brown
307

The Watcher at the Window
Donald R. Burleson
321

Coming of Age
Joel Lane
330

Picking Up Courtney
Tim Waggoner
339

Watchmen
Aaron Sterns
352

Contents

Gardens
Melanie Tem   365

Under the Bright and Hollow Sky
Andrew J. Wilson   375

The Dove Game
Isobelle Carmody   399

Tiger Moth
Graham Joyce   423

About the Authors   435

About the Editors   445

INTRODUCTION

BY DENNIS ETCHISON, RAMSEY CAMPBELL
AND JACK DANN

Tales of Terror from Three Continents!

This was a subtitle we three editors discussed for this anthology, and it pretty much sums up our intentions for the book.

We set out to illustrate how vast and international the scope of the genre has become and the vitality of writing to be found in it as the new century begins. To that end, each editor solicited a third of this volume's contents in his own country of residence—Ramsey Campbell in Great Britain, Jack Dann in Australia and Dennis Etchison in the United States. Our intention was to present the familiar and the experimental, the traditional and the avant-garde, the quiet and the vividly shocking, in a field whose boundaries are no longer rigidly defined and where literary values coexist with the leading edge of popular culture. There is no need for a narrow, constricted theme to inhibit the imagination, for dark fantasy is truly an international fiction without limits.

We were struck not only by the range of the tales we've collected, but also by how some of their themes echo across the world. The big city and its fears are present in tales by Tony Richards and Scott Emerson Bull, while Aaron Sterns discovers the supernatural under the masks of a familiar urban profession. Russell Blackford shows us how vampires have grown up with the city; the late Cherry Wilder has fun with a related and perhaps more civilized species. As Michael Marshall Smith reminds us, however, urban menace need have no supernatural excuse, and Gary Fry elucidates some of the moral horrors involved.

Some of our authors touch on science fiction. Robert Devereaux and Fruma Klass are speaking of the future, we hope, although in both cases it's uncomfortably close to the world we know. Kim Newman's satirical nightmare also illuminates the way we live now. Peter Crowther and Melanie Tem warn us that our childhoods may still lie in wait for us, and George Clayton Johnson finds another dark route they can take to adulthood, while Joel Lane deals with a generation gap that has turned cultural too. Nor is old age necessarily a refuge from anything—Steve Rasnic Tem's surreal piece tells us that—but Ray Bradbury, unpredictable as ever, suggests how even death can be an occasion for fun.

Ghosts are here. They appear in the trenches of the First World War in the story by Chris Lawson and Simon Brown, and in Graham Joyce's story they offer the protagonist a second chance. They revenge themselves on a racist in Stephen Dedman's contribution, and steal identity itself in Donald Burleson's, but despite her title it is no traditional specter Lisa Tuttle has for us. Sara Douglass tells of the power of witchcraft to exact a fitting revenge.

Not all our contents are fantastic—Thomas Tessier and Terry Dowling demonstrate the continuing vitality of the conte cruel—but the bizarre has been our keynote, whether in the marine upheaval Rosaleen Love envisions, the backyard ogre Gahan Wilson depicts, or Adam L. G. Nevill's household that might almost have been dreamed by a fevered Mervyn Peake. Simon Brown's femme fatale is a rare example of her species, and Janeen Webb's angel brings visions, as tales of terror should. Tim Waggoner's terrible old lady undermines reality itself, as do the cosmic horrors conjured up by Andrew J. Wilson, literary gamesmanship by no means lessening their power. Stephen W. Nagy might even make us wary of playing the recent DVD of a famous musical, just as Mike O'Driscoll leaves us afraid to hear. On the other hand—we have six between us—Isabelle Carmody offers the unrivaled pleasures of the enigmatic.

And now, having stirred the cauldron, we three depart into the gloom. We only chose the ingredients, the authors—their magic did the rest. Their dreams and nightmares have lit up our imaginations, and now we cast their spell on the world.

The Hanged Man of Oz

BY STEVE NAGY

Knee-high grass dominated the scene, thick blades uprooting the foundation of a sagging cabin, pushing aside cobbles in the shaded road. Trees circled the clearing and an abandoned orchard lay behind the cabin, straight rows masked by weeds and windrows of dead leaves and forgotten fruit.

A pastoral display except for the people posed throughout—two middle-aged men, one dressed as a hobo, the second clad in a dirty threadbare uniform; an old woman sporting too much rouge and mascara, skinny legs visible beneath the hem of a little girl's dress; and a dead man, hanging from a tree, his feet twitching at odd moments in time with some unheralded tune raised by the wind whistling through the forest.

Obsession is an art form.

And if you're lucky it's contagious.

Denise and I got together for dinner and drinks at her place. Our first date, although we saw each other in the apartment hall every day. I lived in 2B. She had moved into 2C in February. I'd made great strides, starting with an occasional nod and shared rides to work. I'd eventually thrown out an off-the-cuff comment about her hair, which she'd shorn from its ponytail length to a flapper-style skullcap. Guys should notice changes like that; it's an easy way to score points.

After that first compliment, the progression from casual to intimate was natural. We left in the morning at the same time, talked about our days, compared notes on work. If you practice something enough, anything is possible. I knew the boy-next-door routine better than when to observe national holidays. And the Fourth of July doesn't change from year to year.

Besides dinner and drinks, Denise made me sit down and watch *The Wizard of Oz.*

"You've seen this before, Michael?"

"Lots of times," I said. "Not lately, though. Isn't it usually on around Easter?"

"Until recently," Denise said. "Ted Turner bought the rights and pulled it for theatrical release."

Oz? God save me. I already regretted the date and struggled to keep an interested expression as Denise gave me the inside scoop. It was like a psychotic version of *Entertainment Tonight.*

When I was in college I worked at a greasy spoon as a busboy. The chef was a compact Italian named Ricky Silva who came across as uneducated, unhealthy and gullible. I stayed late one night, and I found Silva pouring over a stamp collection in a back booth. I questioned him about it, saying something crass because the idea of Silva as a philatelist didn't match my preconceptions. He told me there were an infinite number of worlds. Each existed next to the other, always overlapping and occasionally intertwining. Learning about his deeper reality forced me to change my opinion of him.

Denise and *Oz* were like that. The places she went and the things she did contained wholly unexpected layers. Up until now I'd only seen her "hallway" face.

But I wasn't in Kansas anymore.

The trivia litany went like this:

Buddy Ebsen—the original Tin Man—almost died from pneumonia, suffering a bad reaction to aluminum dust from his makeup, which let Jack Haley jump into his metal shoes.

The Cowardly Lion's costume was so hot Bert Lahr passed out at least a dozen times.

The Munchkins raised so much holy hell on the set that Chevy Chase mined that aspect for *Under the Rainbow.*

Shirley Temple led the pack for Dorothy's role. Probably because everyone considered Judy Garland too old and a poor box-office draw. The movie lost money, costing about $4.6 million and earning only $4 million the first time out.

Studio executives cut a groundbreaking dance number that showcased Ray Bolger. They believed audiences wouldn't sit through a "children's movie" if it was too long.

Faulty special effects burned Margaret Hamilton at the end of her first scene as the Wicked Witch. This was shortly after Garland arrived in Oz. Hamilton tried grabbing the ruby slippers, but was thwarted by the Good Witch, an actress named Billie Burke. Hamilton dropped below the stage and right into a badly timed burst of smoke and flame . . .

It went on and on and on, everything you never wanted to know. Peccadilloes, idiosyncrasies; in other words, crap.

Then Denise told me a story about the man who hanged himself during filming—and she claimed the final print showed the incident.

"What? You're kidding me. I've never seen a dead guy."

Denise licked her lips, imitating a poorly belled cat. "Not everybody does. It's like those 3-D pictures where you cross your eyes."

"Prove it."

Denise paused the video. Onscreen, Dorothy and the Scarecrow were in the midst of tricking the trees into giving up their apples, frozen seconds before stumbling across the Tin Man.

"It's at the end of this section. I'll run it through once at regular speed. Let me know if you catch it."

She hit PLAY. Dorothy and the Scarecrow freed the Tin Man, did a little song-and-dance, fought off the Wicked Witch and continued their trek. I didn't see anything strange and shrugged when Denise paused it again.

"Nothing, right?" She rewound the tape to a point immediately after the witch disappeared in a cloud of red-orange smoke (this time minus the hungry flames), then advanced the video frame by frame.

Our date had progressed from strange to surreal, and I couldn't wait for an excuse to leave.

Then I saw *him*—the hanged man.

Dorothy, the Scarecrow and the Tin Man skipped down the road. Before the scene cut away to the Cowardly Lion's forest, the jerky movement of the advancing frames highlighted activity inside the forest edge.

A half-shadowed figure moved in the crook of a tree about ten feet off the ground. I thought it might be one of the many birds spread throughout the clearing and around the cabin, but its shape looked too much like a man. The next frame showed him jumping from his perch. His legs were stiff, as if bound. Or maybe determination wouldn't let him go all loose and disjointed at this defining moment. Before his feet touched the ground, they wrenched to the right. Whatever held him to the upper branches swung his ill-lit body back into the shadows. I think I heard his neck snap, although with the tape playing at this speed there wasn't any sound. Even at regular speed I knew the only sound would come from the three actors, voicing in song their desire to see the Wizard.

My heart raced and for a minute I worried that its syncopated thrum might attract the Tin Man, prompting him to step into the apartment and take it for his own.

"I can't believe it," I said. "It's a snuff film."

"Awesome, isn't it?" Denise restarted the film. I couldn't interpret her smile as kind; it seemed too satisfied. "I stay awake some nights," she said, "letting my mind experience what it was like. The studio buried the whole thing. Can you imagine the bad press? I even think Garland started drinking because of it."

On the television screen, Bert Lahr made his appearance. His growls matched the rough nature of Denise's monologue. As the film continued I offered small talk, made Denise vague promises that I would see her in the morning, and left as the credits rolled.

"I feel as if I've known you all the time, but I couldn't have, could I?"

"I don't see how. You weren't around when I was stuffed and sewn together, were you?"

"And I was standing over there rusting for the longest time . . ."

I knew I was asleep, sprawled on my couch. The past five days had stretched me to the limit. I always had a headache. Aspirin and whiskey didn't kill the pain. My conversations with Denise were forced; she mentioned the movie at every opportunity.

We'd had a second date. I agreed because Denise invited two friends from her work. Stan and Lora were nicotine addicts, rail-thin and shrouded in a pall of smoke. I think Denise brought them along so she could (one) look good in contrast and (two) so she had someone to turn to if things went sour with me. We hit a club and during a busy night on the dance floor I demonstrated I wasn't a klutz. I guess you could say it was the modern social equivalent of an Army physical. Denise and Lora exchanged approving nods near the end and Stan loosened up enough so that he took a minute between shots of tequila and his chain-smoking to talk to me.

Between all the alcohol and nicotine, I got a contact buzz and found myself obsessing about the hanged man and the way he disappeared into the shadows. Denise was still attractive to me, but I couldn't forget how pleased she'd looked as she talked about the death.

My thoughts hid me beside the Tin Man's cabin, watching the trio skip past. I would move onto the road. The hanged man was visible ahead. They must have turned their eyes to follow the road as it bent to the right because they didn't see him.

But I did.

Denise had seemed like her old self in the mixed company, and I assumed I was overreacting. So I agreed to a third date. Instead of a rerun with the mystery man in the trees, I got Stan and Lora again and a nice restaurant. I was almost happy when I saw their wan faces.

Almost. Denise and Lora left to powder their noses, and Stan asked me a question.

"How did you like the movie?"

"What?"

"You know what I mean. You look like you haven't had a good night's sleep in a while."

"How do you know that?"

"Denise is predictable. I'd be more surprised if she hadn't shown you the film yet."

I gulped my beer. "You've . . . seen him?"

Stan shrugged. "What about it?"

"The guy hanged himself. She seems so glad."

"Someone dies somewhere every second. Get used to it. Life will get a lot easier if you do."

Before I could ask what he meant, Denise and Lora returned from the bathroom.

I had the dream again the next night. It started at the same point. The Tin Man finished his dance, stumbled off the road, collapsed in a heap on a tree stump near the cabin. The others rushed to his side, Technicolor concern painting their expressions.

No one noticed me. I couldn't hear everything they said. It *did* seem to change from night to night, probably because I could never remember the dialogue verbatim.

The Wicked Witch screeched at the three adventurers from her perch on the roof above, surprising me again. I crouched and prayed she wouldn't see me. She tossed a fireball at the Scarecrow and even from this distance I felt the heat. The Tin Man smothered the flames under his funnel hat, but not before the silver paint bubbled and blistered on the edges and several of his fingers.

The Wicked Witch took off on her broom. Smoke billowed like a tumor in her wake. No trapdoors this time; my position offered an excellent view behind the cabin. Her flight left a rough scar across the sky that traced the road's path toward the Emerald City and beyond to the land of the Winkies.

"I wonder how many she'll kill when she gets home?"

I jumped from my crouch. The Scarecrow stood beside me. Dorothy and the Tin Man remained in the road. Instead of the concern I'd seen earlier, they appeared curious.

"What are you doing?" I glanced toward the trees. The hanged man swung from his rope, as solid as a mirage, flirting with the shadows. I turned back to the Scarecrow. "You're supposed to be on your way to the Emerald City."

The Scarecrow, who looked less and less like Bolger, dropped his gaze and shrugged. The simple gesture produced a sound reminiscent of dead leaves. "I'm not supposed to tell you," he said, his words more rustle than speech.

Dorothy and the Tin Man, poor doubles for Garland and Haley, edged toward the bend. "We have to go, Scarecrow," the not-Garland said. "There's not much time left and we're expected."

The Scarecrow joined them. "I'm not supposed to tell you, Michael," he repeated. "Talk to Stan." He glanced toward the trees one last time as he and his companions moved away. "Stay away from the Hanged Man."

I woke drenched with sweat. I don't know what had happened after the three left. Maybe they found the Cowardly Lion, became a quartet, maybe not.

Stay away from the Hanged Man.

Even the memory of those words hurt.

Talk to Stan.

What was I involved in here? Were my dreams random subconscious processes? Talk to Stan? I didn't even know his last name. I only knew Denise's—Fleming—because the apartment manager had glued labels to the lobby mailboxes. When we met, we exchanged greetings and first names. Surnames never came into it because right from the start we were always personal.

Too many hours remained until dawn. I left the apartment and hit Kroger. The big grocery on Carpenter stayed open all night—and its video selection included *The Wizard of Oz.*

I wanted a copy because . . . because I wanted privacy. I'd need Denise soon enough to find Stan, if I gathered the courage to broach the subject. The hanged man was a drug and I was a junkie. If I had my own copy, I might control the addiction. I'd first seen him with Denise and everything stemmed from that. I'd entered one of Silva's infinite worlds; privacy might let me create a new perspective.

The shadowed streets looked different than they did during the day. The late-night wind didn't touch the trees. Each moved on its own, apple hoarders, ready for a rematch.

"Just wait," a voice rasped beside me. "It gets worse."

I shouted and slammed the brakes. My car swerved, shuddered to a halt and stalled. I turned and found myself facing the Scarecrow.

"What do you . . . what do you want?" I tried sounding angry, but my voice shook.

My Scarecrow smiled and the maw formed by his mouth—old burlap, leather and rotting hay—made my stomach turn. "I won't hurt you, Michael." He nodded toward the back. "But I can't speak for her."

I twisted in my seat and craned to look. A shape huddled there, its outline weird and broken by too many angles. I fumbled to turn on the overhead dome light, but the person in the back actually *cackled* and I leaped out of the car and into the deserted street.

I tripped before I'd gone a half-dozen steps. Scrambling up, I looked over my shoulder, expecting pursuit—and saw nothing. The door was open and the dome light revealed the empty interior. The only sound was the chime that signaled the keys were still in the ignition.

This isn't happening, I told myself. *The Scarecrow was in the passenger seat and the Witch—yes, the Witch—was in the back.*

A soft noise broke the breathless silence. I saw something slowly swinging in the shadows of the trees across the way. I knew the noise was a rope creaking under the strain of a dead man's weight. I retreated to my car, more scared of what hid outside than of my elusive passengers.

The residential speed limit was twenty-five. I did at least fifty and ran every red light getting home.

Two hours more till dawn.

I shredded the box wrap and popped the tape into my VCR. My head throbbed with too many ideas, as if I'd overdosed on coffee and Tylenol. I let it play and tried to clear my mind. I tried to tell myself there was no place like Oz. And this time the scene ran the same as I remembered it from my childhood.

The Tin Man stumbled and landed on the tree stump. Dorothy and the Scarecrow ran over to help. The Wicked Witch made her threats, threw her fireball, bolted in a puff of smoke. The three adventurers danced off down the road.

There wasn't any sign of the Hanged Man.

There was movement among the trees, but I could see it was a long-necked bird moving one of its wings. Was there something different on Denise's tape? I didn't consider myself gullible but I didn't trust my eyes. I rewound the tape and played it again, cursing myself for doing that.

The Tin Man collapsed on the tree stump. But he didn't resemble Haley. His fingers and hat were burned, warped by some tremendous heat, even though the fireball lay moments in the future. Dorothy and the Scarecrow ran to help him. But she looked middle-aged and the Scarecrow was the rotting bag from my car. Once, all three stared at me from the screen. The picture tube thinned, a gauzy sheet no thicker than the dust coating its surface.

And the Wicked Witch screamed to life on the roof—a gangrenous, misshapen version of Denise.

I stopped the tape.

I waited in my car for two hours before Denise exited the apartment. I didn't want to meet her in the hall. She had started the avalanche of fear that buried my senses, and I wasn't ready for a direct confrontation.

Stay away from the Hanged Man.

Talk to Stan . . .

I stayed at least a block behind her. She worked at a department store in the mall and liked to arrive early. I parked in the side lot. She was inside by the time I walked to the front entrance. I hovered there, wondering if I was too late. Entering the store wasn't an option. If Denise caught me inside, I didn't have any excuses. She'd know I followed her. Besides, I worked at a union job shop, creating ads on a computer, and I caught hell when I missed a shift.

Ten minutes later, Stan entered the lot.

I ran over and hovered as he locked his car. I'm not sure what I expected from him.

"I need help," I said.

"What are you doing here, Michael? Don't you have to work?"

"I'm taking a sick day."

Stan nodded, lit up a cigarette. I could blame my imagination, but I thought his hands shook. "So? What are you doing here?" he asked again. He didn't seem in any hurry to get to work.

"The Scarecrow told me to talk to you."

Stan didn't laugh. His mouth twitched, though.

"You know about it."

He shoved past me. "You're crazy," he said, walking briskly toward the store.

I followed, grabbed his arm. I glanced around the lot to see if anyone was watching. No one was close.

"Don't call me crazy," I said. "The Scarecrow popped in and out of my car like a damned ghost and he brought the Wicked Witch along for the ride and I'm scared. This is all Denise's fault and you know something. You asked me about the movie. Don't dare tell me you don't know what I'm talking about."

Stan jabbed his lit cigarette against my hand as I held his arm. I jerked it away, hissed with pain, put my mouth over the burn. Stan backed up and pinned a sneer on his pale face.

"Get away from me, Michael." He paused. "If you don't, I'll tell Denise."

I stood there, silent, and watched him leave.

This time I observed the speed limit on my way home. A ghostly Dorothy rode shotgun. Toto sat in her lap. I didn't recall seeing the mutt before. A taxidermist had worked him over, mounting him to a wood base, so he traveled well, no tongue-flapping out the window, no prancing from one side to the other, nails digging into your thighs. The Scarecrow and the Tin Man held the rear seats.

All four were quiet, which didn't bother me. Maybe the daylight silenced them. I parked in my slot and killed the engine. When I climbed out, chaff and aluminum dust and the ripe scent of a dead dog wafted from the empty interior.

The apartment hall was empty. I pressed my hands against the cold surface of Denise's door. The number and letter glimmered in the fluorescent lighting, incandescent with a promise that felt like prophecy. I knew now that I *wanted* to see. The knowledge might release me.

My fingers ached where I touched the door, as if the wood sucked at my bones, robbing them of warmth. The 2C pulsed and my breath frosted the air, crystallizing in my chest until I forgot to breathe.

Then my legs buckled under fatigue and gravity and the door answered my weakness with its own, selling its solid soul so I could fall through into the reality that lay beyond.

Dry grass rustled beneath me as I fell to my knees. A brick-paved road ran past, its surface a river of yellow pus baked solid under a neon-strobe sun. Disease festered in the scabbed cracks, more efficient as a contagion than as mortar.

The Tin Man's cabin sat across from my position, wearing its abandonment like a badge. The logs sagged, eaten by dry rot and unable to sustain their weight. Years had passed since glass sealed the windows and thick cobwebs, choked with dead insects, served as the only curtains. The stone chimney wore moss and ivy like a fur coat, its only protection against the cold. Large gaps riddled the roof's green slate like open sores. In the places where there were not yet holes the sun glinted off shallow pools of water.

I stood and crossed the road, glancing left and right along its bumpy length—no one was visible in either direction. Not the intrepid trio nor their hanged observer.

Light fell through the rear windows and the roof, illuminating the room. The sun had almost died in the west, but it was enough so I could pick out the familiar details of Denise's apartment.

From the front window to the door, I recognized the vague outlines of furniture. A mildewed couch slumped on broken legs. Two rickety crates supported several planks that served as a table, with an apish skull still wearing shreds of flesh as a centerpiece. Instead of the entertainment center, a cauldron sat before the fireplace, its mealy contents still bubbling.

A mask hung above the mantel like a trophy stuffed and mounted by a hunter. The facial lines were soft, the cheeks frozen in a perpetual smile, spawning dimples at both corners. But the eyes were empty and soulless, the mouth a toothless hole, and both sucked away whatever resemblance to humanity the mask had ever possessed.

It was Denise.

I backed away from the cabin, dazed. Before I knew it I'd crossed the road to my original entry point, just as a dark shape moved across the cabin roof, catching my eye. The Wicked Witch froze, straddling the peak like an Impressionist vision of the Statue of Liberty, broom held high in place of a torch.

"It took you long enough, Michael," she said, her smile as uneven as the road. "I thought I'd need to send someone out after you again."

"I don't know what you're thinking, Denise, but I'm finished with these dreams."

She cackled. "Stubborn to a fault. I love that. The longer you doubt, the closer I get. Eventually it will be too late . . ."

I walked toward the cabin, my first steps tentative as loose bricks threatened to turn my ankles. I stopped once, crouched, pulled one broken piece loose, steeled myself against the slimy texture as I clenched it in my fist. I needed a weapon. I didn't think this ball-sized brick would hurt her, but it might serve as a distraction.

"You're right. I don't believe." Debris littered the yard between the cabin and the road and matched the landscape of my chaotic dreams. "You've drugged or hypnotized me, I don't care which. It's over."

From behind the trees, the Scarecrow moved into the clearing. Dorothy and the Tin Man skulked in his shadow.

"Calling in your troops, Denise?"

Age lines shredded each of their faces, turning grins into something as old as the brown apples piled under the trees, something as calculated as the way the trees' prehensile branches reached out, straining against the roots that kept each woody demon in place.

"Her name isn't Denise," said the Tin Man, brandishing an ax that looked freshly honed. "I don't think she has one."

"Names don't matter here," said the Scarecrow.

"Is that why you told me to talk to Stan?"

The Scarecrow cringed, glanced at the Wicked Witch. His companions backed away. I looked at the Wicked Witch too, expecting her to nail his straw frame with a quick fireball.

"You warned him?" she asked.

"No! No! I was only trying to prepare him!"

The Wicked Witch leaped off the roof, black dress billowing behind her like crows hovering around a fresh kill. She landed in the middle of the road, nimble as a black widow.

Forget the rock, I thought. I needed something bigger if I wanted to come out of this alive. I crouched beside rubble from the chimney, dropped my brick and grabbed a discarded ax handle from where it lay half-buried among the weeds.

The Scarecrow trembled and begged. "Please don't hurt me! Please!"

The Wicked Witch formed her hand into a claw. Eldritch flames sprouted from her bitten nails and knotted into a pulsing globe.

"I release you, Scarecrow! I give you your freedom—in death!"

She hurled the fireball and the Scarecrow tried to block it with upraised hands.

The ball hit him and ate his body up in seconds.

The Wicked Witch stepped into the yard, blocking my way to the road, as the Tin Man and Dorothy circled the Scarecrow's smoldering remains. If I braved the apple orchard I'd have to fight them both, one armed with an ax, the other with a dead dog.

"This is taking too long," the Wicked Witch said. "It's time for you to join me, Michael."

"I'm not going anywhere, Denise." I waved the ax handle before me.

"My name is not Denise. I can't remember my name. It's been such a long time since I heard it."

"But if you're *not* Denise . . ."

My words trailed off. I let my eyes trace the lines in her face. I barely recognized the woman I'd flirted with in the hallway. She might be there under the thick cheeks, the warts, the bony chin and green skin, but there wasn't enough to convince me.

"Then . . . I must be the Wicked Witch!" she said.

I swung my weapon and reached for the roof. The handle cracked when it hit, cut my hands as it splintered. The Tin Man was nearest the cabin and he screamed. His voice squeaked. *You're going to need to oil more than that, buddy*, I thought. My blow shook the roof's remaining boards and the water puddles washed into the yard, striking the Tin Man. He scrambled into the road, metal limbs clanking, joints squealing from friction. The shower streaked Dorothy's makeup, washed her brown tresses blonde and knocked Toto from her arms.

The Wicked Witch smiled.

She raised her claws to meet the deluge that ran across her body, black rags clinging to her stick frame. The shape beneath was suddenly too skeletal and bulged in all the wrong places, cancerous and demonic. She licked the stagnant moisture off her lips with a leprous tongue, slurping at the algae.

"Yeah, right," she said. "Like no one's ever tried water before."

I tried to run but a tree stopped me. Not one of the apple trees. Those were back by the cabin.

The Wicked Witch screamed—"Get him! I won't lose two today!"—and I looked over my shoulder, trying to spot a pursuer. When I turned forward again I ran face-first into a lightning-split oak.

As I lay there dazed, my audience assembled.

"You can't get away, Michael," the Wicked Witch said.

"What do you want?"

"I was thrown out of my land a long time ago and I can never go back." She gestured at the forest, the ramshackle cabin, and the rotting orchard. "This is my home. This is my reality. This is my dream."

I shook my head. "A dream?"

Dorothy wiped her face and left fingerprints in the wet mascara and rouge. "Oh, much more than that. We play our parts here and keep her from loneliness."

"Stan was one of us," the Tin Man said. "He served his time. When she tired of him, she let him serve her outside."

"Be quiet, beehive!" said the Wicked Witch, pushing him aside. "You'll learn my ways soon enough, Michael. You're going to replace him."

"You're crazy." I pulled myself up against the split trunk. "I'll never do anything you say."

"That's why I love you, Michael." She motioned toward the tree. "Lift him up."

A noose dropped over my head and cinched tight. At the other end, hidden among the leaves, an orangutan jumped into the air, guiding its descent with spread wings as it hauled the rope across a thick branch.

My neck snapped.

The Witch's obsession traps us here, and her magic forces us into these forms. When I dream I'm still in my old life, but it fades as her obsession burns, tarnishing the memory. She watches us as we try to amuse her. When she tires, I may stop hanging myself. And someday I will escape.

Her madness is contagious.

The Bone Ship

BY TERRY DOWLING

When Mrs. Davinon brought in the tea and the plate of dark coconut-frosted cakes, Paul Rodan lost his concentration all over again. He had hoped he could manage the old traveler's trick: half-closing his eyes and imagining where else he could be. In England, certainly, that went without saying, inside like this where it was cool enough. Somewhere in the United States, San Francisco in the summer, yes. In Africa perhaps, Johannesburg or Tangiers, even parts of Asia, but in the highlands there, out of the terrible humidity.

It was a favorite game, and it had only just started to work when Mrs. Davinon arrived with the tea and the cakes and ruined what was possibly his final chance for now. The ceilings of her house were high enough, this spacious parlor large enough, cool enough, tastefully furnished enough, and the ceiling fan gave it the right cosmopolitan touch (India was there then; India, or it might have been Singapore, Shanghai or Hong Kong), but the woman's alarming accent and the plate of wretched coconut and chocolate sponge cakes brought him back to the parlor of a two-story Victorian (onetime) mansion in Parkes, in central-western New South Wales, in Australia of all places. In Australia! The Gautier-Davinon search had led to Australia. Who would have thought?

"How do you take your tea, Mr. Roddin—is it Roddin?" the woman asked, looking to Paul like failed gentry in some period film—wearing a neat, once stylish gray dress, flat shoes, closely coiffed hair still brown enough amid the grey, a good face with sharp dark eyes. She had to be in her sixties, either that or life in this godforsaken town had been especially cruel. A doctor's wife, going by the dull bronze plaque beside the front door: DR. C. DAVINON, and widowed by all counts, judging by no mention of a husband in their phone call, and no sign of one since he'd arrived. Or even a doctor herself, though probably too old (and too old-fashioned) to be practicing any longer. It explained the house: once stately but now almost beyond her, both woman and house hopelessly *déclassé*.

"Rodan, Mrs. Davinon. Rodan. Like the flying creature in that Japanese monster movie, if you know it."

(Japan, yes! A stretch, but he might have been in some old embassy building in Kyoto or Osaka, and wished that he was, that the search had led there. There were some good bone ships in Japan. But not the Gautier ship. Not the *Felice*.)

"I can't say I do, Mr. Ro-dan," she said, pronouncing it out with too much inflection, too much emphasis, letting him know she was a dutiful study. "I don't keep up with the latest films anymore." She offered him the cakes and he took one. "But like I say, I only hope I'm not wasting your time. There must be other Davinons."

Oh, there were, there were, as he knew only too well—in Montreal and Ontario and in Marsala on Sicily. In Madrid, Trieste and Buenos Aires. Hundreds in Paris, thousands all over France. But the research and the search had led here, to Parkes in this horrid, blazing Australian summer.

He wiped crumbs away carefully. "The facts are quite conclusive, madame," he said, realizing he sounded frightfully formal. Something about the old house, about this quaint, premature relic of a country doctor's wife, seemed to make it appropriate. "As I said when I phoned, all the evidence points to the Davinons in Parkes. I am very hopeful."

More than hopeful. That was why it had been a phone call from Sydney, no letters of introduction, none of the usual polite inquiries. He was sure of his facts and he was on a time limit. Others were on the same trail.

"Well, we're the only Davinons in Parkes. The family has been in this house since 1845." She pronounced it as "Davinnens" as if to rhyme with "paraffin," one more vile atonal anglicization Paul had lived with for so long. It was Paul's single rebellion: keeping to the French "Duh-vin-non," with its stress on the second "n."

And now the woman was frowning with polite concern. "When I said on the phone that my great-to-the-fourth-grandfather brought his father's things from Paris, I tried to make it clear that they've been looked over again and again."

Paul made himself conceal the excitement he felt, the very real wave of—yes—agitation that came over him. So near, so very near. It was such an intimate, urgent feeling.

"But they took nothing away you said, Mrs. Davinon. You said they looked through the papers but you and your husband allowed nothing to be taken."

"That's right. Charles was very strict about it." She leaned over and poured him more tea. "Apart from the historical society people, everything has been kept in the attic untouched for sixty years. But looked over again and again before that."

"So you were with them while they made this recent examination?"

"Of course." Again Mrs. Davinon frowned, and Paul cautioned himself. Too keen. He was being too forward, too keen. "But, then again, Mr. Ro-dan, we did not search them at the door."

Paul made himself smile and nod, taking the rebuke. "I am deeply sorry, Mrs. Davinon. I meant no offense. I have come a long way in the hope of at last settling this mystery in my family's history. A long way in time—the years spent making such a search—and now in space, traveling here to your wonderful country. I apologize again if I seem—too eager."

His hostess seemed mollified. She gave a smile and a nod of her own; it was all so courtly between them. "There are no valuables. Charles and I checked. Everyone has checked. Just papers and a few oddments."

Oddments, Paul almost parroted, but was able to stop himself. He nodded again, showing interested respect while his thoughts raced. So near, so near. Bettelmann and Lucas were half a world away, chasing their leads, quizzing other Davinons in other lands, sending out their letters and interminable e-mails, making their phone calls. He could take enough time. And he could use force if necessary. That was why he hadn't registered at a motel in town yet; this way there would be no trace. Just the hire car paid for in cash, using the false ID, the false name. Easy to fob off. He was a museum acquisitions expert by profession, he would say. Discretion was always essential. There were reasons.

So he sat sipping the awful tea, nibbling one of the—what were the horrid things called: lillingtons? livingstons? Then, judging his time, he continued. "It is nothing valuable in the monetary sense, Mrs. Davinon. It is information, documentary proof about the fate of a model of a ship. More clues perhaps. My own great-to-the-fifth-uncle was involved with your ancestor in connection with it."

"And it's to do with this ship?" Mrs. Davinon said.

"Model ship. Exactly."

"Then what are you looking for? You must explain it, Mr. Ro-dan. I'm sure I present as a country doctor's wife and must strike you as very provincial by your practiced European standards, but I assure you I am a sharp customer by my own lights and I love history. That's part of why Charles held on to his father's things. They've been passed down. I belong to the local historical society here. Some of our meetings are held in this very room. I may not have all of your conservationist's gloss, but I am active enough."

My, isn't that wonderful, Paul would have said ten minutes, five minutes earlier, but now she had cautioned him with her boast of being a "sharp customer," and the glint in her eye warned of a native cunning. As dangerous as intelligent people were, Paul had found those who thought themselves intelligent often presented a much greater danger. They were obdurate, more willful by far, usually less tractable.

Instead, Paul nodded as if to a peer. "May I just say as one sharp customer to another that it is a relief to be with a woman who understands the absolute importance of custodial care, madame. You are being most kind." He deliberately laid on the continental charm, though in subtleties, he liked to think, not broad strokes. It had always worked for him before. He wanted coffee and pâté, but now, smiling wonderfully, he held out his cup for more tea as if it were ambrosia, and took another of the wretched lillington things. He was Paul Louis Rodan, *former* museum acquisitions agent, now freelance raider of history and resolute builder of a history of his own, and he was very close to owning the Gautier ship, the *Felice*. Bettelmann and Lucas be damned!

"Now I must have the story you have only hinted at, Mr. Ro-dan," Mrs. Davinon said, and reached down and brought up a small tape recorder. "If you have no objections, I will tape what you tell me. For my own records."

"Not at all, madame." (If it came to force, that could easily be disposed of.)

The Bone Ship

Paul waited till she had set it next to the tea service on the table between them and switched it on. There was none of the "Testing, testing" that amateurs so often went on with. Mrs. Davinon had already practiced with it. It made Paul even more circumspect. She was indeed a sharp customer.

"Madame, are you familiar with what are called Prisoner of War Models—models of sailing ships built by prisoners interned during the Napoleonic Wars?"

"Only in the most cursory fashion. I know there is some mention of it in the papers upstairs. Or, rather, *a* model ship is mentioned. It is made of bone."

"Exactly. Between 1793 and 1815 the English were constantly at war with the French. During this great struggle, as you may be aware, Dartmoor Prison was built to house over eight thousand French prisoners of war. Americans, too, fighting on the French side. Other prisons were used, Bideford, Norman's Cross and the like, even old castles and the hulks on the Thames mudflats, but my ancestor, Giles Gautier, and yours were interned in Dartmoor in May 1807."

Paul made an appropriate hesitation at that point, hinting ever so slightly at an emotional stake in what he was saying.

"Go on, please, Mr. Ro-dan."

"Many French sailors were conscripts, so you had bakers, tailors, farmers, and skilled artisans imprisoned side by side with experienced seamen. It wasn't long before the more enterprising of these found they could augment their rations and earn money by making toys and selling them first to the trusties, then to the English officers and gentry who learned about them. These toys soon led to more desirable objects like model sailing ships, miniature replicas of specific vessels currently engaged in the fighting. If only you could see the beautiful model of the 120-gun *Brittania* at the Maritime Museum in Dartmouth, fifty-one inches long, or the *Ocean* in the Science Museum in London, or the fifty-two-gun *L'Amatone* in the South Shields Museum—"

"I'm sure. Please continue, Mr. Ro-dan." Only the accent ruined her queenliness, that and her insufferable, almost willful mispronunciation of his name.

"Some of these models were made of ivory and tortoiseshell, sometimes mahogany, but a great number were made from bone."

"But not human bone!"

"No, madame. Sometimes whalebone, but mutton bone mostly, salvaged from refuse bins or the cookhouse, sometimes bought from the prison market if there was one. The sailors and shipwrights provided details to the jewelers and other craftsmen who then did most of the work, and they divided the profits. It became quite a cottage industry, quite a production line: some hands carving the planks, others doing the fine work using nails shaped into chisels, others preparing the rigging with threads from their garments or their own hair. The English commissioned models of particular ships, and helped provide brass rivets and fine woods for the detailing. There are supposedly several here in Australia. I know one very fine bone model belongs to the Moxon family in Brisbane, recently restored by your own Australian master model shipbuilder, John Larkin. The largest, in the Waterman's Hall, London, is said to be seven feet long, and—"

"And where do Giles Gautier and Phillip Davinon come into this?"

It brought Paul up short. My, but the woman was quick. There they were: the names of both their respective ancestors.

"Dartmoor was terribly overcrowded. While many of the model makers lived very well indeed, other prisoners suffered in absolute squalor. They were meant to be maintained by their respective governments, but this simply didn't happen. Many human skeletons were found when the camp at Bideford was excavated for the new gas works."

Mrs. Davinon looked suitably aghast. "So human bones *were* used?"

It hadn't been what Paul was going to say at all. He'd just meant to illustrate the range of conditions at the POW prisons in preparation to explaining the Gautier/Davinon connection, working round to what was done way back in 1807 in that dismal overcrowded cell block the poor unfortunates had christened the Oubliette.

"Not at first. But there were factions, you understand. Arrangements between model-making groups and particular trusties. Favors and preferential treatment. Giles and Phillip were both on the *Felice* when she was taken. They were with thirty-six other prisoners added to a prison block called the Oubliette. It was already filled to capacity; people sleeping on the floor, fighting over scraps of food. But Giles was a watchmaker, and your great ancestor, Phillip, a master mariner, and they began work on a model of the *Felice*, reinventing the wheel as new model-makers often had to do, scrounging whatever they could, but in the most horrendous circumstances. The Oubliette was full of troublemakers—hence the name: a place to put people and forget them. Giles and Phillip were accused of trying to be better than the rest and were both beaten for it. Their first model was wrecked during an incident, possibly an attempted escape. Whatever actually happened, rations were reduced as general punishment. No longer were even mutton bones allowed for their use. No metal pins and fittings. Nothing."

"How did they manage?"

"Other fine bone ships were made under similar trying conditions. The schooner *Alyson*, the sloop *Deirdre*—using bone pins and glues—"

"But the bone, Mr. Ro-dan! The bone!"

She *did* have a bone ship here. Paul was sure of it. This rush of emotion gave her away; her very real concern that a prized heirloom was made from the bones of humans.

"As you suspect, madame. They used human bone. It was all they had. On burial detail, they would retrieve bones from the lime pits, whatever they could get."

"And the result, Mr. Ro-dan? The outcome?"

"Is what I am hoping you can verify for me, Mrs. Davinon. My sources say that a second model was begun but not completed: a thirty-five-inch model of the *Felice*, just the hull and main deck and very little else. The footings for the masts were barely started. Apparently my distant uncle and your ancestor had a falling out, or they were separated to other cell blocks. Stories differ. Some say disease took them, some say they died during repatriation back to France, though in 1807 I don't see how that could be. It's far too early. At any rate, both men perished; at least their names were dropped from prison records. There were no homecomings recorded after the war. All we know for certain is that the unfinished hull of the *Felice* was given over to your family in Paris, and that—so far as my sources show—it was brought here to Australia. I am hoping I am not mistaken, and that you have it in safekeeping here and are simply being appropriately cautious with a stranger."

Mrs. Davinon gave what looked to be a sympathetic smile. "Such a thing would not be for sale, Mr. Ro-dan."

"I accept that, madame. I do assure you of it. I am a *former* acquisitions agent, as I said. No longer a collector of anything more than the history of the Prisoner of War Models as they relate to the Gautiers and the Rodans."

"And the Davinons."

Paul didn't miss a beat. "And the Davinons, most assuredly. The names are inseparable. I meant only that it is my own family search that brought me here. I can only hope that you might let me see it and photograph it and publish its history, both for its own sake and as part of our shared family histories. It would mean a great deal."

Mrs. Davinon put one slender hand to her throat and looked off across the parlor, as if surrendering to her own run of emotions: thoughts of a model made of *human* bone, recollections of her lifetime with Charles, of his father's stories of old and precious things, of the trap of years that had left her here now in this particular lacuna of time.

Paul set his cup down as gently as he could, but the smallest *chink* doing so brought her back in an instant.

"More tea, Mr. Ro-dan?"

"Only if you will have some too, Mrs. Davinon. As I say, in both senses, it has been a long journey. Your hospitality is wonderful."

"Perhaps you would prefer coffee instead?"

Hah! A truce. Paul seized at it. Coffee, at last. But better yet, a chance to be alone while she went to make it, a chance to rally and consider his best options, to give her time to consider his requests.

"I'd be most grateful. A Frenchman—you understand how it is with coffee."

Mrs. Davinon rose. "Of course. Excuse me a moment."

Paul rose, being his most chivalrous, the cavalier, the attentive and gracious guest, but Mrs. Davinon beat him to the tray and carried it off to the kitchen.

He sat down again, listened to the deep ticking of the clock on the mantel and the distant sounds of her moving about in the kitchen. Somewhere in this house, no doubt up in the dim stuffy attic, sat the model of the *Felice*, probably locked away in a trunk, the stark white hull wrapped in packing, nothing much to show anyone, but real. No longer just the rumor, no longer just the tantalizing listings in old editions of Filiger's.

The smell of brewed coffee came to him through the hall. Avignon, Paul told himself, his favorite little café, or André's in Marseilles, though too many of his competitors went there now, and lately to keep an eye on him. They knew how accomplished he was. But brewed coffee. It would do. In Parkes, in a blazing Australian summer, it would do.

Finally Mrs. Davinon returned with the tray and set it down between them. On it were fresh cups, a teapot and a glass plunger of coffee. He waited for her to settle, waited during the pouring and serving, paced himself with quick thoughts of Amsterdam and Berlin, Prague and Istanbul. The coffee smelled wonderful. He made sure he sipped as she did, mirroring her body language, being *with* her, courteous guest, completely in her hands and at her pleasure. He made a single sound of appreciation—totally genuine—and tried to seem relaxed.

"I have the story a little differently," Mrs. Davinon said, surprising him.

"Pardon, madame?"

"From what Charles's father had passed on to him, it was Phillip who was the watchmaker, and your Giles Gautier the mariner who provided the specifications."

"What's that?" Again Paul was thrown, but at least it was all coming out now. He leaned forward, composing his face to show quiet interest, not the genuine startlement he felt.

"And you are correct: the two men were not repatriated. As Charles's father explained it, they were being transferred to a prison hulk on the Thames—it often happened with recalcitrants—and the prisoners managed to take over the prison barge. They almost succeeded in making their escape, and were out in the Channel when the pursuit ship *Llewelyn* fired on them."

"I am fascinated by this," Paul managed to say. "I knew nothing of it."

"But *before* that happened, Mr. Ro-dan, our ancestors were both *thrown* over the side by the other prisoners. My ancestor perished. Yours was rescued, it seems, and lived long enough to tell of his experience of looking up and seeing the hull of the prison barge overhead as he swam up toward the light."

"That's where my accounts resume, Mrs. Davinon. The hull reminded him of the *Felice*—or, rather, of the model sitting on the window ledge they used as their workbench. In his oxygen-deprived state, Giles felt he was swimming back to the real *Felice*, reprieved, born again. I knew nothing of them being tossed overboard. It is incredible."

"What else you may not know, Mr. Ro-dan, is that when they were cast over the side, they were tied together at the waist and told that only one would be allowed back on board. Only one, you understand?"

"Surely not, madame—"

"I can forgive it. It was long ago. Perhaps they were never friends, just two men trying to do a model ship and stay alive. The survivors from the barge picked up by the *Llewelyn* said it was what had happened. They let the one who killed the other back on board."

"I'm shocked. I had no idea. I'm so sorry, Mrs. Davinon—" Paul didn't know what else to say. All this had thrown him. The fatigue from his drive down from Sydney, from his flight from Paris, was finally catching up with him, the lack of sleep, the determination to keep ahead of the others. Suddenly he was exhausted.

"Please, Mr. Ro-dan. I didn't mean to upset you. Each would have been desperate to kill the other. People do these things to live. But we can make a truce between our families now, can't we?"

"But of course, madame. *Merci, merci mille fois!* I don't know what to say." The sudden weariness was confusing him. All this way, all this effort, and now this. His search was over.

Mrs. Davinon rose from her chair. "You look tired, Mr. Ro-dan. So at least let me show you the hull that was never finished, that was passed on to my ancestor's family by a kindly ship's officer aided by a sympathetic trusty. You can come back and look over the papers another time."

"Yes, yes. That would be splendid." Paul set his cup on the table and stood, steadying himself on the arms of the chair, then followed the woman toward the dark-timbered double sliding doors at the far end of the parlor. He felt odd, leaden was the word, definitely strange. It was as if he were weighed down.

"I keep the *Felice* in here."

In here. Not up in the attic then, not wrapped up and tucked away. She had the ship down here.

Mrs. Davinon slid back the doors to reveal what had once been a dining room with double sliding doors at each end. No doubt the kitchen lay beyond the second pair; it made sense. What made no sense, what startled Paul in his growing stupor, was the stark white hull of *Felice* atop a narrow, six-foot wooden pedestal of the same dark timber as the doors. It stood in the very center of the room, in a room whose walls were painted the deep rich red of old blood. Dark timber, dark red walls, the almost glowing, bleached white of the *Felice*.

But it couldn't be the *Felice*. Paul fought to make sense of it. This wasn't thirty-five inches. This was sixty plus inches, five feet long or more, a huge impossible version.

"As you can see, I've made modifications," Mrs. Davinon said. "It always seemed so small before."

Paul stumbled, actually fell to one knee. He was seriously unwell, all the stress, all the travel. All the years of searching.

"I'm ill," he managed to say, but even as he forced the words he saw the truth. Not ill; he was drugged. The coffee had been drugged.

He fell to the floor. He couldn't prevent it. He lay looking up at the monstrous white hull, seeing it like—like—why, like Giles Gautier must have seen it swimming up after killing Phillip Davinon so long ago, imagining it to be the *Felice*.

"But why?" The words came out slurred and wrong, but Mrs. Davinon understood. Of course she understood. Through shifting, blurring light he saw her go past the great white hull of the ship to the other set of double doors and slide them back.

There, in a glance, he saw the operating table pushed back against a far wall, in a horrid few seconds saw the two figures strapped, propped up in wheelchairs, two men, both securely gagged with white surgical tape, with their legs and arms missing and their eyes wide with drug-numbed terror. Bettelmann and Lucas.

"This—can't just—be—revenge." He dragged out the words.

"Of course not, Mr. Ro-dan," Mrs. Davinon said, just a blur and a voice now. "It's completion and closure, with those who know the worth of it assisting. The ship will be finished!"

Paul tried to fight the deadness but was being swallowed by the depths of the bloodred room, so that all he could do was lay looking up at the bleached white hull of the *Felice*, as if looking at it from beneath the surface of the ocean.

"Masts and spars, Mr. Ro-dan," he was sure he heard the voice say. "I must have my masts and spars!"

Li'l Miss Ultrasound

JUNE 30, 2004

Mummy dearest,

It's great to hear from you, though I'm magnitudinously dis-
traught that you can't be here for the contest. Still, I'm not complaining. It's extremely better that you show up for the
birth—three weeks after my little munchkin's copped her
crown!—and help out afterward. The contest is a hoot and I
want to do you proud, I *will* do you proud, but that can be done
from a distance too, don't you think? What with the national
coverage and the mega-sponsorship, you'll get to VCR me and
the kid many times over. And of course I'll save all the local clippings for you like you asked.

It made my throat hurt, the baby even kicked, when you mentioned Willie in your last letter. It's tough to lose such a wonderful
man. Still, he died calmly. I read that gruesome thing a few years
ago, that *How We Die* book? It gave me the chills, Mom, how
some people thrash and moan, how they don't make a pretty picture at all, many of them. Willie was one of the quiet ones though,

thank the Lord. Nary a bark nor whimper out of him, he just drifted off like a thief in the night. Which was funny, because he was so, I don't know, *noisy* isn't the right word, I guess *expressive* maybe, his entire life.

Oh, before I close, I gotta tell you about Kip. Kip's my ultrasound man. I'm in love, I think. Kind face on him. Nice compact little bod. Cute butt too, the kind of buns you can wrap your hands halfway around, no flabby sags to spoil your view or the feel of the thing. Anyway, Kip's been on the periphery of the contest for a few years and likes tinkering with the machinery. He's confided in me. Says he can—and will!—go beyond the superimposition of costumes that's been all the rage in recent years to some other stuff I haven't seen yet and he won't spell out. He worked some for those Light and Magic folks in California, and he claims he's somehow brought all that stuff into the ultrasound arena. Kip's sworn me to secrecy. He tells me we'll win easy. But I'm my momma's daughter. I don't put any stock in eggs that haven't been hatched, and Kip isn't fanatical about it, so it's okay. Also, Mother, he kissed me. Yep! As sweet and tasty as all get-out. I'll reveal more, next missive. Meantime, you can just keep guessing about what we're up to, since you refuse to grace us with your presence at the contest.

Just teasing, Mummy dear. Me and my fetal muffin will make you so proud, your chest will puff out like a Looney Tunes hen! Your staying put—for legit reasons, like you said—is a-okay with me, though I *do* wish you were here to hug, and chat up, and share the joy.

> Love, love, love, mumsy mine,
> Wendy

Kip brightened when Wendy came in from the waiting room, radiant with smiles.

Today was magic day. The next few sessions would acquaint Wendy with his enhancements to the ultrasound process. He wanted her confident, composed, and fully informed onstage.

"Wendy, hello. Come in." They traded hugs and he hung her jacket on a clothes rack.

"You can kiss me, you know," she teased.

He shook his head. "It doesn't feel right in the office. Well, okay, a little one. Mmmm. Wendy, hon, you're a keeper! Now hoist yourself up and let's put these pillows behind your back. That's the way. Comfy? Can you see the monitor?"

"Yes." Eagerly, she bunched her maternity dress up over her belly. Beautiful blue and red streaks, blood lightning, englobed it. A perfect seven-months' pooch. Her flowered briefs were as strained and displaced as a fat man's belt.

"Okay, now," said Kip. "Get ready for a surprise. This'll be cold." He smeared thick gel on her belly and moved the hand-held transducer to bring up baby's image. "There's our little darling."

"Mmmmm, I like that 'our'!"

"She's a beauty *without* any enhancement, isn't she? Now we add the dress." Reaching over, he flipped a switch on his enhancer. Costumes had come in three years before, thanks to the doctor Kip had studied under. They were now expected fare. "Here's the one I showed you last time," he said, pink taffeta with hints of chiffon at the bodice. There slept baby in her party dress, her tiny fists up to her chest.

"It's beautiful," enthused Wendy. "You can almost hear it rustle." What a joy Wendy was, thought Kip. A compact little woman who no doubt would slim down quickly after giving birth.

"Okay. Here goes. Get a load of this." He toggled the first switch. Overlaying the soft fabric, there now sparkled sequins, sharp gleams of red, silver, gold. They winked at random, cutting and captivating—spliced in, by digital magic, from a captured glisten of gems.

"Oh, Kip. It's breathtaking."

It was indeed. Kip laughed at himself for being so proud. But adding sparkle was child's play, and he fully expected other ultrasounders to have come up with it this year. It wouldn't win the contest. It would merely keep them in the running. He told Wendy so.

"Ah but this," he said, "this will put us over the top." He flipped the second switch, keeping his eyes not on the monitor but on his lover, knowing that the proof of his invention would be found in the wideness of her eyes.

Eudora glared at the monitor.

She had won the Li'l Miss Ultrasound contest two years running—the purses her first two brats brought in had done plenty to offset the bother of raising them—and she was determined to make it three.

Then she could retire in triumph.

She had Moe Bannerman, the best ultrasound man money could buy. He gestured to the monitor's image. "She's a beaut. Do you have a name yet?"

"Can the chatter, Moe. I'll worry about that after she wins. Listen, I'm dying for a smoke. Let's cut to the chase."

Moe's face fell.

Big friggin' deal, she thought. Let him cry to his fat wife, then dry his tears on the megabucks Eudora was paying him.

"Here she is, ready for a night on the town." He flipped a switch and her kid was swaddled in a svelte evening gown, a black number with matching accessories (gloves and a clutch purse) floating beside her in the amniotic sac.

Eudora was impressed. "Clear image."

"Sharpest yet. I pride myself on that. It's the latest in digital radiography, straight from Switzerland. We use intensity isocontours to—"

"It looks good. That's what counts. We win this round. Good. Now what about the swimsuit?"

"Ah. A nice touch. Take a look." Again his hands worked their magic. "See here. A red bikini with white polka dots."

"The sunglasses look ordinary, Moe. Give her better frames, a little glitz, something that catches the eye."

"I'll have some choices for you next time."

She shot a fingertip at him. "To hell with choices. You get the right ones first time, or I'll go to someone else." She'd heard rumor of a new ultrasound man on the horizon, Kip Johnson. He deserved a visit, just to check out the terrain. Handsome fuck, scuttlebutt said.

"Yes, ma'am. But take a look at this. It'll win us this round too. We show them the bikini, a nice tight fit that accentuates your baby girl's charms. I've even lent a hint of hardness to her nipples, which will most likely net you a contract with one of the baby-formula companies. But watch. We flip a switch and . . ."

Eudora had her eyes on the screen, her nicotine need making more vivid the image she saw. It was as if the kid had been suddenly splashed with a bucket of water. No twitch of course. It was all image. But the swimsuit's fabric lost its opacity. See-through. Gleams of moisture on her midriff. Her nipple nubs grew even harder, and her pudendal slit was clearly outlined and highlighted. Moe, you're a genius, she thought.

"Cute," she said. "What else you got?"

Thus she strung the poor dolt along, though his work delighted her. Dissatisfaction, she found, tended to spur people to their best. It wouldn't do to have Moe resting on his laurels. People got trounced by surprise that way. Eudora was determined not to be one of them.

When they were done, she left in a hurry, had a quick smoke, and hit the road. The judge was due for a visit. There were other judges, of course, all of whom she did her best to cultivate. But somehow Benjamin—perversely he preferred the ugly cognomen "Benj"—was *The Judge*, a man born to the role.

Weaving through traffic, she imagined the slither of his hand across her belly.

Benj walks into the house without knocking.

In the kitchen he finds her dull hubby, feeding last year's winner (Gully or Tully) from a bottle. The beauty queen from two years prior toddles snot-nosed after him, wailing, no longer the tantalizing piece of tissue she had once been. Her name escapes him.

But names aren't important. What's important are *in utero* images and the feelings they arouse in him.

"Hello, Chet," says Benj.

Stupid Chet lights up like a bulb about to burn out. "Oh, hi, Benj. Eudora's in the bedroom. Have at her!"

Benj winks. "I will."

He winds his way through the house, noting how many knick-knacks prize money and commercial endorsements can buy. Over-the-hill, post-fetal baby drool is all *he* sees on the tube once the little darlings are born. It never makes him want to buy a thing.

"Why, Benjamin. Hello." She says it in that fake provocative voice, liking him for his power alone of course. As long as he can feel her belly, he doesn't care.

"Touch it?" he asks in a boyish voice. "Touch it now?" He thickens below.

"Of course you can," says Eudora, easing the bedroom door shut and leaning against it, her hands on the knob as if her wrists are tied.

Stupid Chet thinks Benj and Eudora do the man-woman thing. Chet wants money from the winnings, so he's okay with it as long as they use rubbers. But they don't *really* do the man-woman thing. Nope. They just tell Chet they do. Benj rubs her belly and feels the object of his lust kick and squirm in there, touching herself, no doubt, with those tiny curled hands, thrashing around breathless in the womb, divinely distracted.

Breathless.

Baby's first breath taints absolutely.

"Touch yourself, Benjamin."

He does. He wears a rubber, rolled on before he left the car. Later, he'll give it to Eudora so she can smear it with her scent and drop it in the bathroom wastebasket. Chet's a rummager, a sniffer. It's safer to provide him evidence of normalcy.

To Benj, normal folks are abnormal. But it takes all kinds to make a world.

His mouth fills with saliva. Usually, he remembers to swallow. Sometimes, a teensy bit drools out.

The baby kicks. Benj's heart leaps up like a frisky lamb. Eudora pretends to get off on this, but Benj knows better. He ignores her, focusing on his arousal, and is consumed with bliss.

JULY 12, 2004

Mummy dearest,

I'm so excited! Kip is too! The contest cometh tomorrow, so you'll see this letter *after* you've watched me and the munchkin on TV, but what the hey.

I could do without the media hoopla of course, though I suppose it comes with the territory. The contest assigns you these big bruisers, kind of like linebackers. I don't think you had them in your day. They deflect press hounds for you, so you don't go all exhausted from the barrage or get put on the spot by some persistent sensationalist out to sell dirt.

Then there are the protesters.

Ugh! I agree with you, mumsy. They're out of their blessed noggins. Both sorts of protesters. There are the ones who want the contest opened up to second trimester fetuses. The extremists even scream for first trimester. What, I ask you, would be the point of *that*?

Then there are the ones who want to ban pre-birth beauty contests entirely. Life-haters I call them. Hey, I'm as deep as the next gal. But I was never harmed by having a beauty queen for a mother nor by winning the Baby Miss contest when I was three months old. All that helped me, I'm sure—my self-esteem, my comfort with putting my wares on display, which a gal has just got to do to please her fella. I don't mind if Kip likes me for *all* of me, and I sincerely and honestly believe he does. But that includes the packaging. The sashay too, though mine's got *waddle* written all over it these days. Hey, I can work off the belly flab as soon as my baby's born. I know I can. I'll slim down and tighten up you-know-where even if it's under the knife with sutures taking up the slack. That's a woman's duty, as my momma taught me so well!

My point is that I'm *all* of me, the brainy stuff and the sexy stuff too. It's all completely me, it's my soul, and right proud of it am I. Well, listen to me gas on and on, like a regular old innerlectual. What hath thou raised? Or more properlike, whom?

> Wish us luck, mumsikins!
> Your loving and devoted daughter,
> Wendy

Kip was alone in his office, making final tweaks to his software. Wendy had been by, an hour before, for one last run-through prior to their appearance onstage.

Five more minutes and he would lock up.

His ultrasound workstation, with its twenty-four-inch, ultra-high-resolution, sixteen-million-color monitor, had become standard for MRI and angiography. Moe Bannerman, last year's winning ultrasound man, had copped the prize, thanks to this model. But Kip was sure, given the current plateau in technology, that whatever Moe had up his sleeve this year would involve something other than the size and clarity of the image.

Butterflies flitted in Kip's gut. Somehow, no matter how old you got, exposure to the public limelight jazzed you up.

Li'l Miss Ultrasound

The outer office door groaned. Maisie coming back for forgotten car keys, thought Kip.

A pregnant woman appeared at the door. Eyes like nail points. Hair as long and shiny as a raven's wing. Where had he seen her? Ah. Moe's client, mother of the last two contest winners.

Wendy's competition.

"Hello there," she said, her voice as full-bellied as she was. "Have you got a minute?" She waddled in without waiting for an answer. "I'm Eudora Kelly."

He opened his mouth to introduce himself.

"You're Kip, if I'm not mistaken. My man will be going up against you tomorrow."

"True. Look, according to the rules, you and I shouldn't be talking."

She approached him. "Rules are made to keep sneaky people in line. We're both aboveboard. At least, I am." Her voice was edged with tease, a quality that turned Kip off, despite the woman's stunning looks. "Besides, even if I were to tell Moe what you and I talked about or what we did—which I won't—it's too late for him to counter it onstage, don't you think?"

"Ms. Kelly, maybe you'd better—"

She touched his arm, her eyes intent on the contours of his shirtsleeve. "I'll tell you what surprises *he's* planning to pull tomorrow. How would that be?"

"No, I don't want to know that." He did, of course, but such knowledge was off-limits. She knew that as well as he.

"They say you've got new technologies you're drawing on. A background in the movies. Maybe next year, you and I could pair up."

Kip reviewed his helpers, looking for a blabbermouth.

No one came to mind.

"In fact," she sidled closer, her taut belly pressing against his side, "maybe *right now* we could pair up." Her hand touched his chest and drifted lower.

"All right, that's enough. There's the door. Use it." His firmness surprised him. It was rare to encounter audacity, rarer still therefore to predict how one would respond to it. He took her shoulders and turned her about, giving her a light shove.

She wheeled on him. "You think you're God, you spin some dials and flick a few switches. Well, me and Moe're gonna wipe the floor with your ass tomorrow. Count on it!"

Then she was gone.

The back of Kip's neck was hot and tense. "Jesus," he said, half expecting her to charge in for another try.

Giving the workstation a pat, he prepared to leave, making sure that the locks were in place, the alarms set.

"Fool jackass," Eudora said. "The man must be sexed the wrong way around."

"Some people," observed the judge, his eyes on her beach-ball belly, "have a warped sense of right and wrong. They take that Sunday school stuff for gospel, as I once did long ago."

"Not me, Benjamin. I knew it for the crock it was the moment it burbled out of old Mrs. Pilsner's twisted little mouth. Ummm, that feels divine." It didn't, but what the hell. Benjamin would be pivotal tomorrow. No sense letting the truth spoil her chances.

The judge's moist hand moved upon her, shaky with what was happening elsewhere. Soon he would yank out his tool, a condom the color of rancid custard rolled over it like a liverwurst sheath. "Yeah, I wised up when I saw how the wicked prospered," he said. "How do you *do* it, Eudora? This is the third sexy babe in a row. Your yummy little siren is calling to me."

"She wants it, Benjamin," said Eudora.

Perv city, she thought. It would be a relief to jettison this creep as soon as the crown was hers. Three wins. She would retire in glory and wealth. At the first sign he wanted to visit, she would drop him cold. No bridges left to burn after her triumph. Let the poor bastard drool on someone else's belly.

Benjamin groped about between the parted teeth of his zipper. Eudora said, "That Kip person's going to spring something."

"Who's he?" asked the judge, pulling out his plum.

"You know. The ultrasound guy that Wendy bubblehead is using. Scuttlebutt says he's doing something fancy."

"Ungh," said Benjamin.

Eudora pictured Kip's office receptionist, her hand shaking as she took Eudora's money. She was disgustingly vague and unhelpful, Maisie of the frazzled hair and the troubled conscience. All she gave off were echoes of unease: he has this machine, I don't know what it does, but it's good because he says it is and because they both look so sure of themselves after her visits. Worthless!

"My baby girl's getting off, hon."

Li'l Miss Ultrasound

"Me too," he gasped.

"You're a sweet man," she said. "Show us your stuff. Give it to us, Benjamin, right where we live. That's it. That's my sweet Benjamin Bunny."

Benj really gets into it. Eudora's belly skin is so smooth and tight, and as hot as a brick oven. He smells baby oil in his memory.

Eudora has no cause for worry, he thinks. Moe Bannerman's a stellar technician. What Moe's able to do to tease naked babes into vivid life onscreen is nothing short of miraculous.

Benj conjures up the looker inside Eudora's womb by recalling what hangs on his bedroom wall, those stunning images from *Life* last year—better than the real thing though a boner's a boner no matter how you slice it.

He dips into Tupperwared coconut oil, smearing it slick and liberal upon her belly, as he does upon his condomed boytoy. Oil plays havoc with latex, he knows, but Benj isn't about to get near impregnation or STDs.

Benj bets Moe Bannerman will carry his experiments in vividness forward in the coming years. Headphones will caress Benj's head as he judges, the soft gurgle of fetal float-and-twist tantalizing his ears, vague murmurs coaxed by a digital audio sampler into a whispered *fuck-me* or *oh-yeah-baby*.

Or perhaps virtual reality will come of age. He'll put on goggles and gloves, or an over-the-head mask that gooses his senses into believing he's tasting her, the salty tang of preemie quim upon his tongue, the touch of his fingertips all over her white-corn-kernel body.

Benj shuts his eyes.

Eudora starts to speak but Benj says, "Hush," and she does. This time the rhythms are elusive but *there*, within reach if his mind twists the right way. The beauty queen to be is touching him, indeed she is, those tiny strong little fingers wrapped about his pinkie. Her eyelids are closed, the all-knowing face of the not-yet-born, lighting upon uncorrupted thoughts, unaware of and unbothered by the sensual filtering imposed by society on the living.

Her touch is as light as a hush of croissant crust. This, he thinks, is love: the wing-brush of a butterfly upon an eyelash; a sound so faint it throws hearing into doubt; a vision so fleetingly imprinted on the retina, it might be the stray flash of a neuron.

With such slight movements, love coaxes him along the path, capturing, keeping, and cultivating—like a seasoned temptress—the focus of his fascination, so that the path swiftly devolves into a grade, hurrying him downhill and abruptly thrusting him into a chute of pleasure. He whips and rumbles joyously along its oily sides once more, *once more, ONCE MORE!*

JULY 13, 2004

Mummy mine,

I'm writing from the convention center, just having come off-stage from Round One, where our little dolly garnered her first *first*! I had a hunch I'd want to disgorge all these glorious pent-up emotions into my momma's ear. So I brought along my lilac stationery and that purple pen with the ice-blue feather you love so much. Here I sit in the dressing room with the nine other contestants who survived Round One. Ooh, the daggers that are zipping across the room from Eudora Kelly, whose kids won the last two years. Methinks she suspects we've got her skunked!

Baby's jazzed, doing more than her usual poking and prodding. Kip just gave me a peck (would it had been a bushel!!!) and left to check out his equipment for Round Two. If I were a teensy bit naughtier, I'd mention how much *fun* it is to check out Kip's equipment, ha ha ha. But you raised a daughter with that rarest of qualities, modesty. Besides which, it would be unseemly to get too much into that, Willie being so recently deceased and all. But life goes on. Oh boy howdy, does it ever!

I passed through those idiotic protesters with a minimum of upset, thanks to my linebacker types. Joe, he's the beefiest, flirts outrageously, but both of us know it's all in fun. Still, he's a sweetie and you should see the scowl that drops down over his face whenever some "news twerp" (that's what Joe calls them) sticks his neck out where it don't belong, begging Joe to lop it off.

There were twenty of us to start with. 'Taint so crowded here no more! The audience sounds like an ocean, and the orchestra—you heard me, strings and all, scads of them, like Mantovani—set all things bobbing on a sea of joy. Kip gave me a big kiss right here where I sit—no, you slyboots, on my lips!!! Before I knew it, I was standing onstage amidst twenty bobbing bellies, all of us watching our handsome aged wreck of a TV host, that

52

Li'l Miss Ultrasound

Guy Givens you like so much, his bow tie jiggling up and down as he spoke, and his hand mike held just so. The judges were in view, including the drooly one—you know, the one whose hanky is always all soppy by the end.

First off, oh joy, we got to step up and do those cutesy interviews. Who the heck can remember what I gassed on about? I guess they build suspense at least in the hall. At home, all I remember is that you and me and Dad used that dumb chitchat as an excuse to grab a sandwich or a soda.

Then Round One was upon us, and we were number 16, not a great number but not all that bad neither. I lifted my dress for Kip—not the *first* time I've done that, I assure you!!!—to bare my belly and of course to show off my dazzling red-sequined panties. For good luck, I sewed, among the new sequins, an even dozen from my Baby Miss swimsuit. The crowd loved my dumpling's first outfit, a ball gown that might have waltzed in from the court of Queen Victoria. It reminded me of a wedding cake, what with all the flounces and frills and those little silver sugar bee-bees you and I love so much. Baby showed it off beautifully, don't you think?

Then Kip played his first card. With a casual gesture, he brought life to her face. Of course, her face *has* life, but it's a pretty placid sort of life at this stage, what with every need being satisfied as soon as it happens. So there's nothing to cry about and no air to cry with if she *could* cry.

Then it blossomed on her face: a flush and blush of tasteful makeup spreading over her cheeks and chin and forehead, a smear of carmine on her lips, turquoise-blue eye shadow and an elongation of her lashes. Huge monitors in the hall gave everyone as clear a picture as the folks at home on their TVs. I could taste the rush of amazement rippling through the hall at each effect.

Then, her darling eyes opened! Just for a second before Kip erased the image. Of course they didn't *really* open, any more than my baby really wore a ball gown. But they weren't just some painted porcelain doll's eyes. Kip's years in Hollywood paid off, because you would have sworn there was angelic intelligence in the deep gaze Kip gave her face—

53

Oops, we just got the five-minute call, mumsy, so I'll cut off
here and pick back up at the next break. Wish us luck! Gotta go!!!

Kip followed close behind a stagehand, who wheeled the ultrasound equipment to the tape marks, locked down the rollers, and plugged the cord into an outlet on the stage floor. Wendy had already settled into the stylish recliner.

"Hello, darling," said Kip, taking her hand. Wendy returned his kiss. "How are you two?"

"Fine." Her voice wavered, but Kip judged it near enough to the truth.

The stage manager, clipboard at the ready, breezed by. "Two minutes," he said. Hints of garlic.

Beyond the curtain's muffle, the emcee pumped things up. A drumroll and a cymbal crash rushed the orchestra into an arpeggio swirling up to suggest magic and pixie dust. Kip squeezed Wendy's hand.

When the curtain rose, Guy Givens strode over. "And here's our first round winner, Miss Wendy Sales. Round she certainly is. And ready for another round, I hope. Wendy, how does it feel to be the winner of our evening wear competition?"

"Well, Guy," said Wendy, as he poked the mike at her mouth, "it feels great, but don't bet on any horse until the race is over's what my momma taught me. All these great gals I've met? Their babies too? They're *all* winners as far as I'm concerned."

"Ladies and gentlemen, let's give the little lady's generosity a big hand." The emcee's mike jammed up into his armpit so he could show the audience how to clap with gusto. Then it jumped back into his grip. "Wendy, with that attitude, you'll be a great mom indeed."

"I sincerely hope so."

Ignoring her answer: "And now . . . let's see your adorable little girl *in her bobby-soxer outfit!*" The tuxedoed man backed out of the spotlight, his free hand raised in a flourish.

Deftly fingering a series of switches, Kip hid his amusement at the emcee's tinsel voice, as the orchestra played hush-hush music and Wendy's child came into view.

A tiny pair of saddle shoes graced the baby's feet. Her poodle skirt (its usually trim-stitched poodle gravid with a bellyful of pups) gave a slight sway. She wore a collared blouse of kelly green. A matching ribbon set off her tresses, which Kip had thickened and sheened by means of Gaussian and Shadow filters combined with histogram equalization.

When the crowd's applause began to fall off, Kip put highlights back into baby's face, an effect that brought the clapping to new heights.

As if in answer, Kip turned to two dials and began to manipulate them. The baby's eyes widened. She gave a coy turn of the head. Then her eyelids lowered and Kip wiped the image away.

The effect looked easy, but the work that had gone into making it happen was staggering. To judge by the shouts and cheers that washed over the stage, the crowd sensed that. Wendy glowed.

"Judges?" screamed Guy Givens into his mike.

One by one, down the row of five, 10s shot into the air. A 9 from a squint-eyed woman who never gave 10s drew the briefest of boos.

Wendy mouthed "I love you" at Kip, and he mouthed it back, as the music swirled up and the curtain mercifully shut out an earsplitting din of delight.

Eudora watched from the wings as the TV jerkoff with the capped teeth and the crow's-feet chatted up her only competition one last time.

The swimsuit round.

Moe's water-splash effect had gained Eudora an exceptional score, but from the look on the ultrasound man's face out there, that insufferable Kip Johnson, she was afraid he was poised to take the Wendy bitch and her unborn brat over the top.

Dump Moe.

Yep, Moe was a goner. Yesterday's meat. Spawn the loser inside her, let her snivel through life, whining for the tit withheld. A dilation and extraction might better suit. Tone up. Four months from now, let Chet poke her a few times. Stick one last bun in the oven.

Then, adrip with apologies, she would pay Kip another visit, playing to his goody-two-shoes side if that got him off. Hell, she'd even befriend his lover. If Wendy had a two-bagger in mind, Eudora would persuade her—strictly as a friend with her best interests at heart—to retire undefeated.

Onstage, that damned tantalizing womb image sprang to life again, this time dressed for the beach. Her swimsuit was a stylish fire-engine red one-piece that drew the eye to her bosom, as it slashed across the thighs and arrowed into her crotch. Nice, but no great shakes.

Then the kid's face animated again. Eudora knew that this face would bring in millions. For months, it would be splashed across front pages and magazine covers. Then it would sell products like nobody's business.

Would it ever!

Instead of repeating its coy twist of the head, the intrauterine babe fluttered her eyelashes at the audience and winked. Then she puckered her lips and relaxed them. No hand came up to blow that kiss, but Eudora suspected that Kip would make that happen next year.

Her kid would be the one to blow a kiss. *Her* kid would idly brush her fingers past breast and thigh, while tossing flirtatious looks at Benjamin and viewers at home.

Eudora scanned the judges through a deafening wall of elation. There sat the oily little pervert, more radiant than she had ever seen him. Another year would pass, a year of wound-licking capped by her triumph, and Kip's, right here on this stage. *Then* she'd dump the drooler. One more year of slobber, she assured herself, would be bearable.

Eye on the prize, she thought. Keep your eye on the prize.

Benj is in heaven. His drenched handkerchief lies wadded in his right pants pocket. Fortunately, his left contained a forgotten extra, stuck together only slightly with the crust of past noseblows. It dampens and softens now with his voluminous drool.

The curtain sweeps open. Midstage stand the three victors, awaiting their reward.

Wendy's infant has quite eclipsed Eudora's in his mind. The third-place fetus? It scarcely raises a blip. Its mother comes forward to accept a small faux-sapphire tiara, a modest bouquet of mums, and a token check for a piddling sum. An anorexic blonde hurries her off.

Eudora's up next.

Replay pix of her bambina flash across a huge monitor overhead. Beneath her smile, she's steaming. He's in the doghouse for his votes; he knows that. But there's always next year. She needs him. She'll get over it.

A silver crown, an armful of daffodils, a substantial cash settlement, and off Eudora waddles into oblivion, her loser-kid's image erased from the monitor.

Then his glands ooze anew as the house erupts. Like a bazillion cap guns, hands clap as Wendy's pride and joy lights up the screen with that killer smile, that wink, oh God those lips.

Li'l Miss Ultrasound

"AND HERE'S *OUR QUEEN INDEED!"* screams Guy Givens, welcoming Wendy into his arms. Gaggles of bimbos stagger beneath armloads of roses. The main bimbo's burden is lighter, a gold crown bepillowed. Wendy puts a hand to her mouth. Her eyes well.

Then it happens.

Something shifts in the winner's face. She whispers to Givens, who relays whatever she has said to the crown-bearing blonde. Unsure what to do, the blonde beckons offstage, mouthing something, then walks away. Wendy leans against the emcee, who says "Hold on now" into his mike. A puddle forms on the stage where she is standing. "Is there a . . . do we have a . . . of course we do, yes, here he comes, folks."

Benj feels light-headed.

The rest drifts by like a river ripe with sewage. Spontaneous TV, the young doctor, the ultrasound man, a wheeled-in recliner, people with basins of water, with instruments, backup medical personnel. Smells assault him. Sights. Guy Givens gives a hushed blow-by-blow. And then, a wailing *thing* lifts out of the ruins of its mother, its head like a smashed fist covered in blood, wailing, wailing, endlessly wailing. Blanket wrap. The emcee raises his voice in triumph, lowering the tiny gold crown onto the bloody bawler's brow.

It's a travesty. Benj is glad to be sitting down. He rests his head on his palms and cries, mourning the passing of the enwombed beauty who winked and nodded in his direction not five minutes before.

Is there no justice in the world? he wonders. Must all things beautiful end in squalor and filth?

He craves his condo. How blissful it will be to be alone there, standing beneath the punishing blast of a hot shower, then cocooning himself under blankets and nestling into the oblivion of sleep.

JULY 14, 2004

Mumsicle mine, now GRAN-mumsicle!

Well I guess that'll teach me to finish my letters when I can. I'll just add a little more to the one I never got 'round to wrapping up, and send you the whole kitten-kaboodle (sic, in case you think I don't know!), along with the news clips I promised.

57

I'm sitting here in a hospital bed surrounded by flowers. Baby girl No-Name-Yet is dozing beside me, her rosebud lips moving in the air and making me leak like crazy. I do so love mommy-hood!

But I never expected to give birth in public. They were all so nice to me at the contest, even that Eudora woman, who seems to have had a change of heart. That creepy drooly judge came up to wish me his best, but Kip rough-armed him away and said something to him before kicking him offstage. I'll have to ask Kip what that was all about.

Oh and Kip proposed! I knew he would, but it's always a thrill when the moment arrives, isn't it? I cried and cried with joy and Kip got all teary too. He'll make a great father, and I'm betting we spawn a few more winners before we're through. We'll give you plenty of warning as to when the wedding will be.

He's deflected the media nuts so far, until my strength is back. They're all so antsy to get at me. But meanwhile Kip's the hero of the hour. There's even talk of a movie of the week, with guess-who doing the special effects of course. But Kip tells me these movie deals usually aren't worth the hot air they're written on, so he and I shrug it off and simply bask bask bask!

I'll sign off now and get some rest, but I wanted to close by thanking you for being such a super mom and role model for me, growing up. You showed me I could really make something of myself in this world if I just persisted and worked my buns off for what I wanted.

I have.

It's paid off.

And I have you to thank for it. I love you, Mom. You're the greatest. Come down as soon as you can and say hello and kootchie-koo-my-little-snookums to the newest addition to the family. You'll adore her. You'll adore Kip too. But hey, hands off, girl, he's mine all mine!!!

Your devoted daughter,
Wendy

The Intervention

BY KIM NEWMAN

A man he didn't know sat quietly at the far end of the long table, but Keith didn't pay him any attention. Vince, his partner, had asked him to step into the conference room for a moment. Daily crises gave Keith and Vince an excuse to get their brains dirty and demonstrate their continuing (if slightly soft-in-the-middle) whiz-kid status to the youngsters they'd employed when the business expanded.

"This is Mr. Leitch," said Vince, nodding at the stranger.

Keith looked at Leitch and back at Vince.

When his eyes weren't on the man, Keith couldn't picture him.

He looked back again, almost rudely, staring.

Leitch was ordinary, of no particular age, reasonably dressed. Keith tried to memorize features, but his mind slid off the face. It was like trying to pick up a paper clip with mittened fingers.

What he did notice was that this was not a normal crisis talk-through. Vince didn't have a terminal running, surrounded by Post-it notes and an open file of spec sheets. He wasn't wearing the lucky hat he always put on for real work. His hair was backcombed over his bald spot. He wore his smart, first-meeting-with-clients jacket.

Was Leitch a new client? Vince didn't arrange first meets without consulting him. Even if a prospect had come up suddenly, Keith would have been filled in before Leitch appeared in the office.

Details niggled.

Vince's avoidance of him this morning, his excuse for ducking out of their regular lunch.

It wasn't just Vince. Rowena, his wife, had been different at breakfast. Even the kids, Jennifer and Jake. They'd all chattered around him, as usual. But the talk was brittle, with a fine edge of hysteria. It never let up. Questions thrown at him every second, tiny decisions for him to make, pretend-problems to keep him occupied.

Mary, his P.A., had called in sick and stayed away from work. She had not seemed to be coming down with anything yesterday.

Keith half-thought everyone was working on something behind his back. He even wondered, non-seriously, if he was about to be on *This Is Your Life*.

Of course, he was too ordinary for that.

What was going on? Somehow, he couldn't ask the question.

Vince didn't ask him to sit down. He wouldn't have, anyway. This was Keith's conference room as much as Vince's. He didn't need to be asked.

Something told him to stay standing.

"Keith Marion," Leitch said, confirming not questioning his identity. "This is an Intervention."

Keith didn't know what the stranger meant.

Leitch unzipped a leather document folder and opened it like a book. Like the book on *This Is Your Life*, come to that. He produced several white papers in blue plastic folders. He slid them down the table.

"These are copies, of course," he said.

Keith didn't look at the papers.

"They are consent forms," Leitch explained. "Would you authenticate the signatures, please?"

Keith sat down now and slipped the top document out of its blue folder. He turned to the last page and recognised Rowena's scrawl. He skimmed over the many clauses, mind buzzing too much to read.

Another form was signed by Vince. There were more, from his accountant, bank manager, the headmaster of the kids' school, his GP, his *parents*.

"This is a *radical* Intervention," Leitch clarified. "Your rights and responsibilities are suspended. Your bank accounts are frozen for the day, but the cosignees will assume responsibility at the opening of trading tomorrow.

Commitments will be fulfilled. The business will continue, until you are ready to reassume a position. So will your household."

Keith looked at Vince, who looked away.

"Your credit cards are revoked, the codes of all computers you had access to have been changed, burglar alarms here and at your house have been reprogrammed. You will please surrender your house, office and car keys."

Leitch produced a small plastic bowl.

Keith made a fist in his trouser pocket, around his keys.

Leitch held out the bowl and fixed him with his eyes.

"We can help you best if you don't fight us," he said. "Therapy has been authorized by people who care about you."

There were two other strangers in the room now. A man and a woman, casually dressed. They were between him and the door.

Through the glass partition, Keith saw the rest of the office. No one working. Everyone peering at the conference room. Mary was here now, in the reception area, smoking furiously.

Keith brought out his keys and dropped them in the bowl.

Leitch smiled.

"A first step," he said. "Every odyssey begins with a first step."

"And ends with a last one," Keith snapped.

There was a pause. Leitch's face shut down, as if not programmed to respond. Then he opened his mouth and laughed. The other strangers laughed too.

Vince looked away, eyes wet with tears.

"Your mobile phone?" Leitch asked.

The woman held up Keith's phone. She must have taken it out of his jacket, which was hanging on the back of his swivel chair in his office.

"I know this will seem overly harsh," Leitch said, "but you must believe it is done in your interests."

The man at the door took a pair of shears out of his coat pocket. The woman gave him Keith's mobile, and he snipped it cleanly in two.

The *snick* sound made Keith's heart jump.

"If you will come with us," Leitch said, standing up.

Vince took upon himself the task of gathering all the forms and returning them to Leitch.

Keith shoved his chair away from the table and stood.

"It's for the best, old son," Vince said. "You know that."

He knew nothing of the sort, but wasn't stupid enough to say so. The man and the woman were watching him, tensed, waiting for a move.

He remembered the heart-punching *snick*.

The woman held open the conference room door. Leitch left first. Keith was encouraged to follow.

He looked back. Vince didn't meet his eyes.

With Leitch's associates bringing up the rear, Keith was walked through the office. People he employed—*had* employed—scurried out of the way, wary of association with him. He didn't know what they'd been told.

In Reception, he walked past Mary. She was trying to light a fresh cigarette in her mouth while one was still burning between her knuckles.

She looked at him, not with shame but pity.

"Keith," she said, then nothing.

Cold fury kept him calm. He would go along until there was an opening. Then he'd be away. It was some kind of hostile takeover. He would have to fight back.

He was walked outside into the car park they called a courtyard. A white van was parked close by, next to his own estranged car. Another man got out of the van and opened the rear doors. Inside, the vehicle was padded, like a lunatic's cell. A stretcher was pulled out. An undercarriage descended.

"If you would take off your clothes and lie down," Leitch dictated. "Constant will see to them."

Constant, the *snick* man, took a large laundry sack out of the van and held it open.

It was a warm day. Faces were pressed to office windows all around the courtyard.

Constant held the sack open wide.

A long pause. Keith saw the *snick* in Constant's eyes and unbuckled his belt.

"Shoes first, I suggest," said Leitch.

Keith undid his trainers and dropped them in the sack.

"Good lad," said Constant.

Keith undressed and put all his clothes into the sack. He was conscious, standing naked, of the stone he'd gained in his thirties. Constant dropped the sack in a bright orange waste bin.

Keith started to protest.

The Intervention

"Out with the old," said Leitch. "It's important. Lie down, please."

Keith got onto the stretcher. It was exactly his size. Constant drew a thin sheet over him and then, with the help of the other assistant, swiftly fastened straps over the sheet.

"It's so you won't hurt yourself," said Leitch. "We've a long journey."

Keith tested the straps. He was held securely. He should have taken his chances with the *snick* man and made a run for it. Back into the office, out of one of the street doors, into the crowds.

Then what? He apparently had no money, no credit, no car, no business, no home.

The stretcher slid back into the van. The roof cut out the sky. The doors were shut and fastened. The strap across his throat prevented him lifting his head more than a few inches.

He heard Leitch and his assistants get into the fore compartment of the van and felt the engine turn over.

The windows in the back of the van were opaque white plastic, letting in light but no information. Gratton, the attendant, sat out of Keith's sight-line, walkman giving out a muted snare drum.

The van traveled over roads of differing qualities, at various speeds. It got shady and then dark, as afternoon passed into evening. A light was turned on. He shut his eyes against its harshness. His mind raced so fast at the beginning that he lost the sense of time. Hours had passed. He didn't know in which direction he was being driven.

Why had they done this to him? Was Ro having an affair with Vince? Were his wife and partner scheming to oust him? It seemed more extensive than that, as if everyone he knew were in on the game. They had his *kids'* signatures, in crayon.

Who was Leitch?

Even now, he couldn't remember the man's face.

"Nearly there, sunshine," said Gratton.

The attendant leaned over into Keith's field of vision and checked him.

"Is that an earring?" Gratton asked, pinching his lobe.

Keith nodded. He had got his ear pierced last year, when Jennifer had hers done. She'd wanted to do her nose, but he'd put his foot down.

Gratton gently took out the stud and palmed it.

"All for the best, mate," he said.

The van parked and the engine shut off. The quiet was unnerving after the lulling grind of the engine. The doors were wrenched open. Keith smelled the country: damp, vegetable, earthy.

It could be Cornwall or Wales or—depending on how late at night it was—Yorkshire. If it were Scotland, night would have passed and it would be the next day.

The stretcher was pulled out of the van. He saw sharp points of light in the black of the sky. Away from town, the stars were brighter.

"A good trip, Keith?" asked Leitch.

Keith turned his head and didn't reply. Leitch stood by the van, looking over a clipboard.

"We're far from the madding crowd out here," said Leitch. "A lot of therapy is getting away from it all. It sounds like old hat, but you'll be surprised how effective it can be. Everything put into perspective. Things seem clearer."

He indicated the stars. Keith felt cold.

"Let's go inside, shall we?" Leitch said, as if Keith had a choice. "It's a homey old place."

Beyond the van was a house, set in its own grounds but not a mansion. Trees grew close to the walls, which were buckled a bit by thrusting roots. A fluorescent globe light shone over the front doorway.

The house was at the end of a gravel driveway. Keith was carried by Gratton and Constant, who were careful not to let the undercarriage castors of the stretcher sink into the gravel. He looked left and right. A thin row of dark trees lined one side of the drive. A long, low, prefab-looking building was on the other, like a factory or college annex.

The stretcher was slid up a ramp placed on the front steps and the woman, Heather, opened the doors. The attendants set the stretcher down. Leitch himself unbuckled the straps.

Keith could have gone for his throat.

But maybe that was the test. If he so much as flinched, tasers would come out and he'd be zapped unconscious.

He needed to pee. And he was shivering.

"We'll get you something to wear," said Heather.

Keith sat up. He was in the hallway of what felt like a small hotel. A corkboard hung on one wall, opposite a mirror in an ugly old frame.

Heather helped him off the stretcher. He hugged his sheet to him. He was led into a small sitting room, where an imitation log electric fire was on. Heather opened a drawer in an old chest and gave him a pair of off-white woolly socks, a drawstring-waisted tracksuit bottom, a yellow pajama jacket, and a mouse-colored dressing gown without a cord. She turned away as he got dressed. The clothes had a hospital feel to them, soft as if washed too many times, slightly stale.

"There," she said, looking at him, "aren't you handsome."

It was something you'd say to a child or a very old person. It wasn't meant.

Leitch looked in. He approved of Keith's clothes.

"Early to bed, with no supper, I'm afraid," he said. "There'll be breakfast tomorrow. Then we can start."

Keith was led upstairs to a dormitory room with six beds, all empty.

"We're not too busy now," said Heather. "All the better for you. You'll have all of us to yourself, working on your behalf."

He was laid down on a bed, professionally.

"Let me see your hands," Heather said.

He showed her his manicured nails. She smiled and clipped a plastic noose around one wrist. It ratcheted tight and connected to the bed-rail. The bed, he now realized, was bolted to the floorboards.

"Just to be extra-safe," Heather said.

She turned out the lights and left the room.

He still needed to pee. He wasn't tired enough to sleep. He wanted to shout. He pulled the plastic cuff, testing it. He could get a foot or so of play in the line, but that cinched the noose into his wrist. Once notched up, it couldn't loosen.

He could roll off the bed, and did. That pulled loose the sheets and blanket—he hadn't slept under anything but a duvet in years—and exposed himself to a wicked draft. The room was dark, but he could feel under the bed. He found a plastic beaker, about a litre size, lowered his tracksuit bottom one-handed, and peed noisily into the container. Then he rearranged himself, and tried to get the bedclothes straight. He lost the top sheet and found scratchy blanket against his face and hands.

He didn't think he slept, but between one blink and the next it was light in the room. He was woken by a *snick* that gave him a panic spasm. Constant stood over him with his shears. Keith could move his arm, and realised Constant had cut the plastic tie. Constant *snicked* the air.

Should he eat the cooked breakfast? It might be drugged.

"I wouldn't let that go to waste, mate," said Gratton.

Keith looked down at the plate. Full English.

He hadn't eaten since yesterday's quick lunch. Hunger was a claw in his stomach.

He tucked in.

"There's lovely."

He couldn't remember the last time he'd eaten anything fried. It was one of Ro's health policies. His body no longer had a tolerance for grease.

The small dining room was attached to a plant-filled conservatory.

Keith looked around, itching for something.

"No papers, I'm afraid," said Gratton, realizing before Keith what it was he was missing. "Can't be doing with distractions. Let the outside world roll on by itself. You have to concentrate on your own problem."

"I don't have any problem."

Gratton smiled, tolerantly. "You're here, aren't you? You must have a problem."

Leitch stepped into the room. He wore a white jacket over jeans, and a big smile.

Keith was suddenly furious.

"What the hell is this all about? Why the hell am I here?"

Leitch sat down at the table, poured tea from the metal pot, shook a thin sachet of sugar.

"Those are questions you have to ask yourself, Keith. You're a clever man, so you know that you know the answers. But clever people can hide things from themselves. Stupid people can't, you know. Their one great advantage. Do you think you've been hiding answers from yourself?"

Keith genuinely didn't understand the question. "That makes no sense."

"Indeed. If you realize that, there's a chink. You're here to make sense of it."

"Where's 'here'?"

Leitch poured sugar into his tea.

"Not important," he said. "The map name wouldn't mean anything to you. Don't look out. Look *in*."

He made fists and held them together against his chest.

"*All the way in*, Keith."

Keith looked around the room, past Leitch's eyes, wondering if there was movement in the conservatory, calculating his chances of making a dash. He looked back at Leitch's bland face, and pushed back his chair.

Beyond the plants, windows were open. He felt a breeze.

He stood up, stretched.

"Good grub," he said, and ran, tipping the table aside.

He felt a thump in his side, then real pain. An expert jab to the kidney. Gratton held him up, so he didn't fall. Keith's legs were unstrung. Pain ran up and down the entire right side of his body.

Leitch still held his teacup.

"I'm disappointed, Keith," he said, sincerely. "You only hurt yourself by refusing to admit that you have a problem. I thought we were making progress, but I see that you were playing the cunning game, hiding in your burrow, squirreling away nuts for the winter. You've let yourself down. And people depend on you, Keith. Love you, need you. Rowena, Jennifer and Jake, Vincent, Mary, all of them. People you don't even think you know depend on you. Clients, officials, tradesmen, suppliers. They all want only for you to get better, to take your place. This isn't torture, it's therapy."

Keith was able to get a footing again. His sock-swaddled feet were flat on the tiles. The pain was going.

"You must understand."

Keith didn't say anything. He couldn't bring himself to nod.

"You must."

Another blow, in the same spot. He'd have doubled up, but he was held fast.

"Early days yet," said Leitch.

Still in the loose clothes he had been given last night, Keith was escorted out of the house and into the long, hutlike building. The windowless space had an old animal smell.

Overhead lights fizzed on. The building had no interior walls or partitions. In pools of light, basic furniture was arranged in basic configurations. It was like a rehearsal hall, with rough stage sets laid out. There were people here, mostly gathered at the far end, where there was no light.

Heather sat at a kitchen table, opposite an empty folding chair. She wore a dressing gown it took Keith a moment to recognise as Ro's.

He turned to Leitch and got no clue.

Gratton walked Keith into the scene and sat him down.

"Keith," Heather said, "this can't go on. The kids have noticed, things have been said at school."

Keith looked at the woman as if she were mad.

"Say something, damn you," she said.

She was doing Rowena, perfectly. The old accent still there, smoothed out by elocution lessons. Heather touched her hair, an exact Ro mannerism.

"You're frightening me," she said.

Keith looked back at Leitch and Gratton. His side still ached.

"You're not my wife," he said.

Tears started in her eyes. "*Keith,*" she remonstrated, almost whining, looking away, making as if to slap the table, then covering her face.

"But you're *not,*" he protested.

The woman began to sob, uncontrollably.

When Rowena's brother was killed in a car accident, she had been exactly like this. Then, he had tried to comfort her, to get close, to make it better.

Now, he froze.

Heather—*not Rowena!* a stranger!—tore her hair, clawed her face, screamed and cried, leaked gummy fluid from her eyes and nose. He folded his arms, cold inside, and watched the act.

He couldn't take this any more.

He stood up and turned. This was just a silly game.

Where Leitch and Gratton had been standing were two smaller people, Jake and Jennifer. Not stand-in midgets. Their faces were round with horror, appalled at what they had seen.

"Daddy," said Jennifer, reaching out.

"No," said Jake, holding his sister back. "Remember, we agreed."

Leitch was with his children.

"This is low," Keith said. "Really low."

The woman was still making a scene, collapsing into quieter, exhausted sobs that racked her entire body.

"This isn't Mum," he told his kids. "This is make-believe. I'll get you out of here, I promise. I won't let them hurt you."

He stepped toward his children. Damn the kidney-puncher. He'd take anything for Jake and Jennifer. It wasn't just him in this trap now. He had to protect the kids.

He really saw their faces and froze.

They were terrified of him. Jennifer broke away from Jake, and ran to Leitch, burying her face in his jacket. He cuddled and soothed her. Jake held his ground, and looked up at Keith, mouth set, defiant. He was white with terror.

"Dad, don't . . ."

The lights went out and came on again.

He was in another rough set, conforming to the layout of his office, seated in front of an old unconnected television set and a manual typewriter. At the edge of the light, Leitch watched, taking notes.

There were no other "actors."

Keith tried to think through the problem. He wanted to call in Vince, to hash it all out. They could crack almost anything.

He had heard of these things. Interventions.

But they were for people with serious drug problems, alcoholics, and addicts of self-destructive behavior. Weak people who excused their bad behavior by blaming it on irresistible compulsion. Randy bastards who called themselves sex addicts, fat fools who said the Devil made them eat too much, downright crooks who alleged poor toilet training made them steal car radios. Keith was not like that at all. He was just ordinary.

He followed Leitch's advice and looked in, searching for a reason.

Until yesterday, he hadn't had any serious problem. If anything, his life had been well above average. Vince, though it didn't hinder him in the business, was in much worse personal shape, divorced and estranged from his daughter. There were no hiccups in Keith's marriage. He had even been secure enough to tell Ro that Mary had a little crush on him. The kids were great, getting on well in school

(*and terrified of him*)

and Ro was contemplating going back to work, not just for the money, but because she wanted to.

Financially, they were set up. No hidden holes in the accounts. No money bleeding out anywhere

(*that he knew of*).

Imagining images on the dusty screen of the pretend computer, he ran scenarios. Vince was in worse shape than Keith had thought, mixed up with one of his daughter's mad slut friends, spending more and more to keep above water, concealing the drain on the business. Vince knew he'd be found out soon, and had set things up so it all seemed to be Keith's fault. His partner, his best friend, had framed him, projecting his own troubles.

Did Vince resent Keith that much? Resent his undivorced wife and unestranged children?

It couldn't be true. It couldn't *not* be true.

Leitch stepped into the light and sat down on a swivel chair.

"Let's talk business," he said.

Had Vince fooled Leitch? Or was the therapist in on it? Keith had to try least-worst scenario first.

"It's not me, it's Vince," he said. "Look closely. Who called you in? Who showed you the books? This is a setup, a conspiracy. *Cui bono?*"

Leitch looked genuinely sad.

"Keith, Keith, Keith . . . listen to yourself. Ask yourself if even you believe yourself. Look at it like the daily crisis, attack it. Think it through."

Keith spent too much time with Vince. There was no space in his partner's life for the scam he'd imagined.

"If not Vince, someone," he said to Leitch. "You, maybe."

"I only want to help you face your problem."

"I haven't got a sodding problem! How many times do I have to say it?"

"How many times *can* you say it, Keith? How many times before it sounds as fake in your ears as in everyone else's?"

"I haven't got a problem, I haven't got a problem, I haven't . . ."

Leitch was right. It did sound fake. Clearly, Keith had a problem, or he wouldn't be here. It was just that the problem wasn't with Keith. It was with . . .

"Everyone else," said Leitch. "The whole rest of world is wrong, and you're right. Hold that up to the light, Keith. Think. Take that step. Admit the problem, and perhaps there's a way past . . ."

He heard the unforced sincerity in the man.

He was letting them all down, he knew. Somehow. In a way he really couldn't see.

But no. He wasn't a boozer, on drugs, a gambling nut, screwing around, abusing his kids, dragging the business down. He just wasn't.

He couldn't think of a problem.

"Leitch, I don't know what you want me to say."

"It's not what I want. This isn't to please me, Keith. In this room, I don't matter. This is your place. What do you want to say?"

"I don't know."

Leitch smiled, with relief. "Super, Keith. That's a half-step. You can admit that you don't know. You understand now how difficult that is for someone like you. Someone used to knowing. It's all right not to know, to have doubts. It's all right."

"I'm so proud of you, darling," said a woman.

He saw Heather, in the freestanding empty frame that represented his office door. No, not Heather. Rowena, face streaked.

He tried to stand.

Rowena stepped back, dark curtaining her face.

"Not yet, Keith," said Leitch. "Later."

More sets, more scenes. Leitch and Heather were his parents, taking him through a rerun of his teenage years, which overlapped with his memory but also contradicted it radically. They talked through his decision to turn down a directorship of the firm he had started with and set up on his own with Vince, Leitch stabbing in harsh questions about Vince's reliability far more vehemently than Dad actually had done.

Then the pair became Jake and Jennifer, eerily dead-on in their performances, wearing tailored adult-sized school-blazers with overlarge badges to keep the scale. They quizzed him about their own lives and interests. It was a struggle to recall the pop bands and computer games the kids were obsessed with, to be rated harshly on his knowledge of trivia that had been a background buzz in his life for the past few years. He thought he knew the names of Jennifer's best friends, in order of preference, but things had changed in the playground and he was working from last month's crib-sheet.

He was sat down at a school desk he was uncomfortable with, and an elderly woman slapped a piece of paper in front of him. When he turned it over and recognized his Geography o level exam, he realized that the woman was Mrs. Boat, his old form teacher from school. On the desk were a pad of lined paper ("use only one side and leave wide margins"), a pen, a plastic ruler, and a box of colored pencils. Mrs. Boat invigilated, holding up a stopwatch as he struggled to draw maps and write essays. He hadn't used a fountain pen to write more than a check in decades. Blotches appeared on his hands and the paper. Twenty-five years ago, he'd got a B grade Pass; this was likely to be a washout, a Fail.

There were no meal-breaks. He was not let out of the long hut.

The sessions went on and on. Days must have passed, but only he got tired. Leitch and his assistants all remained fresh.

He played real games with Constant and Gratton and mostly lost. One-on-one basketball, arm-wrestling, pool, snakes and ladders, dominoes, the mirror game, I Spy, Risk, Cluedo, Campaign, hopscotch, twenty questions, truth or dare, darts.

Heather, as Mary, tried to seduce him in his "office," while Rowena and the kids watched from chairs outside the circle of light. He resisted, though the woman, surely improvising, became more and more blatant and wanton. After an hour of this, Leitch let Rowena and the kids go, assured Keith that this was a time-out for them and that if he wanted to take advantage of the opportunity no one would be any the wiser. He also winked.

Exhausted, he kissed Heather on the mouth. She slapped him.

Leitch and his real lawyer, Simon Manfred, took him through the basics of sexual harassment legislation. They read long legal documents aloud, interpolating brand names of household cleaning products somewhere into every sentence, never repeating, always managing to conceal them so that sense was preserved. He found himself listening for "Lemon Jif," "Daz," and "Persil," missing what was actually being said, which became more and more serious. Legal complications were set out which could bring his whole life crashing down and land him in prison.

That ended, and he was in a sit-com. Rowena and the kids—the real ones—sat around the breakfast table, providing a laugh track as he tried to get through to them. They must have been brainwashed. In the end, he threw the props around, smashing things. His family found this utterly hilarious.

He collapsed and slept, for maybe ten seconds.

He woke in complete darkness, handcuffed to something with a wiry, hairy arm. It jittered, chittered and leaped, landing on his ribs with a lot of projectile weight. Hairy all over, it smelled rank. He was jerked into a sitting position as the thing bounded off. He was dragged across a bare earth floor. The creature screeched and banged his wrist over and over against the ground. Keith lay limp, dreading long fingers that might come for the soft parts of his face.

It was all over. They were just going to kill him now.

A light came on. Leitch was sitting on a milking stool next to him, a black-furred, pink-faced animal in his lap, stroking and petting and calming. Keith was handcuffed to some member of the monkey family, smaller and more spidery than a chimpanzee.

"This is Kiki, my spider monkey," said Leitch.

That made sense.

Keith couldn't believe he'd had that last thought.

"You see the metaphor, of course," said Leitch. "It's not quite literal. But if we'd put Kiki on your back, you might have been seriously injured. She's a strong little thing. But you get the point. You must be used to the feeling that a part of you is beyond your control. Potentially dangerous, potentially frightening. But also exciting, entertaining, cute as a button. You can't blame Kiki, and you have to love her, but she's not good for you. No, dearie, you're not. Sorry, but you have to say bye-bye to Keith now. There's a good girl."

Constant snicked the plastic cuff. Keith had two leftover noose-bracelets on his right wrist now. Leitch passed the spider monkey to Constant, who carried it off.

"Now, Keith, how would you like some crack cocaine?"

Keith shuddered.

"Just joking," said Leitch. "Time for tea and bickies though."

Keith sat, dissociated, stunned. Around him, everyone had a tea break. Ro rationed two biscuits apiece to Jennifer and Jake, knowing Keith usually slipped them sweets against her program but not really minding. Gratton and Mary lit up cigarettes and went to the far corner of the hut, where Keith could swear they were flirting. Vince sat as far away as possible, whispering into a mobile phone that hadn't been cut in half. Constant worked at the crossword of a newspaper, which was missing its front pages. Leitch slurped his urn-decanted tea like a connoisseur. Other people milled about, some familiar, others not.

"Going well, isn't it?" said Manfred, cheerily. "It's rather fun."

Nobody brought Keith any tea.

Mrs. Boat came back with his exam paper, covered in red ink.

"A 'D,'" she said. "Good thing it was only the mock. You'll do better under real fire."

He stared at his essay on Swiss crop rotation. Red scribbles on blue blotches.

He couldn't see how any of this was helping.

Leitch finished his tea.

"Back to work, everyone," he said.

Chairs were put in a circle, and Keith was love-bombed. Everyone told him how he or she really felt about him, mostly with tears. They all reminisced out loud about the most perfect moments of their relationship. Manfred remembered in convincing detail a weekend of walking in the fell country that Keith could have sworn he and Ro had gone on with Vince and his ex. Then, they all told him when they had started to notice the problem.

Nobody said what the problem was.

But they had all noticed it. Jennifer haltingly recounted the months during which she had gone from being afraid *for* to being afraid *of*, and how the nightmares had got out of control. Jake talked about the shame he had felt at school, when word got out and his friends' parents told their kids to put distance between themselves and the Marion family.

Vince, amazingly reluctant and halting, said the morale of the office was affected. The business might suffer.

Leitch said nothing, but looked at Keith throughout, fixed.

Heather kept asking Keith how he felt, after each little speech. He felt less and less.

The session seemed to go on for hours, days. It was an impossible shift.

No one else got tired.

A well-dressed man, who turned out to be Keith's tax inspector, ran over the case notes for the last five years, flagging odd slips. Keith had made more errors in their favor than his. Only a few pounds were astray, but the man was meticulous. Also boring.

Mrs. Boat said Keith had potential but was easily distracted by extra-curricular activities and could do better. Fair only.

Mum blamed herself. She admitted that she'd always known, but hadn't wanted to face it. But she would stick by him, would see him better. Dad agreed with her.

Ro said she had thought about leaving.

Finally, Leitch spoke.

"It's a house of cards, Keith, and you've built it. You've developed highly sophisticated systems for dealing with your problem, for hiding from it and behind it. They work, and will work for years. But it's only a house of cards. It will collapse. The machine will run down. It's up to you. All of us here have taken it as far as we can. We have to hand the weight back to you. There's a lot of love in this circle, and it's there for you. But it's not unconditional. You have to reach inside, to make a break, to make an admission. Now, is there anything you want to say?"

Keith was cold inside.

He made the words in his mind. *I have a problem.* He knew the reaction that would get. The gathering-around, the tearful hugs, the firm handshakes, the shoulder-claps, the restoration of rights and responsibilities.

He had no spit in his mouth. His tongue was old leather.

He could only creak.

Expectant eyes were on him. His lips went in and out.

"I . . ."

Breaths were held.

Could he lie? Could he fool them?

No, firmly, no. He could not lie.

He shrugged, and sat quiet.

The disappointment waves were worse than blows. His family and friends and associates were all too drained to react. They had poured out so much and this wasn't the ending they had yearned for. They bristled, resenting him for not backing down.

Leitch made a mark on his clipboard.

Vince got up and walked away from the circle. Jennifer began to cry, softly. Mum and Dad held hands. Rowena looked at him with something close to hatred.

"You're a strong man, Keith," said Leitch. "Strong and clever. It's worse for you because of that. You've incorporated the problem into your makeup. You've put up thick walls around yourself. You're in real danger. This place is your last stop before the void. Deep down, you know that. We certainly do. That's no threat. Just a statement."

"Daddy, *please,*" said one of his kids.

"Come on, mate. Get it over with."

"Keith, Keith . . ."

"It can't be that difficult."

"Just say it, Marion."

"Son . . ."

"Out with it."

"Dad . . ."

"Come on."

"You could do better."

"You can do it, Keith."

"Now, please."

Voices from the circle, overlapping, rising.

Inside him, a wall was dismantled. His stomach was ice. His mind floated, far off, then clicked back, into sharp focus.

"Okay, all right," he said. "I've got a problem."

A beat. Quiet. Incipient rapture. Shining faces.

Leitch still looked expectant. Keith didn't get it.

"I admit it, Leitch. I, Keith Marion, have A Problem."

Leitch nodded. "Good," he said, "*good*. Progress. Breakthrough. Now, Keith, you have a problem."

Dead inside, Keith looked at the therapist.

"So, Keith," said Leitch, "what are you going to do about it?"

Blake's Angel

BY JANEEN WEBB

Then cherish pity, lest you drive an angel from your door.

—William Blake, *Holy Thursday*

Inside the iron mesh cage, the angel was shaking.

A fine drizzle had begun falling from a steely-grey sky, and a sharp wind had sprung up, whirling grit and candy wrappers and greasy food scraps along the grimy alley. The angel shivered. His wings ached where they had been clipped, and he shuddered again at the remembrance of dirty secateurs and the foul breath of the men who had pushed his face into the filthy ground to stifle his screams. He hoped his wounds were not infected. Another bout of trembling took him, a rush of heat and a cold sweat that told him he was hoping against the odds. He tried not to radiate his distress, determined not to call for help. That was how they'd caught him, dropping their rank net as he struggled with the lock to release Alisha. God only knew what they'd done with her now.

The angel-seller's booth was at the far end of a ragged line of street traders, obscured by a tangle of ducts and pipes, beside heaps of empty cardboard boxes and wooden shipping pallets, well away from prying eyes. The alley stank of slops from the food vendors' stalls—the reek of rotting cabbage and congealing chicken blood mixing with the pungent smells of heavy spices, of curry leaves and fenugreek and cumin. A tomcat had pissed at one corner of the angel cage, marking territory and adding to the stink of the neighboring medicine stall with its stands of tiger balm and antler velvet and rhinoceros horn and bull's pizzles for virility, with its ginseng roots and mounds of bark and leaves and its strange homunculi floating in specimen jars.

At the front of his booth the trader lounged, smoking a roll-your-own and pausing occasionally to spit through yellowed teeth. Once in a while he swiped a damp rag across the grubby glass-topped counter displaying angel-wares: feathered earrings, necklaces and bracelets of beads and angel feathers, woven angel headbands. A revolving stand offered key rings, bookmarks, pens, little terra-cotta angel statues with glued-on feathers. From the grimy striped awning dangled clusters of charms and amulets made of genuine angel products—feathers, hair, skin. There were long single feathers bound with red and gold thread, for luck; round wheels of shorter feathers radiating from bunches of herbs, for healing the sick; silver pendants with a lock of angel hair inside, for courtship. And at the back, carefully wrapped against the dirt, there were pure white angel-feather bridal fans, for marital harmony. On an upturned crate behind the stall, a wrinkled old lady sat, sipping tea and muttering to herself, rocking to and fro while she stitched the recent clippings from the angel's wings into such a fan, a special wedding order.

The angel felt sick.

A sudden flurry of activity announced that someone, a tourist, a prospective customer, had blundered into the alley. The traders swooped, crying their wares, offering remedies, bric-a-brac, heart's desire. A pimp in a grubby T-shirt and even grubbier jeans sidled out of a doorway, said something; the newcomer blushed, shook his head, kept walking.

The angel locked his fingers through the wire mesh, climbed a little way up the rocking cage to watch the man's progress, glad of any distraction. There were rumors, he knew, of a man who frequented the markets and bought caged creatures just to watch them fly free. One glance told him this was not the man.

This man was short, stocky, and round in the belly. His crumpled white cotton shirt was stained dark at the armpits; his baggy khaki trousers were shiny at the seat and knees. He looked embarrassed as he waved aside the importuning traders, but he made his way steadily toward the back of the alley, toward the angel-seller's booth.

The angel-seller affected to look bored, flicking his rag about, miming disinterest as the man approached.

Blake's Angel

The customer stopped at the angel-wares counter, looking furtively about him. His domed forehead was beaded with perspiration, and he smelled of sweat and cheap white wine. He put down the scratched leather briefcase he was carrying, tucking it safely between his scuffed loafers.

The trader slouched, elbows on the glass countertop. "You want to look, mister?" He pointed at the cabinet. "Plenty pretty things. All authentic." He held out one of the amulets. "Look at this. All real angel-feathers. Guaranteed. I can give you a certificate."

The customer cleared his throat. "No. Thank you. I'm not looking for trinkets or artifacts." He leaned toward the trader, said softly, "I heard, that is I was told, that you might have, you know, *live* specimens?"

The angel's heart sank.

"Who told you?"

"A friend. At a workshop. I've come a long way." The man mopped his mottled face with a once-white handkerchief.

The trader looked the customer up and down, evaluating. "It'll cost you," he said.

"I know. I can pay." He squirmed around, pulled a worn leather wallet from his frayed hip pocket.

The trader leaned farther forward, conspiratorially. "Maybe I can help you. You come around the back." He edged out from behind the counter, unlatched the side gate, gestured toward the grimy cages obscured from public view by the canvas of the stall.

The customer put away his wallet, picked up his briefcase, squeezed his bulk through the little gateway. He took a few steps in the direction of the cage. The angel hung there on the wire, eyes averted.

The customer stared. Despite his recent rough handling, the angel's beauty was breathtaking. He shone like a gilded icon in the greasy light of the alley. The skimpy white robe that the trappers had draped about him when they stole his clothes hid nothing of his perfectly muscled form, and his darkening blue-black bruises served only to accentuate his flawless creamy-white skin. He had a mop of shining golden curls that rippled to his broad shoulders, and his averted gaze showed the customer a faultless profile that seemed carved from alabaster.

The man looked abashed. He simply stood and gaped, absently pushing grubby, nicotine-stained fingers through his thinning white hair. "My God," he said at last, "it really looks like an angel."

The trader grinned, exposing his yellowed teeth. "Genuine angel," he agreed.

The customer paused, peered, adjusted his rimless spectacles. He stroked his little white goatee beard, looked nervously around him. The alley was quiet, except for the low mumbling of the old lady, who had deliberately turned her back.

The angel could smell the little man's need, could taste his hunger, and his fear. He fought down his own nausea, and turned his head. He raised his impossibly blue angel-eyes to meet the watery pale blue human ones that observed him.

It was the customer who first lowered his gaze. He fidgeted, jingling his keys in his trouser pocket. The lonely sound echoed in the alley.

"OK?" said the trader. "We have tea now."

The customer said nothing as he was shepherded back towards the front of the booth. Right on cue, the old crone hobbled up to the counter with a tray, which held a chipped teapot and two little round cups. She backed away again, and the trader poured. Jasmine-scented steam wafted upward, and the customer took the proffered cup, relieved to have something to hold in his hand. He sipped in silence for a moment.

"Genuine angel, very beautiful," the trader began again, nodding judiciously. "You have questions?"

The customer cleared his throat. "I'm a poet," he said. "I'm looking for inspiration. Is this angel inspirational?"

"Ah," said the trader. "I thought you looked like a sensitive man. We get a lot of artistic buyers." He smiled his crooked smile. "Yes, he's one hundred percent inspirational. It's what they do best. Just look at him."

The poet glanced back toward the cage, the longing plain in his worried face.

"And the women," the trader said, leering. "The women are drawn to them. You'll be a very popular man with the women." He winked.

The poet swallowed uncomfortably, ignoring this direction. "Does he sing?" he asked.

"Oh, yes, but he won't do it here in the cage. He is just captured. When he is recovered, he will sing for you. Celestial music." The smile was back. "Ask anyone."

"You know I can't do that. The angel trade isn't exactly legal, is it?"

The trader shrugged. "If you want the angel, you buy him. No one will stop you. It's up to you."

Blake's Angel

The customer seemed nervous again, twisting the cup in his hands. He looked about him, obviously weighing his options. He took a deep breath. "How much?" he asked.

The trader wrote a figure on a scrap of paper, pushed it across the counter to the rotund little man.

"You're joking," the poet said.

The trader spat deliberately into the gutter. "Very rare specimen," he replied. "Tall, well muscled, pure white wings. You've seen for yourself."

The poet named a lower price.

"For that," said the trader, "it would be more profitable to break him up for parts." He swept a hand across his display case.

The poet paled. "You wouldn't," he said.

The trader shrugged. "These are all genuine." He patted the glass, then took up his pencil stub once more to write another figure. He smiled as he slid it across the counter. "I have overheads," he said. "If he doesn't sell . . ." He let the implication hang in the fetid alley air.

The poet swallowed hard, countered once again, a higher bid this time.

The trader shook his head, then produced a grubby calculator from beneath the counter. "I tell you what I'll do. You seem like a genuine buyer," he said. "For you, special price. I work out my margin."

He tapped away, then held out the calculator for the poet to see.

The poet's shoulders sagged. "You guarantee he's inspirational?" he asked.

"Absolutely. One hundred percent," the trader replied. "You can't go wrong with this one."

The poet was sweating now. He typed in a slightly lower figure. "That's my final offer. It's all I've got."

The trader spat again. "My children will not eat tonight. Make me a little bit better offer."

"Sorry. That's that then." The poet sighed, picked up his badly scuffed briefcase, preparing to depart. "As I said, it's all I've got. Take it or leave it."

The trader held out a dirt-streaked hand. "OK," he said. "Deal."

The poet took the hand gingerly. "Deal," he replied.

The trader pulled a dog-eared receipt book from under the counter. "What name do you want on the delivery docket?"

"What? Oh, sorry. Williams. Blake Williams." The poet inspected his fingernails. "And I'm not local. I'll want him shipped."

"That'll cost extra."

"How much?"

The haggling process began again.

In the cage, the angel listened, aching with disease and despair.

Night fell. The angel could sense his brethren loitering nearby, drawn by his anguish. Strange shapes in lumpy overcoats that concealed the telltale wings, they waited, poised and light-footed, to see if they could help. He tried again to damp down his pain, to deny his captors their lure. "Wait," he sent. "This is a trap." It was hard, so hard, for them to see a fellow creature suffer, to go against their very nature, to turn away. But tonight they managed it.

The angel-cage was hoisted into darkness, and the nightmare journey began. Ten days later, the angel sat hunched in a corner, heartbreakingly beautiful, tethered by an iron chain to an iron bedpost. The ankle cuff chafed his smooth white skin, raising ugly red welts. The fever had passed, but he was still weak. He needed to rest. He shuddered to remember the crate, the stinking livestock lorries, the jolting darkness, the motion sickness. Passed from one smuggler to the next along the angel network, he'd finally been delivered to the poet's grotty attic apartment in its seedy downtown neighborhood. Now his new owner was showing off his purchase to his closest friends.

George and Katrina lived in the ground-floor apartment of Blake's building, and they'd seen the packing crate arrive at the end of the day, watched it hauled ungently up the narrow stairs. They'd immediately dropped by, agog with neighborly curiosity. Now they stood, holding freshly filled wineglasses, staring in astonishment at the exquisite winged creature shackled to the bed. The angel glowed golden in the grey city light, the richness of his presence making the poet's modest apartment seem even shabbier.

"So the rumors we've been hearing are true, Blake," said George. "You've actually bought a real live angel."

"As you see."

George peered at the quivering angel from a respectful distance, but Katrina stalked right up to him. She slid a crimson-painted fingernail down his bare arm. The angel flinched. His blue eyes blazed. "He's absolutely gorgeous," she said.

"Don't, Kat," said George. "You'll frighten him."

"Nonsense, darling," she purred, reaching up to stroke a shining, white-feathered wing. "He knows I like him." Her red-lipsticked mouth widened into a dreamy smile. "Maybe I can help you clean him up, Blake. Give him a nice hot soapy bath, or something?" The way she eyed the bulge in the angel's loincloth was downright predatory.

Blake cleared his throat. "That won't be necessary, thank you." The words sounded more formal than he had meant them to. George looked uncomfortable.

"Suit yourself," said Katrina. "I'm only trying to help." She sauntered back to stand beside George, still gazing longingly at the angel.

There was an awkward silence, in which all three regarded the dejected acquisition. It was George who broke the impasse. "He doesn't look very well," he ventured.

"I reckon it was a pretty tough trip," said Blake, relieved to steer the conversation back into safer waters. "And I'm not sure what to feed him. I should have asked. I tried fruit, but he hasn't touched the apple. He's had a little water."

"I heard they don't survive well in captivity."

"He'll be all right. He just needs time to get used to a new environment, that's all. He's probably pining."

"Pining?"

"They're social creatures. He's lonely because he's separated from his flock." The poet poured out more wine for his friends.

"Well," said Katrina, her voice low and throaty, "he won't be lonely with *me* around. I'll always be happy to keep him company."

A fleeting expression of appalled understanding crossed the angel's perfect face. He huddled closer to the bedpost.

Again it was George who spoke. "So why the chain?" he asked. "His wings are clipped. He can't fly out of the window." George appeared genuinely distressed. "He looks so miserable. It can't be right to keep him chained up like that."

"It's the iron," Blake replied. "It keeps them grounded to the earth. They can't escape while they're bound with iron."

"Is that how they capture them, then?"

"Sort of. They lure them close to an iron cage, then they net them. They use pain for bait. It's the empathy. They're drawn to suffering. They can't stop themselves. They have to try to help. It's their nature." He grinned. "So I reckon he'll respond to my misery and help me over my writer's block." The smile vanished. "He'd better. He cost me my life savings."

"I'm sure he'll be just wonderful," said Katrina. She tucked her free hand under Blake's arm, snuggling close, conspiratorial. "And I'll visit him every day while you're working, so he won't be lonely."

"Well, I still think it's wrong to cage something so magnificent, so . . . pure," said George. "You can see he doesn't belong here. Show some pity, Blake. Let him go."

"No." Blake's jaw stiffened. "Not till I get my inspiration. Then I'll think about it. Maybe."

George looked down at his glass, fiddled with the stem. He could not bear to meet the angel's blue gaze. "Well, let's hope that's sooner rather than later, then," he said.

"Don't be so grumpy, darling," said Katrina. "Blake's just told us how valuable the angel is. You can't expect him to pay all that money, then just set the creature free. He might as well throw his money away."

"Would it make any difference if I offered to buy him from you?"

"No. He's my angel and he's not for sale." Blake forced a smile. "Give it a rest, George. I thought you'd be pleased for me. It'll all work out, you'll see."

George drained his glass, suddenly aware that he needed to be away from the sight of the chained angel. "Well, thanks for the drink, Blake," he said. "I'll see you around. Are you ready, Kat?"

"Not yet, darling, I'll just stay and finish my wine. I'll be down in a little while." She kissed him lightly on the cheek as he turned to leave.

Blake topped up her glass, and Katrina draped herself languorously across the end of the bed, almost touching the angel. Teasing. The angel shrank from her, furling his injured wings more tightly about himself. Blake swallowed hard, but did not comment. The bottle was emptied, and the talk turned to other things.

Weeks stretched into months. Living in the same room as an unhappy angel had not improved the poet's temper. Neither had Katrina's constant visits. She just couldn't leave him alone, always popping in with this or that transparent excuse. She knew Blake worked naked, but she didn't care. She barged in whenever she felt like it, which was all the time. She'd even insisted on afternoon tea, complete with angel cake, for God's sake. Blake's patience was wearing very thin. He was still blocked, and drinking heavily. He sat at the table, staring balefully at a silent keyboard. Once again he addressed his captive, continuing his drink-sodden monologue. "So you still refuse to help me, then? You know you'll never get out of here unless you do, don't you?"

The angel remained hunched, silent. He touched the tin water dish with a wary toe. His wings drooped in defeat.

"What sort of angel are you, anyway? They promised me you could sing. 'Celestial music,' that's what the trader said. That's what I paid for."

A faint smile sketched itself across the angel's pallid face. He shook his head, miming: "No."

"No? You mean you can't or you won't?"

The angel shook his head again.

The poet hurled a bottle at him, missing by a wide margin. The angel shrugged, spread his hands in a universal gesture: "Please, no."

The poet raised an unsteady hand, menacing. "Well," he said, "you're bought and paid for." His face took on a look of drunken cunning. "If you don't inspire me *very* soon I can always sell you back for spare parts."

The angel's sigh was almost audible.

He lifted his head, straightened his stooped shoulders, smoothed his wings. Decision shone plain in his beautiful, pale face.

He cleared his throat.

And he began to sing.

The first pure notes, high and sweet, dropped like clear honey into the dank air of the attic apartment. The hum of the traffic receded.

The poet peered blearily over the rim of his wineglass, and smiled. "That's more like it," he said.

The sound swelled, wordless, clean and sad, filling all the building's space with its aching melancholy, growing in magnitude until it seemed the walls trembled.

Downstairs, George and Katrina stopped to listen as the unearthly music flowed through their apartment and out to the street.

"It's wonderful," said Katrina. "I knew he'd sing eventually. I'm going right up to see."

"Maybe you were right," said George. "Maybe it was just a question of time. I've never heard anything so beautiful." Tears were starting in his eyes.

"You're such an old softie," said Katrina. She gave him a quick hug. "Are you coming up to Blake's with me?"

"No, not yet. I don't want to intrude. I'll listen from outside for a while."

"Suit yourself." She was already out of their apartment, taking the stairs to Blake's attic two at a time.

George headed for the street, where a curious crowd was gathering.

The volume of the angel's lament increased; he sang of his shame, of his sorrow, of his longing. He sang of torture, and of death.

The poet was weeping now. It was not gentle. Great racking sobs convulsed his chest; hot tears ran unheeded down his red-veined nose. He gulped for air. "Stop it," he cried. "For pity's sake stop it."

The angel sang on, unheeding. Window glass shattered.

Katrina dashed into the room. "The door was open," she began.

Blake cut her off with a gesture. "Not now," he moaned. "Not now."

She stopped, open-mouthed, in the middle of the room. The angel towered over her. He stood erect, his ankle chain stretched taut. His feathers had regrown, and he held his huge, shining wings outspread, filling the tiny apartment. He seemed totally unaware of her intrusion.

The sound soared.

The apartment walls began to crumble, wide cracks spidering up the bricks and mortar, plaster fracturing, timbers snapping and splintering. A fissure opened in the pavement below. A fire hydrant burst, sending plumes of frothing water high into the air.

And still the angel sang. The barrier was broken. From all over the city, other angels joined their brother in his chorus of grief. His solo voice swelled into a choir.

The roof caved in. Katrina shrieked, unheard, as a roof beam crashed down upon her. The poet was buried where he sat, sobbing, head in hands. Golden light poured from the ruined building, illuminating the cloud of plaster dust that rose into the night sky. Somewhere in the distance, sirens wailed.

The music changed. The lament became a hymn of praise, spiraling upward to the heavens. The chains of iron snapped.

Draggled and dust-streaked in the wreckage, the angel wept.

And flew free.

The Obedient Child

BY GEORGE CLAYTON JOHNSON

The sleeping child's breath perfumes the still air.

It is not yet dawn.

Dreaming, she does not hear the click of the screendoor latch, nor does she hear the careful footfalls in the narrow kitchen outside her small bedroom.

She comes groggily awake to the feel of strong arms gripping her, blanket and all, feels herself lifted and clutched to his chest, feels his fingers touching her lips.

"Shhh . . ." he says warningly, "you'll wake your mother."

The idling car is waiting, its windows all steamed over, a man, a blurred bulk, behind the wheel. He leans back to open the rear door as the old man appears out of the darkness, carrying the drowsy child.

Once inside, with the small girl across his lap, the door pulled quietly closed, the old man gives crisp instructions. "Straight ahead to the first dirt road and take a right. I know a place."

The small girl snuggles closer in his arms, her eyes closed, feeling his warmth and smelling the familiar scent of tobacco and sweat, listening.

"Is that her?"

"It's her, all right. You got the money?"

The man behind the wheel reluctantly passes back an envelope, which the old man shuffles through greedily.

"Now we're talking," says the old man, putting the envelope under his coat with his free hand.

"Let me see her," says the driver, glancing back over his shoulder.

The old man lifts the girl's chin gently. "Are you awake?"

The child opens her eyes.

"I want you to meet somebody. He calls himself Ed. Say hello."

"Hello."

"Say pleased to meet you."

"Pleased to meet you," says the little girl sweetly.

"Did you know Ed here told me how he used to know your mother when they were just little kids like you are? He lived next door. They used to play together. Isn't that right, Ed?"

The child's face becomes animated. Her eyes are wide. "Really?"

The driver's face is flinty. "You talk too much," says the man grimly.

"Calm down. She has the right to know. After all, who's she going to tell? Her mother? Isn't that the idea? So she'll know why?" To the child he says, "I only met Ed here this morning, having breakfast at that all-night grease pit. I noticed the way he walked when he came in. He's got a limp. The damnedest things come up when you're talking to some stranger you never expect to see again. He told me all about what happened to him and what he was after. The more he told me, the more I knew what I needed to do. I offered to help him."

"For money," says the driver.

"There's always that to consider," says the old man genially. "Turn right here and slow down. It's a washboard for the next half-mile. That's why nobody comes out here. It's perfect. A person could yell their head off and never be heard."

The roadway beneath them at once becomes rough and rutted. The driver's fingers grip the wheel as he slows the protesting car to a crawl.

Her curiosity aroused, the little girl sits up straighter, watching the line of trees juddering by through the weeping glass. She wiggles off the old man's lap and props herself in the corner of the car seat from where she can watch the old man's face. Dressed only in a little white slip and panties, the small girl is oblivious to the cold. The old man picks up the blanket from the floor and wraps it carefully around her shoulders.

Her attention is caught by something shiny. She points at his bulging overcoat pocket.

"What's that?"

He digs in his pocket and comes out with it. "A ball of twine."

"What's it for?"

"To tie things up. It's made of hemp. Very strong."

"Can I see it?" wheedles the little girl. "Please?"

He hands it to her. "Don't break the wrapper. I want to keep it like that for a while."

"Thank you, Grandfather."

"Grandfather?" The driver is surprised.

"All the kids call me that. I kind of like it. See how obedient she is? She's just like her mother."

"Obedient? I call it sneaky. You've got to be a born sneak to pretend to be goody-goody all the time." The man snorts with disgust.

Turning his attention to the child, the old man says, "Don't let the way Ed talks bother you. He's got his reasons. Did you know that Ed here once lost a couple of toes? Cut clean off by a lawn mower in an accident."

The child's eyes are wide. Attentive.

"It wasn't no accident," says the driver coldly. "She did it on purpose, just because I got a little water on her dress. How easily you say 'lost a couple of toes,' as if it were nothing. Why don't you say 'permanently crippled' and see how that sounds? Even with special shoes I limp wherever I go, all because of a cruel little girl who knew damn well what she was doing."

His hand reaches down between the seats to grip something nestled there. He squeezes and lets go, squeezes again and lets go. He puts his hand back on the wheel with a grunt of satisfaction.

"Just a little farther now," says the old man, leaning forward, his hands on the back of the seat. "There's a place with a bunch of trees. There it is. Pull over here." To the little girl the old man says, "You stay here till I call you. I got something to talk over with Ed." He plucks the ball of twine from the girl's fingers. "Come on, Ed, I'll show you what I was talking about. Don't worry about her. She'll stay put," he says over his shoulder, slamming the door behind him. "She knows I'll reward her if she's good. She's well-trained."

The driver sighs heavily and climbs reluctantly from behind the wheel, opening and closing the car door, following the old man between the slender saplings.

"See this here tree?"

The old man strips the crisp cellophane from the ball of twine. He quickly ties a small slipknot, forming a loop on the loose end, and begins to pay out a couple of feet of cord.

"My idea is, you loop this piece around her wrist, like this."

He slips the loop around the man's wrist and pulls it tight. He begins to move quickly several times around the medium-size tree, still talking.

The man begins to lunge against the slender twine but it holds him fast. His breath explodes in a cry of surprise.

"Then you go around the tree a couple more times, like this," he says, pushing the protesting man against the tree, pulling the cord tight with surprising force with each circuit, wrapping the cord again and again about the man and the tree, trapping the free arm until the squirming man is helpless. "I learned this watching a spider one day," he says wisely.

Tying off the cord, the old man takes a penknife from an unseen pocket to cut it. He stows the ball of unused twine in his coat pocket.

"Now, what about that foot you been talking about?"

He crouches down and begins to strip off the man's boot, undoing the laces and then the sock to peer at the naked, wriggling foot in the early light.

"Not this one? Then it has to be the other."

He begins to take off the man's remaining boot.

"What are you doing? Wait a minute. Let's talk about this."

"I want to see what it is that made you so mean."

Off comes the other boot and then the sock.

"Well, lookie here."

He peers at the damaged foot. Two of the small toes are mere nubs covered with scar tissue colored an angry pink.

"She sure did a job on you, all right."

"Please untie me," begs the man, weeping.

"By damn. You still don't recognize me. Hell, I'm the one who put the idea in her mother's head. I never did like you, even when you were just a little kid next door. You were too much of a crybaby."

The man's eyes are dumbstruck.

The old man ignores him.

"Now let's see what you were playing with in the front seat."

He goes to the car and opens the driver's door. He fishes between the seats and comes out with a compact pair of garden clippers. A latch holds the hooked, spring-loaded jaws of the tool together until ready for use. Weighing the instrument in his hand, he looks at the girl, who has thrown off the blanket and is watching him intently.

"Please, Grandfather, can I get out now?" she says sweetly.

"Sure, darling. Can you handle the door yourself?"

"I think so."

"Use both hands. It will be easier."

The door is pushed open and the girl clambers out to stand beside the old man. Then she follows him to the sapling where the other man is tied. The sun has begun to rise above the distant horizon, filling the glade with golden light, filtering through the slim trees in bright shafts, bringing color to the meadow and the trees beyond. The chill goes out of the air. There is a sudden shrieking of meadowlarks in different keys, all with the same melody. The animals and insects begin to stir.

"Why is he tied up like that?" asks the child.

"To teach him a lesson."

"What lesson?"

"You can't get ahead trying to get even."

With surprising agility he bends down and grips the man's good bare foot, prying the toes apart, bringing out the garden tool. He trips the little catch on the handle and the wicked jaws spring open, ready to bite. "I think I'll keep these. They'll come in handy when I trim the fruit trees. I guess we can leave you here. You won't bother anybody. I've got your keys. I can leave your car downtown someplace."

"Oh God, what are you going to do?"

"Same thing you planned for her." His strong fingers pry the man's toes farther apart, selecting one for attention. The teeth of the clippers clip.

With the sudden pain the man screams and begins to sob.

"One more to go," says the old man to the child. "Do you want to help? It's messy."

"Yes, Grandfather." There is an eagerness in her voice.

"It will take two hands. Do you think you can do it?"

"I can. I can do it."

"Well, all right, then."

"My God, what are you talking about?"

The old man hands the garden tool to the small child. "Be careful," he says. "Those blades are sharp."

"I know how. It's just like a pair of scissors. Watch me."

The man struggles against the restraining net of cords but can only writhe and twist helplessly.

"For God's sake, have a heart."

"It's what you had in mind for this little girl, isn't it? For what her mother did to you? It's simple justice!"

"Now, Grandfather?"

"All right," he says to the child, "but just the little one. I'll hold him. Stand back and don't get anything on your dress. You know how your mother is."

Holding the clippers carefully, the little child bends forward studiously to her task, grunting with the effort, as she closes the handles.

The man screams piteously. "You can't leave me here," he sobs.

The old man takes the tool from the girl's hand, ignoring the man's cries. "Good girl." To the man he says, "I'd look out for bugs if I was you. They like blood."

Opening the car door, helping the little girl inside, he says, "I've got an idea. What do you say we pick up some ice cream and take it home with us? Your mother will be awake and we can tell her all about what happened."

"Goody," says the obedient child contentedly. "I love you, Grandfather."

"I love you, too, little partner."

Sounds Like

BY MIKE O'DRISCOLL

Holly is crying in her sleep again. For the third night running Larry Pearce listens from across the hall knowing that the right thing to do would be to go to her, to soothe her nightmares away. But instead, he tries to ignore her cries, the way he did last night and the night before. Only this time the harder he strives for silence, the more the sound gets under his skin. Judith stirs beside him but doesn't wake. He wonders if she's somehow immune to the cadences of childhood fear. Maybe it's simpler than that, maybe she doesn't want to remember what it's like to be a child because of all the things that scared her back then. Larry wonders if Holly already has some kind of insight into fear and that her cries are an attempt to articulate that understanding.

After thirty minutes Holly's still crying and Judith hasn't moved. Larry slides out of bed, pulls on a pair of shorts and pads out to the hall. He hesitates at her open door, watching as a shaft of orange light from a streetlamp falls through a crack in the curtains and touches Holly's face. He moves closer and stands at the foot of the cot, listening to sounds too ancient to come from the mouth of a baby.

He's struck by her smallness, how alone she is and despite not wanting to listen, he wonders if it's this isolation she's trying to communicate. He realizes that he's holding his breath, trying not to add to the noise she's making. Judith should be here. Not that she'd have any better understanding of

Holly's intent, but her presence alone would confirm that he's not imagining any of this. These sounds are a language he doesn't understand. They might be saying help me or I'm scared or make them go away. Something like that, but he's only guessing, really he has no idea.

He sits in a child's seat beside the cot even though he's way too big for it. His vision is a little blurred, but it's a few seconds before he realizes there are tears in his eyes. He's not sure why. What he knows is that Holly is scared and that he should help her but he doesn't know how. He's scared too but in searching her face for some clue as to her meaning, all he sees is a smile, the kind that says "sweet dreams in progress—do not disturb."

Is that what he's hearing—the sound of her dreams? No, it's something more concrete, something he can almost touch. Her eyelids move but the little REM flickers reveal nothing of what's going on inside her head. She rolls over onto her stomach, but the sounds persist. He wonders if there's something wrong with her, if she has a medical condition, a syndrome or something he doesn't know the name of. He's not as clued up on childhood illnesses as he should be. It's too easy to leave such matters to Judith. Not that he doesn't care—after all, he's the one watching over her right now. But even so, he feels he's there under false pretenses, because he's not able to give her what she needs. She wants someone to take her fear away, someone to tell her everything will be okay. Larry can't tell those lies. All he can tell her is to look for the silence inside herself, the one safe place.

As if to point her in the right direction, he reaches through the bars of the cot and touches her brow. His fingers tingle at the strange current flowing beneath her skin. He's surprised at the nature of the revelation. Don't say anything else, he whispers, keep it to yourself. Other parents might welcome such honesty but not Larry. Such openness in one so young worries him. He thinks about the future, when she's older and all the pain she'll have to face. He stands and withdraws from the room, but her sounds follow him back to his bed. Even when he crawls under the sheets and holds his hands against his ears, he can't retrieve the silence.

Larry's job is to listen. Ten hours a day, four days a week, sometimes five. He listens and occasionally, when the situation warrants, he makes an intervention. That doesn't happen often; mostly it's just listening, which means he's doing a good job. What Larry does is monitor calls—eavesdrops, for want of a better word, on the conversations between his team and the public. It's called

Quality Control. You have a problem with the service provided by his employers, you call the center. A technical assistant takes your call, listens to your problem and tells you how to resolve it. Larry listens to the two of you talking. His unseen presence on the line ensures his team are prompt, polite and helpful, and most importantly, it ensures they don't take longer than ninety seconds to deal with your call, because by then there's another customer on the line with some new problem. Of course ninety seconds is not written in stone. Some queries can be dealt with in as little as thirty or forty seconds, but others can last much longer. Those kinds of problems require more thought, maybe even a consult, before they can be resolved. But even then Larry expects his team to take no more than three or four minutes, five tops. These longer calls are balanced by the shorter ones so that over the course of the day they average out at about ninety seconds each. You'd be surprised at the amount of information that can be exchanged in ninety seconds, if both parties are on the ball.

Sometimes people call the center because they have nothing better to do than waste Larry's time. It's this kind of call that usually prompts an intervention. They're not having technical problems, at least not with the service the company provides. They have other motives that don't concern you. They're pranksters, or they love the sound of their own voices, or they're lonely and want someone to talk to. Whatever. You're not the Samaritans and while they're using up your valuable time there are other people with real problems who can't get through. Too many calls like that, Larry stresses, can mess up the rhythm of your day.

Larry supervises a team of thirty technical assistants, each of them taking, on average, forty calls an hour. That's twelve thousand different conversations a day he's responsible for. Of course, he can't listen to them all and he wouldn't want to. What he does is he switches between them, flitting from one conversation to another, staying just long enough to make sure your call is being dealt with in a proper and efficient manner, and if it's a new assistant, probably monitoring the length of time it takes to deal with the problem. He'll listen from his own workstation, or sometimes he'll move about among the team, motivating them, even though they shouldn't notice his presence at all if they're really focused. Motivation is important because the vast majority of calls are pretty dull and repetitive. Doesn't matter what the problem is, they've heard it all before. Unless your problem has nothing to do with their service, in which case it isn't their problem and he'll make an intervention. He will cut you off.

That's about the only time in the day Larry gets to himself. Those four or five seconds of silence between cutting off a caller and deciding where to go next. Usually when he flits from one call to another, the transition is instantaneous. Well, maybe to a scientist there would be some measurable gap in time, a nanosecond or something, but to a layman, the transition would appear seamless. But when he's intervened, when he's taken a unilateral decision to terminate a call, Larry likes to take a few moments to reflect on what he's done, be sure in his own mind that it was the right decision. After all, he may be called upon to justify his actions. He calls these his moments of quiet. You'd be surprised at how few such moments there are in the day, all of which tells you he's good at his job.

This morning he cut a woman off for no reason at all. Then he took thirty seconds before moving on to another call. For the rest of the day he was expecting someone to point it out, to ask for an explanation, but nobody did. Not his boss, not anyone. Which means he got away with it.

When he gets home from work, after they've eaten, Judith wants to talk. It doesn't seem to matter what about and Larry understands that being alone with a child for twelve hours a day means she looks forward to adult conversation. It's no good telling her that he's listened in on four hundred or so adult conversations that day and that not one of them was in the least bit interesting. Irony doesn't cut it with Judith. Besides, he knows what she'd say. She'd say, "It's all right for you, you get to interact with other people." As if what he does is interact. Not by any stretch of the imagination does Larry think that listening to conversations between people who are unaware of his presence can be seen as interacting. The closest he gets is when he cuts them off. Still, he usually makes the effort for Judith, figuring that one more conversation won't make a great deal of difference in the scheme of things. Besides, he doesn't have to say much, the level of his participation being dictated by how much or how little she has to tell him. It's not that he doesn't have an interest. He loves Judith and he wishes there was some way to make her believe this without having to say it all the time. It matters to him that Holly's started teething, or that she sleeps through the night. He doesn't want to miss out on these important milestones. It's just that he needs time to himself. Not because he's solitary by nature, but because after listening to all those calls, he looks forward to some quiet time, a time when he can just switch off and listen to nothing but silence.

Sounds Like

But tonight his heart isn't in it and when Judith tells him that Holly took her first unassisted step today, he pretends he hasn't heard.

She throws a cushion at him, playfully. "Hey," she says. "Are you listening?"

Larry says nothing. The news is on the TV but the sound is turned right down.

"I said Holly walked on her own today."

He tunes into the quiet between her words.

"Larry," she says, and he recognizes that note of irritation in her voice. "Did you hear a word I said?"

He's trying not to, but he doesn't tell her that. It would only encourage her and tonight, more than anything else, he needs the balm of silence.

"What's the matter with you?" she persists. "Why are you being like this?"

He wants to close his eyes but he's aware that would be the wrong thing to do. It would exacerbate the situation. Instead he focuses on the reflected lightbulb on the TV screen, how it floats inside the head of the woman reading the news. Every time she speaks, it's like she's having a bright idea.

"For God's sake talk to me," Judith says. He wishes he could but it's just not possible, not right now. How can he make her see that it doesn't matter a damn what she's saying, or what the newsreader says about poverty or the Middle East or that disaster in some place he's never been. He doesn't need to hear their words to know what they're saying. Their lips are moving but the sounds they make are the same as always.

Finally, Judith leaves Larry alone in front of the silent TV. One by one he notes all the household sounds and filters them out of his consciousness. The hum of the fridge, the rattling of pipes, the ticking of a clock, the tired creaks and groans of the walls. As each sound disappears he sinks a little deeper into the silence, where everything falls into place. He understands why people try so hard to keep the quiet at bay, why they need to make sense of everything that registers on the aural plane. They're *afraid* of silence, because they see it as a second cousin to darkness, or darkness itself.

Sometimes they speak to Larry as he drives home along the M4 toward Swansea. The stereo is switched off and he won't even be thinking about music. All he'll hear is the engine and the roar of overtaking vehicles, noises he can tolerate well enough. They come from outside, like the stink of sulfur pouring into the sky out of Port Talbot Steelworks. It wouldn't make sense to get pissed off about them. But then what happens is, it will start raining and he'll try to ignore it for a while, try to see through the blur but eventually it'll get so bad he won't be able to see a damn thing and he'll have to turn them on. Then it's, you know, that sound, *swish, swish,* and the drumming of the rain on the roof, and soon it just becomes too much and he finds himself reaching for the dial. He turns the music up loud to drown out those other noises. But Larry's not fooled—he knows it's a front, a fifth column of sound, behind which lurks the residue of the day's talking, and sometimes the whisper of conversations still to come. It wouldn't matter so much if they had something new to say but it's always the same. They're saying we are here, we are alive, we want you to know that. As if this is something he might have missed.

Larry is woken by Judith's screams. No—that's not strictly true. He's been awake awhile, thinking about last night. He'd been immersed in a world of total silence in which his other senses were predominant. He was able to catch the scent of the city in all its subtle gradations; he saw tachyons penetrate the ceiling and pass through his body; he felt the cool slipstream of the turning world brush against his skin; even his thoughts were soundless, registering only as impulses somewhere in his brain. Until Holly started crying. He'd lain in the ruins of stillness, listening to sound bleed from her, understanding finally what it was she mourned, what she would so rarely retrieve. And as he'd listened, his heart breaking from the sound of her hurt, he told himself he would not let it happen, he would not let the world steal her silence.

And now it's Judith who feels compelled to announce her pain to the world. At first he doesn't know how to react. He's never heard her scream before, which may be why he's confused, why he's still lying in bed instead of rushing to see what the matter is. But even as he thinks this he moves into action. He jumps up and runs naked across the hall to where the sounds are coming from, to Holly's room. And there's Judith holding Holly in her arms and she's screaming and there are tears streaming down her face and though she's looking right at him, Larry believes she doesn't see him at all. That's when he notices how quiet Holly is, how quiet and still and pale. And he feels something horrible, a sharp, cold pain stabbing at his heart, and he tries to speak but the words get all jumbled up with fear and come out like the howl of a beaten dog, but it's a sound that says all there is to say.

Sounds Like

His daughter is dead.

Later, an ambulance comes to take her body away, something Larry finds strange because he associates ambulances with rescue, salvation and repair. But Holly is beyond all that. He finds it strange that he's using the word "body" instead of Holly or daughter or child. The police are very kind and considerate—they ask him hardly any questions and none at all of Judith.

The coroner's inquest returned a verdict of Sudden Infant Death Syndrome, which, Larry discovers, used to be called "cot death." Most such fatalities occurred between the ages of two and six months, whereas Holly was nearing her first birthday. Death was probably due, the coroner said, to a number of contributory factors, including the failure of the child to breathe because of reduced brain activity during sleep. Her death was more than likely peaceful, he said, as if that would make it easier for Larry and Judith to bear.

But Larry thinks he was wrong. Holly didn't suffer from reduced brain activity during sleep—on the contrary, she was far too active. How else to explain her sleeping sounds? The sounds that kept him awake so many nights? It does no good but he can't help thinking that he should have acted sooner to help her discover the quiet she craved. In truth he had so little of his own to give. Now she's gone and her absence is a sore that corrodes his heart. Despite his pain, Larry has to be strong for Judith's sake. If they're to get through this crisis, then he must give her all the support she needs. This is hard but not impossible—he loves his wife, loves her so much that the thought of being without her causes him anguish.

In the first months after Holly's death, Judith retreats into herself. She becomes quieter, more contemplative, and Larry takes this as a good sign. Some evenings they sit together over a Chinese take-away and eat without talking. He watches her as she eats, looking for signs that might indicate she's turned a corner. He finds himself hoping that this apparent numbness, this absence of feeling, is something more—a genuine silence.

One evening he asks her if she'd like to have another child. When she looks at him he sees the conflicting emotions in her eyes. For a moment he wonders if this was the wrong thing to say, then she puts a hand on his shoulder and says, "It's not that simple, Larry."

She's right in this observation, he believes, but when she tells him it's not just a matter of getting another child from the baby factory because the first one, the one that didn't work, was still under guarantee, he's not sure she really comprehends. It's not that Holly didn't work, but that she worked too well. He doesn't say this; instead he says, "I'm not saying we should have another child to replace Holly—no one can take her place. But if she were still alive we'd have been talking about another child anyway. All I'm suggesting is we bring it forward."

"I . . . I don't know if I'm ready," she says, her hand falling to her side. She begins to turn away but he reaches out and pulls her close.

"Please, Judith, I need this as much as you."

She says nothing but there are tears in her eyes, big, fat, luminous tears that well up and roll down her cheeks. She's crying but she makes no noise and for a moment he thinks she understands. But as he watches the tears fall, he sees himself reflected in them, his own face, huge and round and screaming, and he knows her silence is only skin deep.

Larry can tell that David isn't going to work out. Technical assistants hardly ever lose their cool, but he's noticed that odd inflection in David's voice that signifies irritation. If Larry's picking up on it, then you can bet the customer is too. Already this morning he's detected that tone four times in David's conversations. Four times is the limit. You hear it more than four times in one day, you take the assistant aside and have a quiet word, try to find out what the problem is. The usual response is they're tired or hungover, or they have a headache. Something small. But in this job, tone and inflection are everything, and if customers sense that their problems are not fully engaging your attention, or that there's something else you'd rather be doing, then they may cancel their subscriptions. At the very least, they'll probably call customer complaints. And of course, as is the nature of these things, complaints come back to Larry. He can't afford to carry people who let the team down and experience is telling him that David is one such person. In fact it's not so much telling him as screaming it in his ear as he listens to David telling someone to shut up a second. At this precise moment, Larry should intervene, remove David from the loop and pass the customer to another assistant. But he doesn't do that. He merely listens to David pouring scorn on the customer's lack of technical know-how, then tunes out and takes a minute to himself.

Of course, words are not the only sounds that signify. This morning he's heard coughing, sneezing and sighing, the tap-tapping of fingers on a keyboard, snatches of hummed melodies, the sound of someone eating or maybe just chewing the end of a pen, the strike of a flaring match and the loud inhalation of a cigarette, the countless variants of respiration, the blurring of background noises into a torrent of sounds that signify the machinery of life. It all seems banal to Larry—this compulsion to produce noise in order to remind yourself that you exist. The question people should be asking, he believes, is where does it all go?

After lunch, he emails David, asking him to drop by his workstation. He's thinking about how to deal with him. Perhaps some kind of reprimand is in order, an official warning. Larry has to be seen to take action. But the truth is he's warmed to David, even has a sneaking admiration for what he's done. Which makes it all the more disappointing when he doesn't show up and Larry discovers that he's already quit.

Judith is upstairs, waiting for Larry to go and make a baby with her. He wants to, particularly as she's ovulating and all, but he can't. They tried last night and afterwards Judith was sure she'd conceived. But while she slept Larry became acutely aware of the sound of her breathing. He listened to the rise and fall of her respiration and it struck him just how much was going on inside her. Disturbed, he tried to block out the sounds. But the harder he tried, the more insistent they became. Unwittingly, he began to separate them from one another, codifying them according to frequency and duration in an attempt to reveal their meaning. He identified an occasional stutter in the otherwise smooth rhythm of her breathing, as if the in-breath had snagged on some obstacle of doubt. He catalogued stomach noises, lackadaisical groans, the almost-silent hiss of a fart, the creak of her left knee, the one she broke years ago in a motorbike accident, the beating of her heart and the insistent tremor of her eyelids as she dreamed. But there was no sound from her womb. Nothing at all.

Larry watches *Seinfeld* on TV. He used to enjoy this show. Now he watches it with the sound turned down because the characters' actions are too loud, as if they don't trust their tongues to say all they need to say. Their limbs flail and clack, their bodies howl in disgust and he's listening to these gestures trying to pretend he's forgotten about Judith, waiting upstairs. He doesn't want to disappoint her. Right now she's happy. At this precise moment she's lying there, naked, or maybe she's wearing sexy underwear, baby-making underwear, perhaps imagining his sperm has already fused with an ovum but wanting to give it another shot just in case. But this kind of happiness is transient. In a couple of weeks, when her period comes on, she'll begin to fall apart.

He didn't ask for these insights; there is a perfectly good reason people's bodies are clothed in skin, and that's to protect them from the knowledge of what goes on inside. How can he explain? How can he tell her that he hears too much, that he can hear what's going on beneath her outer layer?

Larry's sitting there, pondering, trying to put off the inevitable, when he hears her calling. So he goes and he does his duty and says nothing about the noises he can hear, and those he can't, going on inside her.

Judith is talking names but Larry catches only half of what she's saying. He's listening to that guy over in the far corner of the restaurant, the fat man with a heart murmur who'll probably be dead inside a month. He feels an impulse to warn him, or at least tell him to make the most of what might be his last supper. But how can he tell a perfect stranger that he hears his irregular heartbeat from the other side of the room? Particularly when he's trying hard to concentrate on what Judith is saying.

"Elizabeth," she says, "if it's a girl."

Sparkling water fizzes down the throat of that young woman at the table by the door. It doesn't drown out the sound of her desire for the guy sitting opposite her. "Elizabeth is fine," Larry says, his attenuated voice lost in the blizzard of noise. The woman at the next table is menstruating heavily. She's a little self-conscious about the smell. Larry wants to lean across and tell her it's the noise, not the smell, she should be worried about, but he assumes she wouldn't appreciate the observation.

"Or maybe Candice?" Judith says, raising a glass of red wine to her lips. Larry flinches in anticipation and she asks him what's wrong.

"Nothing," he says.

"What did I just say?"

"Names, you were choosing names."

She frowns and he hears the dry scrape of her skin creasing. Be still, he wants to tell her, be perfectly still but before he can speak she says, "What's the matter?"

He can hear someone in the toilet, taking a piss. An elderly couple sitting at the window stare at him and Judith, smiling and whispering behind their liver-spotted hands. They're talking about love but Larry hears death whistling between their bones.

Sounds Like

"Larry, are you listening to me?"

He nods and watches as she licks a residue of wine from her lip. He doesn't want to spoil things for her tonight so he acts as if the sounds she's making are completely normal.

"Your face," she says, quite loudly. "You look so serious."

He forces a smile and even though he tries to keep it quiet, he's pretty sure she must have heard it. Still, it's not enough. She says, "What are you thinking about?"

He's thinking, How would it be for all of us here to live, if only for a while, in the silence? He says nothing in the hope of setting an example and for a brief moment he thinks maybe they understand. But Judith shatters his illusions by saying, "I'm not getting through to you, am I?"

Even as she speaks her words become distorted, amplified beyond meaning, and he wants to explain why this is happening, how it's because of this need she has, they all have, to avoid the truth. But he keeps his mouth shut because he doesn't want to add to the volume. Already, the walls are vibrating beneath the immensity of sound; it pulverizes their senses and everyone just sits there, pretending there's nothing going on.

Outside, the streetlamp hums orange. Nothing strange in that. Larry's sure he's heard it before—five years he's lived in this house overlooking the bay, so it stands to reason. What's different now is that he's aware of this particular sound, that it's impinging on his consciousness. He's considered the possibility that he's imagining it, but no, he really is hearing light. This isn't normal. Normal is, no matter where you live, coexisting with noise. After a while it gets so that unspecified, individual sounds merge into one constant thrum that blurs so far into other sensory input that people no longer register it as sound. But this illusion of quiet disturbs them, so they produce more sound to fill the void, as if this is the only way they can affirm their existence. And still there's so much they can't bear to hear and these sounds are filtered out into a shapeless background of unwanted information. But the more noise they shut out, the more that's produced to replace it, in an infinite regress. Larry's lost this ability—he can't stop himself from hearing. It's not just the obvious sounds like voices or television or telephones, like traffic and screaming, or the waves breaking out in the bay, but the more subtle ones, the sounds most people never hear.

Right now, walls of sound are closing in and Judith doesn't even know it.

How can she lay beside him and not care that each hiss of her breath, each beat of her heart, is a reminder of what's slipping away? He leans across and tells her "be still," but his words make no impression. He hates this intransigence, this selfishness that allows her to deflect the truth she doesn't want to hear. Having failed to make her see things from his point of view, he turns away and hears the radio alarm whispering three-thirty even before he sees the LED display glowing red in the dark. He shuts his eyes not wanting to see the numbers when they change, but he hears it anyway, the sound of another minute gone. What he doesn't want, what he's fighting against, is counting, because with Larry counting means counting down. He already knows where that will lead.

The bed creaks as Judith turns and drapes an arm over his stomach. He draws a sharp breath, fighting panic, lifts her arm and rolls out from underneath it. Sitting on the edge of the bed, he grabs the pillow and covers his ears. He breathes softly, not hearing anything. Beginning to relax, thinking he's found the silence, he becomes aware of a new sound. Except it's not really new. In fact, it's all too familiar—the modulated sound of his own autonomic functions, those regulatory processes over which he has no control. Terrified by this heightened awareness of self, Larry sinks to the floor and pulls a sheet over his body to cloak himself in silence. But it's no good because these internal processes refuse to go quietly about their work. But there's something else more awful than hearing them, something he can't bring himself to acknowledge.

With an effort of will, he climbs back up onto the bed, thinking perhaps Judith will know what to do. But she's just lying there, oblivious, like she bears no responsibility, sleeping through his fear, just as she did through Holly's crying. That's not right, Larry feels, a mother not hearing her child's night-time fears. Maybe Judith has infected him with her noise. Maybe it's not enough that she has to talk to him every evening after work, that she insists on filling his head with the emptiness of her days, but even while sleeping, she deflects on to him the babble she's afraid to hear. Every night, this constant need to remind him of her presence. As if he could ever forget. He should talk to her about it, see if she's open to compromise. But there's already too much noise in the room, sounds that the darkness intensifies, lending them more power than they have in the light of day.

These are some of the things Larry hears: beads of sweat rolling down his chest; the dry crack of snapped twigs, which are the spasms of his facial muscles; his stuttering breath, like the hesitant query of a nervous child; a heart beating with the irregular rhythm of a broken piston. Even when, after an hour or so, he's managed to bring his body under control, he can still hear things it shouldn't be possible to hear: the creeping of insects in the walls, the scuttle of a spider across the ceiling, the babble of microscopic bedbugs in the sheets. All trying to tell him a truth he already knows.

When it was just Judith Larry could hear, it wasn't so bad. On a good night it was still possible for him to withdraw into his own silence. That's all finished now. Even here at the far side of the room there's no getting away. The noise outside doesn't begin to compare with the noise that fills the room, the source of which he can't even see. He's trying real hard to think this through, trying to find some way to drown it out. Judith's there but she's no help at all. In her sleep she rolls onto her side, facing toward him. There's a smile on her face, prompted, he imagines, by some dream of contentment. He zeros in on her left eye that seems more animated than the other. He wonders if, in the same way that the light entering one eye is translated into a recognizable image by the opposite visual cortex, this movement of Judith's left eye signals a dream taking place on the right side of her brain. It's like she's having two dreams at once, with one somehow amplifying the effect of the other. Maybe that's how she does it, how she infects him. She dreams unwanted sounds into his head.

The logic of this is irrefutable, so Larry returns to the bed, grabs a pillow and presses it down on Judith's face. At first she doesn't react, which bothers him so he presses down harder until she begins to resist. She reaches up and clutches at his arms, scratching, but he just brings more weight to bear, forcing the pillow tightly against her, doing his best to ignore her muffled protests, not even flinching when her nails draw blood from his arms, just concentrating, riding out the frantic thrashing of her legs against the mattress, refusing to be cowed by the tremendous noise she's making until, after a couple of minutes or so, she's still.

He lifts the pillow and stretches out beside her, breathing hard but that's okay because he knows something has changed. He stares up at the ceiling, at that strip of orange light and he's pleased at the way it just sits there, not moving, not making any sound. He takes this as a good sign, a sign that he's on the right track. His chest rises and falls and his heart pounds out a kind of triumphal message, which is understandable, but really he feels better now that things are quieting down.

When Larry wakes he feels renewed. He showers, eats some breakfast, goes to work. It turns out to be one of those days. Every second call is a major crisis, like sunspots are fucking up Earth's atmosphere or something. You can forget ninety-second averages today if things continue on like this. After the fourth consult Larry turns down the volume and listens to dead air for an hour. That's a big improvement. It allows him to stay focused, helps him get through a difficult shift.

He leaves work a little early, intending to make up the hours tomorrow. He hurries home and makes a cold sandwich. The phone rings a couple of times but Larry ignores it, probably for Judith. He watches TV with the sound turned down, having no problems at all understanding what they're saying—the same as last night and the night before. Come midnight he goes upstairs and there's Judith, a little pale, waxy even, but perfectly silent. He gets into bed and finds her somewhat cold and unyielding when he tries to push her over to her own side, but that's okay, the main thing is the quiet.

Next morning, Larry finds himself thinking about David, even missing him. Rather, he misses what David's absence represents, which is silence. Without consulting Larry, the company has given him a replacement. This replacement is really on the ball though, you have to give her that. Not one call so far over ninety seconds. As she's new, Larry's been monitoring her calls and counting—ninety, eighty-nine, eighty-eight, eighty-seven, eighty . . . so far he's only got down to twenty-two. She's cheerful and efficient and he wishes she worked someone else's shift and left quietness in her place. It proves to be a difficult ten hours, made tolerable only by the cumulative total of seventy-three minutes of dead air he listens to, dead air created out of the exceptional number of interventions he's forced to make.

On the way home he stops off to buy a Chinese take-away—noodles, chicken and red peppers in a black bean sauce, some crackers. Picks up a mid-price Chardonnay at the off-license next door and lays everything out on the kitchen table. But he just picks at the food, a taste here, a nibble there. He has no real hunger to satisfy. When the phone rings he disconnects it and throws it in the bin along with the leftovers. The TV is on, but, feeling jaded, he decides to have an early night.

The following day is not so good. It starts off brightly when Larry wakes at dawn and the whole world seems perfectly silent, but it's just an illusion. Strangely enough, it's not the sound that alerts him but the smell. It's coming from Judith. Only after he's noticed that does he hear the noise. That feeling of almost joy he had just a moment ago has completely vanished and now he's confused. In fact, his brain is hurting with the effort of trying to figure out his options. He makes a decision. He gets out of bed, walks across the hall to Holly's room, lowers the rail to her empty cot and climbs in. It's cramped, but the sheets are cool and it's quiet, which is what Larry needs right now. It doesn't matter if he sleeps late, he's not working today. What's important is to lose himself in the quiet. He's not sure why Judith has started making noises again, but at least he's put some distance between them. He's got a feeling that when she realizes how little impression she's making, she'll fall silent again.

Larry manages to sleep for a while. At least he thinks it was sleep. He's not sure because he's finding it hard to tell the difference. He lacks the appropriate terms of reference at the moment. Despite his patience, Judith hasn't let up for one second. The irony of it is she's louder dead than she ever was alive. The sound of her is filling the house top to bottom, like something's really bugging her. When he crosses the hall and looks through the open door at the ruin on the bed and sees the topographers of corruption crawling over her grey skin, he recognizes the truth he's been trying to avoid. He hears it in the awful drone of the flies and the soft hiss of her putrefying organs, but more than that, it's revealed in the sounds of his own treacherous body. There it is in the dry rasp of his frown, and in the rush of air through nasal cavities, in the melody that flows through larynx and trachea and into his lungs. It's present in the strange harmony of spleen and gallbladder, the industry of pancreas and liver, the dance of his heart. But this is just scratching the surface. Beneath these are a host of more complex sounds: the surge of blood through veins, its tides dictated by something other than the moon; the whine of stretched sinews and the grind of bone against bone; the whiplash of a blinking eyelid; the snowfall of flaking skin. Sounds like life ticking away, sounds he was never meant to hear.

Larry figures that he may have to resort to something a little more drastic if he's serious about getting things back to the way they were. He finds what he's looking for downstairs in the living room and sits awhile, reading up on the subject. His research is no more than rudimentary, twenty minutes at most, but to do this properly would take more time than he has. In the kitchen he selects the most appropriate tool, then it's back upstairs. He sits in front of the dressing table and stares at his reflection in the mirror, feeling out of place. This is where Judith would sit to put on her makeup, disguising things she didn't want to see. We can choose not to see, Larry thinks, but once we hear truth talking, we have no choice but to hear it out. Unless . . .

He picks up the carving knife, opens up the *Family Medical Advisor* and takes another close look at the anatomical drawings. Understanding what he has to do, Larry takes hold of the top of his left ear and hacks it off. Blood spurts and pours down his neck, sound falling out of him. Quickly, before fear overwhelms him, he slices off the other one. Looking in the mirror, he wonders if, at the end, Judith accepted the real meaning of sound. We are made of it and each sound heard is another piece stripped from our lives. He holds the knife out till the tip of the blade touches the glass. And he looks into his eyes and sees a true silence staring out, dark mouth moving in affirmation. And of course it sounds like nothing he's ever heard before.

The Wind Sall Blow For Ever Mair

BY STEPHEN DEDMAN

"Kick it! What are ya, a poofter?"

The old man stares straight ahead. His neck has been broken for nearly a minute, and one of his eyes has swollen shut, but he hasn't passed out. Most of the kicks have come from behind, as though his attackers are scared of seeing his face. This boy is different, though; he stands before the old man's battered face, his boot a few inches from his chin—and then hesitates.

"Kick it!" the boy's father yells. "Ya scared his teeth are going to scratch yer boot? Kick the black bastard!"

The boy stares down. His father has been promising him a game of football for his birthday, says he'll give him a new rifle if he manages to kick a goal—a .303 to replace his pissy .22. The old man had been gotten drunk, taken from his camp while still asleep, and buried up to his neck in the paddock. The boy steps back, then kicks out and up; he misses the old man's chin, smashing him in the cheek instead. A sarcastic cheer goes up from the other team—his uncle's side of the family. The boy grits his teeth, and kicks again with more power, more accuracy, and the head snaps back until the one good eye is staring straight up at the crows circling overhead.

Lady Jayne Randal was twenty-seven years younger than her husband, unless he really *was* dead, in which case it was twenty-six years. Her secretary was probably ten years younger still and a few drinks more sober, and his blond hair was a damn sight more convincing, but it was probably better not to mention him. "Do you have any new evidence that Sir John was murdered?" I asked, as though there'd been any *old* evidence.

"No," she replied, calmly enough. "But he's been missing for a year tomorrow, and there's been no word from him; if he were alive, he would have found some way to contact me long ago. The stories the Opposition tells about him going into hiding are crap; he had nothing to hide, no reason to run. Besides, you reporters have been looking for all that time; have any of you found a damn thing?"

She knew we hadn't. Whether you believed that Sir John Randal had been murdered, or had absconded to some country where he was safe from extradition (Spain was the popular choice), you took it on faith. I glanced at the secretary, who remained professionally impassive, just another expensive piece of furniture. I managed not to sigh. "Lady Randal, there's an old saying among police. If there's no suspect, there might as well not be a murder. When there's no body either . . ."

She glared at me. "You want suspects?" The secretary was jolted out of his impassiveness, and opened his mouth to speak, but Lady Jayne was faster. "What about the blacks who tried to kill him a few months before he disappeared? Have you tried speaking to them?"

"I haven't," I replied, "though I'm sure the police did. No one was ever charged."

"You talk to that singer," she said. "That Rose woman. She was there then, and she knows John was assassinated; I'll even bet that she knows who—"

The secretary had turned bone-white, a fight-or-flight response; he finally managed to catch Lady Randal's eye, and she hesitated.

"You're referring to Karen Rose?" I asked calmly.

Lady Randal drew a deep breath, but her secretary answered for her. "There was an incident sixteen months ago," he reminded me, "on one of the Aboriginal encampments on Cape York Peninsula. Somebody threw a spear at Sir John; fortunately, they missed, though not by very much. The assailant was never identified, but Karen Rose was present, standing near Sir John, and it is likely she saw who threw the spear."

I remembered the incident, and thought of pointing out that it was a throwing stick, not a spear, and that at least half a dozen people sitting near the "assassin" would have had an even better view, but what would it have accomplished?

The secretary stopped me in the driveway on my way out to my car. "Please don't forget to send us a transcript of the interview, and a copy of the article before it's printed," he said, a little anxiously. There was actually a bead of perspiration on his brow; I wondered how much it cost.

"If it *is* printed," I replied, nodding. "It's not exactly news, Mr. . . ."

"Wood, and it's imperative that this be resolved, before more people start to believe the nonsense about Sir John having fled the country, or any of the other ridiculous stories that the Opposition is spreading . . ."

I smiled. "Would you rather I told my readers that Lady Jayne accused Karen Ross of murder? I have it on tape, and it would make a lovely headline."

He turned ghost-white again. He was close enough that I could smell Lady Jayne's perfume on him, close enough to throw a punch that might connect, but while he was in better shape than I was, he didn't look or sound like a street fighter. "I'll talk to some friends of mine in the police," I said, "and maybe to Karen Rose. If I can find a story, I'll print it—and yes, I'll be sure to send you a copy. Off the record, where do *you* believe the old man is?"

The blood had started to seep back into his designer face, but at that, he took a step back and snarled. I guess it was a dumb question at that; it would take a brave man to sleep with Randal's wife thinking the Toecutter was still alive, and Wood didn't seem that brave. "Thank you for your cooperation," I said smoothly. "Good day."

I noticed a pair of ravens sitting on the gateposts, obviously confident that Sir John—a keen shooter of wildlife—wasn't coming home. "Nevermore," I muttered as I drove between them. They didn't reply.

A few klicks from the estate, I pulled into a truck stop and looked at my notes. Sir John Randal—Jack the Ripper or Randal the Vandal to the Opposition and the Greens, the Toecutter or the Headkicker to his colleagues— would be seventy-two if he were still alive. Unlike most proponents of family values, he hadn't divorced his first wife; she'd died in a three-car pile-up in '81. He'd been Deputy Premier for thirteen years, Minister for Police and Aboriginal Affairs for even longer. Finding a cop who'd speak against him would be nearly as difficult as finding an Aborigine who'd mourn him. Fortunately, I knew where to look.

I was humming along with the song playing on the radio before I recognized the voice: Karen Rose. "In behint yon auld fell dike," she sang, "I wat there lies a new slain knight; And naebody kens that he lies there, But his hawk, his hound, and his lady fair."

I listened to the rest of the song as someone described what they were going to do with the knight's corpse. I wondered if that was what had spooked Lady Jayne.

"Got a blanket for you, Jimmy," the sergeant says as he walks into the tiny cell. "You ready to sign this confession yet?"

The Aborigine looks away from the window, but says nothing. The cell is ancient; the only light comes from the sliver of moon outside.

"Come on. I know you can write; Father Todd taught you. He must be real disappointed in you, Jimmy. It isn't just trespassing this time, or drunk and disorderly, this is murder. A white girl. Pretty girl, rich, smart. Politician's daughter. You know what they do to abos who do shit like that, Jimmy? They hang the bastards."

"I didn't do it."

"Maybe, maybe not, but I know you abos stick together, all one big happy family, right? Well, you know the saying, Jimmy; you look like a crow, sound like a crow, hang out with the crows, you get shot like a crow. So unless you tell me who killed her, it looks like you're the lucky fella. Old Man Mills says he seen you talking to her a couple days ago, and who d'you think people gonna believe, you or him?"

"She's not dead," says the Aborigine.

"What's that?"

"You know it as well as I do," says Jimmy. "She just run off because she couldn't stand living out here anymore. Got bored. Went down to the city, or Surfer's Paradise, or somewhere. Hitchhiked on a truck she saw going south. That's all."

"How d'you know that, Jimmy? A little birdie tell you?"

"Everyone knows," he says, "even you. I bet her father knows it, too."

The sergeant smiles. "That so? Well, you can tell him when he turns up here in a few minutes. You know who Mills is, Jimmy? He's not just another station owner, he's the local member. You know what that means?"

"Means he's a prick?" suggests Jimmy.

The sergeant actually laughs at this, then slides his truncheon out of his sleeve into his open palm. He slaps Jimmy across the face, then slips the rubber truncheon back up his sleeve as the younger man reels back. "That's a good one, Jimmy," he says. "Yeah, he's a prick, and you got balls—at least, you got 'em for the time being. Problem is, you don't have the vote. Now Mills, he can stand up in Parliament and say whatever the hell he likes and people read it in the papers. Who the hell do you think's going to listen to you?"

Jimmy stares out the window and shakes his head. "You got no body. No body, no murder. You say it's a murder and you got no body, homicide detectives from Brisbane going to come up here and take over, and they'll listen to me."

The sergeant takes the blanket in both hands and rips it lengthwise. "Look at that," he says, "destruction of government property. That means I can keep you here without having to charge you with any murder." He slides the truncheon out of his sleeve, and brings it up sharply into Jimmy's crotch. The Aborigine pitches forward, hitting his head on the bars. The sergeant strikes again, once to each knee, then once to each elbow. While Jimmy writhes on the floor, he knots the torn blanket into a noose. Jimmy struggles to his feet and looks out the window again.

"You going to sign?" asks the sergeant.

"No."

The sergeant sighs. "Pity. Mills don't like wasting time; would really help me if I had the confession signed. Maybe I should just make your mark myself."

"And what'll you do when she turns up alive?"

"You're right, that might be a problem." The sergeant shakes his head, then ties the other end of the blanket to the cell door and tries to throw the noose over a crossbeam just below the ceiling. "You ever seen anybody hanged, Jimmy?" he asks. "If it works according to plan, this knot hits you behind the ear and knocks you out, and it breaks a few bones in your neck and cuts off oxygen to the brain. Only takes a few minutes to die, but it's not pretty; audience sees you jerking about on the rope, hears you wheezing, and if they're downwind they can smell you as you piss yourself, shit yourself, and come in your pants at the same time . . . You want your family to have to see that?"

Jimmy doesn't reply.

"Course, something usually goes wrong. Some people, especially if they're skinny like you, can take quarter of an hour to stop breathing, and you sound like a dying pig and jump up and down like a fucking yo-yo. Sometimes, the knot rips off part of your face. And if you're real heavy, the rope can take your

head clean off." He looks at Jimmy when the noose falls onto the right side of the beam. "What's out there that's so fascinating? Mills here already?"

"Birds," says Jimmy.

The sergeant squints into the darkness. "Can't see any."

"They're black," says Jimmy, "like me."

Sean was sitting in the pub when I arrived, nursing a lemon squash and watching a pretty young backpacker in an Aboriginal art T-shirt and bitten-off jeans knocking back beers with a truckie and his mates; as soon as I walked in, he nodded to me and asked softly, "Thirsty?"

"A little."

"Get a drink, and take it out to the beer garden; I'll see you there in a minute."

"You want one?"

"No, we won't be staying." He stood and walked over to the girl. I couldn't hear the conversation over the Slim Dusty song on the jukebox, but the truckie certainly didn't seem to like it. I ordered a 2.2 and left the room, and saw Sean and the girl walk out together towards his Land Rover after less than a minute. The girl didn't seem happy, but she wasn't protesting either. Sean beckoned to me and I trotted over to the car.

"Mike, this is Julie; we're going to give her a ride. You can leave your car here; no one's going to give you a ticket." He smiled thinly, stepped up into the driver's seat, and put the detachable light bubble on the roof, turning the Rover into a police car. Julie looked at me nervously, then scrambled into the back. Sean kept up most of the conversation as we drove north to the next town, telling Julie what to see, where to stay, all in a deliberately light tone that probably didn't fool her, either. All I learned about her was that she was from Munich, had been hitchhiking around Australia for two weeks, loved the bush and the rain forests and the beaches, and spoke English better than half of my colleagues. Sean let her off outside a youth hostel and carried her backpack in for her.

"What was that about?" I asked when he returned to the car.

"I just derailed a train," he said tersely, turning the car around.

"Come again?"

"I may've just saved that girl from a gang-bang. Quaint little tradition they have in some of these country pubs; if a girl says yes, it's assumed she's also said yes to all your mates. Pulling a train." He put his fist up, yanked down as though tugging on a lavatory chain. "Ah, Queensland. Beautiful one day, prehistoric the next. So, what brings you up this way?"

I stared at the trees that zipped past. Sean and I had been at Uni together in Brisbane, where we'd both failed to get into law. He'd joined the police force and had promptly been transferred out to the country, which he hated. "Do you remember when Randal the Vandal was talking at a tribal meeting and someone threw a club at him?"

"Well, I wasn't there," he said. "It was up near Cape York, if I remember correctly—but I read all the reports. Randal wanted Homicide brought in, but someone, probably Davis, managed to calm him down. What about it?" He started slowing down.

"I was just talking to Lady Randal. She says Karen Rose was there."

"Apparently she was," he said. "So?"

"Why was no one ever prosecuted?"

Sean shrugged, then pulled up by the side of the road. "Call of nature," he said, stepped out of the car and over some roadkill, and beckoned for me to follow.

"Sorry," he said, when we were three or four meters from the Land Rover. "You never know when they're bugging the cars nowadays. Sure, someone threw a chunk of wood at Randal; he kept looking at a couple of girls, thirteen, fourteen years old, and it didn't go down well. But if the guy had meant to hit him, he would have, believe me."

"And Rose?"

"Was there, but I think that's all there is to it. Randal was trying to talk the tribe out of making a land claim; she was there to help speak for them . . . and maybe for the publicity. For the tribe, not just for herself; I think Randal would have rather kept the whole thing quiet, but the journos like to flock around her. She looks better on TV than he does. Did." I smiled; I'd seen photos of Rose, and she was undeniably pretty if you like your women tall and thin, whereas Randal weighed a good hundred and thirty kilos. "But the cameras weren't on when the missiles started flying."

"What do you think happened to Randal? Off the record?"

Sean sighed, leaned against a gum tree (don't ask me what sort, I'm a city boy too), and watched two ravens fly across the road. "Damned if I know. I used to think he'd just run ahead of some scandal, but the scandal never broke, and I think someone would've seen him by now; he sort of sticks out. Shit, people see Elvis every damn week and he's been dead for years. So maybe the old Headkicker *was* murdered, but I don't know by whom. Organized crime, maybe; they know how to get rid of bodies. By now, he may be playing a supporting role in a thousand pepperoni pizzas."

"Thanks," I said sourly. Dependence on junk food is an occupational hazard of journalism. "You said the scandal never broke. Was there a scandal?"

"Maybe. Would you call kicking someone's head off and playing soccer with it scandalous?"

"He did *that*?"

"You thought it was just a nickname?" Sean shook his head. "Look, at worst this is ancient history, by Australian standards anyway, and it may even be an outright lie. The story is that when Randal was a kid, about sixty years ago, his old man and *his* old man and a few friends and relatives buried an old Aborigine up to his neck, then took turns in kicking his head until it came off. Then they played football with it. Another quaint local tradition, though one that was more honored in the breach than the observance even back then—which would've been the thirties. I haven't heard of it, or anything even remotely similar, happening since I've been here, for what that's worth."

"Jesus. How old would Randal have been? Eleven?"

"Twelve or thirteen, according to the stories. Of course, this is just squadroom gossip, you understand; there are probably no living witnesses, and if it was ever written up anywhere, it's been shredded."

I nodded. Randal had long been loudly in favor of harsher penalties for juvenile offenders, but even so, it would take more than this to bring him down. "Anything else?"

"Sure, and this is only about forty years old, when Randal was a cop not far from here. Prisoner supposedly hanged himself in his cell when he was custody sergeant."

"Aborigine?"

"Uh-huh. Anyway, Internal Affairs looked into it; the guy had never even been charged, and Randal barely got away. He may only have been guilty of neglecting to keep an eye on the prisoners, or he might have hanged the guy himself or been an accomplice . . . anyway, enough Aborigines started coming forward with stories of having been beaten that Randal started to look really bad. So they transferred him to the Gold Coast."

"Some punishment," I said sourly.

"Maybe, but they knew they had to keep him away from the Aborigines.

He was also turned down for promotion every time he asked, sometimes *before* he asked. He stuck it out for a few years until whatsisname, Mills, decided to retire, then he quit his job, went home, and ran for his seat. The rest is history." He drew a deep breath.

"Jesus," I muttered again.

"Look, his cuts to health care have probably killed dozens of people," replied Sean. "Maybe hundreds. And you want to talk about gun laws? Tobacco advertising? Kicking a man's head around the backyard like a football was just a rehearsal."

"But it might be enough to kill his attempt to run for a Federal seat . . ."

"Maybe, maybe not. But there's more, the usual questions about paper bags full of money that somehow managed to get past security and land on his desk, stories about him being seen at some of the state's more expensive brothels, that sort of thing . . . and one big incident, this one not long after he'd been made Minister for Police, maybe fifteen years ago."

"Another murder?"

"No, a rape, a gang-bang. He was visiting a police station and they were having a party, someone had just been promoted, and there was a girl, black, in one of the cells, apparently in for prostitution or drunkenness or something minor . . . again, this is just a rumor, because if there ever was any written record, it was destroyed, *but* . . ."

"What?"

"The girl's name—and I heard this story years ago, before the name meant anything—was Rose. More recently, I've heard it was Karen Rose, though I have my doubts about that; she would have been pretty young at the time."

"How young?"

"Thirteen at most, but she has three older sisters, and God knows how many cousins with the same surname. So I don't think it was her . . ."

"But she would've known about it?"

Sean shrugged, then nodded. "*If* it actually happened, yeah. Don't quote me on any of this, okay?"

I stopped at a Trax on my way back to the office and bought a copy of Karen Rose's CD, *Garden of Girls*. The song I'd heard on the radio was "The Twa Corbies," the only track she hadn't written herself. I unearthed the huge poetry anthology I'd bench-pressed in my days at Uni and never thrown out, and found a transcript.

Stephen Dedman

As I was walking all alane,
I heard twa corbies making a mane;
The tane unto the t'other did say
"Where sall we gang and dine to-day?"

"In behint yon auld fell dike
I wat there lies a new slain knight
And naebody kens that he lies there
But his hawk, and his hound, and his lady fair.

"His hound is tae the hunting gane,
His hawk tae fetch the wild fowl hame,
His lady's ta'en anither mate,
So we maun make our dinner sweet.

"Ye'll sit on his white hause-bane
And I'll pike out his bonny blue een
Wi mony a lock o' his golden hair
We'll theek our nest when it grows bare.

"Mony a one for him makes mane
But none sall ken where he is gane.
O'er his white bones, when they are bare,
The wind sall blow for ever mair."

According to the notes, "making a mane" just meant moaning, a "fail dike" was a dam made of turf, a "hause-bane" was a collarbone and "theek" meant thatch. It was difficult to read it without shuddering, and hearing the relish in Rose's rendition made it even more unnerving.

I realized, listening to the other tracks, that I'd actually seen her perform, a few years before, as an opening act for Yothu Yindi. "The Twa Corbies" hadn't been part of her repertoire then, and I wondered what had attracted her to the song. I glanced at the photo on the back of the CD, which showed her sitting in the bush, wearing black jeans and a land rights T-shirt. There were black birds—ravens?—sitting in the trees above her, a whole flock of the damn things . . .

The Wind Sall Blow For Ever Mair

Wasn't there some other word for a flock of ravens? A skulk, or a murder . . . no, that was crows. An unkindness of ravens, a murder of crows.

They had buried the old man and his head in the same hole; the days when such heads were taken to England as trophies were long gone, even then. The old man holds the head onto his neck until the flesh regrows, concealing the wound with scar tissue. He hears the voices of his family, hears an old prayer that had been forgotten until now, unwanted in a world whose young gods were said to prize forgiveness above justice, even for the unrepentant. He smiles, revealing shattered teeth.

With his one good eye, he sees a black bird silhouetted against the moon, and he follows it as it flies towards the city. He meets his nephew a few miles down the road, outside a cemetery, with another crow sitting on his shoulder. "Jimmy?"

The younger man nods, as carefully as though his neck were still broken. "Can you hear singing?"

Thought and memory circle around their heads. Older gods call for sacrifice. Blood calls to blood, calls for blood. The two men and the two crows head south.

It wasn't much of a story for all my travel, just a note that it'd been a year since Sir John Randal had walked out of his Brisbane office late on the afternoon of November 11 and softly and suddenly vanished away. His Merc was still in its bay under the building, though the tape from the security cameras had been wiped before he'd been reported as missing. His staff had assumed that he was going home, and as no taxi driver had admitted to taking him as a fare and he was neither an enthusiastic walker nor a believer in public transport, it was thought that he'd met someone near the building and been whisked away to . . . wherever. While he hadn't been pronounced dead, the party had called a by-election three months later, and his replacement was already in trouble for making racist remarks; seems the public will put up with that sort of bullshit from an old man, but not a young woman. All I was really doing was recapping what most people already knew, and my sub muttered under her breath for a while, cut it down, and consigned it to page five. Karen Rose had not been available for comment, but one of my sources told me she'd be in town on Saturday night for a rehearsal, and probably at a birthday party for one of her nephews in the afternoon. He gave me a list of places to try, and I found her late in the day at a roadside picnic ground, standing on the sidelines of a kids' soccer game and acting as umpire.

She wore faded 501s, well-traveled Blundstones, an old Steeleye Span T-shirt, a black Akubra hat with a land rights badge, no makeup, and no jewelry apart from a digital watch and a whistle on a cord around her neck. A few dozen people, most of them Aborigines aged zero to maybe seventy, sat around a barbecue and some picnic tables nearby; the food, grilled fish and a bubbling casserole, smelled delicious. Feeling horribly out of place, I walked up to her, being careful to walk noisily. She turned to look at me when I was about three meters away.

"Ms. Rose?"

She smiled politely, taking in my T-shirt, shorts and empty hands. "If you're after my autograph, I don't do body parts."

I smiled back, and flashed my press card at her. "Michael Griffin. Just wondered if I could ask you a few questions, off the record."

"What sort of questions?"

I hesitated. "That song, 'The Twa Corbies.' It was something of a departure for you; I was wondering why . . ."

"I loved the song the first time I heard it, and I thought I had the range to do it justice. You know it's a satire, a reply to an older English song called 'The Three Ravens'?"

"No."

"The three ravens can't get near the dead knight because his hawk, hound and lady stand guard over him until he's carried bodily to heaven. The Scot who put together 'The Twa Corbies' was a little more cynical. I didn't expect the single to become a hit, but I'm not complaining."

"You sang it very well," I said. "Still, it's not the sort of song your fans must have been expecting."

She shrugged, busy watching the kids. "My white ancestors were Highland Scots, and don't try to tell me *they* were never persecuted."

"I won't," I promised. "I'm descended from Clan Donald on my mother's side, and I know the English nearly wiped us out after Culloden—not as absolutely as they did the Tasmanian Aborigines, but not for lack of trying."

She glanced at me for an instant. "You're not a music critic, are you? What do you really want to ask about?"

"Sir John Randal."

She rolled her eyes. The kids yelled as someone scored a goal against the wind, the adults around the tables applauded, and suddenly the trees around us seemed to explode with black birds. "Jesus!"

She laughed. "They're only crows; they won't bother you unless you're dead."

"I thought they were ravens. What's the difference?"

"Ravens are pure black. Crows are dark brown, or have some white in their makeup somewhere." She shrugged. "I guess that makes me a crow." The crows settled back into the trees, and the squabbling died down. "What about Randal?"

"His wife thinks you might know what happened to him."

She turned away from the game and looked me straight in the eye. "Do you believe her?"

"No, I think she's desperate not to admit the truth about him, so she's grasping at straws . . . but so is everyone else."

"And what do you think the truth is?"

"I don't know. I know he'd been offered a fairly safe Federal seat, and a cabinet post if he'd won, but I've heard a few stories that might have come out if he'd run. I think he probably decided to get out while the getting was good, save himself the humiliation."

"What sort of stories?"

"Off the record?"

"Sure."

"A rape, and maybe two murders."

She glanced over at the family gathered around the table; there were two men staring at me, motionless men with scarred faces and necks. One was ancient, the other in his early twenties, but both had incredibly old dark eyes. Everyone else was busy watching the kids kicking the ball around. "I know the stories," she admitted, "but I didn't think anyone else did. Is there any evidence?"

"Not as far as I know . . . and if we tried to publish any of the stories without it, we'd get sued out of existence."

She nodded, and glanced up at the crows in the trees. "I wish I could help you, but I can't."

"Pity. It would've been good to tell the public the truth, but I guess it's not important, now."

"No . . . I hope you're right, that stories like that could cost him an election, but I don't know. There's a lot of people who would've voted for him anyway, and that would have been . . ."

"A disaster," I agreed.

We both watched the game in silence for a minute or two, and then I reached for my wallet and handed her one of my cards. She took it without even glancing at it, pocketed it. "I'd best be going," I said. "Thanks for talking with me."

"Thank *you*," she said. "I'm giving a concert in town next month; I can leave some tickets at the box office for you, if you like."

"Thanks . . ." I saw something hurtling towards me, and stopped the soccer ball with my foot. Someone applauded. I grinned, and picked the old leather ball up. It was a few pounds heavier than I remembered a soccer ball being, and it felt as though something was rolling around inside it. I hesitated for a moment, feeling everyone's gaze on me, then threw it back to the kids.

Karen smiled. "Looks like they could use you on the team."

"Nah, I'm just a spectator," I said as the ball was immediately surrounded by enthusiastic children. "Besides, it looks to me like this game's already won." I nodded at the two ancient-eyed men who were watching me and walked away alone.

"The Mezzotint"

BY LISA TUTTLE

> It was a rather indifferent mezzotint, and an indifferent mezzotint is, perhaps, the worst form of engraving known.
>
> —M. R. James, "The Mezzotint"

The front of the bungalow was like a crudely drawn face. The two windows on either side were big, square eyes and the red brick arch around the front door was a lipsticked mouth wide open. It was a squat, ill-proportioned face, with neither nose nor chin and a roof like a hat jammed over a low brow. The first time she'd seen it, Mel had imagined it in a 1930s cartoon. Even then, in love with the occupant as she was, it hadn't seemed to her a friendly house—she'd imagined the cartoon house sneering at Betty Boop, giving her a hard time—and today, in the gathering darkness, with half-drawn curtains over lightless windows giving it an idiot's blank gaze, it looked even less welcoming than usual. She had to steel herself to step into the gaping mouth of the unlighted porch to let herself in.

No cooking smells greeted her. As she hung up her coat she could hear the faint, insectile scuttling sound of Kieran's fingers on the computer keyboard. She walked down the hall and opened his office door.

He was in profile, sitting at his desk, attention fixed on the screen as he typed, and he spoke without looking around. "I thought you said you'd be late?"

"It's nearly eight now," she said, carefully noncommittal.

"Oh, right. Okay, I won't be much longer."

On the screen were lines of type, what looked like dialogue. Curious, she stepped closer, trying to read it, but his annoyance, vibrating like a wire in the room, stopped her. She knew he hated her "spying" as he called it, and they'd had far too many quarrels lately. Wanting peace, she turned away, saying, "Shall I start dinner?"

"Just give me a few more minutes, love." His voice was gentle.

As she was about to go out of the room, she noticed a picture hanging on the wall beside the door. It was an old engraving of a house and its grounds, by moonlight. She'd never seen it before, although it did remind her of something. It was the sort of thing Kieran used to buy at country auctions or in junk shops for a pittance and then sell on for a vastly inflated price. Before he got into website design, he'd told her, he had made his living trading in art, books and other collectibles, but since Mel had moved in with him, there'd been no time for the visits to junk shops or the trawls around country market towns that had been a feature of their courtship. She thought of the amber necklace he'd given her two months ago; a few months before that, there'd been a beaded handbag. Was he buying again?

"Where'd you get this?" she asked.

"What?" He sounded harassed. "Just a mo'." He clattered away at the keys, then shut down the screen. Then, with a put-upon sigh, he swung his chair around and faced her. "What?"

"This picture. When did you get it?"

"*That*? I've had it forever."

"But I've never seen it before."

"It's always been there."

She turned to look at him: no sign of a tease, and he wasn't defensive. Yet it couldn't be true.

"Not always," she objected.

He raised his eyebrows. "It came with the house," he elaborated. "I don't know where my parents got it from. It was just there, as long as I can remember."

"Then why did I never notice it before?"

"How should I know? Well, why should you have noticed it—it's not that interesting. Just an old mezzotint of a house . . ."

The word *mezzotint* raised goose bumps.

He noticed, and grinned. "Mezzotint doesn't mean haunted picture, my darling," he said rather superciliously. Kieran had ten years on Mel and quite naturally adopted the role of tutor. He'd read so many books and seemed to

know so many odd and interesting things, especially about art and literature, that at first she had been grateful. But lately it seemed he only told her
things she already knew, or didn't want to hear.

"Yes, I know," she said quickly. "I know it's a type of engraving." Her eyes
went back to it. "But it is awfully like the mezzotint in James's story, isn't it?"

He shook his head. "Not at all. There's no spooky figure, for one thing."

"There wasn't one at the beginning of the story, either. It only changed
later."

"Hmm. Well, all I can tell you is that in, oh, thirty-seven years at least,
that picture has not changed in any way. Although I suppose I might not
have noticed if it did. I have to admit I don't spend a great deal of time looking at it. It's not a terribly *interesting* picture." He cleared his throat. "Look,
I'm sorry I haven't got dinner ready—I didn't realize how late it was getting
to be. Why don't I get us a take-away. What would you like?"

Although she was still curious about the picture, she gave it up for the
moment.

"Indian," she decided. "You can order; you know what I like."

"I *know* what you like," he said with a lascivious grin.

She smiled back, not to offend.

After he'd gone out for the food, Mel went straight back to look at the
strange mezzotint. The first thing she did was take it off the wall. A greyish
wisp of cobweb, two or three inches long, clung there, and the rectangle of
wall paint that the picture had covered was discernibly a different shade
from the rest of the room. Clearly, the picture had been hanging in that same
spot for years. She put it back carefully just as it had been, not even brushing
away the cobweb.

So he hadn't lied. But why hadn't she ever noticed it before? After all, she
had been living in this house for more than six months, and although she
didn't spend much time in Kieran's office, until this moment she had been
confident she could close her eyes and reliably describe the contents and layout of every room. Back at the start of their relationship, she'd been eager to
know everything about him. On her first visits to his house she had studied
it for clues to his past and his character—she had practically memorized it.
Except for the bedroom, which she had redecorated, nothing much had
changed since she'd moved in. Nearly all the furniture, artwork and books
were his, and much had been his parents', coming along with the two-
bedroomed bungalow he'd inherited from his mother.

Mel closed her eyes and summoned up memory. It showed her nothing at all on that wall.

She opened her eyes. It was an odd place to hang a picture, just above a light switch; she would have been afraid of driving the nail into the electrical wiring. The heavy, black-framed engraving was wrong for the narrow space—it was too heavy and dark, and nearly as wide as the wall itself. She knew little about Kieran's parents—they had died before she met him—but she was surprised that his own aesthetic sense hadn't forced him to rehang the picture, which would have been better placed in the sitting room, or even on the far wall of his office, swapping places with one of the smaller water-color landscapes.

And why had she never seen it before? She was a visual person, alert to her surroundings. She noticed things others did not. She simply would not, could not have missed something that big.

She was starting to get spooked. In the M. R. James story, the mezzotint had changed every few hours, revealing a secret crime from the past. But it had turned up in the usual way, with a provenance, sent by a well-known dealer through the mail, offered for sale at a particular price . . . it hadn't just teleported into a room, the way this one seemed to have done.

Should she believe Kieran and mistrust her own memory? Did Kieran really remember it from his childhood, or only think he did? Was it some kind of trick?

Her heart hammering, Mel left the room, closing the door firmly behind her. She wished she could lock it, although how much effect a locked door would have on something that could materialize at will she didn't know. She was being silly. The thought of Kieran's ridicule stopped her from barring it with a chair: Was she really afraid of a *picture*? What on earth did she think it could do to her if it got out?

She went and found Kieran's first edition of *Ghost Stories of an Antiquary* and perched on the edge of the couch in the sitting room to read "The Mezzotint." She'd first read the M. R. James story at the age of ten or eleven, coming across it in a moldy-smelling paperback with a disembodied hand on the cover, a collection of horror stories bought at a jumble sale. She couldn't remember the other stories, but "The Mezzotint" had given her nightmares. How sinister the title had seemed to her—that strange, hissing word—even after she'd read it (such was the gulping, rapid, half-comprehending way she'd read at that age) she'd thought the mezzotint of the title was not a haunted picture, but the vengeful, skeletal, robed creature who had crept across the lawn by moonlight and stolen away a child. For years she'd believed *mezzotint* was a type of monster, a word like *ghoul, ghost,* or *vampire* for a terrifying supernatural being.

As she read "The Mezzotint" again, as an adult, Mel was surprised by how unserious it was. It was narrated in a casual, conversational manner, with a lot of irrelevant chat, and jokes about golfing, university life and servants. The horror story she remembered was still there, but it was presented at a remove, in a few paragraphs, as something that had happened long ago and elsewhere to people all dead and gone. All emotion was safely distanced. The horror was only an idea, a notion to be enjoyed.

Kieran came in and saw what she had been reading. "Still think that's *the* mezzotint?"

Mel shook her head. "Different house."

"Shall we go see if ours has *changed*?"

She did want to, but he was teasing, so she grinned. "Maybe after dinner. We don't want our food to get cold."

"Oh, yes, and it'll be so fascinating we won't be able to tear ourselves away!" he cried in a northern-accented falsetto.

"It was so different from the story I remembered," she said once they were settled at the kitchen table with their food. "Not as scary as I'd thought. The idea that a moving picture is scary—well, I guess, in the olden days, before cinema—"

"They had motion pictures," Kieran objected. "That story was written no earlier than 1900. Edison invented his kinetoscope, when was it? 1893," he answered himself, tearing off a piece of nan.

Mel shrugged. "Okay, so they knew about movies. The mezzotint wasn't a film, anyway—it just kept changing to a different still picture. If somebody today saw it they'd be, like, 'How'd you do that? How does it work?' They wouldn't be *scared*."

"That's because we have the technology, and it gets smaller and less detectable every day," Kieran said pedantically. "And then you read about things, or you see them in movies, and you just accept it all. Look at flat screens. Look what you can do with a good computer program. With high resolution . . . but the picture quality wouldn't matter so much with an engraving, because you haven't got the color and it doesn't have to look like real life. It would be easy to program five or six different scenes to change at regular intervals throughout the day. Then you can give somebody in a windowless office views of mountains, or the rain forest, or whatever you like," he concluded, digging into his rogan josh.

Was that it? No, the mezzotint was just a picture, not a flat screen disguised as something else. The only thing that needed explanation was where it had come from . . . or why she could not remember having seen it before today.

Their conversation moved on to other things: what she'd done at work that day, what was on TV that night. She liked to keep Kieran abreast of office gossip, to share what she did, even though he'd never met anyone she worked with. He didn't talk about his work; he said programming didn't make for conversation. He could give her the URLs and she could visit his websites if she wanted. Sometimes he told her jokes or interesting factoids he'd picked up on his Internet trawls.

After the washing-up, he agreed to go back to look at the picture with her, although he professed himself baffled. "I don't know why you're so interested in it all of a sudden."

"Just because I never was before."

Although he joked, she honestly *was* relieved to see no change in the picture. It still showed a medium-sized, squarish, very plain house, without the parapets or porticos of the manor house in the James story, and with only two, rather than three, rows of plain sashed windows—none of them open. There were a few trees and bushes and a lawn in front, but no figures.

"What is the house—do you know?"

"No idea." She thought he hesitated.

"But . . . ?"

He shrugged. "Oh, well, when I was a kid I imagined it was the house my parents *used* to live in, before I was born. I don't know where I got that idea from; I don't remember that I ever asked them. I just remember wishing we lived there. This was such a poky little place . . . I loved the idea of two stories, and all those rooms, with a lawn big enough to play cricket on. . . ."

She turned and looked at him sharply. "You lived *here*?"

"Yes, of course, I told you."

"I thought your parents came here after they retired." Although, as she spoke, she couldn't recall him actually saying so. Maybe she had just assumed, since all of their neighbors were pensioners, and this tiny seaside bungalow, all right for a couple, had never seemed like a family home.

He shook his head. "No, I've always lived here. This was my bedroom."

She felt a dizzying sense of shock, of betrayal. *Always?* "But what about—you told me you lived in Bristol, and Brighton—"

"Yes, of course. And London. As an *adult*. I never lived anywhere but here as a child. When I grew up, of course I left home. First to art college, then there was the girl in London, the job in Brighton, then after a bit I went back to London, and then a few years later Brighton again—but I've told you all this before."

Of course. "And then, in the end, you came back here again." She heard the querulous tone in her voice, tried to soften it by going on, "It seems strange, that's all, that you'd *choose* to live in a place you hated."

"I never said I hated it." He was annoyed now. "It was just small for three people, that's all. I never had any privacy. It's different now. I'm grown up. Wanting to live in a house like that was a kid's fantasy. I could never afford anything that big, not in reach of London. This is big enough for two, and convenient for London and Brighton. And since I don't care about playing cricket anymore, and I know how long it takes to mow a lawn that size, I much prefer a small garden."

"But even so—you could have sold this, bought someplace else, taken your time, shopped around . . . moving house is such a big thing. . . . Where were you living when your mother died?"

He stared at her. "Right here. Looking after my mother."

Her mouth was dry. He had never said anything about this before. She was absolutely certain he'd told her his mother had died suddenly. "How long were you looking after her?"

He shrugged. "Eighteen months? I don't know. More than a year, less than two. She had a stroke, about a month after my father's funeral. She recovered a bit, but she couldn't live on her own. So I had to come. I'd just been living in a rented bedsit, anyway. I let it go. So you see, there was no place to go back to. When Mum died, this *was* my home. And, as you say, moving house is a big thing." He was watching her with close concern. "What's this about, Melly? Do you want to move?"

She shook her head mechanically, hardly hearing him as she tried to concentrate. His role as the devoted carer, his mother's nurse—no, he'd never mentioned that before. As she remembered it, he'd been living not in a bedsit, but as the tenant/lover of a woman called Kelly. A flat in Highgate—rather a nice one—but the relationship was in trouble. So when his mother quite suddenly and unexpectedly died, leaving him her house, he hadn't thought of selling it, or invited Kelly to share it, but had taken the opportunity to end the relationship. *That's* what she remembered. Had he lied to her then? Or was he lying now?

"Because if you do, that's fine," he went on. "I'm not absolutely wedded to this place, whatever you may think. I'm happy to move, if that would make *you* happy. Would a joint mortgage make you feel more secure? I'm sure we could find someplace that would suit us both." He took her in his arms and held her close, murmuring into her hair, "I want you to be happy, Melly, I really do. I know I'm a selfish bastard sometimes, but I really do care about you. I love you. You're not like the others. I want you to stay."

They made love later that night. Mel didn't want to, but it had been nearly two weeks since their last time, and Kieran was making such an effort that she sensed it would be more trouble than it was worth to refuse. It went on rather longer than usual, because he was being so careful and sensitive, and in the end Mel faked an orgasm just to get him off her. He fell asleep fairly quickly after that, but she lay awake, finally free to think the things she couldn't when he was watching.

When he'd said, "You're not like the others," presumably he'd meant the women who had come before her, the ones he had loved and left. How many had there been? Mel didn't know. When they'd first become intimate and were exchanging histories, he had mentioned various names. Only four or five of them had really mattered, he said, and he'd only lived with two. Yet details, even names, varied from time to time in his accounts. When Mel called him on inconsistencies, he flatly denied them. She could hardly argue that it was Susan, not Fiona, he'd lived with in Brighton, or that Fiona had been the bookseller and Kelly the teacher rather than vice versa. She'd never known any of them, and if his stories changed, and he seemed to be mixing them up and getting the details wrong, well, wasn't it more likely that *she* was the one with the bad memory? It made her uneasy, but surely it was unimportant what he remembered about his former lovers. They were all in the past, and had nothing to do with her.

Even if he was guilty of forgetting, or even rewriting, his past, she didn't think he lied to her. Although he had what seemed to her a fetish for privacy (she thought of the locked drawers of his desk), she had no real reason for thinking he had any dark secrets to hide. He was still sexually interested in her (it was only she who had changed in recent months) and there were no suspicious phone calls, no weekends away. Occasionally he went out in the evenings for something computer-related. (He'd explained that most of the people he dealt with had day jobs.) Once every two or three months he might spend the whole evening out, leaving in the late afternoon, going up to London for drinks with colleagues, not getting home until well after midnight. She didn't think he was hiding an affair in those infrequent, boozy evenings.

No, if he was having an affair it had to be during the day. He worked alone at home, spending hours in front of the computer, but also finding time to do the laundry and a bit of housework or gardening; more often than not he was cooking dinner when she arrived home. Yet he did go out occasionally, to run errands or just to stretch his legs. From the mileage on the car she knew he must sometimes go farther afield than the local village, and although he hadn't told her where he'd found them, she assumed that at least a couple of the gifts he'd given her in the past year—the amber necklace, the beaded evening bag—had come from unmentioned, solitary trawls through the antique markets or second-hand shops of Brighton or some more distant country town.

If he *did* have another lover, it would have to be someone content with occasional daytime assignations, someone who would never call in the evenings, or expect to see him at the weekend. What sort of woman would put up with that, and where would Kieran have met her?

Mel turned over abruptly in the bed, sickened. Of course Kieran didn't have another lover. What was she thinking?

The mezzotint disturbed her. It was a warning. If it had truly been there all along, why hadn't she seen it before? What else had she missed about this house . . . about Kieran? For some time now she had been uneasy in the relationship. She didn't know why, she couldn't find a reason, and maybe there wasn't one, but her feelings had changed within a month or two of moving in with him. And now, she thought, self-loathing, I'm trying to find some reason to blame Kieran because I've changed.

The next morning Kieran told her that he'd be out when she got home from work. He had a meeting over in Lewes, and they might go for a curry afterwards.

"You don't mind if I'm out for dinner?" He regarded her anxiously, and although he was *always* like this when he went out in the evenings by himself—concerned that she should not feel neglected—Mel felt he was watching her more closely than usual, and wondered if he sensed her disloyal pleasure at the thought of an evening without him.

"No, of course not!" she exclaimed vigorously, hoping she wasn't blushing. "I'll be fine!"

She was rarely in the house by herself. It was an opportunity that might never come again. So, as soon as she got in from work, Mel made a beeline for Kieran's office.

The title to another M. R. James story sprang to mind: "A Warning to the Curious." She didn't remember the plot of it, but the title seemed appropriate to the tale of Psyche and Cupid, the story of a woman who had lost her lover because she had insisted on gazing upon his hidden face.

The mezzotint still hung on the same wall. Her eyes slowly scanned the picture, searching for change, a different scene, any detail out of place, but it was unchanged from yesterday, as far as she could tell. Her heart pounded painfully hard as she gazed around the room. She was reminded of childhood games of hide-and-seek, and scarier games. She kept expecting that he would jump out at her: it was a trick, a trap . . . And what, anyway, did she expect to find? She felt guilty and frightened but determined.

The office looked much as ever to her, untidy yet organized. Probably there were different books, pamphlets, operating instructions, CDs and diskettes scattered about in different places, but that was normal. If there were secrets here, she thought they would be in the locked drawer of his desk. He kept the key to that on the keychain that he always carried with him. If there was a spare key, she didn't know where it was.

Nevertheless, she went and sat in his chair at his desk and tried the drawer handle, just in case. It was locked.

So that was that, she thought with relief. As she moved her hand, she jogged the computer mouse. The machine gave an electronic cough and the screen swam back to life, blossoming into color.

She gazed at the rows of short-cut icons that would take her to his word-processing program, to his diary (if he kept one), to all his e-mail files and folders. She could find out which Internet sites he'd visited in the past weeks, track down what he'd been doing yesterday when she'd interrupted him. She could open work folders, personal files . . .

There was too much choice. She was still sitting, paralyzed with indecision, when the screen saver came on and suddenly, instead of looking at green tiles studded with icons, she was staring at the house from the mezzotint.

It had been done in shades of grey, like the original, but it wasn't still. Screen savers *weren't*—they needed moving pictures. Clouds slowly drifted across the night sky, revealing and then concealing the moon. A star twinkled. A bat flapped past the windows.

Mel let out a sigh and shook her head, baffled and impressed. He must have spent all day on it! She waited to see what else it would reveal, although she knew she really should walk away now. She'd have to pretend surprise when he showed it to her.

A figure appeared at the edge of the screen, running toward the house. She was surprised: instead of a skeletal figure in a robe, this was a very modern-looking man in a hooded tracksuit and running shoes. He reached the door and went in, and the screen went black.

Mel frowned, leaning toward the screen. In response, it lightened again. The scene revealed now was totally different. She realized she was inside the house, in a cavernous, rather gloomy room incongruously furnished with dumpy old sofas and chairs, a TV and video, stereo system, overstuffed bookshelves—she recognized some of Kieran's things, even his pictures in miniature hanging on the shadowed walls, but before she could look more closely her viewpoint was rushed away, toward another door, and then down, down, down a steep, dark staircase. Even though it was only computer graphics, she felt a fearful, vertiginous rush as if she really was descending much too fast.

And then she was in the basement—or would dungeon have been a better word? The graphics were much cruder here; it was like a nasty comic, the sort for "adult readers only." Women's bodies, naked and leaking blood, lay twisted in awkward poses on the stone floor.

She wanted to look away, she wanted *out*, but she had to try to understand what she was being shown. She had been looking for secrets, and here they were.

Words appeared, in lurid green, flashing slightly, above each body.
Susan, it said above one. (*Beaded evening bag*)
Over another, *Fiona*. (*Byron's letters*)
Kelly. (*Silver earrings*)
Sharon. (*Amber necklace*)
Jasmine. (*Pink pashmina*)

She knew what it meant. Oh yes, horribly, she knew, even though she'd never seen the pink pashmina. (Was it bloodstained? Or simply put aside for another day?)

She reached for the mouse, jiggled it, and at once the horrid dungeon scene faded away and she was back staring at the green tiles and icons of Kieran's desktop. She was panting as if she'd had to rush up those stairs to get out. She felt dizzy and sick.

Get out, get out . . . She knew she had to leave the house at once, run away, although her head was swirling and her legs felt too weak to support her. But she knew what she had to do. In her mind, the bungalow and the house in the mezzotint, the house on the screen, became one. She had to get across that huge, cavernous living room—she could see herself doing it—and get to the door, which receded like a door in a nightmare.

Don't think about it—just do it!

She knew she had to move, but it was strangely difficult, a huge effort just to push herself away from the desk and Kieran's softly humming computer. She managed to swing the chair around—and there he was in the doorway, watching her, not saying a word.

She got up, knowing words were useless now, and he came in. He was between her and the door, blocking her escape.

Her eyes flew to the picture on the wall and, yes, she was there, she could see herself inside the house, a tiny figure, pushing open a window, awkwardly clambering out, then fleeing across the empty, silent, moonlit lawn, running for her life.

Yet even as she watched herself escape from one house, in another Kieran's big, blank face was coming closer and closer, looming over her: she was shrinking, or he had become as big as a house. His eyes were wide open, two windows: she could look straight in. She looked inside and saw no one. No one alive.

The Lords of Zero

BY TONY RICHARDS

Somebody once pointed out that, though it can be blamed for bombing half of London flat in 1940, the Luftwaffe can hardly be held responsible for the way that parts of it were redeveloped.

The Craven Estate provides a case in point. Put up in the mid-sixties, and expected to be temporary even then, it still exists today, a fortress of five dismal dozen-story blocks set in a ring. Its colors? Aged, rain-soaked concrete grey, with only prison-green paintwork to break up the monotony. Its location? A bad part of East London, vaguely near the river. Its reputation? Nobody, given the choice, goes near the place.

I had little choice.

A collection of circumstances—broken marriage, a failing, only half-started literary career—had left me facing the prospect of homelessness. Apart from the streets, there were only two options. I could move into a hostel, sharing a room with half a dozen others. Or . . . the local authority was running a new scheme. It was trying to rejuvenate the worst of its public housing by moving fresh blood in. I could have my own small, single-bedroom flat—at a location of *their* choice—for what amounted to a peppercorn rent.

When I heard it was the Craven, I still had to think about it hard.

Don't get me wrong—I'm no softie. I grew up near the Docklands, long before they were redeveloped, got in my fair share of fistfights as a teenager, and am reasonably streetwise. Such wisdom advises you to stay away from certain places, though. They're not controlled by the local authority, nor the police, nor the government. Darker forces are in charge, there. And you cross their path at your own peril.

It was the writing that made up my mind in the end. I'd have privacy, at least. How could I do any work at all in a shared room?

My first day on the Craven surprised me, in some respects. The flat was exactly what I had expected, cramped and sparse, with lots of mildew on the ceiling. I could easily imagine it as some monastic cell, though, and envision myself doing some deep thinking and a lot of great work here. It was *beyond* my window that took me aback. It was all so . . .

Perfectly normal. Trouble-free.

Kids played on the unmown, grassy area within the five tall towers. Old people sat on the few benches and chattered. Women went back and forth with shopping bags. Not a hint of trouble. Not all day.

I was sure that it would change come evening, though. And, my work finished, I planted a seat next to my window, turned off most of the lights. And waited, for the nature of the place to transform.

It was late December, so twilight came early. Of the streetlamps below me, only two came on. Shadows swallowed up the grass. A fierce wind threw drizzle up against the pane for half an hour, but even that stopped. No one moved down there now. There were plenty of lights on in windows, but all of the curtains were drawn. My reflection was the only human shape that I could see at all.

Nothing happened. Nobody appeared. There was not so much as a distant shout, or the crash of a thrown bottle breaking.

After some hour and a half, I had convinced myself that, maybe, the estate's whole ugly reputation had been based on past crimes, past events. It appeared to be a safer place by now. I put some of the lights back on and cooked myself some tinned spaghetti. And then, having been inside all day, decided to investigate the local pub.

By one of those miracles of architectural planning that were well meant at the time but cause residents no end of grief, there is no direct route from any of the flats onto the street. You have to go into the central area I'd been watching all day, and from there through one of the dark chasms in between the blocks before you reenter the normal world. I suppose the layout was intended to create "defensible territory," but all it really does is leave most people trapped. I was down the damp, foul-smelling stairwell, hands thrust in my pockets and my head tucked low, and was marching round the corner of my building, when there was a movement. A large shadow. My head turned.

And they were all around me in another instant.

Eight of them. I couldn't even tell where they had come from.

People always describe, in such circumstances, their hearts thumping, their breath speeding up, or the hairs prickling on the backs of their necks. But that's not the reality of it. It's in your legs. They suddenly feel so heavy, so rubbery, simultaneously stiff and quite disjointed. Your feet become hard to lift. Run? You do not see how you could manage it. Lash out with a kick? The same. All you *really* feel capable of is sitting down on the spot. Which is, naturally, the last thing you should do.

Eight of them.

All of them big. All of them white. Dressed much the same—black T-shirts, khaki jackets, jeans, boots. All with very close-cropped hair.

They stood there, studying me.

I lifted my hands a little.

"I'm just minding my own business, guys. I don't want any trouble."

"Guys?" one of them said. I couldn't tell who.

"Finks 'e's in America," came another, quietly hostile voice.

I was trying to figure out, now, which one of them was the leader. Couldn't tell. Which ran quite contrary to my teenaged street experiences.

"'Oo are you, then?" came a third.

I kept looking round, wondering who exactly to address.

"I live here. My name's Rob. I . . . moved in today."

"You some kind of poof?"

Two years of marriage and literary chats round dinner tables had worn the edge off my Docklands accent. If I tried to revert now, though, they would spot it like a shot. I could feel myself starting to shake. My throat was getting tight.

"No. I'm minding my own business, that's all. I'm just going down the pub."

"On yer own?"

"Yeah. . . . yes. On my own. Is that some kind of problem?"

"Sad git, aintcha?"

"Look, I'm sorry." I drew myself up as straight as I was able. "I'm *really* not looking for any trouble. I'm just new round here. I only wanted to go down the pub."

The gang no longer looked like eight people, by this juncture. More, a single entity. I could feel its numerous eyes study me harder. The voices had stopped completely now.

If a blow came, it would probably be from behind. I tried to ready myself for it, knowing there was no way to avoid it. And if I could manage to stand that, keep my wits about me, then maybe I could surge forward, plow my way out through the ones in front, and give myself the chance to run. My legs seemed far readier now.

They didn't seem in any rush, however, this group of young men. Were taking their own sweet time. And that, in itself, implied a lot. That this was *their* territory. That their rules applied here, and they did here as they pleased. They were the lords and masters of this place, and you passed through here only at their sufferance.

I had pretty well given up on the idea of escape by now, abandoning it in favor of the hope they wouldn't kill me. There's a certain point, in confrontations such as these, where you become stoical because there's nothing else to do. They were either going to start hitting me now, or throw in some more insults and then start. My limbs quite rigid, I waited.

It wasn't a noise that drew my gaze off to the right an instant later. Nor was it a movement in the corner of my eye. More like . . . ? The awareness of a newly arrived presence. Just an instinct. A correct one, as it next turned out.

A few yards away on the grass, where the least of the light reached, a *ninth* figure was now standing. Just a dim shape, charcoal grey against the blackness. A male shape, just as tall as these thugs but much thinner. Was it another of them, or someone come to help me? And if the latter, how? There was no way of telling.

"What'cher lookin' at?" one of the gang asked me.

"Don'cher look at 'im," grated another. "You're not fit to look at 'im."

And a hand came up from nowhere, struck my cheek. Only a hard tap. But it was intended to make me avert my eyes. Why? The leaders of gangs always preferred to be up-front, visible.

"Sorry," I managed to get out. I could still make out the moveless figure in the corner of my vision.

The Lords of Zero

"That's better," the first voice that I had heard told me. "That's more like respectful. Goin' to the pub, are ya? You'd better naff off, then."

And the next instant, there was a silver flash. I felt my cheek being hit again, although there was no pain. And, the moment after that had happened, they were gone.

I stood there quite blank and numb, uncertain what to do. And then, I was back to the stairs, almost without knowing it, going up them three at a time.

My door slammed behind me and I fastened all the locks before going through into the bathroom. Leaned over the basin and dry-retched and gasped for a full minute. Then I raised my head, enough to study myself in the faded mirror.

It *had* been a blade I'd seen, but it had only taken the smallest of nicks out of my skin. A solitary bead of blood stood on my cheekbone. Otherwise, I was wholly untouched.

There was a bottle of cheap scotch by my desk, and I took a pull from that now, before summoning the courage to return to my window. My living room was still dark; I was certain I would not be seen.

The gang was nowhere in sight. Yet—in the exact place that I'd first spotted it—the dim, thin figure was still there. Even from this angle, from four stories up, I couldn't make out any more of it than I had done the first time. Could make out no features. Just the dimmest of shapes, darkness against dark.

Did it lift its head, then? Did it look back at me? I couldn't be sure of that either.

And then one of the two working streetlamps flickered and went out, and even the outline disappeared from view.

The next few days I got to see a lot more of the gang, though always from a distance, and in daylight, and through glass. I'd learned my lesson by now, doing my shopping and errands around noontime, fetching in cans of beer to pass the evenings, and forgetting about any pub. Life on the estate trundled along pretty much as it had done on that first day. Except that, every once in a while, the eight kids would suddenly appear.

Kids seems a strange word for young men who outweigh you, are much taller than you, and look as though they were born on the weight bench at the local gym.

As I said, they were all crop-headed and wore something like a uniform. And being white, you'd have expected them to be some kind of neo-Nazis. There was none of the usual regalia on their jackets, though, nor the mandatory tattoos. And—though half of the women who passed them by were Pakistani or Bengali—not a single retort passed their lips, nor was so much as a sour glance thrown. The gang ignored the immigrant women just as much as . . .

Well, just as much as they seemed to ignore everything else.

The kids playing on the grass appeared beneath their notice. The occasional postman or paperboy went by them unmolested. Youths like these are almost always on the lookout for some trouble to get into. A window to break, a pensioner to rob, a fight to pick. But these particular ones? Plain nothing. They would just appear for a half-hour. Stand beside the grass, motionless, not even talking among themselves. Then disappear the way they'd come.

So what did they do with their lives? I started to wonder. Maybe they were waiting for the night, each time I saw them. Maybe only that brought them alive. It was a theory that I was in no hurry to test a second time.

Of the ninth member of their gang—possibly the leader—there was not a sign at all.

Saturday afternoon arrived and I began to realize something. They were standing there like statues around ten to five when a crowd of little boys came spilling out of a doorway, all wearing claret-and-blue caps and scarves. And the little kids all started yelling, "Hammers, Hammers, Hammers are the best!"

And I realized that the soccer had just finished on the TV, that the local premier league team, West Ham, had won.

It got no reaction from the gang, none whatsoever. And soccer is almost a religion on estates like this.

But these guys didn't seem to care.

What did they have? Jobs? Education? Prospects? None of the above. And what did they believe in? Not even the vilest, most debased of all convictions—those ones centered around race and nationalism—seemed to hold any allure for them. If these eight were self-appointed lords and masters, as I'd first thought . . . then of *what*?

Masters of nothing. Lords of zero.

I didn't once, in all that time, see them again at night.

The Lords of Zero

Sunday came and I finally got down to the local pub, in time for the pre-lunch drinking session. Several people standing at the bar turned out to live on the Craven.

"Council *put* you 'ere?" One of them grinned sardonically. "What, you upset them or something?"

I turned the discussion, gently, to the subject of the gang. The whole atmosphere became much cooler.

"They won't 'urt you, if it's in the day," a man in his fifties with the physique of a hod-carrier finally informed me. "Just steer clear of them at night."

Which, considering the layout of the estate, was a difficult trick to manage.

"But . . ." I pressed on. "What the hell do they *do* all day?"

Most eyes turned away from me.

"Wait," the same big man explained, before putting down his drink, unfinished, screwing up his face and walking out.

By the time that evening arrived, I was at my window once again. The last remaining streetlamp buzzed on slowly, casting barely enough light to see by.

But enough—after three-quarters of an hour—to reveal some movement. One large shape appeared, and then another.

All week they had turned up in a single group, the whole eight. Now, though, they each put in their appearance individually.

They might have been brothers, they were so alike in height and build, though I'd been close enough to them to realize they were not. Were they brothers in another way, however? And if so, then what?

Eight of them. Where was the ninth? Where was the figure who had turned up that first night and had . . . saved me, then? Or simply watched?

Once they'd all gathered, they began walking out across the grass.

I had never seen them do this before. Normally, they remained at its outer edge. But tonight, they moved on forward like explorers in a shallow jungle. I could imagine their heavy boots shushing through the unmown fronds, although I could not hear it. Imagine the trail of prints they left behind. What were they doing now? It seemed as pointless as everything else that I'd seen from my high window.

They came to a halt at the center, where the grass was at its very thickest. Two of them bent down. And began lifting wooden planks, having to drag them free of all the clinging foliage. There was something boarded-up down there.

The pair of them worked quickly, till they'd cleared sufficient space. And then they began stepping down, their legs and then their torsos disappearing by degree. They had revealed a flight of stairs. The others followed.

I was watching, now, with utter disbelief. Gawping, and then glancing quickly at the windows all around me. Mostly lit. But all of them with blinds and curtains drawn.

And was that to stop anyone from looking in . . . or looking *out*?

What was down there? I struggled to think what had been here before the Craven, before bombs had razed this whole area flat. Tenements. Victorian ones. Overcrowded, filthy ones, redolent of crime and squalor and disease and misery. They had to have basements. Maybe this one had survived.

All the gang had gone down now. I glanced at my watch, and glanced again a dozen times before ten more minutes had passed. None of the big young men reappeared. Whatever they might be doing down there, they were, again, in no rush.

I wondered. And my heart thumped slowly in its cage of ribs. I had not been outside in the dark since that first night. Realized that I'd be crazy to go now.

I ached to know, though. Ached to understand. Because I felt that whatever they were up to down there, it might well explain the strange behavior I'd seen all week. The sheer impassiveness. The interest in nothing.

Probably just drugs, I told myself as I crept down the stairwell, my pulse speeding up. Wasn't that always the explanation these days? One peek. One sniff at the air emerging from that hole, and I'd be satisfied, and go back, lock my door.

The grass seemed to cling around my ankles as I made my way across. And I kept looking around the whole while. Expecting, any moment, the ninth member to appear. What was I doing out here?

I stopped by the hole, crouched partly, every muscle set to spring up and run in a split instant. I could see the first few crumbled, brick-built stairs, but could smell nothing. I could hear some voices, though.

Not the way I'd heard them that first night. Not the rise and fall of sharp aggression. These were monotones. Almost like a chanting. They seemed to be filtering from very deep inside the earth, and I could pick out not even a single word.

The Lords of Zero

Very, very carefully—as frightened as I'd ever been in my whole life—I started to descend again. This new stairwell curled around, so they'd not see me immediately.

A dim light started showing by the time that I was halfway down.

And I could hear the voices far more clearly. I was sure they belonged to the gang. And yet they were not speaking English.

I froze up completely. Tried to tell which language it was, and could not. Sometimes smooth and flowing. And then—out of nowhere—harsh, guttural. Like Arabic, though it wasn't that. Some tongue—I was certain—very old.

Another half-dozen cautious footsteps and then, crouching down again, the cellar came in view.

It was wholly bare, just aged brick. And one of the gang had lit an ancient, rusted storm lantern, placing it at the dead center of the floor. All eight were facing away from me, toward the far end of the room, where the shadows were the densest.

And were kneeling.

The ninth member of the gang was in a straight-backed chair there, gazing back at them. And he was still in silhouette.

Flickers from the lamp were washing over him.

But he was *still* in silhouette.

I should have been able to pick out some details of his features from this distance. But . . .

How much closer would I have to get, I numbly wondered, before I'd be able to see who he was?

Just one of the gang had been doing most of the strange chanting. Now he stopped and ducked his head. The figure in the chair straightened a little, almost imperiously. Raised a narrow hand.

And seemed to begin issuing commands, in the same odd tongue. Every time he paused, the whole gang nodded.

I remained still, rooted to the spot. And my head felt like it might burst, there was so much blood now pulsing through it. I could only watch, and try to comprehend.

What had been here before the Craven? Victorian tenements. And before that? I struggled to remember.

Nothing. Nothing urban anyway. Just marshes, bleeding off into the Thames. Empty, flat places, quite vast. The only sounds, the wind whining through the tall, stiff grasses and the birds calling at night.

These eight kids. They possessed . . . precisely nothing. They looked forward to nothing. They believed in nothing. Emptiness. Pure zero.

And if nature does abhor a vacuum, maybe supernature does as well. Maybe it, too, is drawn toward voids.

There was no telling precisely what the figure at the far end of the room was, though I knew it only came at night, and I could take a guess.

But that didn't really matter, now did it? Not to the eight boys. What counted to their young minds was—it was *something*.

Did I make a move? A noise? It stopped talking and looked across at me now, although none of the gang turned.

It studied me carefully, without any apparent surprise. It had, after all, seen me before.

Then it raised its right hand. Crooked its finger. Beckoning.

I understood.

Me? Myself? No marriage left. No real career. No family. No home. Prospects, realistically, quite bleak. Very little to look forward to.

I understood.

And, without even having to think about it, shook my head.

It gestured again, more impatiently this time. And again I refused, and backed up a couple of paces.

How could something without features look so disappointed, sad?

The gang all turned to me as one, their faces pale and their eyes burning.

"'E doesn't just ask anyone," one of them said. I couldn't tell who, in the shadows.

"Next time we see you," another put in, "well, we'll finish what we started."

And then I was running, up the stairs, across the grass. Out through a gap between the blocks. Fully expecting the eight of them to be hard on my heels.

They weren't. They'd stayed behind.

I hit the open street, skidded on a loose paving stone, almost fell. And then I was running once again, leaving everything behind. My paltry few possessions, even my new manuscript. Everything save escape was forgotten.

Within an hour, I was checking into a hostel near Tower Bridge, just starting to calm down.

There were four other men in my new room, one of them fast asleep, another hunched and slightly crazy-looking, but the last two amiable and chatty. The fluorescent lights were bright, and the whole place smelled of cheap, bad cooking. There was loud music coming from next door and I could hear somebody insisting that it be turned off.

Me? Myself? I just sat down on my bunk and took it all in slowly, savoring it. True, it wasn't very much. But it was normal, and was something.

More than zero.

Smoke City

BY RUSSELL BLACKFORD

She was *hungry*; she was *thirsty*.

Her sound system blared out Raptor Jouissant's *Deathbird* album on data dot—the track was "Tyrant Lizard"—as the powerful little Merc swished along in the dark, on the wet road, well within its capabilities. Driving summer rain washed across the tinted screen, wipers bat-bat-batting it away. Meridien turned into a narrow one-way street, then spun the wheel to the left, braking in front of a shiny new grid that blocked the entrance to an automated car park. She waved her key pass and the grid swung up to let her through.

She parked the Merc, switched it off, then marched quickly to a glassed-in elevator lobby. Silvered doors opened for her, and she touched a pad to take her to The Black Blade's third-floor entrance.

Nearly midnight—time to hunt, time to feed. She was hungry and thirsty for blood.

Four time zones away, three of the Chosen played virtual reality games in Dirk's spacious, single-room loft, handing around a set of Damiano Kombat goggles. They wore their flicktrooper gear, black and urban grey, seeing who could amass the most kill points in allocated ten-minute bursts. Right now, shaven-headed Toledo Steel wore the goggles; Principality and beautiful, blond-bearded Dirk watched her strut her stuff.

With shiny metal skin rings implanted in her face and hands, Toledo was like a whirring machine. She was too tall to look the part of a gymnast, long and skinny as a whip, but she moved like a blur on Dirk's padded blue gym mats, performing high-speed *muay-thai* actions against a sequence of invisible opponents. Now and then, she threw herself onto the mats, rebounded to her feet, moving sideways as well as forward, lashed out with an untiring series of spinning kicks, combinations of punches, elbow blows, groin- or rib-crushing knee blows.

Dirk's wide street-front window was smart glass that converted, with a spoken instruction to his cybersystem, into a video wall shutting them off from the outside with its dreary night life or deadly sunshine. The same 3-D images presented to Toledo by the Kombat goggles were displayed on the screen. In a stark, cratered landscape, successive blue-skinned bipedal lizards, eight feet high, with long, razor-sided tails, emerged from one or another crater—and attacked. Each reptiloid moved through one of the goggles' inexhaustible set of fighting routines, slashing with claws and tail. On the video wall screen, Toledo's stylized nude, sexless image counterattacked and killed, dispatching reptiloid souls to Smoke City (if only the VR monsters had souls and memories to send to their true deaths). She moved faster than a merely human eye could have followed, with a Chosen One's near-instantaneous reflexes.

Principality waited her turn to use the goggles.

The Black Blade was four levels of dancing, with bars, the noise of small-time miracle bands, of excited fish people, tiger kids and flicktroopers drinking jugs of beer or alcoholic cola. Layers of smoke. The sweet burning of cloves and marijuana. On floor two, a dot jockey played recorded syntho music with a monotonous dance beat. Shiny metal stairs led up or down, and Meridien chose *up*. On floor three, a band strutted the corner stage, five Korean musos wearing loose, gauzy white clothing, and playing from jacked-in Wires, while young people danced, many of them half-naked to display dramatically morphed bodies.

Meridien drifted among the radical bio-implants of the fish people—the teenage roe girls and their boys, their *sharks*. She moved, with the aimlessness of plankton, amidst limbs and heads and torsos adorned with tusks, dorsal sails, oddly placed fins and fur and feathers, skin-jewels and ivory scrimshaw. The tiger kids were strikingly pierced; they displayed niobium hooks, ribbons and blades, so that metal bristled defiantly from every available inch of their fiercely tattooed skin and stringy musculature.

Meridien was dark-haired and very pale, with a tattooed lightning bolt, three inches long, on each bare shoulder. Her flicktrooper gear advertised her as a street fighter. She wore black jeans and matching Nikes, a gunslinger belt with silverchrome studs and a long knife pouch hanging off it, a light grey T-shirt with the arms taken out. She knew how others saw her, like some dangerous, captivating snake: her lean body, narrow hips, the threat implicit in her knife pouch and the fingerblades on her left hand.

Around her, the morphed children danced. Some cut their flesh with blades—some of them could flickdance, healing as they cut, in a kind of hypnotic state, but others merely bled. No one stepped in to stop it; the city authorities could respond to the flickdancing craze, but not control it. During her long lifetime, the world had come too far. A group of girls wanted to dance with her; they were little roe, late teens, a few years younger than Meridien had been when she was Chosen, centuries before—and ceased growing older. Cropped hair. High-heeled mules. Calf-length, gauzy skirts and bare upper torsos to show off finny implants. She didn't mind them. They gave her camouflage while she scouted the room for prey.

She made a decision. A boy in his early twenties. Dressed in flicktrooper regalia, much like Meridien's own, but with compromises. His hair was dyed brightly in salaripunk style, scarlet red hanging loosely to his shoulders. The pretty child was middle height, skinny, maybe one hundred sixty pounds, with no implants that Meridien could see, not like her own fingerblades. But he had the flicktrooper look. Some kind of sheathed blade hung prominently from his belt. He'd also have martial arts credentials—something to look forward to. He was dancing with a group of sharks and roe and a tall black girl wearing flicktrooper gear far more aggressive than his. She was tall, with pumped-up, oiled muscles. Even more than Meridien, she *looked* the part of a street fighter, and the boy was clearly enthralled.

Meridien tacked and weaved her way across the dance floor. She caught the boy's eye, just for a moment, then glanced away. A big, lean shark stepped into her path and wanted to dance. He was wearing tight jeans, leopard-skin boots, lots of implanted niobium rings, and a built-in dorsal sail. *So wearisome, alas*—he'd be the kind of lover that always wanted to get on top. Still, she danced with him awhile. When the music stopped, Meridien said to the shark, "What's your name?"

"Feend," he said—then laughed. "That's with two *e*'s."

"I see." He had a nice body, perhaps he would do for tonight . . . no, she'd stay with her plan.

"What about you?" he said.

"Mmmm?"

"Your name?"

She shook her head vaguely. "Listen, Feend."

"What?"

"You see that little coterie?" She nodded in the general direction. "Do you see them? The group with the flicktrooper types—the black gal and the sort of salaripunk guy."

"Yeah?"

"Do you like her? Do you think she's pretty."

He shrugged. "Sure."

"Would you like to fuck her?" She could read his thoughts, his feelings like an open book. Of course he would want the girl. The very idea made his pulse race. Dealing with humans was easy.

"Well, sure," he said again, breaking into a grin, just like she knew he would. "What's going on?"

"Come with me, then." She took his hand. "This is your lucky night."

The music started up again as Meridien and her new friend joined the group. *Just a little concentration, fine-tuning impulses here . . . and here.* Feend approached the flicktrooper girl, who looked him over appreciatively. The long-haired boy stepped impulsively after Meridien as she turned and walked away—just as she wished. His soul was cradled now, rocking securely in the gentle darkness of her mind. Like this, up close and intimate, she brought out the best in people.

They danced through five songs, and he tried to kiss her. She laughed and dodged his lips, but didn't back away. Next time he tried it, she let him—she opened her mouth, and their tongues swirled together. He tasted like mangoes and beer. As they kissed, he touched the side of her breast; she pressed herself to his groin; he cupped her breast as the kissing lingered. He was confident, intent. And ever so young.

Next time the music stopped, he said, "Want to go back to your place?"

Snap!

Teasingly, she said, "No."

"Where then? My place? I'm kind of paranoid about where I live. It's not very salubrious." Making a joke of the word.

"What's your name?" she said.

"What's yours?"

"You first, my friend."

"Okay. I'm Number Two. Now it's your turn."

She laughed. "In that case, you can call me 666." He frowned at that, as if to say *very funny*. "Come on," she said, "cheer up. If you can use an alias, so can I." Then, after a pause, "Your place, Number Two, not mine. Don't give me a hard time about it."

They found the Merc and she drove to his apartment near Civic Station. "I love this car," he said as its engine hummed and the wipers bat-bat-batted at the goddamn rain. "You must be a rich gal."

"I do okay. I get what I want."

"You're a strange one. You even talk funny. I'm not sure why I'm trusting you."

She laughed. "Trusting me? With what, *mon cher*?"

For one of the Chosen to watch another playing with the Kombat goggles was always astonishing. *Could I do that?* Principality knew that she could, indeed, perform as well as Toledo when it was her turn, yet she could never get used to it. Perhaps she'd become blasé when she'd lived for centuries like the ageless woman who'd Chosen her, the elegant undead called Meridien. Meanwhile, their powers seemed like those of demigods.

The game was set at the highest point of the equipment's capacity, a level beyond anything a player was expected to reach—one that demanded speed and reflexes faster than was physiologically possible for a human. But Toledo defeated reptiloid after reptiloid, whirring and blurring, making her moves, doing her dance of Shiva.

After ten minutes, the video wall showed that she had sixty-three kills, two better than Dirk had managed. Toledo unclipped the goggles at the back of her head, passed them over to Principality, stood panting and smiling with her hands on her knees. She'd never beaten Dirk before, and he looked disgruntled behind his wispy beard. "We're both going to beat you this time," Principality said.

"No way," he said.

Principality held their record: sixty-seven kills. There was never much between any of their scores. Yet, even more than Toledo, she hated coming last. They all did.

Then, before Principality could clip on the goggles, she found herself leaping instinctively to one side as something smashed the door like match-wood, and rushed straight at them, faster than even they could move, firing a lightweight SLR rifle on full auto, bullets chipping the walls, sending up dust, smashing equipment, shredding furniture, cracking the armored glass of the video wall. It was a *skin*, a thing of featureless, flexible military armor. The rifle noise was deafening. Holo movies never suggested how *loud* military weapons were in real life.

They made love in the dim light of a bedside lamp. Number Two had miniature niobium barbells piercing his nipples, and his circumcised penis was tattooed in shades of blue and green. Meridien straddled him and took him into her body; she lowered herself to take him right up inside. Lifted and lowered.

He moaned softly. "That's good."

"Is it? Just watch me. Hands behind your head. That's right. This is a treat. This is what I do when I have no one to fuck." She stroked her pale breasts, one in each hand, under around, then down, pulling her nipples, making them go long, careful with her fingerbladed left hand. "Keep still; just watch." She pulled her breasts outward for him, then squeezed and pulled her nipples some more, for him and for herself. Just for the moment, as she lowered once more into the hollow of his body, she started to move luxuriously from the hips. She looked at Number Two's eyes, then at her fingers, on her nipples. "There's a direct line from these to my clit," she said and he grew harder and bigger inside her; boys liked that kind of talk. "Okay, let's go."

He gasped. "It's lovely."

"Yes." She rode him fast, still pulling on her nipples. "We're going to *come*."

Her orgasms were like huge breakers rolling in from the ocean. He shuddered along with her. When she bent forward to kiss him, he smelled musky and sweet. His hair was soft, something to remember about him.

Afterwards, they mopped themselves with paper tissues. "That was wonderful," he said sleepily.

"*Merci*, Nicky."

He tensed, moved away from her on the bed. "How do you know my true name?"

"Would you believe me if I said I can read minds?"

She watched him watching her. Watched his expression as he saw her face rearrange itself—exposing her as something far more dangerous than he ever imagined. Her smile bared long pointed teeth like a wolf's.

Nicky rolled from the mattress onto his feet, rushing for his jeans and knife belt. Meridien got there before him, and kicked his clothes away. He crouched into a *muay-thai* stance. "You're cute in a way," she said. "I like to give a sweet boy like you a nice time before you go to Smoke City."

"What the fuck is this? What are you?"

He swung at her with fists and feet, trying to get closer to damage her with knees and elbows. But she'd already moved out of range. She saw every action in his mind before it happened. Meridien loved her work.

"It's no good, Nicky." Then she slashed at him faster than he could see, raking his chest with her fingerblades. When he stopped to feel for blood, he made the mistake of looking down. She took her opportunity, grasped him in a front headlock, her forearm like a metal bar across his mouth. He tried to bite her—which seemed so ironic and made her laugh aloud. Meridien moved forward and down from the hips—and back from the shoulders—a swift, powerful, snapping movement of her body.

"Did no one teach you to fight?" she said as he sagged in her arms.

But he was still alive, blood pumping in his arteries and veins. Her mouth found his throat and she *drank* him. *At last. Ever so sweet.* His young blood flowed through her in satisfying waves like another long, luscious orgasm.

Then there was one last action to take. He was very nice, of course, but not enough for her to Choose. She looked for a deeper compatibility. There was nothing closer to her than her own Chosen Ones, bonded to her for eternity. Alas, he'd experienced her bite and now his body would try to regenerate. That was why she carried a knife.

He was a pale, desiccated thing. Meridien propped him against a badly painted wall and lifted his head by its long, scarlet hair, tugging it a few inches toward her, making an easy stalk of the neck. She knelt slightly to one side of him, calculating the angle quickly as she raised her twelve-inch knife, then chopped just once, with more-than-human strength. She kissed her severed trophy on the mouth, then placed it tidily beside the slumping corpse.

With her soul's eye, she saw a kind of smoke rise and dissipate. "*Adieu,* brave Nicky," she said.

All finished. All gone.

Gone to Smoke City.

Most bullet wounds did little harm to the Chosen, but they could *hurt.* Principality found herself dodging, anticipating the skin's intentions, her reflexes faster than thought.

The skin stopped firing and aimed a blow at Toledo Steel with the gun's fiberglass butt. Toledo rolled away. The skin was only a man, but suited from head to toe, almost featureless, its shimmering dermis the same electric blue color as a virtual reality reptiloid.

All at once the Chosen responded; they changed, jaws growing longer, baring feral teeth—

Dirk reached to his knife belt, drew out his special blade, the long, slender dagger that gave him his name—

Toledo found her own gun, a Browning pistol, and she was firing back from a position on the floor—

Principality jumped over the skin as it spun into a crouch. She tried to run outside, but it outpaced her in a straight line. She stepped from its path, catching its unconscious thoughts, anticipating its action.

They exchanged feints, then Dirk ran at it, dagger in hand. The blade failed to penetrate its armor, slipped aside, though it was only a glancing blow. Still using the rifle butt, the skin landed a brutal blow on Dirk's chest, and he fell. In the same movement, it swung at Principality's ankle and she stumbled, crashing face-forward into a wall, blocking the impact with both forearms. It kept close to her, like a glove, kicked her in the ribs, in the back. She felt bones cracking. Toledo had stopped firing as they all fought close up. "Get away from it," she said. "Principality, get away from it."

The skin dropped Principality and rushed at Toledo, giving her a clear shot at it. As Toledo fired, it slung its rifle across its back and leaped; Toledo half-anticipated, so it got her arm and shoulder rather than head and neck. An exchange of blows, and Toledo went down. The skin grabbed her pistol and shoved it into a belt about its waist from which hung other paraphernalia in silvery pouches and sheaths. It shrugged the rifle back into its hands, ready to fill the room with a long burst of rapid fire. All its targets had been slowed effectively.

Principality checked herself. She'd taken bullets and blows, but no bones were cracked badly enough to immobilize her. She tried to stand, but that was still too difficult. She probed at the skin's mind, looking for emotions she could magnify or tweak, some trace of sympathy or mercy, but found nothing of the sort. The man in there was deeply indoctrinated, committed to his mission. There was nothing for her to work with.

For a moment, it seemed easiest to accept death, to go to Smoke City. Doubtless the skin had plenty of means to send them there. Even a Chosen One could be killed forever if its neck was severed, or its brain or heart sufficiently damaged.

If she could just move, there was now a clear path to the door. Her body was mending. She found her feet.

Back at the dance club, Meridien was troubled. In the riot and carnival, she could pinpoint nothing; yet she sensed malevolent thoughts, something that meant her harm and was confident of success.

The Black Blade's lowest floor was a huge, free-form venue full of dazzling, spinning mirror balls, holos that suddenly appeared, in the semi-darkness, from nowhere and then vanished—Asian- and Welsh-style dragons, giant dancing scorpions, caves of glittering blue ice, laughing clown heads that winked like the dummies of a senile ventriloquist—all layered with fogs of many different colors, emerging from different machines scattered in multiple corners. Laser lights flashed, searched, zapped, strobed, reflected from the spinning mirror balls, plunged like light sabers through the insubstantial holos. On the stage, a miracle band made the amps roar, made them pound and screech, yelp, cackle, trill, laugh, made them sing, or weep, all the colors of sound—every imaginable noise—woven into a heavy rhythm and a kind of melody, while the crowd laughed and shouted, laughed and cried. The musos were like buzzing, roaring motorbikes going full throttle.

All that was irrelevant, for the dangerous thoughts came closer, something that wanted to hurt her, something disciplined and military that she mustn't try to fight. Something that vowed her destruction and had her measure, something with the awful strength of machinery.

She got the hell out of there.

A knot of dancing tiger girls parted to let her through as she leapt seven feet to the sound stage, brushed past a security guard and the bewildered musicians, who seemed to move in slow motion. As she glanced over her shoulder, something followed through the crowd, seeming to flow like molten glass, moving with impossible speed. There were cries of "Stop! You can't go there! No!"

Meridien zigzagged behind the stage and ran to a door that led to the dressing rooms. As more shouts and confusion went up, the thing was at her heels like a shadow. She managed to slide the door, slam it behind, then continued running. A moment later the thing ran straight through the wooden door.

She found another door, leading to an alley. Outside it was still pouring rain. Water swirled in the gutters. She was on a landing thirty feet above the street. She vaulted the metal stair rail, dropping unhurt to the roof of a car—buckling beneath her as she landed—then to the flooded pavement. The thing leapt over her, pivoted to face her, cutting off her escape.

Her fear took on substance and shape. It had a vaguely human form under a tight-fitting but strangely molded suit that covered its wearer from head to toe, color-morphing as it moved. Except for the fat-torsoed, full-chested body outline, and a kind of bump high up on the curve of its back, between the shoulders, no features were visible. It wore a mesh belt full of pockets, pouches, obscured devices.

The skin-thing rushed forward. She drew her knife and the skin rushed onto the blade at the speed of a motor car rather than anything alive. The blade glanced from something rock hard. The skin stabbed and slashed at her with its open hands; she made it miss. When it charged again, she used its own momentum against it; she flipped it over her in the air as she hurled herself backward, but it turned round its body axis and landed on all fours like a giant cat springing from a tree. On its next rush, she jumped over it;

but it tucked into a roll on the alley's broken concrete, sprang upward like a water fountain and spun like an ice skater, landing to face her again. She had the advantage of catching its thoughts, almost like living a second in its future. But it was so fast. She couldn't damage it, couldn't outrun it. It gained a grip on her T-shirt, twisted the fabric in its hand, pulled her toward it. Her blows were ineffectual as it reeled her in.

Close up and intimate, the skin spoke to her, a grating electronically distorted voice in her ear. "There's a crackdown," it said. She saw at once what it all meant, saw it there in her enemy's mind. National governments acting in carefully planned unison, sending in their troops in micro-motored armor to eradicate her kind like vermin. It was a crackdown on the Chosen, simultaneously across the world, with no time for communication among the targets. How fortunate she was: it was night here in her time zone. Others would have been caught helpless in their daytime sepulchers. *She* wasn't helpless yet. Was she?

They traded blows and the skin had the better of it. She blacked out for an instant and found herself lying in the flooded gutter. The skin held a long, glittering, bladed weapon, something that had evolved from a meat cleaver.

Meridien closed her eyes. Everything earthly fell away from her. She was no more than smoke. Without a body, everything that made her Meridien would soon vanish in the wind, the fate of the truly dead.

She was a smoke of memory in Smoke City.

Principality shrugged off the scraping of pain, prepared a desperate rush for the shattered door, with a clear path this time; but the skin fired bullets through her at the same time as it flew at her across the room as though expelled from a cannon. Toledo was badly hurt—broken bones—no help from that quarter. As the skin knocked her down, fought with her on the floor, drove those cruel blows into her, Dirk came after it once again with his one-molecule-sharp, diamond-coated knife.

The skin drove a terrible rifle-butt blow right under Principality's ribs, and she blacked out.

Smoke City.

The souls of the dead are less than smoke on the wind. Bodiless, sexless, mere scattering memories without the glue of life to bind them. This is the true death—this nightmare, this fading into nothingness.

Meridien tried to remember: soirées, cities. *Paris, Moscow, New Orleans, Bangkok.* Conversations with poets and artists and rock musicians. Lovers, mere meals, and Chosen Ones. Centuries of experience, of knowledge and desire and intimacy—blowing, now, like less than dry leaves.

Smoke City.

She experienced it, and rejected it.

Some had come back from Smoke City. Certain legendary sorcerers had bound themselves to the material world with objects of power—amulets or carvings prepared with sacrifice and excruciating pain over many human lifetimes. Such beings could go inward, waiting for a young or frail soul to pass by, then dispossess it of its body. Though she was not such a sorcerer, Meridien had lived for four hundred years and did not face her true death meekly. She had her own special creations, those things she was closest to, her own Chosen, the souls of her soul.

Before she could blow away into the emptiness of eternity, she reached out for the earthly plane, thinking again of cities and lovers, of the night's beauty, the glittering of chandeliers, the sweetness of kisses, and the satisfying sensuality of warm, living blood. She reached out with all the strength of her memories and her years.

She came to her senses.

But what was she doing *here*, still fighting the skin? This was Dirk's loft apartment, thousands of miles away. Her body was in pain, as if her bones had cracked and broken and were now scraping against each other, wearing each other away. She stood without volition, her movements unsynchronized with anything she was thinking or attempting. She'd started to run toward a shattered door; someone was controlling her like a marionette. All she could feel was pain, no real kinesthetic sense. She'd worry *why* later.

At the other end of the room, Toledo Steel lay badly hurt. Dirk moved slowly on a gym mat like he'd been bludgeoned. He picked up his long knife where he'd dropped it. The skin saw her running; it fired on semiauto, and two bullets pierced, entered and exited her body at her waist. At almost the same time, the skin reached her, bringing her down in an unequal collision. It struck her with cruel blows.

She realized: it was not the same skin as she'd fought, the one that had sent her to Smoke City—same shape, same structure, same movements, but this one was slightly larger than "her" skin. Somehow, she'd teleported here, right into the middle of another such fight. Then it was obvious.

This isn't my body, either.

They were fighting on their knees, her body still acting of its own accord, out of Meridien's control. More blows fell, and she felt more bones crack, felt the insult to her heart and lungs. A terrible blow ripped under her ribs as the skin struck her with the rifle butt, yet she stayed conscious. She could suddenly make her own movements, could try to fight back.

All at once Dirk had come after the skin with his knife. *No, I tried that.* The skin turned to him, and Dirk flicked out of the way of a *muay-thai* hook kick. As they feinted and struck, the skin seized Dirk's left shoulder in one hand, the other still holding its rifle. Meridien knew the terrible strength of that grip. At the same time, Dirk stabbed at it. His highland dagger's slim, ten-inch blade pierced the armor at the shoulder, and blood squeezed out for a moment, before the diamondoid cloth resealed. The skin stood stupidly for several seconds, then tightened its grip and threw Dirk across the room one-handed. A moment later it followed, snatched the knife; it forced the weapon through Dirk's eye, into his brain, leaving the Zytel pommel sticking out of the Chosen One's face like a huge, malformed scab.

Then it shifted its attention to Meridien.

Principality dreamed, dreamed that she was Meridien. She was Meridien, somehow teleported across a continent. And she, Meridien, was now in control of Principality's body. Except no, she dreamed that she was Principality dreaming she was Meridien, dreaming she'd been teleported into Principality's body. No, not that either—

The skin was onto her and she had to fight it. She came awake, rolling on the gym mats to the other end of the room, as the skin fired at her; she found her feet and half ran, half tripped to the bodies of Dirk and Toledo Steel. The skin fired a burst of bullets at her again, but again she made most of them miss. Hastily she tore the diamond blade from Dirk's skull. The skin made a mistake. It pounced. Principality caught its intention and *moved*; the skin almost missed, catching her at the right side, like a speeding car hitting her. She held the diamond-coated blade outward, wrist and hand and knife pommel all braced against her own chest wall. The skin fell onto the blade—like sticking a charging boar—at the same time as Principality's head whiplashed against the chipped and cracked surface of the armorglass window. Thunder and lightning tore through her head; she lost all volition.

Meridien wanted to fight the thing, but this body that so resembled her own seemed too battered for the task. The skin was onto her. She stepped around it and rolled away on the floor. Once again, she blacked out for a moment.

Suddenly she was holding the knife, where the skin had impaled itself upon it. *What had happened?*

With her remaining strength, she tried to twist the blade in more deeply, to the hilt, beyond if that were possible. It was such a better knife than her own for this kind of work, some trick with amorphous deposited diamond. The weapon felt beautiful. She gripped it with both hands, holding and squeezing and pushing for all she was worth. Then pulled it out and stabbed again through the armor.

She had a fine new body as hardened and tough as the one she'd left behind. She knew whose it was. *Principality.*

My beautiful Chosen One.

She stabbed yet again with the frictionless blade.

She sent the skin to Smoke City.

When the world restored itself, Principality was gripping the knife, holding it in both hands where it was lodged deep in the skin.

Someone had held the knife for her as she passed out, then done more good work. *Meridien. You're in my head.* She looked about at the carnage, then felt with her mind through the surfaces and depths of her body. She was a mass of cracks, breaks, tears, bruises and partially healed bullet holes. Only one bullet had lodged inside her, in the thigh muscle near her groin. Others had passed straight through her body's tissues.

Moving gingerly, she removed her knife belt and sat against the video wall. She undid her black jeans and shimmied them down over her hips and past her knees. The inside of her thigh, where the bullet had penetrated, was lumpy as if a hard-boiled egg was wobbling around beneath the surface of her skin. The flesh was bruise-blue and pulped-looking, though not actually bleeding. She stuffed the hem of her bloodied T-shirt between her teeth, then cut into the insulted flesh with Dirk's knife. Swift, sure movements, teeth gritting the fabric, pushing the agony away from her. Then she had what she wanted, a blood-smeared expended bullet. She stood and pulled up her jeans, panting from the effort.

Now there was nothing much wrong with her except a ferocious hunger from all her body's efforts of exertion and self-repair.

And one small, nonphysical thing. *Meridien, I know you're with me. We've got to get out of here.*

This was the stuff of a nightmare. Weren't they supposed to fight each other for control? But it didn't feel like that. She was herself, as Meridien must have been *her* self when Principality had blacked out—they had not yet mixed or fought. But something was changing now, more like inspiration than possession. Memories adding, centuries of them, memories of foreign nights, strange faces, poetry and kisses, blending in like insights or the remembrance of lost time, attitudes adjusting as necessary. They were growing into something new, a fusion, something that had no wish to fight itself.

And they were stronger than the humans had thought.

This loft was like an abattoir. She had to get away, let her body recover—whoever's body it now was—go where she wasn't known.

She unclipped Dirk's knife pouch from his belt, then clipped it to her own. She wiped his dagger on his jeans. Satisfied, she sheathed the blade. She found one of Dirk's clean T-shirts, three sizes too big for her but that didn't matter. She could see how the skin's rifle disassembled. She packed its components in a black leather traveling bag, then cleaned herself in the bathroom as well as she could in the brief minutes she allowed herself. Her face changed to a more human appearance.

Toledo would recover if no more skins came to finish the job. Dirk had gone to Smoke City.

There was no time to worry about them. Soon it would be dawn. She must shelter from the burning sunlight. Somewhere safe and anonymous. Then she could plan her vengeance.

Straightening her body that would have been dead many times over if it had been merely human, she walked from the room and downstairs into the dark hours of the morning. The moon and the city lights shone reassuringly.

Smoke City

There were scattered raindrops in the cool air. Night in a huge metropolis. *Vive la vie!*

Meridien-Principality signaled a yellow taxicab. From the front seat, the driver looked at her curiously as she stood on the pavement. She must still be an evil sight. She needed to sate her hunger, then hide from the sun.

She sat in the rear seat. "Where do you live, driver?" she said.

"Why are you asking?" But a street address came to the front of his mind. That was all she needed—still so easy dealing with humans. She punched through the plastic barrier behind his seat and then her forearm was across his throat.

"Drive," she said. She told him his own address, laughing. Images in his mind of a family waiting for him—a young, pretty wife, sweet little children—at the end of his shift. *Ah, yes!* She needed to gorge. "*Chez vous,* driver," she said with a reckless laugh. She tightened her hold on his throat, turned up the volume of his fear. "Take us to your place."

They drove into the dark.

Moments of Change

BY THOMAS TESSIER

Not long after he retired, Larkin began waking up around two o'clock in the morning. At first he thought it was just a fluke, but it soon became a regular occurrence. He would lie still in the dark for some time with his eyes closed, but he could not fall asleep again. Finally there was nothing to do but get out of bed. He would potter about the house, make a snack and drink a glass of milk, and perhaps watch television. Sometimes he sat out on his back porch, listened to the night sounds and waited for the colors of dawn to emerge slowly from the darkness.

The only nights of the week this didn't happen were Friday and Saturday. It was his longstanding habit to play cards and have a few drinks with old friends at the Hibernians on those nights. Larkin wouldn't get home until well after midnight and then he would sleep without interruption until eight or nine in the morning. But the rest of the week, he went to bed a little past ten and fell asleep quickly, as usual, only to wake up about four hours later.

It worried him, but he didn't like talking to a doctor about it, and he wanted nothing to do with pills. No doubt it was some kind of reaction to his retirement. After so many years of living according to a predictable schedule, he now had a lot more loose time on his hands. But that shouldn't have been a problem, really. He liked being retired. He was happy to get away from the daily grind.

Moments of Change

And it was not as if he didn't know what to do with himself. He had already picked up a nice little part-time job at a liquor store in town. It was only three evenings a week, 5–8 P.M. (plus an extra half hour after closing, to stack the empties out back for collection). It was something to do, he got to see plenty of people he knew, and he was paid in cash.

He had no one else to worry about. He and his wife had drifted apart back in their forties. Actually, Larkin hadn't moved at all; Peggy was the one who'd done all the drifting, convinced that she was entitled to more out of life. She found it in an elderly widower who could not stand living alone and who had some money. The guy thought he was lucky because to him Peggy was still a young woman. The only thing about it that surprised Larkin was how little it bothered him at the time.

He had a daughter, Sue, but she lived half a continent away, down in Texas, with her husband and two spoiled kids. They usually came east for a visit once a year, and Sue called him every couple of weeks or so for a brief newsy chat. That was fine. Whenever she tried to persuade him to come down for a visit, he gently but firmly resisted. Larkin was a lifelong New England mill city kind of man who wanted no part of Texas, thanks all the same—his buddies at the A.O.H. always got a big kick out of hearing him repeat that.

He soon adjusted to the sleep situation. The first week, he nodded off for nearly two hours after lunch. It wasn't intentional, it just happened, and the sleepiness came over him quickly. Next day, same thing. Then Larkin decided that instead of getting a sore neck in the easy chair, it made more sense to stretch out on the couch. These naps extended to around 4 P.M. He realized that he was sleeping about the same number of hours he always had, only now it was split into two shifts. That was okay. Those afternoon hours often felt slow and useless anyway.

The one thing that continued to bother Larkin about this was the fact that he had nothing to do when he woke up in the middle of the night. It didn't take long for him to grow dissatisfied just sitting around, waiting for the morning paper to arrive. Television made him impatient. Somehow, at that hour of the night, idleness felt wrong. Maybe it was the dark outside, the quiet in the neighborhood, but doing nothing made him feel like he was merely waiting to die, which he was not.

The solution came to him the evening he carried his recycling bin to the curb for collection with the garbage the next morning. Bottles and cans. He gazed down at a couple of soda cans he'd thrown in the bin. Curious, he strolled around the block, casually glancing at every bin he passed. Sure enough, most of them contained several empties, each one worth a nickel. A lot of people couldn't be bothered lugging their cans and bottles down to the supermarket and popping them into the machine. For what—fifty, seventy-five cents a time? They wanted the empties out of the kitchen, the bin was handy and it meant that the stuff would be recycled anyway. The easy choice.

Shortly before 3 A.M. the next morning, he put a box of black plastic trash bags on the passenger seat and drove around the neighborhood, more out of curiosity than anything else. In less than two hours his car was full, and when Larkin redeemed the empties later that morning he pocketed twenty-seven dollars and change. Not scale, but not bad. It was something to do.

It didn't take long for him to learn the trash collection route—which neighborhoods put their bins out on which night. The cops got used to him, some of them even waved or honked, and he came to recognize many of the newspaper delivery people who were on their own rounds. Larkin learned where there were dogs to be avoided, and to be quiet—rattling bottles and cans seemed incredibly loud at that hour. Two-liter containers took up too much space, so he only picked cans and small bottles. He steered clear of drunks and teenagers, and never had any trouble.

He usually stayed at home when it was raining, but a light drizzle didn't bother him. Larkin discovered that he enjoyed being out at night. The air was cleaner, and the relative absence of noise and cars and people was quite pleasing. The darkness and streetlights combined to make buildings that were old and dreary in the daytime look somehow younger, fresher and more hopeful at night. The city's residential neighborhoods felt like they belonged to him again in a way that he hadn't experienced since he was a boy.

By early September Larkin had been going about his nightly rounds for almost five months. He'd seen some things. People storming around behind their blinds, shouting at each other, banging furniture. People drunk in front of their televisions, sometimes slumped forward, chin on chest, or head tilted back, resting on the top of the chair, mouths open, snoring at the ceiling. The older woman in a long white nightgown who came out onto her front porch and began to sing loudly in some strange foreign language—amazed, Larkin stood and gaped at her for a minute or more from the other side of the street, until her husband rushed out in his pajamas and yanked her back inside the house.

There were animals, too. Besides rats, which were to be expected in certain areas, Larkin also sometimes spotted a small group of deer moving through the yards, a skunk, or a possum. There were a few places where he often encountered raccoons trying to get in the tall green garbage bins. The first time, he tried to shoo them away, throwing a few sticks and pebbles at them, but they didn't move, they only stared and hissed at him. That was enough for Larkin, who got back into his car and went on to the next house.

The wind was whipping the trees and the first sweet taste of autumn was in the air the night he thought he saw a fire. He was on Utrecht Street, in a neighborhood of old triple-deckers and faded brick commercial buildings. Bonder Nickel Plating and Behlman Anodized Products were gone, as was Dinkle Pipe & Tube. Larkin knew guys who had spent thirty or forty years of their lives in those mills. Now the whole area was dotted with vacant premises and junky little storefronts like Ruben's Neon Tattooz, the Kowloon Gardens (carryout only), Cabo Verde Travel, and Exaltation Church Goods.

It was a small house, not much bigger than a cottage, with asbestos shingles that had gone grey decades ago. It was perched by itself on the crest of the small hill, where Utrecht turned sharply and looped back down toward West River Avenue. Larkin no longer stopped there because they never put anything redeemable in their bin. But as he slowed his car to make the turn, he noticed a flickering red glow in the ground-floor window on the side of the house.

He was sure it was a fire. Somebody fell asleep while smoking, or maybe it was faulty wiring—these old dumps were all firetraps. He pulled his car over to the curb, turned it off and rushed across the street. The rest of the house was dark and there was no streetlight nearby. He tripped on a rock in the rutted driveway and almost fell. The window was closer to the back end of the house. Before he got to it, he heard the voice. Snatches of foreign words, half-spoken, half-sung.

Uncertain now, Larkin edged slowly closer to the open window. He peered through the screen. A small bed or cot stood in the middle of the room. There was a body on it, covered with a plain white sheet, on which cut flowers were strewn. The red glow came from dozens of votive candles in red glass jars that had been placed all around the room. The voice was that of an older woman, short and stocky, who circled the bed with slow, exaggerated steps and movements, as if she were enacting some ritual, her hands held palms-up, shoulder high, her gaze ranging up toward the ceiling and then down to the floor.

Larkin glanced around, fearful that someone might see him, even at that hour and in that place. He felt awkward, as if he shouldn't be there. Someone must have just died, and this poor woman was doing whatever they did in her peculiar religion. Saying good-bye, praying for the soul of the departed. It looked strange, but it was her business, not his.

But he couldn't turn away and leave yet. The woman appeared to be so happy, so full of joy. There wasn't the slightest hint of sorrow or loss in the expression on her pudgy round face. Her skin was doughy white, but there were patches of redness clearly visible. She put her hand into a bowl on a side table and then sprinkled some dark powder on the body. She took more of the powder and sprayed it randomly about the room—Larkin saw sparks in the air as the grains fell into candle flames and were consumed in sudden flashes. The woman's movements were faster and jerkier now, and she gasped for breath.

She picked up a small brown bottle and drizzled some liquid on the body. It didn't look like water. Then she poured some into the palm of her hand and splashed it on her own face, slapping herself loudly as she did so, giving her skin an oily sheen that lit up with the glow of the candles. She continued to chant and sing—the language was unknown to Larkin, but he sensed an escalating urgency in the rhythm and tone.

He realized that he was actually touching the window screen, so he pulled back a few inches. He raised his hand to his forehead and felt a tiny grid impressed in his skin.

The woman went into a corner of the room and immediately came back with a bottle of what looked like wine. She splashed it generously over the body, dark red blotches spreading across the sheet. Some of the powder ran in the liquid, forming thin black lines.

The woman fell silent. She took a long drink from the bottle, wine streaking down her chin and throat. She sat on the edge of the bed, beside the body. She gazed at it for a few moments and then carefully pulled the sheet down from the top of the head.

Larkin saw the face of a young woman, a girl really, maybe eighteen or nineteen years of age. Dark brown hair. Almost pretty, but her skin had a yellowish cast and looked unnaturally shiny.

The older woman took another large mouthful of wine, and then she spat and sprayed it all over the dead girl's face. For a few moments she sat and watched, as if she expected something to happen.

The woman seemed to slump into herself. She pulled the sheet back up over the girl's face. She sat down on the floor with a thump, and buried her face in the sheet at the side of the girl's body. She cried and moaned to herself.

For several minutes the sounds she made were soft and muffled, misery suffused with resignation. But they gradually became louder, and then turned into jagged, spasmodic grunts of wild exertion, like someone struggling to lift an enormous weight. The woman shuddered uncontrollably every few seconds as another animal grunt ripped loose from her—it almost looked as if she were having a seizure.

Beneath the sheet, the girl's hand and arm rose from the bed. Only a matter of inches, but enough to shock Larkin. He was completely caught up in what he was seeing, unable to move or think.

The older woman's sounds and convulsions were more frantic now. The slim shape beneath the sheet appeared to increase in size, like a balloon that was being filled with air. The girl's entire body moved an inch or two, then again. The arm swung slightly, the head and shoulders rose stiffly, as unnatural as the movements of a wooden puppet. The sheet fell away as the girl awkwardly forced herself up—Larkin saw that she no longer resembled the same young person he'd seen just minutes earlier. She looked alive, not dead, her skin pale but not yellow or waxy. She was much older, the flesh on her arm loose and flabby, her fingers short and thick, her throat collared with jowls. Her hair was dull and thin, her eyes vacant slits.

Now the older woman was silent and still. She raised her face from the sheet—it was the face of the young girl, alive, slender and attractive, her hair longer and darker. It was as if they had changed places, or somehow each had been transformed into the other. The girl leapt up from the floor, a knife in her hand, and repeatedly stabbed the other woman in the chest and stomach. There was no cry, no blood, nothing but the sound of the knife, a faint rustle, like paper being shuffled. The older body finally sank back on the bed and was motionless. The young woman stood up, leaving the knife where it was. She closed her eyes, hugged herself, and smiled.

Larkin edged away into the night.

————

He drove up Utrecht Street at least once every night, but the house was always dark. There were signs of life—the position of the old Civic in the driveway varied slightly. In the daytime, the car was always gone and the house appeared to be locked up, no one home. He drove by a couple of times right after he finished work at the package store—lights were on, but he never actually saw anyone.

It bothered him, but it wasn't the kind of thing you could talk about with anybody else. Larkin often doubted himself, wondering if he had actually seen all that he remembered seeing—but it was too vivid, too real, and it would not go away.

Ray Stanton in the Assessor's Office helped him a little. The owner of the house was listed as Amelia Krogh. It had been built in 1928, and the Kroghs had been there since the mid-fifties, a couple of generations. It was a boxy little place. The room Larkin had seen was right there, on the floor plan on file in City Hall. 12 × 12.

Even if he could meet the woman—what would he say, what could he ask her? Two weeks went by, and still he had no idea.

Donald Lynch was the name on the business card—a New England Heritage real estate agent. Larkin couldn't even remember meeting the guy. It must have been years ago. At the Hibernians, if the last name was any indication. Larkin came across the card when he was looking for something else in his desk. He checked the phone book, including all the surrounding towns. He called the office number shown on the card. It was still the same office. A woman named Sandy told him that Don had moved on some time back. Not that it mattered, but—good.

It was a Saturday morning, just about a month after the night he had stood at the window of the little grey house on Utrecht and witnessed that—scene. He wore a tie and sports jacket, and he had Don Lynch's card in the breast pocket, ready to be plucked out and handed over. The Civic was in the driveway. Larkin knocked on the wooden frame of the screen door. He rapped again, harder this time. At last he heard someone approaching. The inside door opened. It was the slender, attractive young woman who faced him, but she looked weak or tired. Her movements were slow and stiff, her breathing was labored, and her skin was very pale.

"Mrs. Krogh?"

"Do you mean my mother?"

"Uh, yes, the owner of the house."

"My mother is dead."

"Oh, I'm sorry."

"No problem. It was a few years ago." She nodded vacantly as she spoke, her eyes never meeting his. Her body swayed slightly, as if she were in some way adrift. "I'm the owner of the house. Amy Krogh. That's Ms., not Mrs."

"Ah, you're the owner. Good."

"What do you want?"

Larkin held the business card up to the screen door and delivered the little patter he had practiced in his head. This neighborhood was finally on the rebound. This house and the land it stood on might be a good deal more valuable than Ms. Krogh realized (Larkin got a kick out of that "good deal" part). She ought to consider putting the property on the market. When he finished, she appeared to be thinking it over.

"How much?"

"How much could it sell for, you mean?"

"Yeah."

"Oh, I'd be happy to give you a price range," he said. "I'd just need to have a quick look around. The number of rooms, sizes, fixtures, heating system. Things like that."

Amy Krogh appeared to think about it for a moment. "Okay," she said, pushing open the screen door. Larkin stepped inside. "Where do you want to start?"

"The ground floor is fine, since we're here already."

"Okay."

Larkin took out a notebook and pen, to look professional. The inside of the house was even worse than the outside. The living-room walls and ceiling hadn't been painted in years, probably decades. The plaster was chipped and cracking in numerous places. There were only a few items of stick furniture with flattened cushions. The carpet was nearly as thin as a bedsheet. Dust had accumulated everywhere.

The dining room was much the same, and the narrow kitchen was hideous—dark, cramped and dingy. There were no signs that anybody lived there—no newspaper and coffee cup on the table, no unwashed dishes on the counter or in the sink. It looked like a stage set for some dull working-class drama, waiting for the performers to appear.

Amy Krogh led him from room to room, but she had almost nothing to say beyond stating the obvious—"This is the living room . . . This is the dining room . . ." She would probably be a pretty good-looking woman, Larkin thought, if she took care of herself. But her hair was not brushed, and she wore a dirty old sweatshirt and baggy gym pants.

The room he most wanted to see was a complete disappointment. The bed was gone, replaced by a ratty sofa, a coffee table and a TV set that stood on an old dresser. Larkin glanced at the window, as if to make sure it really was where it was supposed to be. He no longer had any idea what he had expected or hoped to find. He scribbled another line in his notebook, made vague noises of approval, and turned away.

He wished he could make some excuse and leave at that point, but this had been his bright idea and he felt obliged to go through the motions. Ms. Krogh stayed close to him as they went upstairs, her hip brushing his a couple of times. The contact was just enough to create a slight pang within, but Larkin immediately banished it. He hadn't thought about sex in a long time and he wasn't about to do anything that might cause embarrassment or trouble for anybody—starting with himself.

The upstairs bathroom was another sight—mildew on the old tiles, heavily stained porcelain fixtures. The smaller bedroom was empty but for a few boxes and cartons.

The larger bedroom had a few pieces of furniture and a double bed. The mattress was covered only with two white sheets. The woman put her hand on his arm as she followed him into the room. Larkin glanced at her and was startled—she looked older and plumper than she had only minutes earlier, more like the other woman he had seen that night. Perhaps it was a trick of his mind, or some confusion.

"This is the master bedroom," she said. "Come in and take a good look around."

"Yes, very nice."

Now she took his hand in hers. Larkin felt a little weak, almost dizzy. The notebook and pen slipped out of his other hand and fell to the floor. He stared down at them helplessly.

"Are you all right?"

"I don't know," he managed to reply.

"Sit and rest a minute."

She helped him to the bed and he sat on the edge of the mattress. All the strength in his body seemed diffuse—he couldn't focus it to do any one thing, not even something as simple as lifting his hand.

"You don't look well," she said. "It might be better if you stretched out for a little while. Maybe that would help."

She leaned over him and gently lowered his upper body onto the mattress. She's older, he kept thinking, but it was as if his mind was stuck on that and couldn't get beyond it. The woman raised his legs onto the bed and then sat beside him. Her white pudgy face smiled down at him. Now he was incapable of even wagging one finger.

"You don't have that many years left," she said with a slight tone of regret. "But every little bit counts."

Not mother and daughter, he thought dimly. Her alone.

"Who was she?" he asked faintly.

"Who?"

"The other woman."

"What other woman?" She seemed genuinely puzzled.

"That night. I saw. Downstairs."

"Ah—you saw that." Comprehension lit up her face and her eyes widened. Then she laughed. "That's why you came. I see."

The woman went to a dresser and got another bedsheet. She began to unfold it and shake it out in the air. The woman looked down at him and smiled.

"Nobody important. She was helpful to me—for a while. Anyhow, the only thing that matters is, you're here now."

The sheet snapped crisply in the air and then fluttered down slowly over him.

The Big Green Grin

BY GAHAN WILSON

The green grin began at one edge of the vacant lot behind a flattened plastic garbage can which had been mauled the previous winter during a sloppy snow removal, then swept through many yards of tousled weeds and scraggly grass grown tall and thick through a hot, humid summer and finally terminated at the lot's other edge amid the roots of a young oak which was the only tree present.

A glistening grackle perched on one of the oak's scrawny branches and blinked thoughtfully as it slowly turned its small, shiny head in order to follow the grin's vast curve. The bird had only noticed the line of the grin cutting through the uneven earth a few wing beats or so ago as it was flying over the lot but would probably have paid it no further attention if the grin had not chosen that very moment to lick the edges of its lips with a broad sweep of the tip of its pointy green tongue.

The tongue's tip was rather small relative to the size of the grin but, in regard to the objects in the very pleasant little neighborhood surrounding the lot, it was alarmingly large. It was, to give just one example, every bit as big as a gleaming red family car proudly parked in front of the small apartment building located directly across the street from the lot.

Intrigued, the grackle had allowed his neat little body to drop gracefully down towards the young oak until he was near enough to grip one of its scraggly branches and then he settled himself and his feathers comfortably upon it so that he could study the grin leisurely and in more detail.

Of course this will not surprise anyone who knows anything about grackles, as they are famous for their lively curiosity and well known to be enthusiastic students of any objects or events which are odd or incongruous.

They also enjoy investigating things which glisten and the tongue, being dripping wet with thick saliva made of green sap, had definitely and very satisfactorily glistened!

After a minute or two of observing the grin do nothing but remain in place, the grackle bent his head to the left to pinch an itchy spot on the upper curve of his wing between the two points of his sharp beak and his bright little eyes caught a movement in a window of the apartment building before which the red family car the size of the tip of the grin's tongue was parked.

A very young blond boy was peering out of the window with the palms of his hands and the tip of his nose pressed against its pane and since his eyes were wide and he wore an amazed expression the grackle was certain that, like himself, he too had seen the big green grin lick its lips with its huge, glistening tongue.

The grackle left off his wing-pinching since the itch had gone away and—with the wonderful detail and clarity which only a bird's marvelous eyes can provide—enjoyed watching a wide variety of expressions cross the young boy's face.

First his look of astonishment faded down into one of intense interest, then that was replaced by a deeply thoughtful sort of frown and following that there came a sly and foxy smile tinged with guilty delight which pleased the grackle very much because it was an almost sure and certain sign that the boy had thought of doing something which would be very interesting to watch!

When the boy left the window with an air of excitement and determination the grackle let his gaze drop to the door of the apartment building and after he had watched it patiently for only a little while he saw it open and the little boy emerge from it just as the bird had expected he would.

But now the boy was no longer alone, now he held the tiny hand of a pretty little girl a year or two younger than himself who resembled him in so many ways that the grackle had no doubt whatsoever that she was the boy's little sister.

The Big Green Grin

The girl was smiling and looking excitedly around herself as she clutched the boy's hand. It was obvious this was a rare treat for her and she was clearly delighted and proud to be out and about in the company of her older brother.

Meanwhile—though the boy was trying his best to conceal it as much as possible—the grackle could easily see vestiges of the sinister and promising smile he had observed before flickering through the boy's bland look of innocence. With great anticipation he watched the boy and girl leave the sidewalk in front of the apartment, cross the road and then enter into the wild late summer foliage of the vacant lot.

The girl hesitated momentarily after wading a step or two into the thick grass and tangled weeds growing up in great profusion from the lumpy earth and asked her brother—she called him "Charlie"—if they really had to walk through this messy place but then he teased her and she pulled herself together and shrugged and marched on gamely.

They had advanced fairly deeply into the lot's miniature jungle when she stopped and bent down to pick up an old discarded doll. Half of its hair was missing and its polka-dot dress was ragged but it still had a sweet, if slightly cracked, expression so she pressed it to her breast and kept it even though her brother scoffed.

The grackle was interested to observe that her big brother was carefully leading her in the direction of the very center of the grin just as the bird had hoped he would. Once again he peered back and forth over the length of the grin. Had he just now detected a faint anticipatory stirring of its lips? He flapped up to a higher branch of the little oak so that he would get the best view possible in case what he eagerly anticipated actually happened next.

Now the brother began to exclaim loudly and point in front of them as if he had just spotted something really interesting and, just as he had planned, that caused the little girl to excitedly move ahead of him in order to see what he had seen. Meanwhile, in a sneaky sort of way, the boy moved directly behind her.

The grackle curled his tongue within his beak and squawked softly to himself as he shifted on the branch of the tree and watched with fierce concentration. The little girl was steadily coming nearer and nearer to the curving center of the big green grin with her big brother moving softly along behind her, carefully keeping just a step to her rear all the way.

Then the bird clutched the branch hard enough for his claws to dig through its bark when he saw her suddenly come to a halt actually standing on the lower edge of the grin with the toes of her best new shoes resting on its vast lower lip.

She knew at once it was something very strange and awful. Her bud of a mouth dropped open and her blue eyes bulged a little in their sockets as she stared down at the thin dark slit spread before her feet and stretching in a smooth and sinister curve far away to her left and right and then out of sight into the thick, sweet-smelling late summer greenness.

The grackle chattered faintly and stirred his dark wings when he saw the big brother slowly and carefully raise his hands up before his chest with both palms pointing towards his sister's back.

Then, with a gruesome unexpectedness, the long lips before the little girl parted with a great sucking and smacking noise to reveal the two long rows of enormous thorns which were the green grin's teeth!

She screamed and dropped her doll and it tumbled down, turning over and over through the air with its tattered, polka-dot shreds trailing pathetically behind until, with an awful accuracy, the vegetable teeth closed just at the right instant for two opposing thorns to pierce the pink plastic torso of the doll with a sharp, startling crack.

The little girl cried out again but this time softly and with concern as she bent down and reached her arms out towards the ruined toy.

Then, just as she bent, as if in some highly complicated, synchronized dance, her brother shoved the palms of his hands forcefully out before him into what had now suddenly become empty space and found himself falling forward and then down and then felt himself landing heavily atop the doll and sprawling upon the locked green teeth which were now all there was between him and the dark, waiting mouth of the grin beneath!

With his hands clawed he stretched his arms forward as far as he could, trying to grab hold of the tangle of weed and grass growing out from the green grin's upper lip but it receded from him as the mouth opened and the teeth once more pulled apart. He felt the doll drop down from under him and shuddered as he saw it vanish into the blackness of the now exposed abyss.

He flipped himself sideways, grabbing the lower teeth and trying to push himself back to safety but they were horribly slippery and terror beat in his chest and raced through his body as he felt his own weight begin inexorably to pull him either into the darkness below or place him properly for the green grin's next ferocious bite!

The Big Green Grin

Suddenly he felt a frantic grabbing at the back of his shirt and after that a determined tugging which was small and did not have all that much force but which was just enough to counterbalance his downward slide and give him the leverage to scramble frantically up the repellent sliminess of the teeth to the green lip behind them and then onto the blessed ordinary earth of the vacant lot!

He looked up at the tear-streaked face of his sister as she helped him struggle to his feet and then the two of them, each leaning on the other, made their way unevenly through the tugging grass and clutching brambles and entangling vines to the smoothness of the road and the surety of the concrete sidewalk and eventually to the smooth, silken safety of the carpet on the floor of their apartment living room.

But the boy would never be able to leave his guilt behind, nor the horror at what he had almost done, nor his gratitude at what she had done and, because of that, his sister would never again be unloved nor unprotected.

To the great disappointment of the grackle!

Both And

BY GARY FRY

As Dr. Thomas Bart drew his lecture to a close, the scar on Graham Hickman's right temple began to itch irritatingly.

"In short, then, to what extent can we humans claim to be the originators of our own activities? We have seen that by employing the concept of joint action it can be claimed that behavior is something that arises *between* individuals. In the words of Merleau-Ponty, 'The objection which my interlocutor raises to what I have to say draws from me thought I had no idea I possessed.' Therefore are we agents or puppets—or something else? Okay, I sense yawns in the theater: admissible in only the second week of term. Dismissed."

Immediately there was a burst of activity, like an army on the march, as first-year undergraduates made their way toward the exits at either side of the lectern. Graham was forced to relinquish his seat in the middle of the front aisle. For him the issue had just grown interesting, and he watched the principal lecturer in psychology pack away his notes. Graham desired to approach—Thomas Bart had published widely in the field—though he lacked courage at this early stage. His mind still reeling with ideas, he begrudgingly joined the throng.

He had yet to make any real acquaintances. Of the few fellow students he had chatted to, none had matched up to expectations. Surely psychology ought to attract the kind of people for whom self-analysis was a necessity, though apparently not. Certainly his peers were nothing like the thugs he had known on the council estate, though he had anticipated more: friendship that warranted the title, intellectual stimulation. The scar twitching angrily, Graham summoned the lift that carried him sluggishly to his flat in the Halls of Residence.

He would start a new job in the morning, and shouldn't be late to bed. The two-hour 4 P.M. lecture this Friday afternoon had furnished him with enough inquiry to get through another evening. However, he had opened a bottle of red and fried himself an egg sandwich—both snatched from the bags his parents had provided, the hateful Hickman's logo—before he settled in the single room to his books. The October dark had drawn in at the window, a threat of storm in the leaden sky. In the light of a lamp he could scarcely afford, Graham opened his illustrated history of the Nazi death camps at the photography.

Here was a container, a vast steel drum, in which the charred remains of human bones were set among ashes. Were the various sticks and ribs and a skull those of a child? Graham turned the page. Good God, here was a wooden trailer on cartwheels loaded with corpses, so many unwanted dolls. What made people do such things? On the next there was a gas chamber; on the next a ditch full of burned scrawny shapes, dead adults of indeterminate sex. Graham closed the book, fingering his temple. *Why?*

From the arm of the couch he plucked a psychology textbook. There was a chapter on prejudice, some of which detailed the notorious study by Stanley Milgram who, investigating obedience, had persuaded American citizens to administer what they believed to be a lethal charge of electricity to a middle-aged man—in fact a confederate of the experimenter—on account of his failure to answer harmless questions correctly. Seated in another room, participants had spoken into a microphone and, at the psychologist's behest, turned a lever to issue increasing volts of the imaginary juice. Screaming from behind the wall had been followed by deathly silence. Though most had protested, and some violently, an alarming number had delivered the entire course of punishment. The findings had been replicated all over the world.

Is this what Dr. Thomas Bart meant by joint action? The chapter didn't seem to support that; it was more about how one individual could impact upon another. There was no sense of the behavior occurring *between* people. Graham sensed that the lecture had been moving beyond Milgram.

He reached for the bottle and took a needful swallow. Lying on the couch he closed his eyes, his mind wandering. Mum would be missing her one and only, though his dad, sole proprietor of Hickman's mini-mart, would busy himself by selling what the dwellers of the council estate relished: cigarettes and alcohol and cut-price frozen meals. He didn't sell knives, at any rate not to children, though in Graham's mind, in the ripple of senseless flesh at his temple, he might as well do . . .

He snatched himself upright, swinging his legs onto the carpet. It was ludicrous to blame his dad for *that* incident. Indeed it was unwise to focus on past events. The secret was to anticipate, and he had much to consider there. He'd been offered the job after a brief telephone interview, a simple role in a factory yard, clearing rubbish one day a week. The boss—an older chap with a wonderful name: Jack Zimbardo—had promised thirty pounds cash. That would be sufficient to remain independent. This thought and the wine spurred Graham to bed.

He dreamed of teenage boys, taller than he and dressed in tracksuits, stooping toward him with knives. More than flesh, they wanted his tie, the red-and-green stripes of the public school. Why had his dad sent him there, a tiresome journey across Bradford even in the Jaguar? Had he been used as a status object, like the Porsche and the two lengthy holidays each year? Whatever the case, the investment had backfired—in the wake of the attack, Graham's GCSE results had been poor—though he didn't believe that this had troubled his dad, who was uneducated, prejudiced, an illegitimate snob. For him knowledge was power. Even the place at university, luckily no longer a polytechnic, was something to brag of in conversation.

Graham jerked awake, his thoughts beating the alarm clock to its shriek. He got up and dressed in robust clothing, checking his wallet for travel fare. He also had a scrap of paper bearing the details of the factory: Dack House Plastics, Witts Road, Huddersfield. He was feeling a little nervous, yet this was nothing positive action wouldn't combat. He made his way to the campus, the town, the bus station. From the inquiry room he helped himself to a free map of the region, located his destination, and attended the appropriate stand. His ride came and he stepped aboard. Within twenty minutes he was approaching the factory.

He alighted opposite a small supermarket and crossed Witts Road. An enormous gateway, whose logo was as tall as a man, was set in a wall of similar height, allowing access to a factory yard. A group of young men loitered near a doorway, smoking amid talk and laughter. As Graham approached, the faces turned his way, putting him in mind of the boys who had done him damage, grown up and capable of so much worse. But this was something else he must overcome.

"Hi, I'm looking for someone called Jack—er, Jack Zimbardo."

Had he coarsened his accent convincingly? One of the lads, a thin youth with a scribble of beard, jabbed his cigarette down an arm of the yard that was wide enough for lorries. "In 'is cell supping rationed tea, like as not!" he explained, amusement tugging at unseen lips. "See that door bottom left? Knock once, salute, an' enter!"

Were repeated military references a running joke here at Dack House? Perhaps Jack Zimbardo had a history in the forces, though might the factory in fact resemble a prison camp to its employees? Graham didn't know what to make of the laughter that was suddenly revived in the gang. Perhaps the best thing was to move on quickly. He offered a noncommittal "Ta," and then stepped down the yard.

The factory was immense, of a depth not possible to comprehend from this one side. It was vertiginously tall. A stiff wind hurried alongside the building. Graham felt the cold, or maybe this was tension, as he knocked at a door whose black paint peeled like flayed hide. Was there a pungent odor of gas? Suddenly a voice spoke up from within.

"Come in, lad. Just on time."

How could the man be sure that it was he? Graham put his hand on the rusted handle to coax groans from the in-swinging door. The whiff of gas grew stronger, and he concluded that this was escaping from a stand-alone heater, burning with a soft hiss. Beside the heater was a table bearing a kettle, various mugs, a jar of coffee. In front of the table sat a bony shape in an arm-chair. The glow from the flames set an orange hue upon the man, who was bald and wrinkled and dressed in dungarees. This, then, was Jack Zimbardo.

"More haste, my boy. What do y' make o' my office, eh? I can tell by y' face you're impressed."

In fact, Graham was thinking how unruly the place appeared—tools piled up in utter disorder, bits of pipe crisscrossing one wall, paint tins, a lawn mower, a huge tub of nails and screws—but then he detected the man's chuckle.

"Yeah, I know, it's a shit tip. But I boil m' water well. Pull up a pew. None of 'em is gonna make me a fortune at Christies."

There was more of that earthy laughter as the man leaned forward in his chair. Shutting the door, Graham looked left in the gloom and saw a stool in one corner that he relocated before sitting in front of the heater. Ten silent seconds later he was offered a mug of something black, strong and sugarless: the man knew how he took his coffee. Curiously Graham felt flattered.

"To your good 'ealth, son," his boss announced, hoisting his own cup in a brief toast. "Though maybe I'm more in need o' that than a youngster like you. By the by, 'ow old is Graham Hickman?"

He'd remembered his name, too—how often had it been mentioned over the telephone? Once? Twice? No more than three times. "Nineteen last June, Mr. Zimbardo," Graham explained before sipping. The coffee was surprisingly palatable.

"Call me Jack. Everyone does around 'ere—among other things."

More laughter. Once Graham had swallowed another mouthful, he drew breath and added, "I got the impression from one of the lads that you have a military background."

There was no effort to conceal his accent here. Why should that be? Indeed Jack's face—a spiderweb mass of lines and folds, eyes green as jewels—displayed no evidence of the predictable response: If you talk like *that*, what are you doing *here*? This was a man who knew things, an impression that was confirmed as his boss began to speak.

"They're cheeky bastards that work 'ere. But yeah, I fought at the end o' the war. I wa' born back in 'twenty-seven, an' if they teach y' maths at that university, you'll realize that makes me seventy-five."

"You must have seen some sights," Graham replied. He had heard of certain old folk never retiring, just carrying on under the auspices of some understanding boss, the better to stave off decrepitude. But Jack Zimbardo looked far from anything of that sort: he was as sprightly as a man half his age.

"Not something I care t' talk about, as the cliché runs."

Graham sensed that it would be unwise to seek further details. There was another pause for drinking, and then the man was staring hard at Graham's face—no, not the face: the side of his head.

"Look like you've been in the wars y'self, son. 'Ow'd you come about that ugly scratch?"

His hand went up to the scar, though there was none of the usual racing pulse. It was fine talking to this man; it was like telling someone who already knew, who might help.

"I was attacked five years ago, by three lads from the council estate where my dad's shop is. They cut me with a knife. The one who used the blade got a suspended sentence, and the two who held me down a fine apiece: fifty pounds to be paid over a year. That's the price the courts put on my ruined life. I was lucky to get to do my A levels, and luckier when the university offered me a place. I've been trying to make sense of this event ever since. That's why I chose psychology."

"Little bastards, the lot of 'em! Don't know why I ever bothered fighting for this!"

There was venom in the man's tone, a sentiment at present shared by Graham. He asked, "Why do people do such terrible things to others, Jack?"

"Why anybody does owt is a mystery." Jack Zimbardo grinned, revealing teeth whose yellow denoted the original set. "A couple o' years ago, we 'ad this chap working 'ere. Nice fella: rough as houses, but would lend you 'is last Rizla. Anyway, the factory got lunatic-busy, so the company 'ired this skinny bugger. Shy? That man'd blush as soon as anyone stepped within audible range.

"Now the funny thing wa', as soon as the latter started, the former became a bully. 'E'd plague 'im every day, though 'e'd never shown any inclination that way before. An' this other chap—never a sharp word t' a white bird—suddenly became violent. Ended up scrapping an' gettin' sacked, the pair of 'em. The rest of us—never knew 'ow the fuck it 'appened! Both men acted according to type in our company. It wa' just when they w' together that summat queer started. It seemed t' be what went on *between* 'em."

Graham jerked alert on the stool: there was that word again. He was too shaken to marshal an immediate response. But his thoughts were rife. In differing circumstances would the boys not have cut him? Who had been actually responsible? Any one of them, all three of them, or maybe what went on *between* them and Graham? It was a frightening thought.

Jack Zimbardo beat him easily to the floor. "Oh well, come on now—philosophy don't pay the rent. Let me show y' the ropes."

Graham added his drained mug to the cup the man had placed in front of his kettle. It was only once his new boss had stood that Graham appreciated how short he was—the bald head reached only his own shoulder height. Yet the man undeniably possessed a manner that transcended his lean frame. He was stooping to a collection of tools.

"You're gonna need these later."

Back upright, quickly as a fox. Graham was handed two quite unremark-able items: a bottle of paraffin and a box of matches.

Then: "Follow me."

Graham did so, out the door and into the yard.

"Do y' know what we do 'ere?"

"The advertisement in the university job-shop window mentioned some-thing about mannequins."

"Right. We manufacture them plastic dolls y' see all decked up in the best that shops can muster by way o' fabric an' a price tag."

"You talk peculiarly."

"Is that a compliment? Y' tone suggests it."

"Very much one."

"Then I'll take it that way. Come on, there's more t' see."

The factory was alive now in a way it had been dead upon his arrival. Steel shutters had been lifted, staff flitted back and forth, and a forklift truck was trundling with a whiny purr. As Jack Zimbardo exchanged greetings ("Morning, old-timer!" his colleagues invariably said, with the habitual reply, "New recruit. 'E'll be dealing wi' the mess y' all make!") Graham examined the interior of the building through irregular openings. There were mannequins everywhere: male dolls with feminized pouchlike groins, nipple-less female models, each an unpleasant charred green. They were stood in corners, laid on desks, mounted on pallets with limbs akimbo—here a leg, there an arm, and heads and torsos aplenty. It was like peak period on a butcher's agenda. Creepy.

Another driveway led them to an expanse of shale, fringed by a margin of lawn. A picket fence separated the grounds of the factory from a council estate. Graham averted his attention to address the phenomenon that had attracted Jack Zimbardo: a metal box, large as a garden shed, yet lacking a roof. It had been painted red, though now the coat was suffering an alopecic malady. As Graham drew nearer, to halt by the side of the man who was rub-bing his aged hands to combat the chill, he smelt a residual stench of burn-ing. He was certain that this cube was the source.

"This is where we 'ave our weekly barbecue!" Graham was told as Jack Zimbardo released a lock in order to lever open the hinged front. The inte-rior of the chamber was a scorched pit, at the bottom of which lay an assort-ment of blackened fragments. "Anything that'll burn goes in 'ere. The rest—metal an' what-not—in a skip on the other side o' the yard. You'll see that later, but y' get the general idea?"

"I think so. I just toss things in, and then when it's full, shut it up and use these."

Graham proffered the paraffin and the matches, to the delight of Jack Zimbardo. "Y' don't know 'ow good it feels to work wi' somebody of some sense!" The man took the bottle and the box and placed them inside the drum. He propped open the door with a discarded wooden pallet. "Just a tip: careful this door don't break free. It'll take your 'ead clean off!"

"I can see that!"

"Oh, and summat else. If y' get any o' them bastards from the estate"—the man jabbed a thumb over one bony shoulder—"then call me over, an' I'll give 'em 'ell! Saturdays 're a real 'unting season for the likes of them council runts. Don't let 'em piss y' about, okay?"

"I'll try."

"Good lad."

There was more, but again Jack Zimbardo exercised restraint. Indeed his boss then struck off in the direction of the factory. Graham had to trot to keep up. Once inside a van-sized doorway, the man produced a key on a fob to release the padlock of a cupboard flanked by more of the charred-green dummies. "Freak you out, these ladies an' gents," the man said, removing a brush and a shovel from the store of gardening equipment. "Use these to gather the litter, an' stack it up on whatever pallets y' can find. We'll get the forklift to dump it in our 'ot 'ouse later. I've got things t' attend to now. Are you gonna be okay?"

Graham nodded. The care with which the old man had spoken had brought a lump to his throat. Graham didn't believe his dad had managed so much in nineteen years. He was handed a pair of gloves before the cupboard was resealed. Then Jack Zimbardo smiled, turning to depart along a corridor formed by reaching, grasping, lifelike limbs. Graham did the same, tugging on the gloves before making for the yard with the brush and shovel.

It was largely a case of getting dirty. He wasn't required to work with anybody else, though as he piled the pallets with gunk, banter was exchanged with some of the lads in the factory. Undoubtedly there was a sense of community at Dack House, but with a raw edge. How indeed would it feel if this—five days a week, including Saturday—was all one had? Graham might enjoy the opportunity to muddy himself up, yet how much was informed by his knowledge that next week he had only books to read? Whatever their acerbic faults, Graham couldn't help but respect the staff.

Bugger 'em! his dad would say, but he was a fool. And Graham's mum, locked in a sheltered existence, knew no better than a child. How much of their attitude, that pseudo-middle-class disdain, had he absorbed? The scar at his temple stirred viciously. He had never forgiven the kids from the council estate, despite an appreciation of the gulf between their experience and the privileges of his own. Perhaps that was why he was here: an attempt to understand a class of people. It would take a while; maybe it would never happen. Unaccountably this worried him.

At twelve o'clock the staff headed for the shops across Witts Road. Dropping metal in the skip that was not for burning, Graham followed at a wary distance. Perhaps the job would be good for him in another sense: it would keep his feet on the ground at university. However little he might ever trust the type of person who worked in factories, he would never forget the desperation they must numb in order simply to go on. Graham bought a salad sandwich, retreating to the cell of Jack Zimbardo. The old man wasn't around—indeed Graham had seen him only at a distance since the beginning of the day—and he warmed himself at the gas while sipping a mug of coffee. It had been a good morning.

That afternoon everything changed. The old man had arranged for the forklift truck to convey the pallets to the skips. The wood and paper and all things generally burnable went in the sooty cube. When this was half-full, and articles were spilling out the front, Graham snatched up the paraffin and the matches, pushing them into the pockets of his pants, before closing the door. What remained to be eaten by the conflagration was dropped from above, crashing within. It was 4:30 and as the sky darkened seasonably, it was time for a light. Graham was instructed to collect a short ladder from his boss's room. Then Jack Zimbardo strolled away, a tangible lilt in his stride. He must be looking forward to something soon.

The steps on one shoulder, Graham was laboring along the cobbled yard when he noticed that the employees were winding down toward closing time. An air of merriment—the weekend starts here—infested the chatter, and a few chaps had even broken into song. All of this matched Graham's turn of mind, and it was with a whistled tune of his own that he rounded the bend that gave on to the area of shale at which the fire drum was stationed.

Then he halted, the breath caught in his throat. His past had returned to haunt him.

Two boys—early teenagers, dressed in tracksuits—were standing to the right of the steel container. They had crew cuts and spotty faces and eyes set in slits. Graham knew at once that they were trespassers from the council estate. A flash of rage, tempered by treacherous fear, sent him charging forward, the ladder a forgotten burden at his side. One of the boys, the taller of the two, had cupped his hands at knee level in order that his lighter companion might insert a foot and be hoisted higher. They were seeking entry to the metal chamber. It was Graham's job to ensure they didn't succeed.

"Hey, you two! Keep away from there!"

Certainly the boys seemed startled, though a second later they were standing slackly and eyeing their assailant with derision. Graham knew this look well, but he wasn't about to be perturbed. Sometimes he forgot that he was now nineteen, that youngsters could no longer threaten him. He blundered to a halt, slammed the ladder against the steel door, and turned on the pair.

"*Get out of* this yard." As his breath grew short, his authority tailed off. He compensated by adding, *"Now."*

"Who sez we 'ave to?" answered the taller boy, smugness in his tone. "You don't own it."

"No, but I've been instructed by the man who's in charge here to keep out trespassers."

"Come an' do it, then," said the other boy, his scalp rusty with ginger stubble. "Touch us, an' I'll get m' dad t' beat the fuck outta you."

"An' mine'll sue y' bollocks off."

That familiar mixture of the illegal and the legal—the latter was a recent phenomenon, as serviceable as violence. These days the kids didn't need to carry anything in their pockets. That was good. If the situation was reduced to the physical, he could handle it. Nevertheless Graham added, "Okay, I'll have to fetch my boss."

"Not skinny Jack?" asked the taller boy. "Old slaphead!"

"Mr. Zimbardo—that is he," replied Graham, stepping away.

"Our friend's already inside y' skip," the ginger-haired boy announced, pointing a skeletal finger at the metal side of the drum.

Graham ceased his movement. "What do you mean?"

"He's called Zed," added the taller boy.

"And he's inside the box?"

"Yeah—climbed in on top o' both of us," explained ginger-hair. "Now you won't be able to 'ave y' fire in time."

So this was their plan. Perhaps they had been causing strife elsewhere in order to return later and scupper the routine of the factory. That dark intelligence angered Graham, so much so that before he was able to govern his reaction he had steadied the ladder against the front of the chamber and begun to climb. The bottle and the box were dead weights at his sides. As he reached the top, affording a clear view inside, he heard giggling from the boys beneath. Then one of them—Graham couldn't be certain which; each voice was equally abhorrent—said something.

"Hey, mister, why've y' got a squashed centipede on the side o' your 'ead?"

Graham jolted so vigorously that the ladder shook. The sudden fright served to defuse his rage, much of which had threatened to see him on the ground and using his senior advantages to attack the boys. A mistake, or it would have been if he'd given in to such vulnerable tendencies. In fact he rubbed his temple, the ruined meat thereon, and readdressed the task at hand. The metal box was stuffed to the brim. In the thinning daylight, Graham could see that pieces of wood and balls of paper and strips of plastic sheet lay in an abstracted clutter ripe for destruction. Could a boy have struggled inside the mass? It seemed likely; there were ragged pockets of space everywhere. Nevertheless not a fragment stirred.

"Hey you, come out of there!"

Whichever one of them, between laughter: " 'E's called Zed."

"Hey, Zed, you need to come out." Was his voice betraying an undertone of malevolence? Certainly this seemed the case as he finished, "I *must* set light to this soon."

Suddenly there came a chaotic clattering. Disorientated, Graham continued to stare at the rubble—still nothing moved—and it was only after several seconds that he realized the noise had come from behind. He swung round, clinging to the ladder, the paraffin and the matches straining against his hips. What he saw in the gloom initially confused him—a figure heading inexorably this way, and two fleeing rapidly. Then his mind assimilated it and he was able to comprehend the situation: the two boys had noted the approach of Jack Zimbardo. They had done—up the slope of lawn and over the fence that backed onto the council estate—the sensible thing. Indeed Graham also had begun to feel apprehensive.

"No smoke yet, son? It's quart' to five. What w' them little bastards up to?"

The man stopped walking, only a pace from the foot of the ladder. He appeared as ambitiously authoritative as he had earlier, though perhaps a tad grimmer—the end of a working day.

"They were trying to get into the box, but only their friend managed," Graham explained, looking back inside the chamber. Beyond the rubbish, he noticed the two boys watching from behind the fence, faces hatched by the wire grid, like criminals in a camp. But they were laughing and calling out.

"*Ha! Look at 'im up that ladder, talking to nobody!*"

"*We w' lying, you know! There's nobody in there at all! Zed's been grounded again for not wearing 'is—*"

The rest of the sentence was masked by the old man's interjection.

"I know these sods all too well—see 'em every fucking week. Zed, 'e's one of 'em. Always up to summat. Never been one for practical jokes m'self." Jack Zimbardo paused, revealing rotting teeth—but this wasn't a smile. After a moment he added, "Pour the paraffin on, son."

"Wha—"

More from the voices at a distance: "*What an idiot 'e looks, standing up there for no reason!*"

And: "*Posh-arse prick wi' a funny fucking face!*"

Shuffling closer, the old man explained, "You 'eard me. If Zed's in there—and 'is buddies say 'e's not, but who knows wi' them buggers?—then maybe 'e'll take us seriously when 'e gets a whiff o' the pure stuff. Now *pour the paraffin on.*"

Graham didn't care for how the man's voice had changed—it was forceful, angry—but immediately he found himself delving into the right pocket of his pants, removing the bottle, spinning off the cap in hands that trembled, though not entirely with tension. He didn't need to ponder what was required next. He splashed the paraffin hither and thither across the fractured surface of the litter. The liquid hissed tartly in the cool late day. It dripped into the chamber. There would be quite an inferno; little would survive its appetite.

When the bottle was empty, Graham sensed Jack Zimbardo stepping up to the cube. Now he was out of sight of the boys at the fence, both of whom seemed to have grown bored and to be contemplating a new strategy. But Graham's attention was fixed on the shadowy way of his boss. The old man had placed his bald head close to the metal and was listening as the wet continued to soak into the debris. Graham watched, mesmerized and aroused, as Jack Zimbardo began to speak in a voice that could be scarcely heard above the constant hum of breeze.

"Are you in there, Zed? You 'ear that damp stuff dribble, eh? Y' know what that is? It's not water. It's summat far worse, summat that when combined wi' a flame goes up like dry wood on a 'ot afternoon. An' guess what my friend 'ere's carrying." The head came up, the voice raised only slightly; the old man was now instructing Graham. "Show 'im, son—show Zed that w' mean business. Give them matches a nice good rattle."

Graham felt his heart rate step up. Nevertheless his free hand went at once into the other pocket to remove the box—and then shake it. Dry wood chattered in the cardboard, audible between gusts of wind. But still there was silence within the steel. The old man grinned, his darkened eyes like chunks of coal. He was staring firmly at Graham.

"If that don't scare 'im, nothing will. 'E can't be in there. We've wasted enough time." Jack Zimbardo pointed casually at the matchbox. When he spoke, his voice was again extremely low. "Strike up one o' them twigs, an' then set the fire going, son."

Certainly this seemed the appropriate thing to do, though some of Graham pleaded in a wan voice, "But—"

"What's *that*?"—again the severe tone—"This is y' job, son. I'm responsible for getting this yard the way it should be. That's why I took you on. Are y' now suggesting I wa' wrong?"

Although Graham had no intention of letting the old man down, that same part of him replied, "No, but what if—?"

"Strike a match, Graham. You 'ave no choice but t' do that. It's what I'm paying y' for."

Averting his gaze, Graham discarded the empty bottle—it fell to the ground with a clap—and then slid the drawer out of its cardboard sleeve, selecting a wooden pin. He reassembled the box before pointing the match at one edge of sandpaper. Just a single obedient wrist movement—that's all the man required. And Graham *had* to do this, didn't he? It was his job; it was what his boss demanded. In fact Graham wanted to oblige, though at an unarticulated level he knew he ought not. In quite another sense, however, the command seemed different here; there was an additional element that he hadn't experienced previously. Graham thought it might be trust. It had been proved that there was nobody inside the chamber. But more than this, there was the man himself. In some intangible manner, Graham had been entranced.

The fingers stirred around the spoke. He sensed Jack Zimbardo glaring, glaring. From behind the fence, the boys had grown suddenly reanimated. Finally they had settled upon an alternative form of antagonism.

"*Oi, scabby-'ead!*" announced the taller of the two, and then, "*Go on, burn the invisible boy if y' dare!*"

Ginger-hair took up the chant. "*Scabby-'ead! Scabby-'ead! Scabby-'ead!*" Soon it became a chorus.

Graham struck the match and dropped it unhesitatingly into the drum.

The remainder of the day blurred by. As the box spewed forth its mouthful of flames, Graham expected the police to arrive. Certainly the boys at the fence had looked shocked when the paraffin exploded, ducking away to safety. Did their parents own telephones? But the only cars to pass were those of the staff, swiftly filing away, another week over and their few pennies to enjoy. Graham himself was paid as the fire lost its rage: thirty pounds cash, as promised. The last he saw of Jack Zimbardo was his stick figure striding through the gates with that familiar satiated hop. At 5:35, with the mass reduced to smolder, Graham rushed for his bus, the journey back, the solitude of a long lonely night. Once inside his flat he resisted a temptation to look again at his books, struggled with some toast, and then fell to bed early, exhausted or worse than that.

He dreamed of his dad, grown old and wise—no, only the former, for he was dressed in a military uniform and working in a death camp. His head was bald, the face a tangle of ingrained lines. His colleagues, folk committing similar such atrocities with equal gusto, addressed him in a peculiar name— something that began with a Z, Graham fancied, but then awoke with a scream. Throwing back the sheets, he was compelled to look at the book. Here was the steel drum, the bones at its singed bottom; there the cart stacked high with corpses; the gas chamber and the burned bodies had Graham reaching for his clothes, dressing at speed. It was twenty-five minutes, nigh on 10:30 A.M., before he was back on the bus, headed for Dack House Plastics, Witts Road.

There were only national Sunday newspapers on a stand outside the supermarket. Any major local story—early-teenage boy missing from home—would appear the following day, in the first edition of whatever passed for journalism in this part of the town. Graham stormed along the pavement to the gates of the factory. It took him only minutes to scale the iron frame, swing a leg over the top and slide down the other side into the yard. There a smell of gas struck him that must have been from heaters similar to the one behind Jack Zimbardo's door. As he moved across the cobbles to the area of shale, he saw blank faces pressed against windows, limbs splayed in rigor mortis. The charred-green plastic mannequins were piled on trolleys, like cadavers awaiting burial. Smoke rose thickly above a portion of the fence that kept out the council estate, though it was only from a chimneypot. The smell of flesh cooking was undoubtedly the supermarket, preparing its meat for the day. Suddenly he had reached the metal chamber.

Was it only bones that didn't burn completely? If so, they would be in there, for the fire had gone out overnight, leaving only a sickening smell. Ash, that must be—of only wood and paper and plastic. The conclusion encouraged Graham to leap up one side of the box, clamber to the top. Once he had his elbows over the rim he was able to heft his torso forward, the better to see inside. Just then, a gust of wind sent soot the way of his eyes. He snapped shut the lids, and it was several seconds—once the morning shriek of autumn had diminished—before he was able to look again, into horrendous darkness.

There was nothing in the box. Just dust and dying embers. No boy had been in there when Graham had lent a light to the contents.

Dropping to the ground. Relieved. Dread done with. They hadn't committed an appalling act, he and Jack Zimbardo, that moment of joint-action. Would the old man have thrown the flame without Graham? More crucially, would Graham without his boss? At any rate together, *between* themselves, they had done so. So who was responsible: either one? The two of them? Or only the circumstances? They had both admitted contempt for the type of people the trespassers from the council estate represented. Suddenly Graham was hearing an echo of the chant—*"Scabby-'ead! Scabby-'ead! Scabby-'ead!"*—and recalling the act it had precipitated. Had *he* been the more culpable, after all? The notion terrified him, though imponderably he felt relieved.

None of this actually mattered. They'd warned the boy. Graham's boss knew Zed well enough to realize that he wouldn't persist in a joke that might endanger him. That both men had savored the moment shouldn't detract from the fact that they had put human morality first. It was perversely pleasant to fantasize about wiping out an unfortunate—there was no sense in denying that, however wrong it felt—but ultimately one shouldn't do it, couldn't do it, *didn't* do it. Decency always won through. He and Jack Zimbardo, they knew better. Graham decided that he was to enjoy a good relationship with the old man. He smiled, clutching his hammering chest with excitement as well as the release of stress. Then, as he turned to head out the way he had arrived, he heard a voice shrill from the council estate.

"*Zed! Zed! Ze-e-ed!*"

Good God, was that a woman? Graham was quickly at the fence, gazing through. On the pavement of a litter-strewn cul-de-sac he saw a teenager in clothing rendered baggy by malnutrition. He had a crew cut and acne and was of a similar age to his friends. On the road behind stood a plump woman in a creased blue dress, slippers wrapped around fat ankles. She had bottle-blond hair and a face as red as fire. Suddenly she was stooping, one hand clenched and holding something, the other reaching for the boy. Oddly she continued to shout.

"*Who'd be y' bloody mum? 'Ow many times 'ave I got t' tell you? When y' out, y' wear this! You're useless wi'out it! Never 'ome for y' tea for one thing— not t' mention all them cars that might run you over! Ev'ryone round 'ere might know of y' affliction, but y' can't gamble on others . . .*"

And she belted him full palm around the side of his head. But that didn't matter—she had preserved what she might have damaged. High in her free hand she held aloft this morning's bone of contention: a small brown thing that, to the lad's struggling dismay, she then rammed into his right ear.

It was her son Zed's hearing aid.

Graham Hickman simply stared, his fingers once again irrevocably at his temple, until the facts hit him very hard.

Love Is a Stone

BY SIMON BROWN

It occurred to Talbot as he was about to make the first incision in his chest that sorcery, like love, was driven by obsession. Once he had the thought, he realized Imogen had told him this many years before, but back then he had not understood.

She had asked, her head resting over his breast, "You will never leave me, Oliver?"

And Talbot had said he would not, his conviction sincere, not yet betrayed by time and fear.

Imogen sighed and traced a pattern on his shoulder with one long nail.

"I am filled with you, my love," she said. "All thought, all breath, every heartbeat, is in your name."

Touched by her words, by the thought of being the object of so much love, his eyes brimmed with tears. He looked down on her fine, pale face, her jade-green eyes, and opened his mouth to kiss her. He stopped when he saw the design on his shoulder: a pentagram raised with his own blood. Her nail had been so sharp he had felt no pain. She saw his startled expression and smiled, then blew softly on the wound. The blood instantly coagulated into black tracery. His intake of breath made her laugh and the design suddenly flared brightly. Talbot felt searing pain and he shouted. Imogen crossed his lips with her hand. A moment later the pain subsided, and his shoulder wore a pentagram scar, raised and livid.

"Love is like this," she whispered, and kissed him fiercely.

As the memory struck, he glanced at the scar on his shoulder, still clearly a brand. He shook his head and readied the scalpel, admiring its steel cleanliness. *This is the most perfect instrument ever invented*, he thought.

Watching his actions in the surgical mirror suspended above his chair, he made a midline incision, drawing downward from a point about halfway along his sternum.

"God!" he hissed as blood pooled around the cut, almost fainting. He swabbed the blood, relieved there were no serious bleeders. He placed retractors and pulled back the skin.

He rested his head back for a moment, gazed up at the sky he could see through his surgery's window. It was a strange creamy color, as if someone had drained all the blue out of it and left nothing behind but the raw, undecorated skin of the air's molecules.

This is nature without its disguise. I knew it wouldn't be beautiful.

Talbot met Imogen at one of those parties later—and somewhat self-consciously—called Bohemian, but at the time regarded as adventurous at best and tediously absurd at worst. The party was held at the flat of another medical student named Jenkins.

As he arrived, Talbot recognized many of his friend's cronies, art-lit types with silk cravats and marijuana joints, and avoided them as he headed into the kitchen to get a drink. He was relieved to see Pat Henschel there. Another med student, short, plump and dour, he was always welcome at parties because he could play jazz on the piano. He was lounging against a serving bench, a long glass of vodka in one hand, watching a group of four people sitting around a square kitchen table. Talbot found a bottle of cheap white wine but no glass. He hung onto the bottle and joined Henschel, who nodded a welcome.

"What's going on?" Talbot asked.

"The bird with the dark hair is a witch," Henschel told him. "She's telling fortunes."

Talbot looked at Henschel's face to see if he was joking, but his friend looked merely bored. "A witch?"

"So she claims. Her name is Imogen."

"Imogen what?"

Henschel shrugged and Talbot turned his attention to the group around the table, noticing Jenkins for the first time. He was sitting opposite Imogen, his hand held in both of hers, palm upward. Two people Talbot didn't recognize completed the set. Imogen herself had her back to Talbot.

"You will spend the rest of your life resenting your own good fortune," Imogen was saying. Jenkins made a half-smile, but wasn't convincing. "You are an irredeemably sad person."

"I don't suppose it would help if I offered you the other palm?" Jenkins quipped, but no one except Talbot laughed, which made Talbot feel a little foolish.

"It would make no difference," Imogen said flatly. "I can also see that you will die violently."

Jenkins's face soured. "Haven't you anything pleasant to say?"

"You will have three children."

Jenkins groaned. "More bad news. I don't want children, thank you very much; the life of a roving bachelor for me, I think . . ."

"You will love your children. They will be the only points of happiness in your life."

Jenkins withdrew his hand. "Well, enough of me," he said lightly. "Someone else's turn. Hie, Pat, what about you?"

Henschel demurred with a shake of his head. Jenkins then saw Talbot.

"Oliver! I thought you wouldn't make it! Want your future told? Can't be any worse than mine."

Talbot was about to say no, but then Imogen turned in her seat and he saw her face for the first time. His first thought was of Elisabeth Siddal, Rosetti's wife and model for many of his paintings. But Imogen's face was built with finer bones. She had eyes the color of the oldest jade, as green as the summer dress of an oak tree. Her beauty struck at him.

"Yes, why not," he said, struggling to find his breath. Jenkins stood up to let Talbot sit down. Imogen took his left hand and studied it for a moment, then looked into his eyes. Talbot couldn't read her expression, but there was something of wonder about it.

"You will be a great surgeon," she said.

Talbot smiled slightly. "I have no intention of being a surgeon."

"Nevertheless."

"And will I resent my good fortune and die violently?" The others in the kitchen laughed, but Imogen stiffened, then pulled away. She stood up and left. Talbot silently cursed himself for his words. He had acted like a brute, and knew it. He followed her out, calling softly after her, but she ignored him. At last he said, "I'm sorry."

She stopped then, turned toward him. Seeing her face again, Talbot was lost for words.

"I could have taken it from that fool Jenkins," she said, "but not from you."

Talbot, confused, was about to ask if she would like a drink when she said, "Yes, thank you. Whiskey."

His intake of breath made her smile. "I thought you had to hold my hand for that sort of thing," he said lamely.

"That's a parlor trick. People expect it."

He misunderstood her and smiled in return. "Lucky guess." He couldn't hide the relief in his voice, but before he could ask his next question she said, "No ice, thank you. Just neat."

Talbot used the scalpel again to cut into the brown, subcutaneous fat, then retracted the layer. This time there was too much blood simply to use swabs. He identified the bleeders and cut them off with artery forceps, then sponged the exposed area. With some difficulty he ligated the bleeders and carefully removed the forceps. The bleeding stopped. He could see the linea alba in the mirror.

After the party he and Imogen went back to her place, a small flat in Kensington. She poured wine from a brass ewer into two glasses. They sat down in chairs and drank in silence: Talbot did not know what to say, and Imogen was watching him with the intensity of an owl.

"This is a nice place you have," he said eventually, starting to feel intensely uncomfortable.

She smiled at him. "It was my mother's. When she died she left it to me."

"Oh, I'm sorry."

"Don't be. She died a long time ago."

"Where do you work?"

"From here." She went to a small dining table set under a window and lifted a green velvet cloth to reveal a crystal ball.

"You're joking," Talbot said. He wanted to laugh.

Imogen shook her head. "Come here. Sit at the table."

Talbot did so, and Imogen sat opposite him.

"Put your hands on the ball," she said.

"I thought you did that."

"Put your hands on the ball," she repeated.

He did so. Imogen placed her hands on his. Her hands were warm and soft. He avoided her gaze.

"You are going to sleep with me tonight," she said. "And you are going to fall in love with me. Desperately."

He jerked his hands away.

"In fact," she said lowly, "you already are in love with me."

Talbot made another midline incision, retracted the tissue, cleaned up the small pool of blood that welled in the exposed hollow. Once that was done, he scraped away a patch of preperitoneal fat, finding the lateral motion difficult while guided by the mirror, where everything was back-to-front. His major concern when operating on other people at this point was accidentally puncturing the bowel, but on this occasion it was accidentally slicing off one of his own fingers.

Her blood flowed across the white alabaster bench like something given its own life, something almost primordial.

"God!" Talbot grabbed Imogen's hand and pinched the cut on her left pointer between his own thumb and fingers. "What were you doing?" Imogen half-shrugged, nodded to the carving knife still embedded in the leg of lamb on the cutting board. "Here, you hold it," Talbot ordered her. "I'll get a plaster for the cut."

He was back in less than a minute with a thin plaster and a cotton ball soaked in a carbolic solution. Imogen was staring at the small river of her blood on the alabaster. As Talbot watched it started moving again, forming itself into a snakelike shape, then slid across the bench and into the sink. The shape didn't pour down the plug hole, it slithered, and then was gone.

Talbot froze, cotton ball and plaster in his hands. He stared at the plug hole for a long time. There was no stain left on the alabaster.

"How . . . how did you do that?"

"How long have we been lovers, Oliver?" Imogen asked innocently.

"Umm. Three weeks."

"And you still don't believe?" She sounded disappointed.

He shook his head as if dispelling some conclusion he didn't like. "Give me your finger." She held it up for him. The cut had disappeared. He slowly put down his fixings. "I think I'm going to pass out," he said.

Imogen put her arms around his neck and kissed him lightly. "No you're not, darling. You're a doctor. Doctors don't faint."

"I'm a student. I assure you that students *do* faint. Regularly." And then he did.

When he woke he was lying naked in bed, the equally naked Imogen beside him. She was staring into his eyes, searching for something. "I'm sorry," she said. "I should have been more careful."

"We need to talk, don't we?" he asked feebly.

"I've been waiting three weeks for you to say that."

Talbot raised the peritoneum wall with a pair of forceps. He used the scalpel to make a small nick in the tissue, then used scissors to cut down the wall's length. He removed the forceps and retracted the peritoneum. In the mirror above, reflected back to him in all their glistening obscenity, were his intestines. With great delicacy he lifted them with one hand and placed them into the plastic bag attached to the side of his chair.

For Talbot, it was a matter of separating what he knew about Imogen and what he knew about the real and physical universe. He could not reconcile his own experiences up to the time he met her—his education and worldview—and his experience of her ability. His existence had fissured into two unequal lives, and he struggled to keep them apart, afraid of what might happen if they should collide.

In the end, the passion in their relationship subsumed all his doubts and misgivings. He could think of nothing else except Imogen when he was with her, her presence the greatest sorcery of all. From their first night together it had felt absolutely right to Talbot, as if destiny had always meant them to meet and fall in love.

More fat-scraping, this time on the posterior peritoneum. Again, using the forceps to raise the curtain of tissue, the small cut with the scalpel and then the scissors. He made the final retraction. And there he was. The heart of the matter.

The heart of the matter was this: What truly ended their relationship? What had made everything fall apart for them? For a long time he had believed it was the night he saw Imogen take a life, but now he wasn't so sure.

They had been walking home together in the dark, after meeting for a meal in a small restaurant not far from the university. Imogen was holding on to his arm and he felt her tense before he heard the footsteps behind them. He stopped, started to turn around.

"Keep on walking," Imogen hissed.

He obeyed the urgency in her voice, but the footsteps behind were getting closer and closer. Even Talbot felt menace in the air. Imogen was starting to breathe hard, and her eyes were closed.

"Don't stop," she ordered him, but the danger he felt kicked in his sense of responsibility. He had to protect Imogen.

"You keep on going," he told her, detaching himself from her arm. "I'll take care of this."

"No—!"

He ignored her, turned around to face whoever was following them. A tall man, thin as a rake, wearing a long raincoat and a wide-brimmed hat, hands hidden in the coat pockets. His face was in shadow, but Talbot could make out the reflected whites of his eyes. Imogen crowded in behind him.

"Are you following us?" Talbot demanded.

The man stopped, but said nothing. He cocked his head, lifted his chin. Talbot could see his face now: big-boned, hooked nose, thin lips that seemed too wide. He pulled out one of his hands to reveal a gun. An old service revolver.

"Your money," he said. His voice was low and flat. No emotion whatsoever.

As soon as he saw the gun, Talbot's knees started to shake. "We don't have much . . ." he started to say.

"Give me your wallets."

Talbot fished his wallet out from his jacket, threw it to the man who caught it with his spare hand. He flipped it open, looked inside. "You gotta have more than this," he said angrily. He pointed the gun at Imogen. "You. Your purse. Quickly."

Love Is a Stone

"No," Imogen said levelly. Talbot couldn't see her, but he could feel her presence by his side. Her body seemed to be generating a lot of heat.

"Give him your purse," Talbot said under his breath. "He has a gun, for God's sake—"

"No," Imogen repeated, and took a step forward. The man automatically moved back.

"I'm not joking," he said gruffly. "I'll use this—"

He stopped in midsentence, looked up strangely at Imogen. He opened his lips to say something again but nothing came out. He collapsed to the ground, his gun clattering on the pavement.

"Crikey!" Talbot grabbed Imogen's arm. "Come on! Let's get away while we can!"

"No rush," Imogen said calmly. "He's dead."

This was Talbot's freshest memory of Imogen. It was then and there she had been revealed to him for the first time, like the way a breaking storm reveals the night sky. But the memory also showed him that the seeds of their relationship's destruction had been sewn when they first met, when he had accepted her in spite of his fear. And in the end, love could never be stronger than fear. He knew that now, in his surgery, only moments away from the final truth, the truth he had been seeking ever since that last night with Imogen. The night she had said . . .

"I will turn your heart into stone."

"I love you, but I can't stay with you. There's no other way." He did not really believe his own words. There was another way, if he had the courage. She loved him, and he knew he loved her more than any words could say. But she also terrified him, and when he was with her his love and fear threatened to tear him apart.

"You are killing me," he told her, and this time believed he spoke the truth.

But there and then in their bed, Talbot was drunk on her, filled with her incredible beauty. He saw her round, white body, full of blood, her red cheeks, her surprisingly small breasts and rose nipples, the vee of dark, moist hair between her legs. He remembered how their whispers had become caresses, and caresses keys to deeper passions. And how those passions had seemed to fuel Imogen's fury, her anger at him, a terrible anger that cut him as finely and cruelly as any scalpel.

She moved herself on top of him, her green eyes shining. "You will live

201

forever," she said, her green eyes brimming with tears. "Forever; as long as my love will last for you."

He laughed, struck by the absurdity of the words. "And this is a curse?"

She did not laugh back. She held his jaw in one hand and closed her fingers. Her nails sank deep into his cheeks. "You cannot begin to imagine." She kissed him again, and he felt his sex stiffen between her thighs. She started moving back and forward, slowly teasing his erection until he held her by the hips to stop her motion.

"This isn't right," he said, shaking his head. He could feel blood in his mouth. "Not now."

She slapped his face and he fell back in shock. Before he could recover her hand was over his heart, her whole weight behind it. He wanted to laugh again, at how ridiculous and childish she was being, but then he felt it. His chest tightening, the muscles in his arms and back contracting so sharply he spasmed in pain. He blinked.

Imogen was gone, as if she had never been anything more than a dream, but for a moment he could still hear her voice.

"Forever."

His immortality was not a dream. He never aged, and unable to stay in one place for more than a few years he traveled the world alone with no one to love, and no one to love him.

And now, seventy years after receiving the curse, he had finally gathered the courage to see for himself what Imogen had wrought.

At first all he could see in the chamber was the duodenum. He mobilized the organ, moving it gently to one side. And there was his heart. Made of stone.

He used the end of the scalpel to tap against the left ventricle, and heard the *chink-chink* of metal against the greenest jade he had ever seen.

Memento Mori

BY RAY BRADBURY

The sequence of light and dark events was thus:

On May 1st, a bright spring day, Henry Abbleby died of natural causes—large gins after small vodkas.

Flowers ensued by the avalanche, and the full membership of the Oddfellows, Moose and Elks, smoking on the way in and tipsy coming out, with fine wines to buffer the not-so-fine funeral canapés.

The Swedish Glee wailed and his relatives lined up, trying not to smile.

During which William Krasnick arrived with his secretary, Guy Chandler, and the congregation sat.

Krasnick and Chandler hardly noticed the odd women in the back row, permanently wrapped in crepe by the yard, crushed under great storm-cloud hats with mists of veil wafting their faces.

Krasnick in his Reserved pew stared at the dark-clad females and said, "Haven't I seen—?" but stopped. "No."

"Yes." Guy Chandler shifted so that Krasnick could rise in pity and descend like justice. "They attended the Hamilton wake last week, the Crewes burial before."

"Oh," Krasnick said. "Relatives?"

"Not quite."

And the rites began.

So much for sun and shadows on May 1st, with more funerals in line.

On May 7th, with rain celebrating yet another departure, Krasnick arrived first and, bored, glanced about.

And there sat those bleak twins beneath their fog-bank veils and midnight hats.

Krasnick glanced up to where lay Willis Hornbeck, a liberal financier who had now financed himself a conservative coffin for clear sailing down Eternity.

"Friends?" murmured Krasnick. "Of old Willie?"

"No," said Guy Chandler.

Then the crowd arrived.

The wake was so large that it adjourned to the Benevolent Order of Elks Hall, where the two blackbird-raven-rook ladies glided by with champagne.

Krasnick whispered, "Anyone *know* them?"

"Haven't the faintest," was the response.

Krasnick moved on. "Who are those strangers pouring champagne?"

"Saw them at Charlie Nutt's grave," someone said. "And Christmas, when we buried Ned."

"God," Krasnick said. "No one knows *who* in hell they are. Not aunts, nieces, sisters, cousins, mistresses. They're just *here*!"

"*Who's* just here?" said a female voice.

And Krasnick beheld a tray of drinks, and a fog-like veil drifting from a vast thundercloud hat.

"*You!*" blurted Krasnick.

"*Indeed,*" said a second voice nearby, a black bodice above fresh drinks.

Krasnick seized two champagnes.

"Wasn't it a lovely service?" said the first voice, buried under the veil.

"Lovely!" said the second.

"Willie's funeral *lovely*?" Krasnick wondered.

"But," cried the first voice. "*He* appreciated it."

"The dead can hardly—"

"Appreciate?" exclaimed the second. "You *feel* their exhilaration in the last row! Don't *you*? No?"

"You miss all the joy."

"Give me," said Krasnick, "two *more*!"

Drinks in hand, he saw the women sail off like a dying storm.

———

What happened next made him, for a time, forget funeral mourners. His board of directors set him free, retired him against his violent will. Suddenly, with time on his hands, he began to notice that the daily obituaries had a curious value. They gave him a peculiar vitality, an indescribable élan.

"Good grief, old Henry Gaddis is dead. I must go see."

See *what*, for God's sake? He didn't *know* old Henry.

But he sent flowers and went late.

The next day Eleanor Stillwell died.

"Didn't know her!"

Yet he observed the dispersal of her soul and the interment of her flesh.

Three more days, three more half-strangers lost in mortuary parlors.

Guy Chandler finally said:

"Why this sudden fascination with mortal remains?"

"Not mortal," said Krasnick, "but the remains that remain when bodies leave and two dark flowers stay."

"You mean the dark raven ladies? Crocs. Two old crepe-ribboned crocodiles. Featherdusters."

"Feather—?"

"Dusters. When I was a child in London, mourners wore big black hat-plumes."

"Featherdusters. But you see *real* tears in their eyes!"

"Glycerin! Why bother?"

"Because, Guy, I am a financier forcibly retired to finance time. I yeast with *ennui*. Then, by God, see these ghosts time their lives by mortuary clocks—my gusto returns. Look!"

Krasnick laid out a notepad.

"Grant Holloway's funeral. *They* were there. Louis Martin's graveside. Ditto. George Crankshaw. Guess who arrived first, stayed *late*? Day after day. Twice on Sunday."

Chandler snorted. "So? Do you tell the police?"

"And say two rootless souls patrol our coffins, toss flowers at wakes? No! I *might*, however, write a piece for *The Times*."

Chandler scanned the list. "Twenty-two goners. Twenty-two featherdusters. Have they no other hobbies?"

"Probably hate films, abhor TV, so why not visit dark sideshows, cheap. Know where they're from?"

"That old Victorian house by the ravine. Don't know their names."

"*I do*," Krasnick smiled. "Mori. Maiden names. The older is M. Mori, the younger Eterna."

"Eterna!"

"But," Krasnick laughed. "Braille your fingers down a tombstone to feel *what . . . ?*"

"*Mori*. Latin? For 'Death'?"

"And if the older sister's 'M' stands for Memento—*Memento Mori*. Remembrance of Death."

"My God!"

"Ah, yes," said Krasnick. "My God!"

Then the weather changed. The rains stopped. The sun stayed late. The funerals ceased.

"Good grief," said Krasnick. "What's God up to?"

Days passed into weeks, with good news erasing bad. Droves of in-patients leaped out of hospitals all smiles. Salk vaccines raged unchecked. Penicillin and sulfa broke Death's bones. Brain-scan films went blind with midnight suns. Coffin makers loitered on streets, hopeful of road rage.

Krasnick, stunned, summed it up:

"The local funeral depot, dear Guy, sports a HELP WANTED. Yangtze flood victims to be imported. Seriously? No. A grim joke. Used to be ten eulogies per week. Now the score reads Life ninety-nine, Mortality zilch. The workaholic mortician has sobered up. The coroner is home harassing his wife. So—"

"So," Guy said, "such abstinence threatens—"

"Our death's-head angels, how can they live—"

"Without funeral meats?"

"*Touché*! After a life of tuberose sermons, Chopin's dirges, what? The graveside guns are still. What will happen to our crepe-corseted ladies?"

" 'Twas the absence of mortality killed the Moris?"

"*Say* it!"

"The absence of mortality—"

Did *not* kill the Moris.

Like weeds that fight concrete burials, the Moris leaped from the cracks.

Next day, with the sun bright, Guy stared out at their front lawn.

"They've not gone mad," he murmured. "The Nevermore girls have found a new matinee. Look!"

Krasnick, at the window, blinked. "Is that who I *think*?"

Memento Mori

For way out by the curb stood the two black-marble ladies with dark stormcloud veils shadowing their cheeks.

"But this," Krasnick protested, "is no funeral parlor. No one's dead, or *sick!*"

"Not *yet*," said Guy.

"I'm healthy as a horse, dammit!"

But at dinner Krasnick ignored his utensils.

"Not hungry," he murmured.

"Cook's made veal with wild mushrooms."

"Aspirin will do. Are they—?"

"Still out front? Yes. Eat your veal to spite them."

But when the veal came Krasnick lurched out onto the front porch.

"You!" he cried across the lawn. "I know your tricks!"

In the dusk the sisters stood bolt upright, their veils clouding their sight with promised rains.

"You!" Krasnick yelled. "You've got no bodies, so you try to *make* some! Scat!"

But the presences stayed rooted as their breath stilled the veils.

Scat, he thought, but turned away.

"One wonders," he said that night, "are there gravestones like these two in every town? In towns with few delights, and TV a deadfall, one might applaud funeral vaudevilles, yes?"

"One might."

"Do they stay in *touch*? If local burials stop, would you be tempted to bus to the next town for some midnight-at-noon soirees? Last-Rites circuits? Dark Greyhound landscapes? With a wild Valentino finale! Recall the mobs, the flower blizzards at his Chicago wake? DeMille might have run that cyclone of tears!"

Upstairs, his bed was a winter snow.

"No!" he cried. "That's Ahab's bunk! Those sheets are *winding* sheets!"

"Who *said?*"

For answer, both looked out to where the silent women sprouted like toadstools.

"Where," said Krasnick, "is my aspirin?"

"Easy does it."

"Easy?" Krasnick swallowed. "Hell, I'm seventy, young, but *fired* by a stupid board that shoveled me down the chute! Guy, make me well! Bring me the want ads. There must be ten *billion* jobs!"

He climbed into the cold winter sheets.

"Hold on." He blinked at the ceiling, his eyes taking fire.

"Damn fool! *Don't* get the want ads. *Don't* read me in the Help Wanteds."

"I won't."

"Do you suppose," Krasnick said, almost wildly, "that the local library has dozens of phone books from across the country?"

"They *have*."

"And if I call, our librarian could give names in Schenectady, Sweetwater, Waukesha? Funeral directors in two dozen cities? Does it dawn on you what I'd *ask* them?"

"How many deathwatch birds fill *your* nest? Do strangers loiter at your wakes? Often? For *years*?"

"Man the phones!"

They manned the phones until the small towns slept. At dawn they questioned funeral noons.

Krasnick exploded.

Jabbering to Oswego and Oshkosh, he glared out at the false family plot in his yard.

"Patience, sleepwalking ladies—your cure will come when I *find* the cure!"

By noon he'd logged three dozen calls, by nap time sixty-odd.

"Guy!" he gibbered. "*Look!* No one's tried this search. In every village and town live Grim Reaper clones of our dire sisters. Women in their seventies, with thundercloud hats and raven bodices, whose notion of off-hour treats is lackluster strangers. Friends, no—strangers! Four a week, one a day! Oh, joy! I've charted sixty towns, where death's helpers harvest crepe. I am the first to call these undertakers and guess at their morbid visitors. No one else ever guessed! Hold on. Wait. Maybe . . ."

"What?"

"I am brooding, Guy, to make a big lightbulb flash in my brain! There! It *flashed*!"

"The light?"

"One thousand watts! Solves both problems—those melancholy ladies and *my* tomorrows! Would you see those marble women cracked and strewn?"

"Yes!"

"Then quick, my pants, my shoes!"

Next dawn the two Moris, ready to head out on their gravewatch, gasped.

"What's that on our lawn?" both said.

With umbrellas glooming their heads like clouds, the two approached the figure by the tree in their yard.

There sat William Krasnick with binoculars crushed to his eyes.

"Sir," said Eterna Mori, "why are you here?"

"Madam." Krasnick focused the glasses. "This grass is city property. Anyone can sit."

"Nevertheless," said the older. "What do you see that causes alarm?"

"Alarm?" Krasnick barked. "No, panic! I see a graveyard hut of cold marble that hides colder Eternity. A tomb with a chiseled name." Krasnick smiled. "What do *you* see?"

"Our home!"

"*Not* marble? No MORI inscription?"

He thrust the binoculars at them.

They looked.

"See?" said Krasnick.

The sisters' hands swiped the air.

"Nothing!"

"How come I spy a *Mori* vault?"

"Liar!"

They fled to the house to slam the door.

"Hear?" Krasnick whispered.

Nearby, Guy said, "I heard."

"Did it sound like a tomb door shut?"

"A tomb."

What happened next reminded Krasnick of a newsreel of soldiers shot, *wham*! and their bodies flopped into graves. Krasnick barked a laugh, then stopped, ashamed. Annihilation? Fun?

All this as he watched the Mori house.

The older sister popped out with a carpet-beater to drive him away. The younger whipped a flyswatter and ran.

Dr. Samuel Craig galloped in and out, his pills rattling.

Two doctors that night.

Three the next day.

Krasnick left.

Next week, two Spring Valley citizens voted for Eternity.

Rumor had it that M. Mori, the older featherduster, wandered into the Coldsnap Ice House, where they found her, a frozen beauty delivered out of a glacier like those myths of maidens shut in winter for a thousand years, unchanged at deliverance. A worker clamp-tonging ice had pulled forth Death, M. Mori, so rimed she could not melt.

Eterna? Some said she, naked, flung wide her icebox door, her bare flesh jumping, then held forever still.

The first funeral in weeks came next day at the Abscond Parlor, Momento and Eterna, two solemn icicles for one price.

The whole town showed. And in the parlor rear? A man suited in black, crepe-sleeved, dark glasses on his eyes.

"Your name, sir?"

The quiet man replied.

"Friend of the deceased?"

"Not friend, foe, relative or acquaintance."

"Would you attend the reception?"

"Just might." The stranger unfolded the front page of the *News*.

Influenza Ravages States. Dozens Die. More Feared.

The stranger smiled and removed his dark glasses.

"Krasnick!" came the cry. "You! And why so happy?"

Krasnick showed his list.

"Kankakee, Oswego, Okeefanokee, York. Dark celebrants galore, ripe to get their dot-coms connected. I've started a pc travel website! Internet midnight-at-noon Greyhound tours. Mausoleum bed-and-breakfasts. Rebirthed, my new career! I'm Chairman of the Board!" Krasnick yelled.

The mourners fled.

"And *CEO*!" he cried.

The Mistress of Marwood Hagg

BY SARA DOUGLASS

Edmund Lewkenor, Earl of Henley, stood at the edge of the battlefield and surveyed his victory. The rain that had blighted the entire day continued to sleet across the grey landscape, and Henley winced at its sudden icy touch across his sweaty face as his squire removed his helm. Henley gestured impatiently and the squire hastened to unbuckle the heaviest pieces of armored plate from about his lord's body, then handed Henley a thick worsted cloak.

Lionel Fitzherbert, one of Henley's senior commanders, materialized out of the driving rain, hunching inside his own cloak. Its lower folds clung about his legs, the material sodden with mud thrown up by the rain.

"Where is he?" Henley said.

Fitzherbert's head jerked toward a depression in the field. "Over there, my lord." He tugged once or twice at his muddied, waterlogged cloak, then let his hand fall. There would be no warmth to be found this terrible day.

Henley shot his commander a sharp look. "Alive?"

Fitzherbert shrugged, too exhausted to find the words for a reply after a vicious battle that had raged for over ten hours.

Henley grunted, looking toward the depression that Fitzherbert had indicated. He hoped the bastard Earl of Chelmsford *was* still alive, for he deserved the full pitilessness of Queen Elizabeth's justice for his unholy rebellion.

Damned Catholics and their Popish plots!

And look to what had their dishonor brought them—the most contemptuous of deaths in this luckless, bemired landscape. Chelmsford had picked a gently undulating and recently plowed field for his battle with the Queen's army, and God Himself had sent His judgment in the form of this rain, turning the soft, giving earth into a clinging black deadly quagmire. Now the field was marred with the dark featureless clumps of corpses settling deeper into the ooze: hundreds, if not thousands, of rebels now manured the sodden earth with their rotting hopes and ambitions. Worse, many of Henley's own soldiers lay mired side by side with their foes, both rebels and defenders made brothers in the cold ooze of their shared muddied death.

"Let's not waste time," Henley said, and together the two men, accompanied by a contingent of men-at-arms, squelched their way toward the central depression of the battlefield.

It was a slow, difficult journey. With every step Henley and his companions sank over their ankles into the battle-churned slime. If Henley had thought the horses would prove faster, he would have ridden, but as it was this field would have eaten the weighty destriers up to their bellies.

As they approached the depression, disfigured with the fallen, mud-covered bodies of foot soldiers and knights alike, Henley saw that several of his men were attempting to lift one of the fallen knights from the field.

Chelmsford? Henley wondered, and hurried as much as he could.

As he reached the struggling group, treading over several corpses as the easiest and most efficient means of covering the final few paces, Henley realized that the fallen man was, indeed, accoutred in Chelmsford's heraldic devices.

"Sweet Lord Christ," Henley muttered as he drew level with the four of his men trying to raise the rebel from the muddied field, "save him to face our Queen's justice!"

And with that mutter, his men slipped and Chelmsford fell from their grasp, his heavily armored body sinking back into the mud.

The rebel baron struggled, his arms waving, his mailed hands outreaching for aid, his helmeted head writhing within the cold embrace of the rain-soaked earth.

A sound issued from within his helmet—a frightful, desperate combination of gasp and gurgle.

"Get his helmet off!" Henley snapped, and two of his men pulled off their leather gloves and, risking their own stability, leaned forward and unbuckled Chelmsford's heavy helm.

It moved, but not enough, and their efforts perversely pushed Chelmsford's armor-weighted head deeper into the mud.

"For the Lord's sake!" Henley said. "Get it off—*now!*"

The two men put in a final effort, and with a grudging squelch the helmet at last surrendered. The men staggered back and the helmet fell into the mud to one side of Chelmsford's head.

Henley drew in a sharp breath, shocked by what he saw. Chelmsford's head was all but submerged in the liquefied soil—it covered his forehead, cheeks and chin and lapped at his mouth.

Chelmsford's eyes, however, were incongruously free of the mud, and they stared at Henley, pale blue, bulging, frantic. The rebel baron opened his mouth, meaning to add words to the plea in his eyes, but as he did so the mud surged and rose up about him, sliding into his nostrils and pouring into the void between his lips, and the only plea that issued from Chelmsford's mouth was a great bubble of air that burst with the stink of escaping marsh gas.

Henley's men leaned down again, horror hastening their hands, but Henley stopped them with a quick gesture.

"Leave him," he said. "*This* is justice, no better."

Chelmsford's eyes, impossibly, widened even further, their pale blue turning to pink as terror burst a score of blood vessels within their orbs.

He struggled, frantic, and the mud gurgled and bubbled in his mouth and flooded his nostrils and the air passages of his sinuses.

"Cursed rebel," Henley muttered. "Accept your fate without grudging." He paused, then placed one of his feet in the center of Chelmsford's armor-plated chest and bore down with all his weight.

Chelmsford had died in his own county, a mere two days' journey from his home base of Castle Marwood Hagg, and it was to Marwood Hagg that the Earl of Henley—together with an armed escort of several thousand men—escorted his body.

It was, after all, to Henley's advantage to ensure that Chelmsford's widow did not harbor rebellious ambitions of her own, or shelter supporters of her lately deceased husband. A viewing of what happened to those who *did* think to challenge Queen Elizabeth's right to rule over the largely Catholic north of England would undoubtedly do these Papists the world of good.

They approached Marwood Hagg as a cold dusk gathered. Crows circled through the low clouds and soared about the crenellated towers of the castle. Silent, sullen peasants stood in huddled groups at the edges of their stubbled fields, watching expressionless as the bier carrying their lord's corpse trundled past.

Sentinels of death, Henley thought, and did not know if he meant the crows with that thought, or the silent, watching peasants.

The castle stood open to them, its gates rolled back, its sentries absent from its parapets.

A single figure stood in the open gateway, and Henley signaled his escort to a halt as he rode forward alone.

"My lady," Henley said, reining his horse to a stop before her.

Eleanor, Countess of Chelmsford and mistress of Marwood Hagg, was a young woman, full twenty-five years her husband's junior. Despite her relative youth, there seemed a quality of weariness about her thin, tall frame, as if she had lived a little too desperately during her thirty-odd years.

She was veiled in grey and robed in scarlet, and beneath her veil her face was pale and lined, as if she had spent long hours in tearless grief. There was no fear nor respect in her brief regard of Henley, but when her gaze settled on the bier at the fore of the escort her composure momentarily deserted her. She took a sharp breath, her cheeks blotching with color. "You have brought home my husband?"

"Aye, my lady."

Eleanor inclined her head toward Henley, in control once more. "Then I thank you, my lord."

And with that she turned and walked into the courtyard.

Henley watched her narrow, straight figure for a moment, then kicked his horse forward, waving to his escort to follow.

They carried the Earl of Chelmsford's corpse to the chapel and it was to this chapel that Henley took himself after he had rested and eaten.

The countess had instructed that her husband's corpse be laid upon the altar and now, as Henley approached, she stood behind it straight and still, her hands clasped lightly before her, the veil folded back from her impassive face.

Henley scarcely noticed her, so appalled was he at the state of Chelmsford's corpse. Instead of being suitably robed and draped, the countess had caused her husband's remains to be stripped. Now the Earl of Chelmsford's white body lay naked atop the altar, his arms hanging toward the floor, his massive belly mounding toward the stone-vaulted roof, his face, hands and genitals mottling and bloating in the first stages of putrefaction.

Henley slowly raised his gaze to the countess. "My lady? Why have you not attired your husband decently and with respect?"

"Because I am mystified, my lord."

"Mystified?"

Eleanor swept one graceful hand down the length of her husband's body. "My beloved husband has died in battle, yet I see not a single wound upon him. How was his death accomplished, my lord, if not through means of foul witchcraft?"

Henley's neck reddened, the only sign of his discomposure. "There has been no witchcraft or foulness in the manner of your husband's death, my lady, save in that he brought his death upon himself in his most vile rebellion against our good Queen Elizabeth."

"*Your* good Queen Elizabeth," Eleanor said softly, "for we do not honor her in these northern counties." Her voice strengthened. "I ask again, how is it that there is no wound on my husband's body? In what manner did he die?"

Henley remembered that instant when his men had pulled Chelmsford's helm from his head, remembered Chelmsford's frantic pale eyes staring at Henley from amid their sea of mud, remembered their silent scream for aid.

And, in remembering, Henley felt no regret for his lack of mercy toward the terrified, dying man.

"He died," he said, his tone icy, "when he fell from his horse into the thick mud of the battlefield. His weighty armor dragged him down, and he drowned, my lady, drowned in the mud as it flowed through his mouth and nostrils and swamped his lungs. Our Lord God vouchsafed unto your husband a death most fitting for his treacherous soul."

Eleanor's entire body stiffened, as if she fought for control. In this effort she was partly unsuccessful, for when she spoke her voice trembled very slightly. "And in his muddied drowning, my lord, did any attempt to aid him?"

"It *was* a death most fitting, my lady," Henley said, "and I had no thought to interrupt it."

There was a moment of utter, cold silence in the chapel, then the Earl of Henley turned his back and strode away.

Behind him, the mistress of Marwood Hagg sagged in horror, and she leaned her hands on the altar so she would not entirely sink to the stone floor.

"My dear sweet lord," she whispered, bending her face close to that of her dead husband's, "they murdered you with *mud?*"

Then Eleanor looked down the chapel to where Henley had disappeared, and both her face and her voice strengthened. "Then will mud dog your murderer's every footstep, my lord. Mud shall consume his hopes, as it has consumed mine."

She buried her husband the next morning. The Earl of Henley attended, for he would not ride out for his home in Suffolk until noon.

By which time, he prayed to God, this dismal weather would have turned into something more conducive to journeying.

Besides, Henley meant to ensure that Chelmsford had a proper Church of England service said over his rotting, treacherous bastard of a corpse. There would be no Papist heresy muttered here.

The small-graveyard attached to the village church stood a half-mile from Marwood Hagg. Like most graveyards it faced east, so that the morning sun could chase away evil shadows and sprites from the sleeping dead.

But there would be little chance of sun this morning, Henley thought, hunching closer inside his cloak. Heavy rain clouds rumbled across the sky, swollen and misshapen as if demons cavorted within their midst, and a hard, biting wind blew down from the north. It made Henley wonder if such foul weather normally attended upon Chelmsford; perchance it was merely the reflection of his dark soul.

He shuddered, and to distract himself studied the people attending the service.

There were relatively few.

Eleanor was still dressed in her scarlet robe and grey veil, apparently unconcerned by her lack of a cloak against the approaching storm. Her entire being was still and silent, and her eyes rested unblinkingly on Henley, who stood on the other side of the black, open grave.

Two women attended her, as well as Chelmsford's estate steward and the seneschal of the castle.

Five peasants, their thick woolen robes twisting in the wind, stood seven or eight paces away, their faces turned toward Henley.

Apart from the priest and a deacon from a neighboring parish, the only other people in attendance were six of Henley's men-at-arms. There not only to protect their lord from any danger, but to manhandle Chelmsford's corpse into his grave.

Back to the mud, where it had died.

The corpse itself lay at the feet of the priest, crosswise to the grave. It was wrapped in a linen shroud, its seams roughly sewn together with twine.

Henley shivered, wishing that Eleanor had chosen to have her husband interred within the church—as would have been fit and proper for a man of his rank. *Why wish to have him interred in the soil, in the open, naked to the elements?*

Finally, impatient and uncomfortable, Henley nodded once at the priest, willing him into action.

The man was nervous, his tongue playing about his lips, his weight shifting from foot to foot.

"Begin," Eleanor said, not moving her regard from Henley.

The priest cleared his throat and the Book of Common Prayer wobbled in his hands.

Henley wondered how familiar the priest was with it.

"As you wish, my lady," the priest said, his voice high and strained and looking down to the prayer book, began the Order for the Burial of the Dead.

He rattled the words out, running them together in a litany of discomfort.

"Speak slowly and clearly," Eleanor said, finally turning her face to the priest, "for otherwise you dishonor my husband!"

The priest halted, swallowed and then spoke again, his voice now wooden and ponderous in his attempts to please the countess.

"Man that is born of woman hath but a short time to live," he read, "and his life is full of misery—"

Eleanor's eyes snapped back to Henley and her veil lifted away from her face in a great gust of wind.

"He cometh up and is cut down like a flower—"

Eleanor bared her teeth at Henley, her face a silent rictus of hate.

Henley was horrified. *What was the woman about?*

"—and he fleeth as it were a shadow," the priest continued, trying his best to ignore Eleanor's actions, "and never continueth in one stay. In the midst of life we be in death—"

Eleanor bared her teeth again, then hissed, her face twisting viciously.

"Be still, woman!" Henley said.

Eleanor's face contorted once more and at her sides her hands clenched into fists.

The priest stumbled into silence and Henley gestured impatiently to him to continue. *Lord God, all he wanted was to get out of here, and leave this maddened woman to her festering anger!*

Another gust of wind rocked the group standing about the corpse and open grave, and this time it bore on its wings the needle-sting of approaching rain.

"Forasmuch as it hath pleased Almighty God," the priest said, his words once again tumbling over themselves, "of His great mercy to take unto Himself the soul of our dear brother here departed—"

Above them the heavens opened, and the rain sheeted down, drenching everyone within heartbeats.

Eleanor shrieked, making everyone start, then sank to her knees at the graveside.

"Continue!" Henley hissed at the priest, who had closed the Book of Common Prayer and tucked it under his robes away from the rain.

Eleanor wailed and tore the veil from her head. Her black hair tumbled over her shoulders and she lifted her face to the rain, her wails growing ever louder and more pitiful.

"We therefore," the priest said, almost shouting now above the sound of the elements and Eleanor, "commit his body to the ground—"

Eleanor screamed and her hands grabbed at the neckline of her gown. She ripped it apart, exposing her creamy breasts to both weather and the shocked eyes of the mourners.

The priest tore his gaze away, fixing it on the grave before him. Despite the chill of the rain and wind, his face had flooded with color. "Earth to earth—"

Eleanor's wails and shrieks rose to an almost unbearable level and her hands buried themselves in her sodden tresses, tearing out great chunks of hair and flesh from her scalp.

Blood poured over her forehead, diluting in the rain to wash in pink rivulets down her distorted, shrieking face.

"For the Lord's sake!" Henley muttered and began to move around the grave, intending to slap some sense into the woman.

"Ashes to ashes—"

Eleanor's cries collapsed into a frightful moaning and her hands tore her robe even further asunder. She smacked at her breasts with open hands, the noise shockingly sharp and hard amid the rumble of the intensifying storm.

The rivulets of blood washed down over her chest and her beating hands smeared blood all over her breasts.

Henley slipped a little in the muddied earth at the foot of the grave and cursed.

Save for Eleanor, Henley and the priest, everyone else had now stepped well back from the grave site, and several had abandoned the service entirely to slip and slide their way through the mud toward the church.

As Henley moved toward her, Eleanor suddenly leaned down to the wet soil, her fingers clutching into the mud.

"And dust to dust," the priest said.

"Dust to dust, *and mud to mud!*" Eleanor cried, lifting her hands and hurling handfuls of the sodden earth into Henley's face. "*Mud to mud!*"

It spattered into his eyes and mouth and stopped him dead in his tracks.

"Witch!" he yelled, reaching blindly toward her.

"The Lord bless him and keep him," the priest shrieked and Henley could hear from his voice that he, too, was now dashing toward the church, "and the Lord make His face to shine upon him and be gracious unto him and give him peace!"

Mud to mud, Henley heard Eleanor's now-calm voice echoing into his mind. *Mud to mud . . .*

"Amen," Eleanor said softly as a blinded Henley's right foot slipped at the edge of the grave and the earl tumbled in, sinking deep into the mud meant for Chelmsford's corpse.

OCTOBER 1583, SUFFOLK

Edmund Lewkenor, Earl of Henley, stood in the great hall of his castle in Suffolk and thought on how the Lord God had blessed him. These past ten months since his return from disposing of the Earl of Chelmsford and his ill-conceived rebellion had been good to him. Queen Elizabeth, pleased at his quick and successful action against Chelmsford, had heaped preferments upon him; he had arranged advantageous marriages for his two eldest daughters; the harvest on all of his estates had proved spectacular; and tonight . . . tonight his beloved wife Alice lay within her birthing chamber, laboring with the child he had conceived upon her on his return from the north and which, so every astrologer he'd consulted had assured him, was finally his yearned for son and heir.

Henley stood alone by the fire in the massive hearth at the northern end of the hall, sipping a fine spiced ale. Behind the screens at the other end of the hall he could see the occasional movements of the midwives as they hurried between kitchens and the stairs leading up to the birthing chamber, carrying urns of warmed water, vials of herbs and quantities of linens.

In the far north, the mistress of Marwood Hagg issued forth from her castle. She walked with great purpose, and upon her face was an infinite peace.

She had garbed herself in the same, if mended, scarlet robe she'd worn at her husband's funeral.

The hurried movements of the midwives did not concern Henley. This would be Alice's eighth birth and her seven previous had all been mercifully sweet and brief (if all ending in the production of yet another daughter). This time, Henley fully expected to greet the dawn with a healthy son and a recovering wife.

Henley took another sip of the spiced ale, his eyes drifting to the great leaded windows in the hall's eastern wall. It was deep autumn now and the wind threw scatterings of dead leaves against the glass.

The fire warmed Henley's back and the ale his belly, and he smiled, content with his lot.

She walked directly to the grave of her husband. Strangely, considering the many months that had passed, the earth still lumped fresh and loose atop the grave.

Eleanor noted the condition of the grave with satisfaction, then smiled, love transfiguring her face into an unexpected beauty.

The Mistress of Marwood Hagg

Disregarding the wind that twisted the robe about her body, she knelt down by the fresh-turned earth.

A sudden, harder gust of wind rattled the windows of Henley's hall. The noise was close followed by a thump from the floor above him.

Henley's cup of ale stilled on its way to his mouth and his eyes cast upward.

Nothing. Henley relaxed. It was just the wind and the timber joists creaking in the cold that blew down from the north.

Eleanor lifted her face to the dark sky and tore the veil from her head, allowing her black hair to unravel in the wind.

As her veil fluttered away, the clouds opened in a violent rainstorm.

Rain suddenly squalled viciously against the windows and Henley jumped, almost dropping his cup of ale.

Frowning, he placed the cup on a nearby table and looked once more toward the windows.

It was dark now, but he could make out the shadowy waves of the rain beating against the thick glass.

It was almost as if it was angry . . . as if it wanted to gain entry into the peace of Henley's hall—*and of his life*—and drag Henley's contentment . . .

"Down into the mud," Eleanor whispered.

She smiled once again as the rain pelted into the loose earth of her husband's grave, but this time something harder and more deadly than love underlay her expression.

Vengeance was the last service she could do her husband.

Unbidden, memories of the horrifying day of Chelmsford's burial flooded Henley's mind: Eleanor's shrieking and self-mutilation; her hurling of the blinding mud into his face; his own tumble into the grave meant for Chelmsford.

It had taken all six of his men-at-arms to haul him out again, the pelting, freezing rain and Eleanor's laughter washing over them the entire time.

When finally he was above ground, shaking with his shock, the cold, clinging mud, and his vicious anger, Henley had ordered his men to throw Chelmsford's shrouded corpse into the muddied hole. Then he had simply stalked away, leaving the bare-breasted and bloodied, but now silent, Eleanor kneeling by the mud pit of her husband's grave.

"Mud to mud," she whispered, and lifted her hands into the rain.

Henley dragged his mind back to the present. He reached for his ale cup, then stopped when he realized his hand was shaking too badly to pick it up.

"What is born in mud," she whispered, "returns to mud."
And in a sudden, violent movement, the mistress of Marwood Hagg buried her arms to their elbows in the cold, muddied womb of her husband's grave.

Shivering with an unreasoning fear, Henley stumbled down the hall only to halt halfway as one of the midwives hurried toward him from a gap in the screens at the other end.

"My lord! Oh, my dear sweet lord!"

"Lord Christ save us!" Henley muttered, then rushed for the stairs.

She smiled, happy and content, the mistress of Marwood Hagg, and wriggled her arms yet deeper into the mud.

Henley's first impression when he burst into the birthing chamber was that it was freezing.

He halted, so disorientated by the icy atmosphere that for a moment he could do nothing but stand and gape at the scene before him.

In the center of the room stood the birthing bed, two midwives huddled about it. Both were moaning and wailing and plucking helplessly at the fabric of their aprons.

His wife lay sprawled atop the bed, its linens in jumbled disarray as her hands groped and grasped at her sides.

She was half-sitting, her legs bent up and apart, her face looking down to what lay between them.

Henley only gradually realized that she was shrieking, and he shuddered, for her frightful shrieks echoed Eleanor's graveside madness.

There was a clap, as if of thunder, and Henley's eyes jerked to the window.

It was open, its panes swinging wildly in the wind and slamming against the window frame.

Rain gusted through, slicking across the floor with arrow-like determination toward the bed.

Alice shrieked once more and Henley wrenched his head back toward his wife. She jerked as if trying to escape whatever lay between her legs, but was too weak and hopeless to do anything more than writhe ineffectually.

Something dark and wet issued across the linens and oozed in clinging fingers down the side of the bed.

Black viscous mud, trickling down to meet the rain-slicked floor.

"*Edmund! Edmund!*" Alice screamed, now half-turning toward her husband, one of her hands held out in desperate appeal.

It was black, coated with mud.

Henley took a step forward.

"Witchery," he whispered, his eyes wide and staring.

"Edmund . . ." Alice said again, her voice now a whisper, and her hand dropped back to her side. Her belly, soft and bulbous from the infant it had expelled, rippled and quivered, as if it continued to expel . . .

"Mud!" said Eleanor, her arms still buried in her husband's grave, her sodden hair clinging to her neck and shoulders. "Mud," she said again and laughed softly.

Henley took the final three steps to his wife's bedside, pushing aside one of the midwives.

The woman slipped in the mud and water on the floor and fell down with a cry.

Henley had no mind for her. He stared at what lay between his wife's legs . . . and then he, too, moaned.

There lay his son, perfectly formed.

There lay his son, lying in a sea of mud that even now continued to flood forth from his wife's body.

There lay his son, covered in mud, *buried* in mud, mud that bubbled and belched as it poured into the infant's mouth that had opened for its first, life-affirming wail.

His son, silent in his agonizing drowning.

His son, staring up at his father with Chelmsford's pale blue terror-struck eyes.

Earth to earth, Henley heard Eleanor's voice whisper in his mind.

He reached down to his son, desperate to rescue him.

Ashes to ashes.

He touched his son's body, and flinched at the coldness and foulness that coated it.

Dust to dust.

His hands closed about the infant's chest and his arm muscles contracted as he prepared to lift the child from the death that enveloped it.

Mud to mud.

And then Henley shrieked, for his arms were no longer his, but were the scarlet-clad thin arms of a woman, and her (*his*) long-fingered pale hands were now clasped hatefully about his son, pushing the infant's face deep into the sea of mud, and now there was nothing, nothing but the clumpish, still form of something covered in mud and the thin scarlet-clad arms buried to the elbows in the mud and the single bubble, that one single bubble of air that burst hopelessly through the mud with the stink of escaping marsh gas.

The remains of his son's life.

Hundreds of miles north, the woman leaned back and pulled her arms from the grave.

Strangely, her white thin-fingered hands and scarlet-clad arms were unmarked by the mud.

Rain washed in sheets over her and the wind as it blew chilled her almost to death, but yet still she smiled.

She rose to her feet. "May you *now* finally have peace," she said to the still, cold corpse of her husband, buried deep within its embrace of mud.

Then, straight-backed and joyous, the mistress of Marwood Hagg withdrew into her castle.

The Right Men

BY MICHAEL MARSHALL SMITH

Jack leaned against the wall, panting heavily. His calves felt stretched and rigid and his forehead was covered with a thin slick of sweat. His lungs felt better than they had ten years ago, when he started making the same journey while still a smoker, but he took no pleasure in this. He hadn't stopped smoking through choice. Jack's life had not been the one being protected. Today his trouser pocket held a packet of Marlboro Lights. Before the day was over, he was going to have one. At least one, perhaps many more.

He knew that Maxwell would be waiting beyond the door in front of him, his eye on some very expensive and accurate timepiece. Maxwell would know the exact time Jack had entered the building, using his PIN to open the reinforced glass door twenty-three floors below. His employer had often commented on the time it took Jack to climb the seven hundred and fifty stairs from the street up to the penthouse. He had never in this time offered an explanation as to why he did not allow Jack to use the private elevator that would have taken him from floor to sky in a lazy minute, opening directly into the apartment. Instead, long ago, when they had first commenced their association, he had merely shown Jack the entrance to the private stairway and furnished him with a code number. It was impossible to access these stairs from any of the floors beneath, which meant it was no use taking the building's main elevator for some of the distance and then swapping over. Jack knew this because he had tried it. From every floor. More than once.

"Don't keep me waiting," said a voice.

At first Jack thought it might just be in his head, an aural hallucination brought on by years of familiarity and the intensity of the occasion. Then he realized it had been relayed by the small speaker in the ceiling. It still surprised him. Usually his boss would at least let him enter the room before his demands started. He hurriedly reached out and punched in the further code required to get through this door, cursing himself for jumping. For doing what he was told. Immediately. Every time.

The door opened, allowing him to step into the wide corridor beyond and then silently sweeping shut again behind him. Four steps took Jack to the threshold of the living room.

The room was bright and airy, running almost half the entire side of the building. It was sparsely furnished, floored in laminated wood. Half-height windows ran along its entire length, affording an extraordinary view of the city below. One of these windows was open.

Stefan Maxwell was sitting in front of it. He was wearing a long black coat, and dressed in a suit that had once belonged to John F. Kennedy. The cut had gone in and out of style several times since, but this made little difference. When capped by a face as rigorously handsome as Maxwell's, any suit would do the job. Fashionability was not in any event the point of the garment. The point was who it had belonged to, along with the fact that it had been stolen under difficult circumstances and at the cost of a human life. Jack knew this because he had been the one tasked with stealing it. Then, too, he had been instructed not to keep his employer waiting.

Maxwell was seated in his favorite chair, a reupholstered Wilhenzüffer club armchair from the 1920s. Jack knew what it had been recovered in, but did not like to think about it, even now.

"Perhaps I'm not the only one who's grown old, Jack."

"Thought you might want an extra minute, that's all." Curiously, and despite everything that had happened between them, this had been true.

"I told you a time," Maxwell said. His eyes were on Jack's. "Punctuality was the only courtesy I required."

Fuck you, Jack thought. Fuck you, you old cunt. He looked away, over to the table in the center of the room. On it sat a collection of files, about nine inches high. It should have made him feel elated. It didn't.

The Right Men

"Yes, those are yours," Maxwell said. "But not just yet."

"So. How do you want it to be?" The old question, a last time. "A cup of coffee first?"

Maxwell nodded. "Of course." The ritual.

Jack turned his back and walked over to the kitchen area. Like the rest of the apartment, it looked like it had never been used. In common with the rest of the apartment, notably the floor, this was because it had been very scrupulously cleaned very many times. By Jack.

He opened the Sub-Zero, which was empty except for a tall glass bottle. It was made of Roman glass. Inside was something that resembled water. It actually was water, in fact, if you ignored the fact that it had passed through three humans before being filtered and stored in the fridge. Jack had buried all three of these humans, and had assisted in forcing the second two to drink the urine of a predecessor. The humans had been young and female, of three different races. What was in the bottle was the last of their product, and Jack was not surprised to see that there appeared to be enough for exactly one cup.

While he made the coffee, using ground beans that had been demonstrated to come from one particular bush, and collected by only one person, Jack was careful to keep his eyes on the task. This was only a habit. Long ago he had wondered if Maxwell's eyes were something to do with the position he was in. He had read about a technique of hypnotism, that of keeping your gaze firmly centered on the bridge of the intended victim's nose while drawing them in with the calm pressure of your voice. He had grown accustomed to avoiding Maxwell's eyes as much as possible. It had made no difference, and he knew now the idea had never been more than an excuse. An attempt to reduce his own culpability, to negate his weakness.

Maxwell hadn't needed hypnotism. He'd only needed Jack.

When the coffee was made he carried it over. The cup was hot enough to produce a mild burn in the fingers, but Maxwell made no sign of discomfort. He had already developed calluses, during a period in which they had experimented with making the cup hotter and hotter each time, to see at what point it became unbearable. Maxwell had been able to affect nonchalance even at a temperature where you could smell a faint burning. The experiment was abandoned. Jack recalled the period without consciously summoning the memory, and the recollection merely floated across his mind and across the other side. He believed it had been acquiring the technique of letting things like that pass without awareness that had kept him sane. Truth was, Maxwell hadn't even needed the calluses. All he'd needed was his will.

"Anything else?"

"One of your cigarettes, I think."

Jack tried not to react, but the other man smiled.

"I know you have some. You're very predictable, Jack. I know how much you resented giving up. How better to celebrate?"

Jack miserably reached into his pocket and pulled out the packet. He tugged the sealer, wrenched off the clear plastic wrapping, flipped the carton and pulled out the foil. He had spent a good deal of the trip up the stairs imagining doing these things for himself. Now it was spoiled. Of course. Like everything else. Everything else in the world.

He lit the cigarette and handed it to Maxwell. The man took a deep drag on it, sucked it down, and then waited. After a moment he exhaled. He did not, like any other man smoking a cigarette for the first time in his life, cough and splutter like a maniac. He merely accepted the discomfort, absorbed it, and waited with interest to see what would come next. Jack had half-expected him to blow a smoke ring, that the man would have worked out how to do it from first principles. However much you hated him, and Jack did hate him, hated him so much that it often seemed the only thing running through his soul, you had to credit his power.

"Do you want to talk?"

Maxwell looked at him, lip twitching. "Talk?" he said, evidently amused. "Why on earth would I want to talk to you?"

Think about the files, Jack said to himself. When this is over, they're yours and it's all over. He shrugged. "Just thought you might. You do talk, sometimes."

Maxwell didn't reply. He took another drag off the cigarette, tapping the ash professionally onto the floor. He sipped his coffee, turned to watch out of the open window.

He still looked good. Exceptionally good for a man of seventy. Astonishingly good for a man of that age who moreover had advanced cancer, whose dark soul had finally metastasized throughout his body. You simply wouldn't have been able to tell. All of the man's will had been turned to negating the effects, the gradual and sticky unfolding. The secondary reason why Maxwell didn't currently have a knife sticking in his chest—or a broken coffee cup protruding from his face—was that Jack hadn't been sufficiently confident that either act would have been possible to carry out. The old man was fast, and strong, and very, very clever, even now.

The primary reason why these events had not occurred was that Jack was simply incapable of them, and Maxwell knew it. Maxwell believed deeply in a certain theory, which Jack by now knew very well. The world was full of men, it ran, but not all those men were equal. A proportion of them possessed something different, something that gave them the potential for being exceptional. This quality had first been established by an academic who had been trying to explain why no American servicemen had escaped from Chinese prison camps during the Korean War. Surely, as the straight-backed heroes of the world, our boys should have been up and over those fences at a rate of knots? The answer was interesting. It had not been due to any lack of vim on the part of the soldiers—thank God, what an unpopular conclusion *that* would have been—but instead to an insight on the part of the guards. They watched the prisoners carefully on arrival, looking for ones who seemed to have more get-up-and-go than the rest. Each of these prisoners, the men who seemed dominant within their group, was removed from the general population and put together in a separate—and heavily guarded—compound. It was quickly discovered that the other prisoners didn't even need guarding. Once the dominant individuals had been removed from their number, the general mass listlessly waited for the end of the war or death. The dominant men, it was established, accounted for one in twenty of the total number. Without them, the rest were lost.

Further research had established that this feature of humanity, and the 5 percent rule, was true across all cultures. Call them dominant, call them alpha males, call them—as Maxwell did, Right Men—they were a fact of life. Some were good; some were bad. The former achieved greatness, the latter notoriety, greatness's evil twin. Most achieved nothing of substance, but were frustrated by birth or happenstance and ended up in the criminal fraternity. All were characterized by the will to power, a measure of charisma, and the need to be right: the overwhelming need to be always and forever Right, at all costs, even unto death and perhaps beyond. History had been forged by these men, by the Hitlers and Napoleons, the Freuds and the Edisons, the Caesars and Stalins. Everyone else followed in their wake.

Maxwell was a Right Man. Jack was not. It was this that had made the difference, more than the files his boss had acquired on his early life, more even than the covert threats made against his remaining family. All of that family was dead now. They could no longer contribute to Jack's internal defenses against culpability. His parents had died of natural causes, five and seven years previously. His wife lay in two different forests. She had been first to go, a decade past. Jack had been present while Maxwell had dismembered her, seen the man introduce his penis into a variety of Janine's body cavities, including her breached skull. Jack had been drugged at the time, but only lightly. He had not much liked his wife. Maxwell had known this. The event sealed the partnership.

"If you were not able to stop me doing this thing, you cannot stop me doing anything. It is better that you do what I tell you. That you work for me. Let me give you direction. I am a Right Man, and so I will always prevail. Always. Accept that, and let me tell you what to do."

Jack had. He had become thief and procurer, a general factotum of evil. In the end he had even earned a nickname from his employer, albeit a derisive one. With brutal and affectionate irony, he sometimes called Jack his "right man." Not because, he emphasized, Jack had become dominant, or because he had any chance of doing so. He was merely the right man for the job, the right man for Maxwell, the man who would do whatever he was told, who was snared both physically and emotionally, who was his for forever and a day. Jack assumed that Maxwell must have had previous right men, and that their bodies would never be found. He had further suspected that he would share their fate at some point, that his boss would suddenly erase him—and that he would never see the event coming. But then Maxwell had fallen foul of some dominant little cell, prey to an expansionist speck of flesh, and everything had changed.

Not quite everything. Maxwell would follow his dream to the last, and that dream was extremity. The best and worst, doing things that had not been done, or doing them better or worse or harder or longer than anyone else. Maxwell had to win. The manner of his passing would be exactly the same, and under his control. Jack understood this was why the window had already been open when he entered the room. It was Maxwell's dream, and Maxwell's death. Jack had only ever been an extra pair of hands. Even after everything, that's all he was.

"We've done such things."

Jack turned to see that Maxwell was looking at him. The cigarette had been dropped to the floor, was gently smoldering on a surface that had seen blood and urine and shit and semen spilt and smeared and wiped countless times. When Jack shut his eyes at night it was generally these things he smelled, the odors now locked behind his eyelids and tattooed on his brain.

"Such things," the old man repeated.

For a moment Maxwell looked almost wistful, and Jack was horrified to realize he felt sorry for him. The dream was over, and there was only one more experience to be had. However purposeful, and perverse, and extreme, it would still be the last. The pity disappeared quickly, a homeopathic dot in a sea of hate.

Yes, they had done things. Such things had they done. Hundreds dead, many more violated in ways that beggared belief. Not everything had involved violence and death, not by a long shot. There had been experiences and tastes and concoctions that any man or woman might like to sample, had they merely the persistence and money and will to seek them out, to bend the world to their desires, to dominate reality itself until it yielded unusual fruit. There were extremes of happiness too, of mere strangeness, of the purely arbitrary. But it was the blood that came back to you, the endless shrieking gallons of it, the slick and sticky lubricant that most people saw so little of, but in which he sometimes felt as if he was lacquered from head to foot. The nights spent in bars, buying drinks and then crossing parking lots with the staggering doomed; the men used and betrayed and dispatched, none mourned with anything more profound than an airy "Just weren't one of the five percent, Jack"; the promises to children that were never kept, all the walks into twilight woods, so many walks, and not one of them ending in a land where everything was candy and puppy dogs.

Jack realized that when Maxwell died he would have no one to blame for his part in all of this; no one still living, at any rate, and he knew that would make a difference. As the man's dominance and power faded, as it must surely do once he was dead, it might become harder and harder to believe that someone else had brought him to this place, that he hadn't been equally to blame. When the Right Man disappears, his followers wake up and remember what they have done, have to find explanations in heads and hearts that are suddenly empty. This was perhaps a third reason why Maxwell had been in no danger from Jack in the last years. Either way, very soon this balm of subjugation would disappear, and when he thought of that, Jack felt afraid.

Maxwell noticed him glancing into his coffee cup. "Yes," he said. "Almost done. Looking forward to it?"

"Just hope it's all you think it's going to be," Jack said, and was surprised to find the sentiment was genuine.

Maxwell smiled, and drank the last mouthful. He stood, and Jack unconsciously took a step backward. Not to get out of range, he didn't think, but just because the man's field was so strong. However widely the gates of hell yawned for him, how the devil himself might be thinking that genuine competition was on the way, you had to concede Maxwell's self-will: the will of a man who would leave his very considerable estate to three political organizations who were known to fund prolifically successful terrorist groups, so that the fun could continue when he was gone; the will of a man who could command his body and mind to do exactly what he wanted and not concede to the demands of cringing flesh; the will, finally, of a man who would choose this way to die.

Jack had no doubt that he would go through with it. No doubt at all. Maxwell had announced it to him on the very day the cancer had been discovered, before it was even clear that he was going to die.

Maxwell was going to leave the world from his own penthouse, from the center of his life. He would not, however, be using either the elevator or the stairs. His final second of existence, his last sortie into the dream, would be experiencing the moment in which his head connected with the sidewalk twenty-three floors below. Most men would pass out before they hit the ground, either through terror or the physiological effects of the descent. Maxwell was confident he would be able to resist these pressures, and Jack believed him. The brain that had created so many events to haunt the world, that had dreamed the horrific and beautiful into life, would be extinguished in contemplation of its own violent dissolution. Like the severed head of the guillotined rolling away from its former body, its last vision would be of the concrete proof of the extreme brevity of this final perception. Unique. Supreme. Completely in control. Utterly Right.

Maxwell walked over to the window. He paused for a moment, looking up at the sun, which was heading westward to join the night at the end of the day. Jack wondered whether he should offer assistance, but knew it would be unwelcome. It was unnecessary either way. Maxwell vaulted up onto the sill with one clean and graceful movement.

He stood there a full minute, poised above death, his coat flapping in the breeze like that of some vampire king. He looked down at Jack and winked, the eyelid's movement slow and lascivious.

The Right Men

"What are you going to do, Jack? How will you spend your days now?"

Jack shook his head dumbly. All at once, he didn't know.

"Good-bye," Maxell said, and dived.

He didn't fly away. He fell.

Jack stepped over to the window and watched him go. All he could see was the coat billowing, as Maxwell rocketed toward the earth head first, ensuring that his brain would be at the point of contact, that the experience would not be marred in some crumpled confusion of limbs. And Jack smiled.

He turned away, picked the files up from the table. The wink had been proof, its lazy slide, the least graceful movement Jack had ever seen in his employer. From that wink, it could only have been seconds away.

Jack knew about drugs. Jack had used many different types, over and over again, watched countless people blink their way to the start of a final week they had not anticipated and could never have comprehended. He'd chosen Neprotabulin today because it was so precisely predictable, because its effects were delayed and then came quickly and stealthily. He knew that the few micrograms he had slipped into the coffee had ensured that the old man had been unconscious within seconds of leaving the windowsill, that the head that had collided with the earth had been incapable of perception.

That the final experience had not happened.

That Maxwell had not felt it. That he had only died.

Jack strode over to the elevator, a spring in his step. The doors opened automatically for him.

He stepped in, pulling out his packet of cigarettes. Maxwell might have sullied the anticipated moment, but he had not destroyed it. For all his power and will, the old fuck was gone. Now that his brain was strewn over several square yards of filthy sidewalk, that was it. The Right Man was dead, and the right man survived.

If Jack smoked enough cigarettes, in time the smoke would cover the smell of the blood. He took a long drag. It tasted good. He didn't cough. He too possessed will, and it was now this will that would prevail.

It didn't occur to him that the old man might have foreseen him using the elevator, not until it was too late.

The doors closed. He pressed the button.

The Raptures of the Deep

BY ROSALEEN LOVE

How I used to enjoy the shimmer of light on water. Now I look out and know it is from there that the terrors that beset us have come. Worms walk on the land and blind white crabs skittle and skuttle and munch and slide under doorways and ride elevators to penthouse suites and adapt to underground tunnels and eat and eat and eat everything that they find.

Crustal plates collide. The earth quakes and people have cell phones and call from the fallen house, the village deserted and all around them fled.

The giant squid came from a trawl a thousand meters down the Manus Trench. They showed it on TV, flopped off the edge of the dissection slab, eyes glazed, tentacles akimbo. An intelligent species, they said, its neural system intricate and mysterious.

Tasted good, stir-fried with garlic and ginger, at least the parts that didn't turn to mush on the haul up from the pressures of the deep. Curious pads on the tentacular tips. The camera zoomed to close-up. Pads too tough for stir-fry.

The sea crept farther up onto the land. Worms island-hopped, crossing species from fish to pigs to human, the way these things do, from Manus to the islands strung out along the coast, one by one, until they reached Moresby, Brisbane, London, Paris, Rome.

It was my job to fit stuff like this together into a pattern. I look at things you won't find in the formal systems of zoology. If I say Bigfoot, you get the lunatic end of the spectrum, but giant squid, oarfish that bask on the surface of the water, monster turtles that walk up onto the beaches, that was my scene. Cryptozoology.

That was how I found myself in the submersible a couple of k's under the sea down the Manus Trench.

Scott drove. I observed. Worked with Scott before, down the Pual Ridge, with the NASA nuclear program. Bad news, that. Dump radioactive waste down a hydrothermal vent, see where it gets you.

I had been with Scott enough times to cope with fear of the submersible, fear of being crushed to death in the deep. I had faith in the vehicle and the equipment. What if it failed? Death would come swiftly. The prospect of a swift death if things go wrong, I could handle that. I was not afraid of my own personal death. But I discovered there are things worse than the death of the individual, and it was on that dive I began to know it.

After Pual, Scott took off and went to work for Tristar. Mined deep under the sea, two kilometers near the hydrothermal vents. Brought up gold, copper and silver. Other stuff as well, squid, fish, worms, mussels, crabs, stuff that exploded on the way to the surface, so that gold came mixed with the shredded flesh of rare and wondrous deep-sea creatures.

There'd been trouble at Tristar. As we sank under the sea, Scott filled me in. "That squid on TV? Get this. That squid was only the beginning. The TV crew came on board. They wanted a squid and we got them a squid."

I looked out into the dark around us. "Nobody goes to all this trouble for a squid." I shivered. We were padded against the cold, but still it seeped through, getting colder and colder as we descended. Our headlights poked through gloom.

I caught glimpses through thick glass, and readings on the sonar, of creatures that came and went, registering as shadows in the glass, on the screens of the panel of instruments.

"The trawl gear went down and the squid came up from a thousand meters, right? That's only halfway to the bottom. Halfway down to the vents on the ocean floor."

At the vents, liquid rock and superheated steam surge from the earth's core. There's a smell that bubbles to the surface round the Tristar mining ships, part bad eggs, part rotting fish.

In my line of business, you soon develop peculiar tastes, at least they seem weird to others. Bella didn't like the person I became when I started work on the trawls. She soon took off. I didn't notice the slide from good to bad. I descended into weirdness without knowing it and others couldn't or wouldn't get used to the weirdness that entered into me, that wouldn't let me go back to whoever I once was, that bright-eyed boy straight out of ecology school, ready to take on the world and change it for the better.

Down deep in the vents, life takes a sulfurous path. Sulfur feeds microbes; microbes form mats; worms grow in the mats; fish eat worms; blind white crabs eat everything. Dark ecosystems exist, with dark thoughts, dark motives, dark desires.

"More to come," said Scott. "Got some black smokers down there, you'd love them. Beauties. Name of Satanic Mills. Roman Ruins." Black smokers form where black steam feeds the red-fronded tubeworms, and crabs claw their way across smoking fumaroles.

"Okay, the trawl goes ahead. We get the squid and bring it up, but the net is weird, full of large holes. The net is tough stuff, monofilament sure, but thick. It just can't break. But it can burn."

First I'd heard of it.

"Tore holes the size of houses, looks like the mother of Jaws got there before us. Get this. They found stones tangled in the nets. The rocks shouldn't have been there. Ocean floor's a thousand meters farther down. What're they doing, halfway to the surface? And they were hot, burning hot to touch."

My field, as I said, is cryptozoology. I study the rare and wondrous, the animals of folklore and personal testimony, not yet the creatures of formal classification in zoology. I study the creatures of the deep that have washed up onto land, here a half-rotten carcass, or the distant sighting of a monster by a sailor exhausted by the night watch, deeply untrusting of the testimony of his senses. They call me when they do not know what it is they are encountering and it becomes necessary that they know in order to do the work of the day.

I never knew about hot rocks until they hit me.

They hit and the submersible juddered to one side with a series of huge jolts to the metal shell. They came like asteroids pounding a spaceship.

Scott moved fast. He kept his eyes on the sonar and dodged through breaks in the blips. He guided the sub like a spacer.

I watched. I listened. I felt.

The Raptures of the Deep

The noise was deafening. Before, the sea had seemed empty, with few things out there to watch us watching them. Now, caught in the wildly swinging headlights, I could see what was hitting us. Rocks like the rocks Scott talked about, but these rocks were covered in wildlife. Large red tube-worms, giant mussels, white crabs skittering. The rocks hit the glass, and I could see the worms squelch up against the glass and disintegrate. I sensed the power of ancient forms of life that followed the path not taken by life that, long ago, had crawled up from the sea to colonize the land.

I looked again at the sonar screen. It wasn't a random pattern of rocks on the screen. The rocks were on the move, but in the same direction.

Scott saw it too and swiftly steered us to one side, out of the tumbling rocks.

Looked like the rocks were heading south. "There's been a bit of action in that direction, down on the ocean floor. New vent opening." Scott pointed to the map.

Rocks on the move? Worms moving south? I could hardly believe what he was saying, nor accept what I was seeing. A vent opens in the cold depths of the ocean. Soon red-fringed worms appear, and giant clams. New life arrives, mysteriously, across the cold dark sea. Life that loves heat travels through deep cold.

"How's it going?" I asked Scott. He was checking out the instruments. "Want out of this?"

"Still looking good," said Scott. Scott was skipper. "We'll keep going."

The sub dived and the rock belt vanished off the screens.

Red eyes glinted at us, red eyes floating in the sea. Millions of tiny red eyes. Mussels and worms floated free in the water, huge worms writhing around the submersible, pressing against the glass, looking in. Worms don't have eyes. Red-eyed shrimps clustered in red fronds, navigator shrimps, shrimps with a sense of direction, showing worms where to go, what camera to slither over, what hatch to prise open, what human to head for, what gut to infect, what . . .

I caught myself falling into panic and pulled back.

Scott sat at the controls, frozen. I shook him.

Worms don't have eyes, but they have worked out ways to see. There's something stirring out there.

Scott was out to it. His eyes were open, but he did not move.

We continued to sink, as if weighted by heavy stone.

Scott passed out. He slumped over the control panel.

I yelled at him, and punched him, and pushed him away from the controls, his eyes closed, his breathing shallow.

If I was in an auto on the highway I'd reach over, try to take the wheel, try to pull the keys out, screech to a stop, anything to stop the vehicle moving.

I did not know how to drive the sub.

They have hit the oxygen supply, I thought, the rocks, the worms. They have done something to our air and soon I shall pass out, like Scott, and never wake up. I am caught in the raptures of the deep. I am narced, like a diver where bubbles in blood and brain bring on a swift descent into drunkenness. I am going deeper and deeper into unknown places. The cold of the sea has entered my bones and the spirit of these dark places has entered my blood and I am enraptured.

From the lofty plateaus of my bubbling thoughts I felt deep pity for Scott. His mind had caved in to the darkness of unknowing. I sought out the other minds out there, minds that were open to me, and I heard their call. I had the desire to go deeper, that exhilaration that cuts in sharply and rides the diver with a madness of the spirit, in which is entwined the intellectual desire to know, to go deeper, and deeper, forever. I must know the raptures of the deep, even if that knowledge kills.

I looked out at the waving fronds of life and knew they were showing us what they could do. They were showing the way the human world will end.

We will come to our natural end, just as the dinosaurs and the woolly mammoths.

The submersible bobbed to the surface, rescued by the dead man's clutch. We came aloft and they said I had bad dreams down there, with the lack of air and the damage to the controls.

I wait, here in my chalet high in the Alps, and look at the world and see the links between this and that, here the rise of the sea level, there an infestation of intestinal worms.

Weird life is coming on land, like it's migrating. It's coming to change our world. Change, when it happens, will be sharp and swift.

What did I see? I saw a whole lot of wildlife where it shouldn't have been, doing things it shouldn't have known how to do, sulfurous life with a kind of instinct, a talent for survival. All life has it. Witness the worms.

The thoughts I have are dark and formless.

They are on the march and they're bringing their environment with them.

The Raptures of the Deep

The first colonists they send out will die, just as with the first Pacific voyagers who sailed out from their homes to distant lands. Some made it to New Zealand; many others died along the way. They're bringing their home environment with them, as once the New Zealanders brought their trees, their dogs, their pigs.

The dark world brings warm stones, clouds of sulfurous bacteria, shoals of mutating worms.

That which is under the sea is coming out onto land. Life that glows with the sulfurous flame will rise up to terraform the earth. They will bring the earth back to where it once was, just as once oxygen-based life took over from those that preferred an atmosphere of methane. Once more the red fronds of the giant tubeworms will waft in bubbles of volcanic gases, at Yellowstone and Rotorua, and the mats of sulfur-munching bacteria spread outward from mud springs to slide over and smother the green plants of the land.

I came back from below knowing too much. Once we were fearful that spaceships would come from the sky, with aliens. But now I know that yes, they are sending their ships to earth, but theirs are the ships that rise up from beneath. We were wrong to think they would come from the skies.

They are all carnivores down there.

Out Late in the Park

BY STEVE RASNIC TEM

Once again, Clarence Senior has let the ball get away from him. The other men gasp when it rolls out of the shadowed circle formed by our beloved trees and into the brilliant sunlight baking the sand paths where the beautiful young people stroll. Jacob, one of our oldest, scowls bitterly. I raise an eyebrow in warning—or I believe I do. Facial control has been more difficult these past few months. Often I'm not sure whether my thin line of mouth is smiling or twisted into some shape less agreeable.

As has been typical for him, Jacob ignores me. "He'll spoil it!" he growls through a swallow of phlegm. "He'll spoil it for all of us!"

I raise my hand to stop him, but too late because I can feel the stirrings of the angled things that dwell at the edges of the sunlit path. It's a terrible thing, worrying that every spat of anger might cause your heart to seize, and then the whole of your works comes tumbling down and there's no more light in you than a dark stone at the bottom of a pond. Finally Jacob recognizes my warning and stops, takes a deep, savored breath as if it's to be his last one. Which it might be, of course. In this park of the world suddenness is the business of the day.

Clarence Senior, as usual, appears to be somewhat lacking in orientation. He trots playfully after the volleyball. I envy the looseness of his stride, something my own arthritis denies me. But I am pleased that one of our own can still play with such reckless abandon.

"He'll get hit by a car!" George cries nonsensically. "We'll all get hit by cars!" This has been George's signature warning since he first started coming to the park. I assume his family has some tragic history related to the automobile, but of course I do not inquire. Men of our age trust each other well enough not to ask. We all assume tragedy and imagine disaster. Perhaps this makes us less sympathetic—certainly it makes us impatient. And burying the curiosity of our youth has become a measure of the respect we have for one another.

Although if truth be told I would say we respect nothing more than the dark, and the half-remembered things which move there.

Now the others are yelling. Of course I have seen this phenomenon before—all of us are quick to panic. It is something that happens to the nerves, I suppose, as the nervous system constantly monitors to determine if the flesh is still alive. Men my age understand the process. There is nothing worse than waking up in the middle of the night to discover that a favorite extremity has died.

"*Get him back!*" Joseph sobs. He is a weepy thing, old Joseph, moreso than the rest of us even though as a group we are a weepy bunch indeed. "*Get him back!*" Again, with that disturbing flail of movement-limited arms. Some sort of stroke, I believe. Strokes are as common among our kind as flies on newly-harvested meat.

"Just stop it! Stop it!" I complain, unable to bear their old-guy whining a second longer. "Can't you just let him play? We have plenty of extra balls—grab a couple and toss them around! Nothing's going to happen to him, or any one of us because of him!"

I do not believe any of this, of course, but it gets their minds off Clarence. He retrieves the ball from a beautiful young woman who has been watching us from the edge of one of those sunny paths. I stare at her for some time, even after Clarence Senior has jogged happily back into our little circle. The other men quickly close around him in case he's been followed.

The young woman is unusual in that she has noticed us. We are not used to being noticed at all, especially by beautiful young women. I wonder if those of us with daughters—Jacob, Samuel, perhaps one or two others—feel the same confused anticipation when a young woman looks at them. I wonder if they suffer from the same temporal dislocation of desire the rest of us experience.

She looks quite familiar. But then all the young women look familiar to me. By the time a man reaches my age he has stockpiled the blueprints of a thousand young women in the caves of his memory, ready for somber perusal during the long lonely hours before dawn.

The young woman's eyes lock with mine and she slips in a quick smile. My heart speeds as a long stem of black insect leg darts from one corner of her mouth and scratches futilely at her chin before her dark red tongue can usher the leg back inside her mouth.

I look away as if with mere embarrassment, as if some part of her garment had slipped away and revealed more than might be decent. When I look back she is gone, but the ground where she stood appears blackened and torn.

Joseph injures himself again. His eyes are always filling with tears and then he can't see more than a few inches in front of him. He runs into things and then he falls down hard. Clarence Senior is always trying to help by convincing him that he isn't *really* hurt. "See, no blood!" Clarence Senior shouts with no small measure of delirium. He says this every time, even when there's blood gushing from the wound. Everything is A-OK in Clarence Senior's world, even though Clarence Junior hates him, even though he has the worst nightmares of us all.

"Throw *me* the ball! Me me me!" George cries, his belly moving independently of his leap. Benjamin the retired carpenter—perhaps the best coordinated of us all—throws the ball and George drops it. No one laughs or complains—it has always been George's job to drop the ball. He staggers back and forth as he attempts to pick it up, frustrated to tears because his knees will not bend properly. If someday he were to magically acquire competence there would be considerable tension generated in the group, for only by comparison do the rest of us remain competent.

Benjamin shuffles after the ball like some huge, shaggy toy run by remote control. No one knows very much about Benjamin—he started playing with us one day as if he'd always been here. He has never spoken. I get the impression that he simply has nothing to say and will not pretend. A far better way of being in the world, I think. The rest of us speak constantly, fueled more by anxiety than idea.

We toss the ball and drop the ball, we run around things called bases, worshiping at each one briefly before being urged on by the impatient cries of our companions. The bases are old schoolbooks, interestingly shaped stones, stakes ripped from the hard hearts of trees and driven almost flush into the ground. Who among us would have the power to execute such a pounding? It has always been here, driven ages ago by some comic-book hero or other. It would be nice to linger, but our fear is that to stop even briefly, to stop at all, would be to invite the fragments of black into our mouths, into our ears and eyes and anuses, until all motion is stopped forever.

So this tired old group of us, we play and we play and we play, pretending to have fun until like toddlers run amuck we collapse into the arms of our mothers at the end of the day.

But, of course, our mothers are not there at the end of the day. Most of us cannot even remember how our mothers died, or how they've otherwise left us. But we think about our mothers often, during these last, long days of play in the park, for we are still the melancholy boys we always were, late for dinner and crying over the day's small, misplaced treasures.

Late in the afternoon Samuel arrives from his job by bright yellow taxi, his favorite mode of transportation. He is the only one of us to continue in a state of gainful employment. He sits down on the graffiti bench ("Peggy loves Frank, but what about God?" "Sing and play all day, but whatever you do don't go past the path at night") for his daily cry, the rest of us gathering around him for our daily pretense of comfort. "They act like I'm *stupid*!" he complains. "Like I'm too old to learn anything new!"

We all pat his back and his knee, more fiercely now, agreeing vigorously although we really have no idea what we're agreeing to. We have never been to Samuel's work and most of us haven't worked a regular job in years. Still we know how it can be out there. Any man knows, past a certain age. The world is something new every day, something you've never seen before, something you feel hopeless to understand. The colors of the world shift their spectrum with each rising of the sun. The mouths of the world mutate the words of the world even as they are formed. "Damn bosses . . . damn wireless whatevers . . . damn computers . . ." We all nod our understanding. Damn whatevers, indeed.

Then there is Willy, standing in his corner of the field waiting for the ball to come to him. He would wait all day if we let him, and more often than not we do, for we enjoy observing his profound patience.

"It's not patience," Jacob declares. "He's just an idiot."

If there is truth in what Jacob says we do not want to know about it. Willy does not appear to suffer the fears that bother the rest of us. Willy has no need for hand-holding. Willy does not appear to need at all. Willy simply stands, and waits, watching for whatever comes next, a ball, or a butterfly, or fragments broken off the shadows and stealing across the lawns.

We try to prevent the ball from coming Willy's way. He would not know what to do with it. He is a watcher, you see.

"He has about a thimbleful of brain," is the way Jacob so delicately puts it. Jacob thinks it is shameful the way I let Willy groom himself: unshaven, hair long and stringy, greasy. Jacob has even brought shampoos and razors to the park from time to time, "to take care of poor Willy. Shameful the way we've let him go like that." As if Willy were an unkempt yard or a dog needing to be trimmed.

But I always wave Jacob away. Willy is not exactly happy, but he is stable the way he is, and some things should not be tampered with.

Again I see the pretty young woman at the edge of our area, watching. I cannot keep my eyes off her. The beauty of young women is something I truly miss, being able to touch them, to admire them openly. Not that there is no beauty in older women, or that the feelings I'm expressing are primarily sexual. But so much is recalled when I see the newness in them, the untutored look as their eyes open up to the world.

A sudden breeze lifts her hair, revealing a sheen of brittle membranes close to the skull. Small nodules like eggs nestle around her ears and above her forehead. Tiny shapes pulse and jerk in the sacs. As one begins to erupt into a flowering of dark, segmented parts the breeze mercifully drops her hair back over the assemblage.

We are all supposed to be having fun here. Even though sometimes we try a little too hard, laugh a little too hard for comfort. But what are you going to do? Far better than the alternative. That is what everyone says. That is what all the old people say.

At five o'clock we line up and the designated adult checks the pockets of the others. We stand at lazy attention with our hands stretching our pockets inside out and sideways so they resemble a pair of large ears. Clarence Senior always requires some encouragement; Willy has to have his pockets turned inside out for him; and nine times out of ten George will be hiding something, so we have to watch him especially carefully to make sure he does not do anything that is going to get him into trouble. More often than not I am the designated adult, a fact that I often resent and can be quite bitter about. In those instances I always have Jacob check my pockets—I never keep anything in there besides some hard candy for the others.

By eight o'clock we are well into drowsy, although most of us will fight sleep with our last breath. We sit up on our bedding and talk about the day's games and share memories of our mothers, now and then twisting our heads around to make sure that a particular piece of night remains respectfully in its place.

Jacob and I are always the last to fall asleep. Sometimes I think it is because we feel a certain paternal responsibility for the others. Sometimes I think it is because we think our alertness will protect us from the inevitable.

In the middle of the night they come for Willy. I am somewhat comforted that he shows no signs of surprise. Surely, this is what he has always been waiting for. Tonight they come as eight or nine squirrels and a large black bird with a broken neck. The bird bothers me most: its head flops and stretches painfully on the narrow strand of neck flesh as it still manages to grab a bit of Willy's pants in its beak and pull with the squirrels to drag Willy's body off into the night. Now and again one of the squirrels will let go and turn its head, smiling at me so broadly I can see that all its teeth are missing.

Some people, I believe, are paid for dreaming. But most, I think, are punished.

In a few days they will come to take another of us. Rabbits, perhaps, or snakes, or shiny emerald-green beetles, or an old dog that so resembles one from our childhood we will be convinced it is the very same. Soon only Jacob or I will be left.

But that is the worst kind of wish fulfillment. How do I know I will be a survivor? At some things the imagination fails.

I know I should not whine about it. It is a natural process that happens to everyone. You can wait for it or you can play with it; you can roll your ball at it or you can run headlong into the cars that seem to be everywhere. But what you cannot do is stop it from coming.

Each morning we awaken to find that life is a bit less understandable. Each morning we awaken to the disappearance of the known. Each morning we awaken to discover that we have missed the last bus for the life to come.

Bedfordshire

BY PETER CROWTHER

The clock in the hallway tells the time,
The saddest hour of the day draws near
And all good children now must climb
The wooden hill to Bedfordshire.

> —Samuel Cleaker (1861–1929),
> *The Coming of Morpheus*

The air is full of our cries. But habit
is a great deadener.

> —Samuel Beckett (1906–1989),
> *Waiting For Godot*

(1) 12 JUNE 2001

Dear Diary,

Last night in bed I stroked Helen's back while I read the newspaper, as I've done ever since we got married. I didn't read much, just scanned the headlines. And I didn't turn around to look at her and give her a kiss before bedding down, the way I usually do. As I was trying to get to sleep, I heard someone moving around outside the room: probably Helen, still restless—it's only her third night away from me—but it could have been Nanny. I didn't get up to look . . . and, thank God, she didn't come into the room.

(2) 16 OCTOBER 1943

"Come in, lad," Meredith shouts, his voice booming into the corridor.

The boy steps into the prefect's room and smells furniture polish, burning tobacco and crumpets toasting.

"Helliwell said you wanted to see me, Meredith?"

"Indeed I do, young man," he says, "indeed I do." His face beams at the boy, his eyes glinting. He wafts his prefect's gown around behind him and stands facing the boy, his back to the roaring fire, a couple of crumpets, cut in half, suspended above the flames on a kind of makeshift pulley. It's warm, that's the first thing that really strikes the boy about the room. The next thing is the table. And the leather straps.

"Now, Bellings, what do you know about cunts?"

"Sir? Nothing, sir."

"Buggery?"

Hands clasped behind his back, the boy shakes his head.

"Close the door, there's a good chap," Meredith says. He turns to the fire, drops his cigarette into the flames and lifts the crumpets onto the hearth.

(3) 4 DECEMBER 1936

"Have you had a good birthday, Thomas?" His mother leans over from the chaise longue and, without affection, ruffles his hair. She doesn't bother that her arms crease the newspaper she's reading.

"Answer your mother, Tommy," Nanny chides.

"Nanny, the boy's name is Thomas. Kindly use it."

"Yes, ma'am." She turns to the boy and though her face is impassive, her eyes are smiling. *Take no notice, Tommy*, they seem to say. "Answer your mother," she says.

"Yes, mother," he says. A part of him feels guilty in some way, guilty for having enjoyed himself. Perhaps, he thinks, it is this feeling of guilt that prevented him from responding immediately.

Over by the fireplace, the boy's father holds a lighted taper above his pipe bowl and then wafts out the flame. He draws heavily on the pipe and the boy watches the smoke waft out of the corners of his father's mouth.

"So," his father says, throwing his head back and allowing a cloud of smoke to drift up toward the ceiling, "how does it feel to be four years old, eh?"

He feels Nanny's hand on his back, gently rubbing him, encouraging him to speak.

"It feels very nice, sir."

" 'Very nice,' eh?" his father says. "What do you say to that, Emily?"

"Capital!" his mother exclaims and, without any obvious reason, they both start to laugh. Nanny pats the boy's back.

"Well, you've had a busy day, young man," his father says, the pipe stem back in his mouth. "Time to bivouac. Nanny."

Nanny moves her hand up to the boy's shoulder and pats it once before gripping tight and turning him around. "Time to climb the wooden hill to Bedfordshire," she whispers in his ear, her voice creaking with smiles.

"I'll be up later," his father shouts after them. Nanny's grip tightens for the briefest of moments and then relaxes again. As they approach the staircase, she pulls him toward her the way she always does at the end of the day.

"It's all right, Nanny," he tells her.

But it isn't really.

(4) 4 JUNE 2001

"Tom?"

"Yes?"

"It's Graham. I was ringing to see how Helen was doing."

"Not too bad, considering. Had her down to the park this afternoon. She seemed to enjoy it."

"Good."

"How's Evelyn?"

"Oh, Evelyn's fine."

"Do give her my—*our*—love, won't you?"

"Of course, of course."

Pause.

"I . . . I don't suppose there's any change, is there?"

"Change?"

"Yes, in Helen . . . in her condition."

"No, no change."

"Oh."

"I don't think it will be long now."

"No, I suppose not."

"Anyway, I must go. There's a lot to do."

"Of course."

"I'll tell her you called, Graham."

"Yes, do that. And tell her Evie sends her love."

"I will."

"I'll call again in a couple of days."

"Right."

"Just to see how she is."

"Yes. Right."

"Cheerio then, Tom."

"Cheerio."

(5) 7 JANUARY 1944

Of course, after just the first visit to Meredith's rooms, he realizes he already knew all about buggery . . . and, indeed, cunts, though Meredith is ever keen to expand the boy's understanding of the development of language.

On each of the subsequent occasions, the pain of the straps cutting into his wrists is more bearable for he has discovered that if he holds himself still, he is able to minimize the pain. At least the pain from his wrists. The only thing that keeps him going is the handle on the closed door, which he watches from the table he is stretched across. In that handle lies the means to his escape when he can no longer endure his education.

He has learned that the first cited instance of the word "cunt" occurred in a London street name "Gropecuntlane" around 1230. It was probably accepted long before that, Meredith tells him breathlessly during one of the boy's visits, for it was first recorded in Middle English circa 1200. Indeed, he tells the boy when he has finished, there are many ancient cognate Germanic forms: the old Norse *kunta*. the Dutch *kunte*, and even the French *con*. "Though such was regarded," Meredith says, "as *une terme bas*.

"Then, in the bawdy tale of Chaucer's Miller," he continues, "the variant '*queynte*' "—he spells it out—"appears: '*Hir quente abouen hir kne.*' "

It is another couple of visits before he learns that the word "bugger" derives from the French *Bougre*, meaning "a Bulgarian": "It carries the sense of 'a heretic' from the fourteenth century and 'a sodomite' from the sixteenth. The term was used by Dan Michel in 1340 in condemning 'false Christians.'

"The sexual application," Meredith explains, at great pains (though not as great as those endured by the diminutive boy) to demonstrate, "is probably a malicious extension in physical terms of the idea of spiritual perversion."

Indeed.

(6) 4 DECEMBER 1936

His father steps into the bedroom, the light from the corridor illuminating him from behind. He is just a dark figure without a face, but the boy knows it's him. And he knows what he wants. He curls up tightly and hugs his teddy bear.

His father closes the door and the room plunges into darkness again.

The floorboards creak as he comes across to the boy's bed.

"Turn over onto your side, young man," he whispers. "I have another birthday present for you." The boy can smell alcohol and tobacco on his father's breath. As he lies on his side, he fixes his eyes on the door handle.

(7) 6 JUNE 2001

Dear Diary,

The doctor came around today and put Helen onto morphine. I always thought it would need to be injected but he's just given her a bottle of what looks like cough mixture. She had one dose while he was here and another one tonight with her tea—just a couple of slices of bread and jam. She didn't want anything cooked. She seems to have lifted a little—her spirits, I mean. But her chest is really bad. Sounds like she's breathing underwater. The doctor says her lungs are filling up quite badly. He says he's amazed I'm able to cope. The Macmillan nurse asked me if we didn't have any relatives that could give me a hand—I know she was meaning children. I just told her there wasn't anyone. She asked me if I had any trouble with the neighbors. I said we didn't and asked why she'd asked. She just shrugged and said she'd heard a lot of noise while she was

Bedfordshire

washing Helen and I had gone to the shops. I blamed it on old houses.

"How did he sound?"

Graham replaces the receiver and shrugs. "Distant."

He sits on the sofa and looks across at the television. The mute sign is on in the top left-hand corner and the picture shows a man behind a desk arguing with a woman standing in front of the desk. Evelyn frowns and stares at the screen. She hits the OFF button and says, "So how is she?"

"It was really strange," Graham says, still staring at the now-blank television screen . . . a part of him wondering if the man and the woman are still arguing, and what they were arguing about. "He sounded really calm. He's been calm ever since Helen was diagnosed but not as calm as that."

"Did he say how she was?"

He shakes his head. "He said he's stopped the Macmillan nurse calling at the house."

"*Stopped* her? Whatever for?"

"And the doctor. Apparently the doctor had taken it on himself to call around most days just to see how she was doing."

"Did he say why?"

Graham shrugs. "Why not? The woman's dying and I suppose he thought it was just common court—"

"No, not the doctor . . . Did Tom say why he'd stopped them calling round?"

"He said . . . he said he didn't want her to be distressed any more by all the visitors."

Evelyn frowns.

"It can't be long now, I wouldn't have thought."

"No," she says, the word filled with helplessness . . . and maybe just a tinge of fear: there's none of them getting any younger, she thinks.

"It's after half-ten. Let's watch *Newsnight*."

"Mmm," Evelyn says, and she switches the TV on from the remote.

The man is still behind the desk and now he seems to be arguing with someone else . . . another man. Evelyn surfs until Jeremy Paxman appears. She removes the MUTE and then she places the remote on her lap.

Dear Diary,

I dreamed that Nanny came to see me last night. I was just coming out of the front room and she was walking along from the kitchen. At first I thought she was cross with me but she smiled. She asked me if I'd given any thought to climbing the wooden hill to Bedford-shire. I told her I didn't know how to get there anymore, not since I had grown "big," and I cried. I think I possibly cried for real, in my sleep, because the pillow was wet this morning. Nanny told me not to be so silly—everyone can get to Bedfordshire if they really want to . . . but they really have to want to go in a very big way. "Do you want to, Thomas?" she asked me. "Do you want to go to Bedford-shire?" I remember wanting to ask her to tell me again about Bed-fordshire but I woke up.

(10) 22 MARCH 1937

"Nanny?"

"Yes, Tommy."

"Tell me about Bedfuddsheer."

He feels her hands on his back, rubbing zinc and castor oil cream into the bruises on his bottom.

"In a minute, darling."

Her voice sounds all creaky, like one of the old floorboards in the attic.

"Are you all right, Nanny?" he asks, trying hard to keep his discomfort out of his voice.

"Just a little tired, my love," Nanny says. "There!" She pats his bottom gently. "Pull up your pajama bottoms now and climb between those sheets."

He does as she asks, wincing a little as he bends down.

"I'm still not sure how you manage to get such bruises just by falling over Hammersmith."

He looks across at the stuffed crocodile and widens his eyes at it, committing it to silence. "He was in the way."

"In the way? He's not very big to be in the way of a big boy like you," Nanny says.

Bedfordshire

Pulling the sheets up beneath his chin, he says, "Tell me again about Bed-fuddsheer, Nanny. *Please!*"

"Very well." She sits down on the side of the bed and smiles as he shuffles himself into a comfortable position. He pulls Teddy from behind the pillow and cradles him in his arms, waiting.

"Bedfordshire is a very magical place," she begins. "It's a place where everybody goes when they're asleep. A place where everything is . . . every-thing is right." She emphasizes the word "right" and watches him frown and then smile at the idea of it.

"It's a place where ice cream grows on trees—"

He giggles.

"—where the sun always shines—even in the night—and everyone plays games all day long."

"And all night," he adds, "if the sun is always shining."

"And all night," Nanny agrees. Then she says, "And, best of all, nobody ever hurts anybody there."

The boy's eyes gloss over with understanding: and in that brief exchange, the two of them looking at each other, they are as equals . . . the four-year-old boy from Kensington and the twenty-seven-year-old spinster from Muswell Hill, with nothing between them, be it years or gender or language. He reaches out a small hand and takes hold of Nanny's hand and, just for a second or even the tiniest part of a second, she thinks he is going to pat her hand and tell her not to worry . . . tell her that pain and him are old acquaintances. But almost as soon as it is there, the thought bursts like a soap bubble.

And he says, "Is it a real place, Nanny . . . Bedfuddsheer?"

She gathers her thoughts and nods. "It's real, my love . . . very real . . . but you can only get there if you really want to. You can only get there when you're really really tired."

His eyelids droop momentarily and then widen.

She tucks his hand back beneath the sheets. "Now, are you really really tired, hmmm?"

He nods and pulls Teddy closer.

"And is Teddy really really tired?"

He makes Teddy nod.

"Then off with the pair of you!"

"Off to Bedfuddsheer!" he says.

She stands up and leans over him, plants a kiss on his cheek . . . warm soft flesh that smells of talcum powder. "Off to Bedfuddsheer!"

(11) 8 JUNE 2001

"Bless me, Father, for I have sinned. It's . . . it's a *long* time since my last confession."

"But now you are here."

"Yes. Now I am here."

"God cares little for *when* His children seek His absolution, only that they *do* seek it. We all stray from the one path from time to time; and although it is better not to stray at all, it is good to purge ourselves when we do stray. Confess your sins, my son."

"Are my thoughts counted as sins, Father?"

"If they are harmful or impure thoughts, yes. Are they harmful or impure?"

"Only to me."

"Would it help for you to share them with me?"

"Perhaps."

"Then, in your own time, tell me."

"My wife is very ill. Dying."

"I am truly sorry to hear that, my son."

"I can't imagine life without her. And I'm afraid that, when the time comes for her . . . for her to . . ."

"For her to go on?"

"For her to *die*, Father. I am not convinced that she will go on anywhere. Does that offend you, Father?"

"I am not so easily offended. But tell me . . . if you do not believe in the hereafter, how is it that you believe in God?"

"I did not say that I believed in God."

"Do you?"

"I don't know. I think I'm just a bugger at heart."

"Pardon me?"

"A bugger, Father. Someone once told me that buggers are actually just freethinkers and religious deviants."

"But you know there's another meaning?"

"For the word 'bugger'?"

"Yes."

"Yes. I know that."

"Tell me, why are you here?"

"I . . . I'm not sure. For help."

"Then confess your sins, my son, and I shall do all I can. You were saying that you were afraid of your wife dying . . . ?"

"Yes. And when she does, I . . . I have decided that perhaps I will not want to continue by myself."

"Death comes to us all, my son, but it comes when God wills it not when we ourselves would wish it. You know—or you may remember—that the Catholic Church regards suicide as a mortal sin for which there is no forgiveness."

"Yes. And does that mean that if there is a 'hereafter' then we shall not be together?"

"That is exactly what it means. But maybe you should—"

creak . . .

"Are you still there, my son?"

creak . . . thud

"Are you still—"

"Bless me, Father, for I have sinned. It is two weeks since my last confession."

"Confess your sins, my daughter."

(12) 2 JUNE 2001

Dear Diary,

I seem to be dreaming all the time, whether asleep or awake. Fragments of the past elbow their way into my thoughts and replay themselves with remarkable clarity. Everything is there—the sounds, the feel, the smells. It is as though all time exists in this house, exists here amidst the stillness as though being gathered by Helen's deterioration. And they are rarely good memories. I can't stop thinking about Nanny. This morning, when I came out of Helen's room, I even thought I saw her, just for a second or two, standing against the wall. It was probably just the light and the fact that I'm so tired. Then, this afternoon, I heard Helen call for me but when I went to the foot of the stairs, the stairs seemed to go up and up forever. I couldn't move but when I blinked my eyes the stairs were back to normal. Helen is very weak. I think it is only her reluctance to leave me to fend for myself that keeps her going. Eventually, of course, even that resolve will succumb. I suppose all that I'm going through is only to be expected.

(13) 30 MAY 1950

"Excuse me . . ."

He looks up at the young woman standing against his table. Nods.

"I was wondering . . . is this seat taken?"

"Wha—" He looks across at the seat on the other side of the table, and the scuffed and dirty briefcase that sits upon it, and then glances around the room. He can feel his cheeks coloring. "Is . . . is everywhere else taken?"

The young woman looks around and nods slowly, curling her mouth. "I think so. It's always busy in here before exams."

He reaches over and moves the briefcase to sit on the floor between his feet. "I wouldn't know," he says.

"Oh, are you a freshman?"

"Considering I've been here more than seven months I would have thought 'freshman' might not be quite the word."

He returns his full attention to the book on the table in front of him and doesn't see her make a face at him.

"Sorry," she says, "I certainly didn't mean to offend you in any way. I should have said 'first year.'"

Without lifting his head, he says, "No offense taken."

"What are you reading?"

He sighs and looks up. She is, he realizes now, quite beautiful, her pale complexion with the tiniest hint of pink on the cheeks and lips, topped with a veritable bird's nest of blond hair cut in the fashionable bob. Her expression is one of interest, genuine interest, and so he doesn't mean to sound pedantic when he says, "Right now . . ."—pointing at the book—"or here at King's?" though, on reflection, he feels that he was.

"Both," she says, a slight smile tugging at the corners of her mouth as she leans back on her chair.

He can't help returning the smile. "*Semantics: Studies in the Science of Meaning*," he says, holding up the book as proof, "written by Michel Bréal in 1900, and translated by Mrs. Henry Cust. And here at King's I'm reading English and Medieval History."

Nodding at him while retaining the smile, she thanks him and watches him return his attention to his book.

"Sounds fascinating. Do you enjoy learning about language?"

For a second, his mind drifts.

. . . the first cited instance of the word "cunt" occurred in a London street name "Gropecuntlane" around 1230. It was probably accepted long before that, for it was first recorded in . . .

"Yes," he says.

When he doesn't say anything more, she says, "Do you want to know what I'm reading?"

He grins. "Right now . . . or here at King's?"

Her laugh is like the tiny mobile of cotton reels that Nanny constructed for the nursery back in Kensington. And he joins in, reaching out his hand across the table.

"Thomas—Tom—Bellings," he says.

"Helen," she says, accepting his hand in her own, her touch cool and exciting. "Helen De Beauvoir Chabon."

He repeats her name, just the first one, turning it over in his mouth like the wafers placed on his tongue by the vicar at St. Martin's. "Hel—"

(14) 9 JUNE 2001, 11:47 P.M.

"—en."

She doesn't respond.

He kneels down beside her bed, taking care not to put any pressure on the sheets, and whispers again, breathing out into the musky fragrance of sickness . . . the sweet smell of piano dust and stopped clocks.

"Helen," he says again, his voice hardly louder than a knife gathering butter—more a suggestion of sound than of sound itself—and he holds his hand out near her face, the fingers clawed in upon themselves as though refusing to touch her head.

When he does touch it, lifting a curl of now-greying hair from her forehead, he sees that his fingers are shaking.

"Helen . . . please don't go. Don't leave me. Not yet."

His hand moves down to her wrist and feels for a pulse.

(15) 15 FEBRUARY 1944

"Ah, as I live and indeed do breathe . . . it's young Bellings!" Meredith exclaims.

He stops in his tracks. He was taking the shortcut to the dormitory block, running around the back of the library—out of bounds—and now wishes he had gone through the main school buildings.

Meredith is standing with Burgess the younger and Oxley, the man-mountain of the prefects' contingent at Woodhouse Grove in this year of our Lord, 1944. They are enjoying a cigarette—Capstans—an activity that is out of bounds outside the prefects' rooms or the Common Room.

"Where are you going, lad?" Burgess the younger inquires.

"To my dorm."

"To my dorm *what*, lad?"

"To my dorm, *sir*."

"Leave him be, Bob," says Oxley. Of the three of them, he's the only one not smoking. "On your way, lad."

"He's not on his way *any*where," says Meredith, grinding the cigarette beneath his shoe. "You're not supposed to be back here, are you, lad?"

He shrugs. A fire lights behind his eyes and it is a cold fire, fueled by the ever-present discomfort in his backside. "I often do things I'm not supposed to do," he says, adding—as he glances down at the flattened Capstan—"as we all do from time to time."

Oxley raises his eyebrows.

Burgess the younger's mouth opens involuntarily and he looks aside at Meredith, then across at Oxley and back at Bellings.

"You're a cheeky bugger, aren't you, lad?" Meredith says, wafting his gown behind his back and stepping toward him.

"Cheeky, perhaps," the boy says, "though not without good reason, I believe."

He can feel his heart beating in his temples . . . a strange sensation but one not wholly unpleasant.

"But I can be a bugger only within the early 1700s context of 'fellow' or perhaps 'customer'—for I am undoubtedly a 'customer' of yours am I not,

Meredith?—and not within the 1340 context of 'heretic,' not the 1550s context of 'sodomite' and most certainly not the context of 'bestiality,' also originating in the mid-1500s."

The three faces stare at him, Meredith's eyes glancing sideways at his two companions. He makes to speak, but the boy has not quite finished.

"And anyway," he says, "you said I was a cunt, and then proceeded to demonstrate what a cunt was for . . . an action which I believe—from your own highly imaginative tuition sessions—must qualify *you* as a bugger." He takes a deep breath and shrugs. "One is either a nut or a bolt, *sir*: not both."

Oxley turns to Meredith and frowns.

"William? What's he talking about?"

Meredith shrugs and blusters.

"What do you *mean* by that, lad?" says Oxley.

Bellings maintains a wide-eyed stare and looks from one prefect to another until he has fixed his own eyes onto each of theirs at least once. "With respect, sir, I do not feel it is my place to say more. In fact, I may already have said too much."

"You're damned right there," Meredith says, and he produces his cane from the window ledge behind him. "I think I'll give that arse of yours a little exercise."

Oxley takes hold of Meredith's arm. "If what the lad says is true, William, you've already been giving it a little *too much* exercise."

Meredith laughs in astonishment. "You don't *believe* him!" He looks over at Burgess the younger. "Bob? *You* don't believe him, do you? The little bug— little blighter is trying to discredit me. He needs a damned good hiding."

"William," says Oxley, tightening his grip, "put down your stick." Meredith tries to shake off Oxley's hand, to no avail. "I said put down the stick, William." He turns to Bellings. "To your dorm, lad."

He nods and moves off, carefully skirting around the trio of prefects.

"This isn't finished, Bellings," Meredith shouts. "It isn't finished by a long chalk."

(16) 9 SEPTEMBER 1967

"Mother," he says, nodding curtly.

"I'm pleased you came, Thomas," she says, dabbing her nose with a tiny handkerchief, its sides decorated with pink lace.

He looks back at the coffin. "I wouldn't have missed it for the world," he says.

Helen tugs at his jacket sleeve.

His mother frowns. "I know you didn't get on too—"

"I made my peace with him," he says, dropping his arm and finding Helen's hand with his own.

His mother nods and dabs some more. "I saw you," she says, nodding to the coffin. "Were you . . . were you saying something to him? When you leaned into the coffin?"

He lets go of Helen's hand and reaches into his pocket to produce a hatpin with a pearl end. "No, I was merely ensuring that he was dead," he says, showing the hatpin to his mother. "And I wish I had the time to spare so that I could stay around until I am similarly assured that he is buried. Indeed, my only regret is that tradition dictates that we have to encase him in soft earth rather than in the concrete he deserves."

"Thomas! How could—"

He leans in toward her, ignoring Helen's tugging at his sleeve. "You knew, didn't you, Mother?"

A woman in a large grey hat passes close by to them and he affects a smile while putting his arm around his mother's shoulder. As the woman nods and moves on, her eyes half-lidded in complete understanding, he says, whispering in his mother's ear, "You knew what he was doing, didn't you? You knew he was—"

He wants to say "fucking me up my arse" . . . wants to go on and ask his mother if she knows that, despite its truly wondrous versatility, the word "fuck" is traceable only to the very early 1500s, and even then with thanks only to William Dunbar, a Franciscan preaching friar, while the far more recent "arse" . . . But instead he says:

"—you knew he was abusing me, didn't you? And yet you let him do it."

"How could you *say* th—"

He holds up a hand to stop her. "I'm going now but I shall see you again . . . though I regret that you shall not see *me*." He brings the hatpin up to within a few inches of her face. "And on that occasion—which cannot come soon enough for me—I shall perform my little test once more." He stands up and looks at Helen. She is looking at him with immense sadness. Turning back to his mother, who has clasped her hands in front of the bosom of her black dress, he says, "Good-bye then." He nods once and turns away. "Time to go, I think," he says to Helen.

He hears his mother's voice call after him: "Thom—"

(17) 8 MAY 2001

"—as!"

Helen raises her voice to try to cut through his grief. And it almost works. But he is too distressed and the tears come with moaning shudders.

"Thomas, I haven't gone yet, for goodness' sake."

"How . . . how . . . long?" he asks, the words coming out in breathless hiccups of air.

"Oh, a while . . . it'll be a whi—"

"How long?"

She pulls her mouth into a sad shape and holds his cheek in her hand. "Three months. It could be six, he said, but three is probably the most we can hope for." She shrugs. "I'm so sorry, sweetie."

"Isn't there something— We'll get another opinion. We'll go . . . we'll go somewhere else—America! They'll be able to do something in—"

"It's gone too far," she says, her voice soft and low. "Tommy, we have to be brave."

He shakes his head, dislodging a tear that falls onto her knee. "I can't," he says. "I can't be brave."

(18) 10 JUNE 2001

Dear Diary,

Amazingly, I managed to get some sleep—just a couple of hours. I woke up with a start, my arm around Helen. She was very cold, like ice. I had been dreaming about Nanny—I think that was what woke me up. In the dream, I was trying to find my way up to the bedroom that had mysteriously disappeared. She asked me why— was I tired, she said. I said I just wanted to find my wife. Her name is Helen, I told her. Then Nanny chuckled and did a side-to-side jiggle with her head. Oh, she said, she's not in there anymore. Where is she? I asked. And Nanny pointed along the landing and I saw another set of stairs leading upwards. When I moved along, I couldn't see the top of the stairs. Where do they lead? I asked Nanny. And she told me they went all the way to—

(19) 28 MAY 2001

"Bedfordshire?"

He straightens the sheets around her chest and gives her the biggest smile he can muster. "It comes from an old children's rhyme: 'The clock in the hallway tells the time, the saddest hour of day draws near . . . and all good children now must climb the wooden hill to Bedfordshire.' "

Her laughter turns into a sputtering cough and he puts an arm around her shoulders, pulling her toward him.

"So," she says, regaining her composure, " 'Bedfordshire' means bed, I suppose."

He shrugs. "That's the way most children interpret it—the way most adults interpret it, too—but I think it's more than that. At least, that's what Nanny used to tell me."

"You loved her, didn't you?"

"She was more of a mother to me than my own mother. She was the one who first got me interested in language."

She nods and looks down at her wattled hands, before tucking them beneath the sheets out of sight.

"I'm glad you decided against going to her funeral—your mother, I mean."

He frowns and strokes a hand through her hair. "Why?"

She shudders. "I dreaded you doing that *thing* again . . . the thing with the hat pin. That was terrible, Tommy. Even though I understood how you must have felt—about your father, I mean—it was still a very . . . a very cruel thing to do. So unlike you."

He chuckles. "I didn't do anything with that pin. I took it with me, just to give him a taste of the pain he had inflicted on me all those years . . . but, in the end, I couldn't go through with it."

"But you told her—"

"I just wanted to hurt her then. Wanted her to feel the anxiety I used to feel . . . every night, lying up there in my bed hugging my teddy bear, dreading the sound of the door opening . . ." His voice trails off.

Bedfordshire

"But standing there," he continues, "leaning over his coffin, I could feel only a profound sadness . . . a feeling that I'd been cheated out of a normal father-son relationship—out of even a normal mother-son relationship. And anyway, he was gone by then . . . he wouldn't have felt anything."

She turns around so that she can look into his eyes. "Where do you think he had gone?"

He shrugs and smooths out a crease in the bedcover. "Who knows?"

"Where do you think I'll go, darling?"

He looks at her and feels his eyes begin to sting. "Please," he says, his voice barely more than the whisper of turning pages, "don't let's talk about it."

"But you do believe I'll go somewhere?"

He nods and stands up, feigning normality by increasing the volume of his words. "I believe you'll go to Bedfordshire, which is where everybody goes when they're asleep . . . and that's all that you'll be: asleep."

She accepts his kiss on her cheek, closing her eyes and making a soft groan.

"And what will it be like?"

"In Bedfordshire? Well, it's a place where everything is right . . . where ice cream grows on trees, where the sun always shines—even in the night," he adds, holding an index finger aloft, "—and everyone plays games all day long. But best of all, nobody ever hurts anybody there. And nobody ever feels any pain."

"Sounds wonderful."

"It will be, darling," he says as he watches her eyes close.

"But there'll be just one thing bad about it," she says dreamily as he reaches the bedroom door.

"What could possibly be bad about Bedfordshire?" he asks, in mock astonishment.

"You won't be . . ." But she falls asleep before she can finish.

(20) 10 JUNE 2001

Dear Diary,

It's a little after midnight, 10 June 2001. Helen died fifteen minutes ago, at a quarter to midnight on the 9th. The house feels still and silent and yet it feels busy. There's no other word for it. I feel her presence all around me, a feeling of nervous energy. I can't even begin to explain the way I feel. It's as though my whole world has stopped and I want to make the pains go away and yet I dare not even move. I don't want to speak to anyone, don't want them to know. I dread people trying to console me. What am I going to do?

(21) 10 JUNE 2001

"Mr. Bell—"

"Doctor, there is absolutely no point whatsoever in pursuing this any further. I have made up—"

"With *respect*, Mr. B—"

"I have made up my mind and, what is more important, my wife has made up *her* mind, and we do not require or even desire any further visits from either your very good self or from the district nurses or from the Macmillan nurses. In short, we don't want anyone to visit. Am I making myself clear, Dr. Henfrey?"

"Perhaps I might speak with your wife . . . perhaps she—"

"My wife is resting, doctor. She is very sick and very tired. I do not want her disturbed, either by people visiting the house or by people talking to her on the telephone."

"I'm afraid I'll have to speak with the authorities about this."

"You may speak with whomever you wish, doctor, but you will not be permitted to see my wife. Good day to you."

He hangs up.

There's a movement from upstairs.

"I'm coming, dear!" he shouts . . . and then realizes that the noise cannot have been made by his wife.

(22) 15 JUNE 2001

Dear Diary,

I have made up my mind. There are still lots of pills left, plus the morphine. It should do the trick. This note is for whomever finds it. Please do not think badly of me. I leave behind nobody to mourn my passing, no financial upset, any creditors or dependents. Thus, being of sound

Bedfordshire

mind and body—though the latter is somewhat more infirm of late—
I hereby give notice that I have decided to relinquish the last true pos-
session I have left. The wooden hill calls to me, far too loudly, so I must
respond.

Goodbye,
Thomas Bellings

(23) 7 JUNE 2001

The old man steps out from a covered section on Charing Cross Road, seemingly miraculously appearing out of thin air, and taps his shoulder. "Hello, Bellings," he says.

Bellings turns around, the rain running down his face. "Do I . . . do I know you?"

Taxis go by filled with passengers and the pavement is all but deserted. The rain hammers down and people pass them by, completely ignoring the shabby old man wrapped in what appears to be an Indian blanket . . . ignoring him as though they don't even *see* him.

"You did," the old man says with a chuckle that soon gives way to a throaty cough. "You might say we never saw eye to eye, as it were."

Bellings shakes his head. "I'm sorry, I—"

"Not surprising," the old man continues, "seeing as how you always had your back to me during our little . . . *tête à derrières.*"

Bellings frowns. There is something about the man but—

He leans forward, his face almost touching Bellings' face, and he says, "I always enjoyed our 'conversations' . . . until you got me expelled." He rests a filthy hand on Bellings's gabardine. "Tell me, are you still as much of a cunt as you were? And still as—how shall I say—*accommodating?*"

"Meredith?" Bellings pulls back and a horn blares from the road behind him.

The old man laughs and coughs a thick lump of phlegm into the gutter.

Bellings glances down and then starts to run off toward Cambridge Circus; Meredith shouts after him, "It isn't finished yet, Bellings. But it's closer now."

He finally finds a cab and when he gets inside, it smells of cigarettes. He looks at the sign on the screen behind the driver—THANK YOU FOR NOT

SMOKING—and frowns. As he watches the rain running down the cab's windows, the image of the old man's phlegm—and the maggots crawling around in it—stays with him. As does the fact that, throughout the whole brief conversation, no rain appeared to fall on the old man.

(24) 12 JUNE 2001

He lies in bed pressed up against Helen with an arm draped around her. She's very cold now. Even though he has the window wide open, the whole room smells of freesia, garden compost and used tea bags. And something he can't quite put a finger on.

The bedroom door opens slowly and then closes. Even though his back is to the door, he sees the light from the hallway table lamp wash into the room briefly.

Thomas!

It's Nanny. But "Thomas"? Why is she being so formal?

He doesn't turn around but hears a whimpering. It stops when he pulls the sheet up into his mouth.

Thomas! she says again. *Helen's waiting for you.*

He pulls the sheet up around his face, covering his ears. But not before he hears her tell him it's time to climb the wooden hill.

The door opens again and then closes.

He waits for a long time before falling asleep. Each time he thinks he's close to dropping off, he feels slight movements from the cold skin he's pressed up against.

(25) 10 JUNE 2001

Brrrinnngg! Brrrinnngg!

He looks around at the telephone briefly and then returns his attention to the bottles on the counter.

Seventeen of the little yellow ones and—

Brrrinnngg! Brrrinnngg!

—a whole bottle of the white ones.

That should do it.

Brrrinnngg! Brrrinnngg!

He looks at the bottle of morphine and shakes it. Just for a second, he wonders if he's doing the—

Bedfordshire

Brrrinnngg! Brrrinnngg!

There's a noise from upstairs.

thuuud

thum

He lifts his head as though watching the noise move along the ceiling . . .

thuuud

thum

thuud

thum

. . . move along the room above him—his bedroom, where Helen is still lying—and out into the hallway. He turns to look—

Brrrinnngg! Brrri—

—at the kitchen door. The noise reaches the top of the stairs

thuuud

thum

and starts down, slowly.

His hands are shaking as he tips the pills into a plastic container. He pours the morphine on top and returns the empty bottle to the counter.

He drinks it down, chewing the pills and

thuuud

thum

swallowing, gulping. He reaches for the sparkling water—Helen's favorite—and washes it down. Then

thuuud

thum

he licks out the plastic container, takes another drink of the water. It doesn't taste so bad. Not really.

The noise stops at the foot of the stairs for a few seconds and then starts up again.

thum

thurrrrrp

thum

thurrrrrp

As the drugs start to take effect, he turns to the kitchen door, watching the handle, listening to the sound of the steps coming along the hallway . . . one good step and then one that sounds as though the foot is being dragged, as though—

Peter Crowther

"Her left leg is useless to her now, I'm afraid. Helen won't be able to get along to the toilet any more, Mr. Bellings."

He looks blankly at the district nurse, mildly irritated—as always—at her use of his wife's name. "Why's that?" he says, amazed as the words come out, sounding so

oh, really . . . and do you think it's going to rain later?

matter-of-fact.

"Her muscles are going, I'm afraid." The explanation delivered with a practiced concern. "It looks as though we're in the final stages."

"Oh."

The kitchen fades and shimmers, walls elongate and then contract, and he feels a lightness coursing through his body.

He watches through half-closed eyes

thum

thurrrrrp

as the cupboards seem to fall in on themselves, leaving only plain white walls.

He glances down and, momentarily, he sees a shape . . . a man, curled up in a fetal position—and wearing a similar jacket to his own, he notices absently—and then the shape grows darker, like a shadow, and disappears.

He looks up and watches the counters fade from view, the drawer handles disappear, the flowers in the vase

thum

thurrrrrp

on the kitchen table—freesia, he thinks, mouthing the word, and carnations—pop out of existence one by one.

"You've been a naughty boy, haven't you . . . Tommy?"

Even though, when he turns around, his face is only an inch or two away from Nanny's familiar face, the first thing he notices

thum

thurrrrrp

268

is that the windows have gone. And the back door leading out onto the garden.

"Nanny?"

Nanny lifts her hands and places them on her cheeks. Then, smiling, she digs the fingers into the flesh and pulls it out like taffy. When she releases the flesh, it springs back into her face: but it isn't

thum

thurrrrrp

Nanny's face anymore.

"Mered—"

Meredith lifts a finger to his mouth and shakes his head, nodding over toward the door leading to the hallway.

As he moves backward, Bellings turns around to face the slowly opening door.

His father is wearing Helen's nightdress, holding it up with both hands as he kicks the kitchen door closed behind him.

" 'Pistol's cock is up,' " his father says, grinning as he recites from *Henry V*, " 'and flashing fire will follow.' "

When the door closes, there is no sign of its outline.

And no handle.

"You know what happens now, don't you?" Meredith whispers in his ear.

A table has appeared in front of him. The leather straps look familiar.

"And for a very long time, too," the prefect adds.

Mr. Sly Stops
for a Cup of Joe

BY SCOTT EMERSON BULL

Mr. Sly and fear were old acquaintances, though when they usually met it was at Mr. Sly's invitation and on his terms. He never expected to run into fear at twelve-thirty on a Tuesday night in a Quik Stop convenience store while he chose between the Rich Colombian Blend and the Decaf Hazelnut coffees, but then fear always did have a mind of its own.

A kid had ushered in fear. He did it when he yelled, "Everybody in back. This is a robbery."

Mr. Sly crushed the empty coffee cup in his hand and dropped it to the floor. Dammit, he thought. He knew he should've just got what he needed and skipped the coffee. If he had, perhaps he could have avoided this, but he needed his fix, didn't he? Now his work at home would have to wait. He'd have to deal with this first.

"Come on, Fat Man. That means you, too."

He turned toward the direction of the voice. The first thing he saw was the gun. The kid holding it wasn't much, just some local Yo-boy wannabe with bleached hair and a bad attitude. The gun, however, was big as a cannon. Mr. Sly hated guns. Blam blam blam and all you had left was a big ugly mess. Mr. Sly preferred knives. Knives required skill and demanded intimacy. Kind of like fucking without all the post-coital chitchat.

"As you wish," he said. "You seem to be in charge."

The kid pointed him toward an office in the back, where Mr. Sly joined the Indian girl who ran the register and a well-dressed woman of about thirty who'd also been buying coffee. He looked for a window or a second door, but there was no other exit. Not good.

"Okay. On the floor!"

Mr. Sly turned to the kid. He had to look downward, since he had a good eight inches on the boy.

"Do you want us sitting or facedown?" he asked.

"Huh?"

Mr. Sly looked into the boy's bloodshot eyes. He didn't see much sign of intelligence.

"Do you want us to sit on the floor or lie on it facedown?"

"Facedown," the kid said.

The two women complied. Mr. Sly remained standing.

"Why would you want us to do that?" he asked.

"Because I fucking said so, okay?"

Mr. Sly shrugged. "That's not how I would do it. I'm assuming you plan on shooting us in the back of the head."

"Maybe," the kid said. One of the women sobbed.

Mr. Sly shook his head. "For what? Maybe a hundred bucks in the register? Where's the fun in that?" He made a gun with his index and forefinger and aimed it at his own temple. "Don't you want to see our faces when you pull the trigger?"

The kid's eyes widened.

"Why the hell would I want to do that?"

"You don't have a clue, do you?"

"Fuck you, man. On the floor! Now!"

"Okay, but I'm going to do you a favor and stay sitting up. If you shoot me, I want you to see my face."

"Just fucking sit down."

Mr. Sly did as he was told, keeping his anger in check. At six-eight, three hundred and fifty pounds, he could easily crush this punk's head with his bare hands, but the gun equalized the situation. He lowered his bulk and sat cross-legged on the floor.

"Now don't move. I'm gonna be right out here. I hear anyone move, you're all dead, okay?"

Mr. Sly nodded.

The kid left the room and started banging on what sounded like the register. The well-dressed woman sat up and turned to Mr. Sly.

"What the hell's wrong with you?"

Mr. Sly smiled at her. He could see she was in the first stage of fear, what he liked to call disbelief. That was when your mind still refused to come to grips with what was happening, although your body had accepted it fully. He could see that by the sweat on the woman's brow and the red splotches on her cheeks. He wondered if she'd wet herself yet. Most of them did and Mr. Sly hated that. How could you enjoy the deliciousness of dread with soggy panties?

"I must tell you that I thought you were rather rude a few minutes ago," he said.

"What?"

Mr. Sly didn't like this woman. He didn't like her at all.

"I thought you were rather rude when you reached in front of me to get that coffee cup. You could have been more patient."

"Are you insane? Any minute that kid's going to blow our brains out and you're lecturing me on patience? Is that all you're worried about?"

"Perhaps not the only thing."

"Well, good. Now will you please cooperate so we'll have a chance of getting out of this alive."

He felt an urge to slap this woman across the mouth, but fought it off.

"Either way he's going to shoot us," he said. "So why do you want to deny me a little fun in the last minutes of my life?"

"My God, you're insane."

"As the day is long," he said, smiling.

They could hear the kid returning, so the woman lay back down on the floor. When the kid came in, he looked agitated.

"There's only seventy-five dollars in the cash drawer. Where's the rest of the money?"

"Told you so," Mr. Sly said.

"Shut up." He motioned with his gun to the Indian girl. "Get up and open the safe."

"I'm not sure I can open it," the girl said, rising to her feet. Tears dampened her delicate brown face. Now Mr. Sly liked her. He loved the diamond stud in her nose and the way her small breasts pushed against her Quik Stop T-shirt. She displayed an intoxicating blend of terror and submission. In the end, these were the ones that really fought back or at least took some dignity in suffering.

"Just relax and give it a try," Mr. Sly said.

"Did I ask you for any help?" the kid said.

"No, you did not. I apologize. I hate it when someone interferes with my work, too."

"Man, you're fucked in the head."

"You don't know the half of it."

They left the room. Mr. Sly could hear them talking, but couldn't make out the words. The woman sat up again.

"You want us to get killed, don't you?"

"Not particularly. I'm just trying to feel him out."

"And your opinion is?"

"I'd say one of us is going to die."

"Oh, terrific. And this doesn't bother you?"

"Not really. Not when I figure you're the one that's going to take a bullet."

The woman's mouth dropped open.

"Excuse me?"

Mr. Sly leaned closer and whispered.

"The way I see it, our best shot is for you to make a move on him. He'll have to react to you, most likely by blowing your head off, but at least I'd be able to subdue him."

"You're insane."

"Perhaps, but it's a good plan."

"It sucks. I end up getting killed."

"I didn't say it was perfect."

"Well why do *I* have to be the brave one? Why don't *you* make a move on him?"

"Because if he shoots me, you'll never be able to take him down. Then you get shot and most likely so does the girl. If I get ahold of him, I'll twist the little bastard's head off. Then at least the girl and I make it."

"It still sucks."

"Look, lady. If you have a better idea, I'm waiting to hear it."

The gun appeared at the door, followed in by the kid. "What the hell are you doing?"

"Plotting your death," Mr. Sly said.

"Man, I am this fucking close to shooting you. And you." He pointed the gun at the woman. "Back on the floor."

"No." The woman straightened her back. "If he sits up, then I sit up, too."

The room exploded with a hail of smoke and coffee grounds. The kid had blasted a four-inch hole in a can of Colombian mix on the shelf above their heads. Mr. Sly's ears rang from the noise. He suppressed a smile when he saw the woman facedown on the floor again.

The kid had the gun pointed at Mr. Sly.

"Next one's gonna be lower. You get my drift?"

"Loud and clear."

The kid left the room. Mr. Sly could smell piss.

"Fear should be our friend," he told the woman.

"Dear God, we're going to die," she said.

Yes, they were, Mr. Sly thought, unless he thought of something soon. He closed his eyes and thought of his walnut chest at home, the one where he kept his knives. He wished he had one now, but he never took them out of the house, because of the risk they presented if he was caught with one. After tonight he might have to rethink that policy, if he got the chance.

"Fear brings clarity," he said. "It fires the brain. I don't mind admitting that I'm scared, but I'm trying to enjoy this experience and learn from it. I don't often get this perspective."

The woman looked up at him, her face a series of red splotches on a pale white canvas.

"I don't want to know what you do in your spare time, do I?"

Mr. Sly smiled. As he did, they heard the gun go off out in the store.

"I guess she couldn't get the safe open," he said.

The woman put her face in her hands and wept.

The kid rushed back into the room. His gun seemed bigger now, as if reacting to some exhilaration it got from firing its shiny missiles. The kid looked wired. Either the drug he'd taken had finally peaked or he finally understood what this was all about.

"All right. Wallets. Jewelry. Anything you got. Dump it on the floor."

The woman sat up and dumped out her purse. Mr. Sly eyed the contents: a wallet, eyeliner, lipstick. A container of Mace landed near his foot. He looked at the woman, catching her eye, then looked back at the Mace.

"Not all that shit. Just the money and credit cards." The kid aimed the gun at Mr. Sly. "You, too. Get your wallet out now."

Mr. Sly studied the gun, figuring the bullet's probable trajectory and the distance between himself and the kid. He reached toward his left back pocket where he kept his wallet. Then he stopped.

"I only have twelve dollars. I really only needed a cup of coffee and some maxi-pads."

The kid's grip tightened on the gun.

"Maxi-pads?"

"Let's just say I'm entertaining tonight and she's in no position to pick them up herself."

"Just give me your wallet."

Mr. Sly looked back at the gun. He wondered if he'd survive taking a bullet in the gut. Given all his fat, he probably stood a pretty good chance of making it, but doing time in a hospital wasn't something he could afford, nor could he afford a few days of questioning by the police. That was all he'd need, some bright cop putting two and two together.

"I can't get it out," he said.

"What?"

Mr. Sly switched hands and reached toward his right rear pocket.

"It's the problem with being fat," he said. "My pants are too tight. I'll have to stand up if you want me to take out my wallet."

The kid took a step back. Mr. Sly could see him sizing up the situation. The kid didn't seem to like it, but luckily greed was still foremost in his mind.

"All right, but get up real slow."

Mr. Sly laughed. He had no choice but to get up slow. His leg muscles strained as they lifted his weight from the floor. He felt like an old grizzly bear raring up for one final attack. He only hoped he looked that way, too.

"That feels much better," he said, stretching up to full height. "My legs were going to sleep."

The kid looked up at Mr. Sly, who now dwarfed him. Some of the kid's cockiness seemed to drain away, but that didn't stop him from sticking his hand out for the wallet.

"You have no sense of fun, do you?" Mr. Sly reached for his right rear pocket. "A man should love his work no matter what line he chooses. Don't you think?"

The kid cocked the hammer.

"Just give me your wallet."

"As you requested."

Mr. Sly stopped time. He could do this when he wanted to, just like a quarterback when he gets into the zone or a racing driver when he pushes his car towards two hundred plus miles per hour. Everything slows down when you're in total control. He watched as his arm came from behind his back. Watched the look of horror on the other's face, then the split-second of consternation when the kid saw that the big man's weapon was a comb, a simple plastic comb. He watched as it tore into the kid's cheek.

The gun went off, but the bullet missed. The kid slumped back against the door and screamed when he saw a generous portion of his skin hanging from the broken plastic teeth of the comb. The woman picked up the Mace and sprayed it in the kid's face. Ouch, that had to hurt on an open wound. The gun fell to the floor and Mr. Sly kicked it away. Then he delivered a finishing blow to the kid's head, letting him drop like the proverbial sack of potatoes.

"Only good thing my drunken daddy ever taught me," Mr. Sly said, shaking the flesh loose from the comb. "A plastic comb can come in handy if you ever find yourself in a bar fight without a weapon."

"Charming," the woman said. She pointed the Mace at Mr. Sly. "Now I think it's time for you to leave."

"Fair enough," he said. "Just let me tie him up first."

The woman kept the Mace pointed at Mr. Sly as he bound the kid's feet and hands together with packing tape.

"We should check on the girl," he said. "See if she's dead."

"You first."

They walked into the store with Mr. Sly leading. They found the girl behind the counter, a purplish welt rising on her forehead. There was a bullet hole in the safe.

"He really was an amateur, wasn't he?" Mr. Sly said as he turned to face the woman. "I'm glad she's okay, aren't you?"

Before the woman could answer, Mr. Sly had grabbed the Mace from her.

"Sorry, but I don't like people pointing things at me."

The woman shrank back against the counter. Mr. Sly read the concern on her face and laughed.

"You didn't believe all that stuff I said back there, did you?"

"Well."

"You needn't worry." He picked up some maxi-pads and threw them into a plastic Quik Stop bag. "Think I'll skip the coffee. I'm keyed-up enough already, aren't you?"

The woman stared at him.

Mr. Sly went to leave, but when he reached the front door and looked out at the empty street, he turned around.

"Mind if I take something with me?"

"By all means," the woman said.

He went back into the storage room and came out with the kid thrown over his shoulder. "And just in case you get a sudden bout of sympathy for our attacker here." Mr. Sly held up the woman's driver's license.

"I can't imagine that happening," she said.

He walked with the boy over his shoulder to the door.

"Wait," the woman called. "I suppose I should say thank you."

He turned and smiled. "No need," he said. "Most fun I've had in years."

Then Mr. Sly went out the door and disappeared into the night.

Finishing School

BY CHERRY WILDER

My mother is Spanish and my father was Hungarian. His death in a plane crash has been considered a freak accident, in any case a disgrace. We have been living here in Bavaria, a widow and her daughter, refugees from Hungary who could not escape when the Uprising of the fifties was savagely put down.

Madre is a teacher of dancing and music; my father, Lajos, was a fencing master. He excelled at many sports, coached a small German group in water polo—they were flying home from a meeting in Austria when the plane went down in a wooded area northwest of Munich. It was the smallest plane I had ever seen people fly in—yes, propellers; and the accident *was* a freak accident. The team was up front but my father sat at the back with one boy who had broken his ankle.

The tail of the little plane broke off, snapped, when the pilot struck a tall radio mast. He managed to land the rest of the machine in a meadow but the swimming coach and the injured team member went careering down into a ravine. My poor young father was pierced to the heart and died.

Although I have read secretly the despised and uncomfortable book by A—S—, I feel that our heritage is so odd and clearly defined it makes me feel safe, protected by a vast warm reddish fog of myth and superstition. Yes, we are connected to the Hlatos, yes, my poor papa was an unresolved person, who could choose his destiny, yes, I myself may soon have to make the most direct choice of all, but I refuse to be daunted. Is it any worse than the heritage of—for instance—the British Royals, poor things, or a New England woman who is heiress to a great deal of "old money"?

My name is Magda Lucia y Flores Kalman. My ambition is to belong to, to live and hopefully to die in, the new Millennium. Dolores, my poor mother, a beautiful woman, a lonely widow, does charity work for a nondenominational rather Green organization here in Hoheim, near Munich. I pray that she finds a decent, handsome German lover or second husband. I pray fervently that she never tries to tell this man—or anyone—the truth. We would be plunged into the whole farrago of superstitious nonsense from the Stoker book and various penny dreadfuls and an archive of films.

My cousin Tibor, who is presently studying Commerce at Columbia, is a film buff. We share a love for long classics—*Dances With Wolves*, *Heaven's Gate*, and for a retrospective or two—Eisenstein, Robert Altman, Orson Welles . . . But of course he has made a study of all the traditional Vampire films.

There goes silent old "Max Schreck" in *Nosferatu*, then our dear Bela, *without* fangs, and Christopher the Tall and endless horrors from Hammer and George Hamilton being funny . . . I do admire Gary Oldman and there are coffinloads of bloodstained offerings from Italy, Russia, Spain, Aspen, Chicago, New Zealand—a brilliant handsome actor/director named Scheib. The problems of those who hold in any way to the fantasies concerning "traditional Vampires" are related to the problems of those researching the Loch Ness monster. One must have two of the creatures in order to breed. An endless spate of unfortunate soldiers in battle, for example, who became Undead, following an encounter on the field—this will not quite do. And neither will a bevy of heroines who encounter a caped and fanged gentleman in the wooded graveyard/gothic pile/gaslit *quartier*.

The Hlatos, even in the direct line, do not subsist entirely upon human blood; they mate with human beings—usually a family connection. Yes indeed there are those who joined the Hlatos through an encounter on the battlefield or elsewhere and they can be described as "*created*," but this is impolite—they are all ageless, rather than simply old. Life has become much easier for them all since the end of the First World War, when blood in plasma form was developed, and our own technicians have made many refinements since then. My poor father who enjoyed his work and loved his family took a measured amount of capsules—as if he controlled some type of anemia—and enjoyed his "wine of life" on high days and holidays. Some of the family are superstitious—there were those who wondered if my father's death by *piercing* was a Christian conspiracy. The Christian churches, Catholic and Protestant, insisted that their symbols could affect the Hlatos. The Vampire Hunters were cruel and deluded.

The females of our line, as savagely caricatured as the males, do in fact have a slightly larger window of choice. We are born mortal, all but a few true Lamienne who possess an extra chromosome. But we remain Maidens until we receive the first piercing—I am sure some genre writer would call it the Kiss of Life. Yes, there are many anomalies. What of my poor father who was a full Hlatos, who died by accident? What of a Maiden who once pierced, does not marry, and so on . . . ? Stories of female "Vampires" are often lewd and kinky—are those slavering beauties in the Abraham Stoker book about to suck Harker's blood or bite off his penis? Then there are the sad threatening creatures like Carmilla—Le Fanu was a good writer and his descendants still work with genre fiction. So one could go on—deploring the awful Polidori, admitting to a certain fondness for L'Estat and especially for Wayland. I must ask the Hlatos if any of our kind did have periods of something resembling hibernation . . .

I must admit to a love of bats of all kinds. On our best family holiday when I was thirteen we stayed with friends in Sydney, New South Wales, and saw the flying foxes, the great fruit bats, come flying past our holiday house on the North Shore in the evening. They had a refuge far away in the trees. Once we went to visit a friend in another suburb and found a bat, a medium-sized quite ordinary bat, flying in beautiful silence around the room—not touching anything, of course. A window was opened and it flew silently into the antipodean night. Do I or any member of my family believe that we can or ever could *turn into* bats? Who are you kidding? Do me a favor! *But*—yes, here it comes, a reservation, not so much a grey area as a red one. How about those relatives in South America? Might the grandfathers, the Abuellos, have a *special relationship* with those blood-drinking bats? Yes, of course I have a theory . . .

But now Madre, sensitive and brave, has shown me a new dress—fashionable but very decent with a slit maxi skirt. It is the spring solstice: we have put things off as long as possible but now I am an old Maiden of twenty. Hlatos Lajos, for whom my father and hundreds of others were named, has come to take me to meet my destiny. At dusk, as the red sun sinks behind the foothills of the Alps, the black BMW comes to the gate of our house. The driver is a woman, in smart grey-and-red uniform. My mother stands on the porch and raises a hand in salute. I wrap a gray knitted stole about me— it is always a little cold in the presence—and slip into the cavernous depths of the limo.

Hlatos Lajos has a beautiful olive-skinned face. Yes, indeed he looks most damnably old but at the same time he looks as if his face has been lifted. An uninitiated person might not see the point of an anti-wrinkle treatment in a very old man. Think for a moment of the wrinkles of an untreated immortal, one of the Hlatos.

"Well, my dear!" he says brightly. "How fine you look! Your mother is a great beauty, of course . . ."

"Yes, Grandpapa, she is a hard act to follow!"

He laughs aloud. I wonder if there are many other "grandchildren" who are meek, submissive, unjolly . . . The great black car goes swooping upward into the hills. I think of the many films with a sinister coach drawn by black horses, with a hooded coachman who sometimes turns out to be The Fiend himself.

"Grandpapa," I ask sweetly, "do you watch moving pictures?"

He chuckles and presses a remote: a twenty-inch monitor lights up on the entertainment panel, beside the dishes of olives and cashews.

"I know your cousin Tibor's little hobby . . ."

We look for a few moments at a generic coach galloping through poor Transylvania, then there is a beep from the driver and the old man turns on a finance report. I observe that he is interested in futures in Argentina. The car must slow down to take a sharp bend and I see a red-and-white sign on the side of the road. It reads INTERNAT.

Internat is short for International School, the general word for a boarding school. The simple boarding schools of other lands are not known here. An international school contains privileged students, often from other lands, the daughters of diplomats, millionaires, financiers, military personnel. I have met a number of girls and young men from similar places and they are not absolutely hopeless, but they have a high ratio of nutcases, poor dears, whisperers, addicts.

Higher and higher we swept up among the dark hills and came to a beautiful lighted courtyard before a splendid house. Yes, it had a touch of mansion, a tower at the back—perhaps part of an older building—but it was neither sinister nor spooky. We sat waiting and a welcome party approached, led by three older women in long dresses and academic gowns. A party of the young women from the Internat followed them. I was still approving but their gear was a little too flowing and overdone. The Hlatos was assisted from the limo by Jacques, the body servant who had followed in the support auto, with the medic, the cook and the two bodyguards.

There was a cheerful procession into the building and I had a place in it. Two of my fellow students came and brought me out—Estralita and Jan, one dark and one fair. I liked them at once. I was expected, I was Magda.

"Yes, well," said Jan in a faint American accent, "there is the ceremony but then we will take you to your room and after that we can have our own fun . . . You'll see!"

Estralita saw that I was faintly apprehensive.

"It is just a little fun," she said in Spanish. "Have you spent much time in an Internat or Female College?"

Oh yes, I had indeed. I tried to be cheerful. We entered the building at the main doors and came into a magnificent lofty hall. We were part of a chorus of spectators. The Hlatos declaimed softly and solemnly before a carved marble pillar that commemorated a certain battle with the Turks, many centuries ago. The Principal, Frau Leibnitz—I knew her from a festival in Budapest—announced that, to the great honor of our finishing school, the Hlatos Lajos would remain here in retreat for three days. The great man was already kneeling at a stone lectern beside the memorial pillar. Not far away stood his special bodyguard, Amaranta. She was a splendid person, over six feet, lithe and muscular. She wore purple-black leather harem trousers and a long matching jacket. She held a spear tipped with bronze.

As we went out, singing an ancient song, "Blest be the double victory! Death and the Foe are conquered," Jan nudged me and whispered: "Of course Amaranta is a true Lamienne."

"That is so cool . . ." I said.

We all went into another spacious hall and sat down at once at long tables for our supper. I counted twenty-three fellow students. Again, top marks for the food: fine bread, a choice of bouillon or asparagus soup, a small helping of chicken with pasta, then a treat—caviar with crackers. The dessert was fresh fruit; we drank mineral water or rose-hip tea.

Estralita sighed, "Wine is waiting, my dear Magda."

We all went out sedately and I was shown to my room on the third floor—yes, very nice, en suite bathroom of course, a Jacuzzi would have been too much to expect. My luggage had arrived and was being unpacked by Fraulein Tina. Would I be cold? Well, I admitted, I had brought along Daisy, a ridiculous sheep, who was in fact a hot water bottle. I pulled her out and my new friends laughed aloud. There was a heavy knocking on the bedroom door.

"Oh, Lord," said Jan, "here we go."

I flung open the door and found a bundle of fun. A tall girl in slinky black satin and a red half-mask. Black hair—a wig—tumbled over her shoulders. She grinned, showing fangs, dripping artistically with a red mouthwash of some kind.

"Magda," she intoned. "Magda must come to her Harkering."

I inclined my head and said in Hungarian, "In the name of the Hlatos!"

The person snarled and went away. The girls hustled me along, what must be must be.

Well, it was what one might expect—pupils do react against their boarding schools. The Merchant Tailors School had a marvelous anticlothing song about wearing woad. Older girls—and we were all over eighteen—might be expected to sneak out, smoke pot. And so on. So my Harkering or initiation featured half a dozen traditional female Vampires with more fake fangs, dripping that red mouthwash. I tried to play along with a certain amount of shrinking and screaming. I was glad when I was "rescued" by another group, the Helsing's Angels, in white, wreathed in garlic plants and waving crosses.

I sat up in my cozy room going over the courses I intended to take in the next three months—excellent stuff on food, cookery and diet, interior decoration, modern art, a history of Venice . . . But the crunch came almost at once. Traditional Vampire rubbish was with us all day and half the night. I took the introductory Venice lecture—the desk I used was carved with a large inaccurate bat, the word *Dracula*, and a cross giving off rays. In one of the common rooms there were board games, Monopoly, Trivial Pursuit, backgammon, Scrabble and so on. There was a revisionist game called Blood Money, a

Monopoly rip-off, where the movable tokens were a skull, a coffin, a bat, a tombstone, and a heart pierced by a stake.

We were four Maidens this semester. I knew two of them, Alenka and Eva, from Budapest, and I knew of Conchita, from Barcelona, a sweet naive girl of seventeen, as well connected as myself. The usual question for the older Maidens was of course: "Are you really still a virgin?" And I could reply with perfect truth: "Yes I am!" Conchita found it hard to grasp that orgasm could be achieved without penetration. I found it as distasteful to be a sex consultant as it was to watch all this Trad Vamp nonsense. The second question among Maidens was: "Do you know who you are going to marry?" Oh yes, I knew that too—thinking of the couch, the red wine and all the films of *War and Peace*, U.S., Russian, BBC serial—so many battles of Borodino, blending into one.

I tried to behave sensibly, step by step. On that first evening I managed to obtain an interview with the Principal, Frau Leibnitz. We sat in her beautiful Art Deco sitting room and sipped dry sherry. I inquired about the numbers— yes, there were four Maidens and ten well-connected young ladies (including Estra and Jan) from families close to the Hlatos who might expect to marry into the clan. They were all rich, of course, and some were already betrothed. This left nine young women who remained at the Internat for another semester. Frau Leibnitz pointed out that they might have family reasons for this. I knew the sort of reasons—a father posted abroad, a messy divorce, with problems about where the daughters should live. Some girls stayed on to take a special course—the semesters were not long.

I became bolder and raised the question of the "Harkering," the insistence on Vampire myths. Frau Leibnitz smiled and refilled my tiny glass.

"Magda," she said, "you have the great privilege of living close to the Hlatos, but perhaps it has made you a little critical. I take all these foolish tales as a childish disobedience—rather like using bad language."

I controlled my paranoia and ate a chocolate biscuit.

"The girls have a number of clubs," she said, "and I am sure they would like you to visit them. Archery, of course, fencing, the Tower, who publish a magazine . . . There is a Wiccan coven and the senior group who have the use of a study, also called the Den—they hold debates."

I agreed to look in on some of these places. My friends Jan and Estra were still waiting in the common room—nobody went to bed early. The scandalous gossip was that the Hlatos support team, lodged in a special guest house, was having more fun than a rock band. I resisted the temptation to make these two friends my spies. We crept off to bed and I left lying e-mail messages of good cheer for my mother and for Tibor.

My ESP was working, perhaps. The group in the Den—not girls but women: a love of power, a wish to control, to frighten poor innocents like Conchita or to encourage radicals. I used my sleep mantra and set off alone after a breakfast in my room. I visited the archery buffs, looked in on the Wiccan coven—too cold for them to be sky-clad. I accepted a sandwich lunch with the editor of *Tower Times* and gave her a short item on the bats of Australia. So I came at last to the Den. Of course I was expected but I would not take a place of honor, a black wooden throne twined with ivy and red poppies. There was a spirited debate in progress about the use of virtual reality.

And there was the leader, the person I had imagined. Her name was firm and crisp, prominently displayed—KATE. Probably Spanish. She must be older than all the present intake. Twenty-five? Twenty-seven? In the entire bevy of girls and women in the Internat she stood out as very beautiful.

Her acolytes included a young teacher who taught music theory and mathematics. The talk was very lively and sensible. I joined in a little and I began to feel foolish. I was the one who was too critical, as Frau Leibnitz had pointed out. I was lacking in trust and in empathy. As time went on I wondered if there was a very simple explanation for Kate and her Den—she was gay and did not wish to marry. At the end of the session I went down to speak to this leader and at once we were alone.

"I am a spoil sport," I said, coming straight to the point, "but I don't care for the 'Harkering' and all the Trad Vamp mythology."

"What does the Hlatos think of it?" asked Kate.

"He thinks of the mythology as nonsense, of course, but I don't believe he knows that there is anything like it in this school."

I looked down at a nameplate on her desk and saw that her full name was Katerina Flores. One of my cousins. Her hair was lustrous and black, loosely tied, and her eyes were a remarkable green, two shades of green.

"What work do you do?" she asked softly and wistfully. "I know you are betrothed to Count Tibor Kallman . . ."

———

"I miss him very much," I said. "In New York I publish a good deal of criticism, book and film reviews, travel notes—even food pieces."

"Can you cook?"

"Yes, quite well—but not so well as Tibor!"

We laughed aloud and I made the luckiest hit of all.

"Kate, you must come to the United States—to California!"

There was a flash of pure excitement in her remarkable eyes.

"The family have excellent connections with the major studios," I said, "and I am certainly not talking of Vampire movies!"

I decided to give this strange woman my own plan.

"Do many students leave without completing the semester?"

"Yes," she said, smiling. "Family trouble. A few have been expelled."

"I will be leaving shortly," I said. "I will ask for an interview with the Hlatos tomorrow. Can I ask a favor?"

"Anything . . ."

"Let me leave the three other Maidens in your care. Conchita is especially innocent."

"Of course, dear cousin!"

We clasped hands upon the tabletop.

A great deal was unexplained, but some information came from my mother when she came to take me to the airport. She wept, blamed herself. These must be the poorest and most reclusive of the Flores clan. Only direct instructions from the Hlatos could release Katerina.

Before this I returned to the great hall with its sacred pillars and requested an audience with the Hlatos. His time in retreat had done him good: he was smooth from his massage, bright-eyed and cheerful. He laid aside the international edition of the *Herald Tribune* and embraced me.

"Grandpapa, I will leave the Internat and go back to the United States. Tibor and I will marry at his friend Andy's house at Martha's Vineyard."

My grandfather laughed.

"Whatever you like, child," he said. "Can you give a reason—besides love, lust, boredom . . .?"

"It is a seasonal thing," I said. "We must go promptly to Argentina on account of my bat studies."

"You will be taking Tibor away from his portfolio, from his studies!"

He was stern, but I had an answer for everything.

"Wouldn't it be a good time for Tibor to examine Argentine futures?"

He put a hand across his ancient eyes and said, "You are too clever, Magda Kallman. Please do nothing to upset the few Abuellos you find on the pampas!"

"Of course not, I promise!"

The Hlatos changed the subject with a little flash of reminiscence. "Always a tomboy," he smiled. "How fine to see her again . . . my Amaranta, my Lamienne!"

Presently we embraced and parted. Now I am sitting in a tree at sunset, thousands of miles from Europe. I can see the light in our hut where Tibor is cooking supper. It was just as well that I did not tell Grandpapa my theory about the Vampire bats. Suppose, just suppose, in distant times, before plasma, there was this bond between clan members and bats. The dear creatures came flying in—ah there is one now and my equipment has recorded it—with a gift of blood.

Jennifer's Turn

BY FRUMA KLASS

Jennifer was waiting for her turn.

Sometimes it seems as if I've spent my life waiting, she thought. *For a ride on the swings. To see Mickey Mouse. For ice cream. For love. For money. But you shouldn't have to wait on your birthday.*

She sighed. *Everyone on the line has a birthday today. That's why we're here.* The line moved forward.

She looked back along the line. It wound around the building, the whole block at least. She couldn't see the end.

The man behind her smiled. He looked pretty good, considering. His long hair was held with a rubber band in a ponytail that somehow made his pink, balding scalp look even balder and shinier than if he'd been just plain bald. But he was wearing a black leather zipper jacket and tight jeans ripped at the knee. All he needed was a flag patch and maybe some beads and he could pass for a hippie from the Sixties. The Nineteen-Sixties. If only his beard weren't so gray.

He smiled again. "I've been on longer lines than this," he said. "Waited a lot longer, I remember a Grateful Dead concert, waited all night and all day. About fifty of us, waited from midnight one night to two in the afternoon, just to buy tickets. Man, Jerry Garcia died, I didn't think I'd ever get over it."

The woman behind him said wryly, "Jerry Garcia? What about Kennedy,

Martin Luther King, *Bobby* Kennedy for chrissakes, John *Lennon?* That didn't bother you?"

"Sure, and Jimi, and Janis, and all of 'em. But the *band,* man, the fuckin *band.* 'Scuse me," he added politely.

"Yeah, but I'll bet you had mattresses or folding chairs or something while you waited." She was wearing a crisp navy blue dress-for-success business suit, circa the Eighties, and her hair was a somewhat startling yellow-blonde.

"Oh yeah," the hippie type said. "Somebody had a mattress and somebody had some cookies and a lot of people had some great weed. It was like—you know."

"Yeah," the dress-for-success woman said. "I know."

I know too, Jennifer said to herself. *A lot of people made fun of us later, like we just sat around all the time singing Kum-Ba-Ya, but it really was great. All the camaraderie, if that's the right word. We didn't really mind waiting then. We were always waiting for something wonderful.*

"Wish I had some of that great weed now," the hippie said.

The success woman laughed. "Can't even smoke tobacco anymore," she said.

"That's different," the hippie said righteously. "Tobacco gives you lung cancer."

"Whatever," the success woman said.

The line moved forward.

Ahead, about a block up the line, there was a commotion. A really old-looking man in a black raincoat lay on the sidewalk, his aluminum cane still in his hand. The small knot of people around him opened up as a Health Service cylinder, a Robo-Med helly, came down quietly from the sky and landed right next to him. Its flat, automated voice could be heard all the way back to where Jennifer stood, announcing that it was there to provide "any treatment you need, sir, from a Band-Aid to a heart transplant. Courtesy of the U.S. Government's Mobile Medicare Service." A young woman in starchy white coveralls moved swiftly out of the helly and over to the old man on the ground. "Let's just pop into the helly, sir, and we'll be in the E.R. in a jiffy," she said.

"No hospital! No hospital!" the old guy was yelling. *Why not?* Jennifer wondered. After all, it was still free for him, all the rest of the day.

A woman easily as old as he was, bent over with that sort of hump old women get (Jennifer unconsciously stood up straighter), cried out, "He's right! He can't go to the hospital! He won't get back in time!" And Jennifer suddenly understood.

He'd lose his place on line, yes. And if he didn't make it back onto the line by five o'clock—cutoff time—he'd never see a hospital again. Or even a doctor. Get a cold, it turns into pneumonia, and you can't see a doctor or get any medical care at all—or even any prescription drugs—because you didn't pass your annual test. No, he couldn't leave this line and come back tomorrow. Tomorrow's line was for people whose birthday was tomorrow. Today's birthday boys and girls had to get their testing, their "annual checkup," as the Medicare people called it, today.

The fallen man was struggling to get up by himself. "Don't help me!" he shouted at the medic. "I don't need any help!"

"Anyone has the right to refuse medical aid," she said stiffly. "Helly, make a note. Patient refused treatment."

"Patient refused treatment," the mechanized voice repeated. "Ten twenty-seven a.m., May ninth, twenty eighteen."

May 9, 2018. I'm 68 years old today. But I'm not old! She looked at the other people on the line. Many of them did look old, even (or maybe especially) the women whose careful blond hair framed taut, surgically lifted, desperate faces. Like the dress-for-success woman behind her. Actually, the hair and the facelifts didn't make them look much younger than the gray-haired, wrinkled women. *But people like* me—*we don't look like them. We wear* jeans, *like we always did. And my hair's perfectly straight, parted in the middle and hanging down my back. Girls used to iron their hair on an ironing board to get it to look like mine. It even has some brown in it. A lot of brown.*

The line moved forward.

We weren't supposed to get old. We even had young names—like Kevin and Stacey and Brandi and Jason. Not the silly names of the generation before us— Francine and Estelle and Bernard, Arthur and Phyllis and Florence. We had nice names. Like Jennifer.

Another bent-over old woman was talking, in a loud voice. She wore a vintage 1990s dress, a little flower print, with a raggedy coat over it and old-lady shoes that closed with Velcro. *Velcro!* You couldn't dress older if you tried. And granny glasses. Migod, you can't wear granny glasses when you *are* a granny! The whole point was to make fun of the old, to show off how young you were that you could wear old-folks-stuff and get away with it. But you can't get away with it when you *are* old.

"It's your fault," she was shrieking. "You goddam Baby Boomers!"

Baby Boomers. As if it's a curse, a dirty word or something. Listen, lady, we've always been Baby Boomers. We've never been anything but Baby Boomers. So what's the big deal all of a sudden?

"We had it good before you came along," Granny Glasses was saying. "Before you turned sixty-seven. We had the Social Security and the Medicare too. Before you came along."

"Bulge in the belly of the snake," said a distinguished-looking elder states-man type. His neat white beard came to a point in the middle.

"Now what the hell you talkin' about," said a motorcycle type with bare arms, big muscles, and a lot of ugly tattoos on them.

The line moved forward. The front door of the building was coming into view now, and you could see when someone went in. You could read the big sign over the door:

Free Annual Checkups Today
Senior Citizens Only

—as if they weren't running the Annual Tests every day, all year round. As if anyone *wanted* the testing.

Granny Glasses was tilted so far forward that her shabby coat—surely too warm for May—was too long in the front, too short in the back. The line was dotted here and there with real oldsters like her, but most of the people waiting were Jennifer's age. Senior Citizens, all right, but young Senior Citizens. I mean, the AARP sends you an invitation when you turn fifty.

Fifty! They figured *fifty* was old—and here she was *sixty-eight!*

"The bulge in the belly of the snake," the elder statesman type said again. He must have been a professor or a lecturer once; his voice was rich and full, and it caught everybody's attention. "Picture a straight line, horizontal, slop-ing up just a little. It's a line on a graph: Population, USA. Here and there it goes downward a little. See—it's dipping. That's the Spanish flu epidemic, a hundred years ago, nineteen eighteen."

Everyone nodded. It wasn't hard to visualize the graph.

"And now the line flattens out. It's the Great Depression, people aren't having a lot of children."

Yeah, you could see that too.

"And suddenly the line turns into a big bulge. It goes up, way up, runs in a big arc for a while and then gradually sinks down again. And now it's running straight again. The line looks like a snake that swallowed, oh, a whole cow."

"Bulge in the belly of the snake," said Muscle Man, clearly enjoying the picture. "That's us."

"Not quite digestible," said the elder statesman.

"And as the snake keeps moving forward, the bulge keeps moving back, back along the snake, no stopping it, right to the *end* of the snake," Granny Glasses said. "Where—"

"But meanwhile," said Muscle Man, "Meanwhile . . ."

"Yeah. Whatever you Baby Boomers are doing, that's what the whole country is doing. You're getting married, marriage rates are up. You're getting divorced, divorce rates are up. Your clothes, your slang, your *music*, dammit—"

"What's wrong with our music?" Muscle Man was defending his generation, apparently.

"It won't go away," Granny Glasses said sadly. "You grew up and got old, but your music won't go away. I am so *sick* of it."

"I just want to get in there, pass this year's test, and forget about it for another year," somebody else said.

Me too.

The hippie behind her began to sing, very softly: *"Oh, where have all the young men gone . . . "* People laughed.

"I sure hope it's easier this year than last," another woman said. She didn't look terribly old, but she was hobbling along with a walker.

Jennifer remembered last year's test. It was simple. The pill was on an open dish, on a small table up a flight of stairs. All you had to do was go up the stairs, maybe ten or twelve steps, get the pill, and bring it down the steps to the nurse. Lucky the pill wasn't in one of those vials with the child-proof cap; Jennifer had never been able to get those open. The joke she had always heard was that the only way to open a child-proof cap was to give it to a four-year-old. Anyway, you went up the stairs, got the pill, and brought the pill to the nurse. The nurse put the pill on your arm, buzzed it with a little electrical pulse, and threw the empty pill case away.

Now your whole body was activated for a year. Whenever you have a medical problem, your body itself sends an alert to a Robo-Med, and you get medical help fast, the best in the world. Free. Fail the test, and you're out of it. No medical help. For anything, even things that could be easily cured, like appendicitis. A doctor feels sorry for you and takes a look, he loses his job and he'll never practice medicine again.

Jennifer stared at the woman with the walker. "But how did you get up and down those stairs last year?" she asked. "I mean, with the walker and all?"

The woman smiled grimly. "I crawled," she said. "I crawled up on my elbows, and I came back down on my butt."

Thank God there's nothing wrong with me. Just a little morning stiffness, especially in my fingers. The joints don't work so well any more. But it's not arthritis. Not real arthritis. Just some pain in the fingers and the fingers don't work so well.

"We're pretty tough," Granny Glasses said. "The weakest ones get weeded out early. But we sure had it better before you joined the ranks."

Walker Woman nodded. "That's right," she said. "See, too many politicians had promised too many times that they'd never touch Social Security. But they never made any such promises about Medicare. So when your cohort came along, it was Medicare that had to go. Remember the ads? 'Who deserves Medicare more—this innocent child or this greedy geezer?' And it was your votes that killed off a couple million greedy geezers." She sighed. "Oh well, now it's your turn. How do you like being the greedy geezers?"

The line moved forward, Jennifer was getting awfully hungry. She'd gotten hungry last year too, but she'd forgotten. Around her, the older people were taking sandwiches and fruit out of their pockets, purses, and backpacks. You couldn't bring anyone with you, so you couldn't have someone go get you lunch. *I'll remember next year*, she thought. *Next year I'll bring food.*

The line moved forward. Some of the old men in flapping raincoats were apparently urinating under their coats. Tired and hungry, Jennifer noticed only when they brought their bottles out from under the raincoats and slipped them into brown paper bags. One at a time, they left the line to empty the bottles into trash barrels, then scurried back to their places, holding the empty bottles under their coats. The line moved forward.

And there was the door, right ahead. The last two people before her seemed to flash past, and it was—finally—Jennifer's turn.

Through the doorway, then, and into a corridor whose lumpy walls were painted nasty green—institution green. Jennifer followed the signs: "Free Annual Checkups for Seniors, Room 111," then "Senior Checkups, Room 111," then, simply, "Room 111."

A friendly receptionist, maybe forty, checked her birth certificate and Social Security card. "Wait in here," she said, waving Jennifer into a large waiting room with straight wooden chairs. Jennifer gratefully sank onto a chair. She had never had any trouble with her feet, but her feet hurt now.

The room was dominated by a huge TV on the wall. It was on, and loud, some European sports program with men on bicycles. There were no magazines. There was nothing to eat. There was, however, a ladies room; Jennifer hurried in and hurried out. *They might have called my name.* They hadn't.

Finally, finally, *finally,* it was really Jennifer's turn. She followed the nurse into a square, open room very much like the one last year. Maybe, in fact, it was the same one. The nurse was young, terrifyingly young. She smiled a cold but proper smile. "Fifty percent," she said.

"I'm sorry?"

"Of my salary," the nurse said. "Social Security tax. Medicare tax. Fifty percent of my salary goes to support you."

"I'm sorry," Jennifer said again.

"Well, anyways, there's your test. You just go and get the pill and bring it to me." The nurse picked up a nail file.

Jennifer looked around "Where is it?" she whispered.

"On the table, against the wall. I'm not going to get it for you," the nurse said.

"No, of course not," Jennifer said vaguely, and went over to the small table against the wall. On the table lay a flat green plate, and on the plate sat a plastic vial. You could see the white pill inside. The child-proof cap bore the words "PUSH DOWN AND TURN."

"I can't open it. I've never been able to open these things," Jennifer said. She had started to cry.

The young nurse was filing her nails. "What a shame," she said.

Mother's Milk

BY ADAM L. G. NEVILL

Exiled like a degenerate king on a cardboard throne, Saul sleeps down here in the gloom, same time every day. All seven feet of his bulk rests. Thick limbs splay among the boxes and acres of bubble wrap. His big head is thrown back and making strangled sounds. There is a moon of a face above a neck tiered with fat, luminous from afar in the dusk of the warehouse.

Left among empty factories on the edge of the city, just the two of us work here in this metal labyrinth, where aisles of skeletal shelves the color of battleships go on forever. Above us the buzzing, fluorescent suns on the corrugated sky bleach our skin. Together, we are neglected by the managers in a distant office block and avoided by the drivers who come for our packages: square mountains of boxes we pack, seal, stack and then stuff into the lorry that is parked inside the giant roller doors at the end of the day.

As I watch Saul sleep until the afternoon period, when our shuffling under the weight of boxes begins again, I fancy I could run away. But he makes sounds like gas escaping whenever I stray far. Through those sticky lids, I think he can see me.

"Saul," I whisper. "Saul, Saul, it's time." My voice is quiet and I keep my distance from the alabaster mass as I try to rouse it. Rising without a sound from sleep or out of the shadowy aisles, he still frightens me.

Before me, an eye opens: a blunt, grey shark eye. Soon joined by another to move inside the doughy curves of his eye sockets. There is a sound from dewy lips as if a billiard ball is passed from one cheek to another. Then Saul speaks. Oversized tongue speech I have learned to understand. Milk. He wants milk. And then we work some more before the pickup.

After lifting the metal flask from the little white table, I cradle the sloshing torpedo in my arms and deliver it to his moist paws. Big hands gently take it with a touch like cold cheese. Turning my face away I hear guzzling sounds but do not watch the feeding. It reminds me of her, the mother. Saul's mother. My mother, she likes to think.

Signaled by a grunt, I collect the flask when he's finished. Watching my own hands tremble on the lid, screwed tightly down, I feel my stomach flop over as I carry the flask back to the little white table. Hunger starts in me with a growl and I can feel Saul smiling behind me. In the past I would only take it in tea, but now there's no resisting such delicious cream. At night I dream of milk.

With the work done, we go again to the place he calls home: a house on the top of a hill, protected by a fence and hidden by the trees and the dark. We are the last people to leave the bus and disembark by the big oaks at the bottom of the hill. Then the bus turns around, almost by itself because the driver never stops staring at us. Old iron bars, with spikes on top, run all the way around the base of the hill, but Saul has a key for the heavy gate I can't move. He opens the gate and we pass through. It slams shut behind us.

Walking in silence, we go through the black gaps between tree trunks. Pine needle and weedy smells rise thickly from the ground. Above, the leafy canopy shuts out the light. Darkness presses against us. Straightaway, I feel peculiar as the odors of the forest pad my brain with a thick creamy drowsiness, flowing through me and over me and getting behind my eyes too. But with nowhere else to go, I follow his shambling up the thin path and into the restless woods where I imagine children running away from the dewy-faced thing in front of me—flitting like little ghosts, the way they did when I escaped and ran blind into the shopping center full of Christmas lights. What a commotion I caused. Seeing my reflection in a shop window made me weep like a baby—a big, fat, white baby. That was a long time ago and I haven't run away since.

Carrying the flask of milk, which is now empty and must be brought home every day, I whip my head from side to side. Birds the size of dogs are flapping out there. They crash about in the undergrowth and their wings make wet leather sounds. I can't see them but Saul told me they're what's left of unfarmed game. Can't picture pheasants. My mind tries to see greeny-blue birds pecking the ground nearby but my heart still gallops inside my mouth when I hear them. Same every night and there have been many journeys up through the trees.

As we climb Saul makes a smell among the huge oaks and conifers. Something bubbles from his flabby body and smells of sulfur. I make the same smell now. It comes from the milk; gallons of frothing sweetness we slurp down.

After passing through acres of woody darkness we come to the houses that have been owned by Saul's family for longer than they can remember. Looking up from the bottom of the hill, you can't see the houses because they are smothered by the trees where the forest suddenly thickens around the two white buildings. Upper boughs and branches then curl over their pointy, red-tiled roofs to blot out the stars. And only when you're in the center of the garden can you see the sky through a small hole, up in the top of the trees, like you're at the bottom of a huge bowl with curved sides and a rim.

After returning from my first escape, I spent ages trying to find the garden gate on my hands and knees, so frightened by the loud flapping in the woods around me. And in the end only my stomach was able to lead me back to the gate and the houses where the milk is kept.

When we pass through the hidden gate and go through the corral of trees the first thing we see is a pale lawn. Milky green grass grows here. It's short and soft, on flat dirt, that is black if you dig down with a finger. The lawn is perfectly flat and smells sweet too. It's amazing, in all these trees is this circle of grass like the top of the hill has been chopped off for the houses and the dances I dream of.

This evening, as soon as I'm in the garden the grass catches my eyes and holds my stare. It grows in my dreams too. Sometimes in the middle of the night I imagine I've woken up facedown and I'm pushing my nose and mouth into the lawn's soft pelt, sucking the sugary blades. Shining under the strongest moons, the lawn often looks like a big pond too. I like to watch it from my window to bring the dreams back. The good dreams; not the bad ones when things move across the bright surface.

Silence and darkness inside the houses now. No lights on behind the windows in the square white walls that remind me of the sheds farm animals live in. There are no flowers or shrubs around the great solid building. It is divided into two houses by a thin inner wall. Each back door faces the milky pasture and leads into the kitchen. Like lonely sentinels the houses watch the sky and are lost to the world below.

In the kitchen of our house, we light the lamps full of pink oil and wait. But never for very long. Over they come, rushing through the back door—the mother and the brother, Ethan. In the days before I drank the milk, I used to wonder what they were doing next door with the lights out. Soon as I started to drink, I stopped thinking about it.

Be humble, stay quiet, lower the eyes; in the mother's presence it is best not to stare. Her shape is vaster than the first son Saul, but the pallor of the flesh is the same. With my eyes on the floor I can see the bottom of the floral dress that sticks to her bulk in places. In the pinky light and rushing shadows I see sparrow legs under the hem, as if her pudding body has been smashed down on two bone pins to stop it rolling around on the floor. But she's fast on those legs. Usually, I barely have time to run upstairs and hide in my room when I hear her feet skittering around from next door.

She speaks to me in a deep voice. With words booming like cannons she says I have done wrong. Moving my eyes, I look at the tiny DAINTY MAID sign on the enamel cooker that is next to the rickety kitchen table. Reading the letters to take my mind off her voice, I see they are made from chrome, like the names on the metal grilles of old cars.

Look at me, little bastard, she says.

I shake my head. I don't want to look. She makes me sick; even more than my own bulbous shape looking out of a mirror. Perhaps this is why there are no mirrors in our house, but in the bus window I can always see what the milk has done to my face.

Shadows flick around her stick legs, made by the quick movements of her short arms. Her gruff voice rises. Slowly, I turn my hot face from the "Dainty Maid" and look at her naked arms. There is no elbow. Dimpled stumps end in baby hands. Puppet fingers move like anemones in a rock pool.

Look at me, little bastard.

This time I obey.

White eyes with purple irises are pressed like studs into the cushion of her face. On top of her head is a messy thatch of fine white hair. Around the wet mouth there is more hair.

Mother's Milk

I have done wrong, she says. Never bring milk and bread home from the outside. How many times have you been told? She thought I was ready. Ready for what? Doesn't she realize I will always hold on to the last bit of myself, what is left of me—the fuzzy images I have in my memory before the milk cravings start fires in my body?

This means she has been in my little room and gone through my things. All alone in the unlit house, cleaning and sweeping while I'm at work, she searches about. I imagine her face when she found the loaf and the carton of normal milk that I brought home yesterday. I bet she screamed.

The telling-off is soon over. She has a good mind not to give me milk tonight. On my face there must be a look of horror. I feel it tighten my podgy cheeks and crease my forehead. But then she smiles. I will be allowed my share after all. Now where is the dirty washing? she asks. I want all of it.

Ethan appears from around the hem of her yellow-and-brown circus-tent dress. Glad to see me and pleased the telling-off is over, he frolics like a puppy. He jabbers at me in his strange buzzing voice that I can hardly make sense of, even after all this time. To please the watching mother, for it is my job to amuse Ethan, I hold a stupid grin on my face until it aches. His small body speeds around the kitchen like a fleshy barrel on tiny legs, covered in old man's hair. Jabber, jabber, jabber. Will he ever shut up? Sometimes I want to smack his little pig face. But he'll only run next door and tell the mother.

After the mother collects the washing in white pillowcases, she leaves the kitchen and returns to her house next door. Saul, Ethan and I sit around the wooden table in the flickering pink kitchen and wait. Our elbows make the table rock where the oil lanterns sit. Light ripples against the brown cupboards, shining on all the glass windows and off the china dishes we are forbidden to touch.

Groaning and yawning sounds start inside us all when we hear her coming back. Outside, she waddles across the lawn to make us wait, like a big plucked goose with no beak and chin feathers.

Milk! Here is the milk, frothing and slopping in big, ivory-colored jugs. It's brought around on a broad tin tray, painted with green, blue and red stripes. Her fetal paws hold the tray under her chin and it always looks so heavy for her. There's one flagon each. Little squalls and squirts of excitement start in Saul, Ethan and me. Warm cream smells fill my nose and I can almost see the little bubbles in the soupy fluid. It's like starving and dying of thirst when you're near the fresh stuff. You have to have it quickly. Slug it down with big gulps and let it thicken inside you, all the way down until your belly is full. There is bread too. Oily bread soaked in cream. Steady boys, she says, but all we can hear is the rushing sound when we close our eyes and feed.

After the meal I run upstairs to make sure she hasn't been stealing again. I know she has been in my room to take my normal bread and milk, which is so bland and thin and makes me sick now. Straight out it comes like a fountain after it touches my stomach. But maybe, I tell myself, outside milk will help water down the strength of her produce.

In the bedroom I go rummaging through the bottom of the cupboard with the mothball smell, to check my little stash. There should be a comb, a wallet and a broken watch in a shoe box. Everything else has gone. There used to be letters held together by a rubber band but the mother took them. This house doesn't have a number and no one writes to the family anyway, but people used to mail letters to the store where I work with Saul. A girl used to send letters and cards for a while too, and I liked the one with "happy birthday" written on it. Big pink letters on the front and a blue number thirty inside.

Although nothing more has been taken from the shoe box, I see the contents are disturbed. The mother's little hands have been in here then. Fortunately I keep the photo of the girl safe under my mattress. I want to remember the girl. Like I do in the store before the hunger grows and I circle the little white table with the metal flask on top. But when I look for the photo of the girl with the charcoal eyes, thin body and long brown hair, the rage comes out. The mother has taken the photo along with the bread and milk.

Anger boils inside me and sweats across my skin. I decide to escape again. These are the same feelings as before, when I ran down through the trees and managed to get over the gate. Back then I wasn't so fat or sleepy and the cold snow kept me awake. I hate myself for taking the milk. If I had left it alone back in the beginning of the tenancy, I would be with the girl I can't remember properly, and not with the mother. My hate adds to the rage.

I run downstairs and smash the milk jug on the kitchen floor. Upstairs, Saul closes his heavy book with a thump that I hear through the ceiling. Ethan appears from under the table to buzz and jabber and run around the kitchen as if the house were on fire. Shouting and slamming, I run from the house, through the back door, and into the garden. Heading for the gate and the woods beyond, I cross the lawn. Anger drives my podgy legs and I don't even care about the pain between my rubbing thighs. My heart gurgles and my little lungs feel raw but I keep running.

Shouldn't have turned around by the gate. I only look to see if Saul or Ethan is following me. They aren't, but I see movement in the mother's house. At the kitchen window is a face, pressed against the glass. What looks like a huge white hare with buck teeth stares at me with pink eyes. It is the father.

My slippery hand goes still on the ring-shaped gate handle. I don't like those eyes one bit. He's the one the mother keeps locked away next door; the one with the hiccuping voice that used to come through the wall at night when I first moved here. He was angry back then and he's angry now, watching me trying to escape. Out come his hiccuping shrieks making the glass tremble, and up go his goaty legs with the hard bone at the end to rattle, scratch, rattle on the glass like he wants to get to me. Now the mother's face appears in the gloom behind the father, all red and howling because she's heard the jug smash. From the mother's kitchen, there is a sound of a door being unlocked and I watch the father's grimace turn into a grin. She's letting him out to catch me.

I run from the gate, back across the milky green grass to our house and don't turn my head. But he's so fast. When I reach the kitchen, I can already hear his bone feet on the tiles behind me, getting louder as he gets closer. Soon, I can smell his goaty breath as he snorts over my shoulder and all I can think of are his yellow teeth and how they must bite with a wooden clacking sound. I want my heart to stop; then it will be over quickly.

Jabbering, Ethan runs into his legs and stops him from catching me. There is a crash behind my back. One of the pinky lamps smashes on the floor and the table skids across the tiles and hits the Dainty Maid enamel cooker. Ethan is hurt and I hear him squeal as the father stamps on his hairy back with those clip-cloppity feet.

Up the stairs I run and hear the mother start to bellow at the father for crushing Ethan. There is more smashing and howling in the kitchen as I slip into my room. The truckle bed goes against the door.

Now I am ill, laid up with a fever, and the dreams are worse. For two days I've been off the milk and it has made me sick. Ethan is outside my bedroom door, buzzing. His words are madness. He is saying the milk will make me better and the mother is angry. When she is angry we all suffer. He tells me the mother has said I am never to go to work again. I have done wrong, she says. I'm a little bastard who can't be trusted.

And I'm hurting inside now; dry and gritty and sore in my throat and lungs. It's like there's broken glass inside my stomach too, cutting my softness, and a little voice tells me to drink milk because it will fill in the slashes and take away the pain. And all I can think of is the creaminess inside the ivory jugs. Cravings make me weep salty tears and I hate myself even more. All I want to do is go back to the time of the debts and say no to the warehouse job where I first met Saul. Then I could also say no to the little room and the sweet, sweet milk.

Back in the days of my early tenancy, I wanted to be sick whenever I saw the milk. Laden with tins and packages of normal food, I would struggle up the hill through the black forest, resisting her. There was no way I wanted to drink that brew with the offal taint and soupy thickness. But every night, it would be brought across in huge jugs, slightly steaming, and left upon the kitchen table for the sons to feed from. The sounds they made when feasting made me think of new accommodation. I would have moved out too if I hadn't touched the milk.

As if it were poison, she would pour my normal supermarket milk away whenever I left a carton or bottle in the otherwise empty Dainty Maid fridge. With no other choice, I got into the habit of storing a little emergency container under my truckle bed. But once, when it ran dry with a last rattle and I had a desire for hot tea to stave off the night cold, I was trapped into tasting her produce. To whiten my tea, I used a teaspoon of her milk from the jug that had been left on the kitchen table. And it was delicious; the best tea I ever tasted. Thick and sweet and warming me up like a shot of whiskey, while filling my belly like a big roast dinner. Then, a few days later, I tried it on some cereal. Just a few warm dollops with my nose turned away from the smell. As I ate, loving spoonfuls wrapped my body in warm feather pillows and filled my head with sleepiness and the promise of good dreams. In secret, I went to that jug again and again, like a drowsy bear who found a honeycomb in a log. Eventually, Ethan saw me and sped next door. When he returned with the mother she was smiling and her cheeks were ruddy. That was the start of my troubles.

If only I'd trusted my instincts. Maybe the last tenant did and escaped. There was another, you see, before me in the little room upstairs with the cupboard, greasy wallpaper, and child's truckle bed that my feet hang over. I have seen his markings and know he had the dreams. Maybe he hid under the bed after dreaming of the dances down on the milky green grass, scratching the last of himself away on the wooden slats beneath the tiny springs. Milk, milk, milk, he scratched over and over again with a nail or belt buckle. He knew the craving, when a thousand fish hooks snag in your belly, and a shrill inside voice screams until it's smashed all the windows in your head. But where is the last tenant now? If he escaped then so can I. Soon.

Locked in my room without the milk, I'm struggling to fight off the rolling waves of yellowy fever. Sometimes my head gets a little clearer, but not in the cool way it used to at work before I supped with relish. When I'm not so sick and can move a bit, I write tiny notes under the bed for the next person who takes this room, drinks the milk, and has their clothes washed by the mother.

The father is outside the door now. Up he comes every day and chitter-chatters like an ape, but I won't let him in. Before I smashed the milk jug the mother used to threaten me with the father. My husband will bite you, she'd say, if you don't go in with Ethan at night. Ethan gets lonely in his little box, but the straw smells like the meaty chairs downstairs and I always hated going in with him. I'll have to wait until Ethan and the father have gone from outside the door of my room before the next escape is attempted.

There are noises too at night. The worst sounds come out of Saul's room.

Since I've been here, Saul follows the same routine. After work and the feeding he always goes to his room, which is next door to mine, to read his heavy books and he never comes out until the following morning. In the early evening when the mother's curfew is announced, by her banging on the walls, the rest of us go to bed and dream. But now I'm awake for most of the night, rolling and turning, I hear her moving up the stairs. I know it's her because their feet make different sounds like their voices: Ethan scrabbles, Saul shambles, the father clip-clops, and the mother skitters like a chicken in straw. Most nights, she scratches up the stairs on her bird legs and goes into Saul's room. It is then I cover my ears, unable to listen to the bumping sounds.

But dreaming is the most frightening part of being a prisoner. I'm never sure whether I'm awake or asleep now and all the good dreams have gone. Stuck in my tiny room, passing in and out of sleep, sometimes disturbed by the shifting sounds the father makes outside—I think he sleeps by the door now—I dream of the dances. The whole garden is lit up by a yellow moon,

the color of the fever inside me, with thin clouds drifting across its brightness. It's as if the stars are closer to the earth too when the family forms the
circle. Croaking and bellowing, Ethan and the father hop and skip round
and round the mother, who moves slowly on her hands and knees with her
face in the grass, while Saul chants things from the side in his singing bark.
He has a book open and sits beneath my window like a white whale glowing
on a strange beach. They are calling out to something in the sky with words
I have never heard and don't understand. But these names and words pull
me from sleep, sometimes with a scream.

When I wake up, I am always standing by the window looking down at
the milky green grass, with my body all moist. The garden is empty but there
is a faint ring still left on the lawn as if it has been trampled down by skipping feet. Then the soft blades of grass straighten themselves, and in the center of the slowly vanishing circle the lawn is silvery with midnight dew.

I could break the window to lick that moisture down. To stop the yellow
fever and parched throat that has stolen my voice. Nothing has passed my
lips for three days and nights and much of my strength has gone. Maybe a
final slurp of the milk will allow me to escape, but you can never trust yourself after swallowing that creamy sweetness.

Fourth day, maybe the fifth, and my room is starting to smell. If I don't drink
soon I'll dry out and die. Feeling my face with slow-moving fingers, I touch
the loose flesh. All over my body the skin has gone yellow. Even the little
white hairs are dying on my tummy. Cramps have taken over from the fever
and sickness, but they're half hidden by weakness.

No matter how stained and sharp the father's teeth are, or how fast he can
run, or how big the forest birds are, I must escape tonight. You see, they've all
been up today and talked through the door. It's no good, staying in there.
Come and drink the milk, Saul said. Tonight is very important, he said.
Everything is ready and you don't want to miss out. We've all worked very
hard to welcome you into the family. Ethan just buzzed and squealed, but the
mother made threats. This is your last chance, she said. If you come out right
now I won't let my husband bite and we'll forget about how bad you've been.
But if you don't come out, I'll put you to sleep for good. I'll put your big head
in a bowl of water and drown you, like the last one. You'd grown so well, she
said. Almost ready. All you had to do was grow some more for the joining.

Rage keeps me awake and I hold the bed against the door with my body on top. Joining will be the end of me. There was glee in her voice when she mentioned it. Let them dance beneath the vapors and the yellow moon. When they gather on the grass, I won't be here.

Now it's quiet outside. I make my move and ease the truckle bed away from the door, bit by bit, while listening out for the father. Silence fills the house. Maybe they're next door. Thoughts of escape give me a shiver and start a dripping in my gut. All I have to do, I tell myself, is go out of the house, leave the garden, run through the woods, and then climb over the gate by the bus stop. And this time I won't come back when the children start screaming.

Peering through a tiny gap between the door and the frame, I can see no one outside between the grubby walls on the landing. So out I go, breathing softly with little shudders in my lungs, into the dark house.

Creamy smells surround me on the unlit stairs, like soft hands reaching out from the stains on the walls. Even the bricks beneath the dirty wallpaper must have milk inside them and I hold my sagging face to stop the spinning in my skull.

I'm getting nearer the kitchen, with the pinky glow and the flicker of shadow against the table and the cabinets, which I can see from the bottom of the staircase. I continue past the old parlor with the horsehair chairs that smell of bad meat. I think of sitting in there for a while to catch my breath and to stop the dizzies, but then the idea of sitting on those fleshy things, surrounded by the silk wallpaper gone brown with damp and smelling of sulfur, makes me go all sea-sicky.

In the kitchen, the lamps are lit but the jugs are empty. I look inside them and dry belches rise to my mouth. My eyes screw up from the hot-fire cramps that pinch my inner softness between tweezer fingers. Nothing in the enamel Dainty Maid fridge either. Vanilla light glows thickly around the frosted-glass shelves and sends me reeling back to the table. I can't stop my snorting sounds or the licking tongue, dry as toast, that comes through my puffy lips to touch the cool ivory jugs.

Then I hear the song. Saul's chant is coming through the kitchen wall that attaches us to the mother's house. Strange barking music with the family's chorus beneath his dog sounds. Slipping to the cold, tiled floor, neatly swept by the mother, I feel their rhythms and howls pulling at my clammy body. Making sucking sounds with my belly, I squirm across the floor and out the back door to the milky green grass.

Now there is a fight inside me between two voices. Something whispers about the gate and escape, pulling my squinty eyes across to the arch in the trees, where the metal ring hangs against the dark planks. But the other voice is screaming.

I go looking for milk.

Crying, I move like a thing, yellow and soft, that has fallen from a fisherman's rough hand into the grass. Slowly, I make my way to the back door of the mother's house. I can't stop myself and the screaming voice inside me softens. That's it, just a sip to feel better, it sings.

The expectation of milk eases the gritty feeling inside the pipes and tubes beneath my skin, and my naked flesh shines under the biggest moon, set low in the night sky over the milky green grass whose caressing blades sweep and brush beneath me, feeding me toward her kitchen. Crawling over the little step before the door, I wince at the roughness of stone against my pale underbelly.

Pink oil has been lit in four lamps inside her kitchen and it's as if I am still on the floor of our house. Things are much the same in here, save for the wooden service hatch set between the wall cabinets and work surface. Little curved dents on the swept tiles, made by the father's feet, make me stand up. The family's song has eased to a halt. A smacking of lips begins on the other side of the hatch.

Snuffling takes over from my dry-mouth panting and I see my hands reach for the hatch. Thick fingers work by themselves to nudge and press about for the plastic hole, big enough for a thumb. The wooden doors of the hatch slide through the runners soundlessly and make a hole for the kitchen light to fall through. Staring into the moving darkness, my eyes follow a funnel of pink light, dropping like a ray through a church window.

Before my eyes, pallid shapes move about the floor. Wet and tangled, the family squirms before the mother who sways back on her haunches. A moist face pauses in its feeding and whimpers a message up to the provider. Another's lips part to show rows of small square teeth before turning away from me. They all mewl, then twist aside, and the pinky light strikes her.

Tiny fingers pinch the hem of the floral dress and hold it under her chins. Her eyes are full of excitement. Unveiled is the swollen belly with its pasture of teats among the white hairs. Opaque tears of sweet milk, so thick and dangly, fall to the family and melt something inside me.

With a broad smile, mother invites me to join them.

No Man's Land

BY CHRIS LAWSON AND SIMON BROWN

The whistle blew and we went over the wall in our thousands, a dark tide of frightened men with tin hats and Lee Enfields.

In the wispy light before dawn we were meant to catch the Hun asleep; we'd listened in the early darkness to our scouts going out and cutting through the barbed wire and I guess the Hun had been listening, too, because we only made a hundred yards before we heard the bugle call retreat.

We were deep in No Man's Land with enemy guns spraying bullets from the trenches ahead, and us marching through gaps in the cut wire like sheep scrambling through the narrowing of an abattoir run. When the retreat sounded we found ourselves bottlenecked. I saw Jimmy almost cut in half, and Ethan catch one in the ear, and the panic rose in us, souring us.

Those of who got out scuttled back through the craters and the barbed wire and fell over the wall and into our own trench. On quiet nights, which was most of them, the trenches were hell, but at that moment—with the Hun's bullets whip-cracking around us—they were the sweetest place on earth.

Eventually the tide of retreating soldiers ebbed, and soon there were no more coming over the lip at all. The trench was less crowded. It felt like half of us were left behind in No Man's Land. Captain Beith raised his periscope over the trench and scanned from one horizon to the other. I saw his lips move as he counted, but after a while he stopped and his face went ashen.

The bullets stopped pinging as the Huns realized the attack was over.

At first, the silence was heavenly. After the constant clatter of guns and the pneumatic sound of bullets hitting sandbags and sometimes flesh, the quiet reminded me of Cornwall, where ocean squalls made a cocoon of silence in the ears.

And then the moaning started in No Man's Land, sounding like a dirge. I wished once more for the crack of a fusillade.

"There's Barnacle!" shouted Frog. He pointed over the wall. Along with a dozen other men I scrambled to see where he was pointing, daring to risk a peek over the trench. Barnacle Jones lay strung across the nearest line of wire. His head nodded. Barnacle, a huge and quiet man, famous back in Wales for his running game with Cardiff, was popular with all of us. The only things he ever talked about were rugby and women, a set of distractions that allowed him to strike up a conversation with everyone from the Yorkshire cook to the captain from Oxford.

"Barnacle! You're only thirty yards from the trench!" shouted Frog.

A tired voice called back. "I'm stuck on the wire, you stupid Geordie. An' my legs won't move."

"Don't worry," Frog called, "I'll come and get ya."

I put my arm on Frog's shoulder. The thirty yards might as well have been thirty miles. "Don't be a fool. You'll get yourself shot for nothin'."

"That's Barnacle, Sam! He's our—"

"Look at 'is stomach."

Frog peered across the mud and saw Barnacle had no chance. Suddenly Frog wept. "What are we gonna do?" he asked.

"Barnacle!" I called over the wall. "Your guts are all out! They're goin' to hurt like hell and we can't come for ya."

"Then end it," he called back.

I picked up Frog's rifle and clasped his hand to the barrel. He looked back in shock and shook his head.

"You're the best shot in the squad," I said.

"I can't do it!" He threw his rifle into the mud and turned his back. No one else would look at me.

Benny, a Jew from a family of tailors in London, looked at me and said, "You do it."

No Man's Land

"I couldn't shoot the Kaiser 'isself at that distance," I complained.

"It's only thirty yards," said Arthur, who normally looked like he would murder a man for a ha'penny. At that moment his face was white and his hands shook like tin sheeting in a storm.

"I'm not sure I could hit an elephant if it was standin' right in front of me. Where's Sergeant Prior?" I asked, realizing there was a way out.

"Haven't seen 'im since the attack," Frog said mournfully.

Barnacle's voice filtered across to us. "Jesus Christ! It's hurtin'! Please *somebody!*"

I swore under my breath, loaded the breech of my own gun, lifted the barrel over the trench, and took aim. The Hun must have seen something, for a few bullets whipped overhead, but not so close to be dangerous. I aimed at Barnacle's back, right where his heart should be, remembering the drill sergeant who told me never to try for a head shot if I wanted to live out the war.

I fired the round, only to see the bullet spray mud five yards to the left of Barnacle.

"Jesus!" he screamed. "Who gave the job to the corporal?"

I took aim and fired again, this time missing by only a yard.

"What is going on here?"

I shouldered my rifle and stood to attention as Captain Beith strode up the trench. His mustache was still flecked with mud from our unsuccessful sortie.

"I asked what is going on?"

Nobody spoke.

"Corporal Meredith," he shouted, only inches from my face. "Was that you wasting ammunition after an order to hold fire?"

"Yes, sir," I said.

"Do you have an explanation, Corporal?"

"Sir, Barnacle Jones is caught on the wire thirty yards from the trench. He is in a lot of pain, sir."

"You know as well as I do that the army cannot condone the shooting of our own men." Then he stepped back from my face and breathed heavily. "Well, Meredith, you have been warned. Should you see a Hun stick his head above the trench, well then that is another matter. Then it would be appropriate to loose a quick shot. Just make sure it's a single shot so that Colonel Haslop doesn't hear it and take a personal interest."

Beith marched on, leaving us to it.

"Did anyone else see a Hun?" I asked.

"Sure did," said Benny, staring through me. "Just over there."

I grimaced and took aim again. I went through the drill I had learned. Set the sight for distance. Shoulder the rifle. Aim with the right eye over the barrel. Squeeze the trigger. The rifle kicked in my hand.

"Jesus!" cried Barnacle. I had blown off his left shoulder.

Another shot rang out from over to my left and I saw Barnacle's head snap back, and then he slumped. The wire held him like a scarecrow. I looked down the trench and saw Gully Magginnen, a Dubliner.

"Mother of God," he muttered as he slid down the trench wall. "And they say Robin Hood was an Englishman."

He crossed himself and mouthed a prayer. When he finished, he looked up to see us all staring at him. "Don't look at me," he said in his brogue. "I like shooting Englishmen."

As evening came the air drifted as cold as Charity, but at least a fog came off the river with it and hid the carnage in No Man's Land. Within minutes, the fog was so thick we couldn't see past ten yards.

The sun was a soft red light hanging above the trench. Along the line storm lamps glowed like distant cities and all else was white.

Just before dark, we heard a wheezing, snuffling noise in No Man's Land.

"What the hell's that?" whispered Frog.

"Nothin' to get spooked about," said Arthur.

But the noise came closer.

"It's the Hun," said Frog. "They're using the fog to get through No Man's Land!"

Sergeant Prior put his hand on Frog's arm. "Let's not be silly, lad."

Just then we heard a low keening, like a dirge sung through a broken face. In our months on the line, we had become accustomed to the whine of bullets, and the sirocco blast of the big shells, and the scream of dying men, but nothing could have steeled us against that cry.

Frog launched himself at the trench wall screaming. He leveled his rifle and let go with a round into the fog.

"Bloody hell!" shouted Prior. He threw himself on Frog and dragged him back into the trench. "What if one of our boys is crawling back?" he shouted.

"S-sorry, sir."

No Man's Land

"Jesus, Frog, never shoot at *anything* unless you can see the damn thing!"

Another cry came out of the fog, coming from a different direction, then tapered off into nothing. Then all was silent. Frog sank deeper into the mud.

The next day, when the fog lifted, there was nothing left to see of Barnacle but his helmet, his Lee Enfield, and a boot trapped in a tangle of razor wire.

We knew the war would never end; it had become a constant, one of the great laws of the universe. We imagined our children fighting in the same trenches a generation from now, with the same rats and bog-water at their feet. We talked about being old men, beards down to our belts, our helmets as rusted as the barbed wire in front of the trench, the wood in our rifle stocks as soggy as seaweed, standing to every dawn and every dusk, waiting—God help us, hoping—for the enemy to charge across the field of bones.

We heard the shells falling on the salient held by the Scots about two miles north of us, a pincushion tattoo that rocked the earth and made soil spurt through the sandbags. "They're catching a wallopin'," Arthur said.

"No worse than usual," said Prior. He never smiled, and never meant anything in jest. Company rumor was he had been a law clerk before the War, and I could believe it.

"They're goin' to attack," Frog said, but he said that every morning and no one listened to him anymore. His goggle eyes made him appear constantly startled, but he was always first out of the trench when Captain Beith blew his whistle. He had an unnatural hatred for the Hun.

"No, they're not," Prior said dismissively. "We'd already be neck deep in the bastards otherwise."

Frog fidgeted impatiently with his rifle until we were stood down. We hungrily set to breakfast. Corned beef and tea; the corned beef was fine, but the tea was a little sour, which meant the water in the can had come from a puddle near a hidden German corpse. If the tea was sweet the corpse was French; if straight it was a Tommy, of course, although we allowed it could be Empire generally. After breakfast Prior got us working on the trench again, filling new sandbags, pumping out water, replacing rotten duckboards. Then we did some rat-catching.

We all went after the rats with relish; we wanted to kill something. Prior used a pistol he'd retrieved from a dead officer from another regiment; the rest of us used pick handles. The rats never squealed; some of them didn't even try to escape. In a way it was like mercy killing, and I remembered Barnacle then and didn't catch any more rats.

Afterwards we cleaned our rifles; we had no gun oil and had to use Arthur's Vaseline that his mum sent him every month. Then we played cards, and Arthur asked if anyone had heard the stories about the ghouls. He sounded like someone with a big secret who didn't want to keep it anymore.

"British or German ghouls?" I asked him offhandedly.

"Can't be ours," Frog said, taking my cue. "No such thing as a British ghoul."

"Could be French," I suggested. "Or Canadian. Australian even. The Australians'd make good ghouls."

Arthur looked lost and Frog took sympathy. "What are these stories, then?"

"Don't know I should say anythin' anymore."

Frog snorted. "Fuckin' suit yourself." He dealt a new hand, and he and I carefully looked at our cards. I could see from the slash on the pattern on the back of one that Frog had the king of hearts; it wasn't an unfair advantage— as soon as he saw the card he knew I knew.

"In No Man's Land," Arthur said, picking up his hand.

"What?"

"The ghouls. They're supposed to be in No Man's Land."

"An' what are they doin' there, eh?" I asked.

"Farmin'," Frog said dryly. "Vineyards. That's what they're doin'. An' then they flog the vin blanc to soldiers on both sides."

"Takin' our wounded," Arthur said lowly. "An' they're Hun and Frenchies and us, too."

"What do they do with the wounded?"

"Eat them."

I'd had enough of this. "Change the subject," I said. "Anyone see where Prior went?"

"The captain called him," Arthur said.

"We're on tonight," Frog said.

"There you go again," I told him, shaking my head. "Prior can't take a piss without you shouting 'up and over.'"

But Frog was right.

This time the geniuses behind the lines arranged an artillery barrage, but buggered up the timing. By the time we were going over the top the last round had fallen seven minutes before, enough time for the Hun to slip back into the forward trenches and man the machine-gun posts. It wasn't just our division in the attack this time, but the whole corps, trying to straighten the line so the salient wasn't so . . . well . . . salient. I remember walking in line, tripping over hands in the mud, for the first ten yards, then my muscles just taking over and me charging. The gaps in the wire were still there from a couple of days before, but we didn't even try that passage. Sappers came up with us and blew away whole sections of the barbed wire. This time we got to the trenches.

I jumped in the first one I came across to get out of the way of the murderous machine-gun fire. There was a Hun there, wide-eyed, and I stuck him real good before realizing he was already dead. There wasn't a mark on him so I guess it was concussion that got him. I had to fire my rifle to get my bloody bayonet out of his chest. There was no one else in my section. I should've gone on right away, but I just wanted a rest. Someone landed behind me. I spun around and almost put a hole in Gully.

"Jesus, watch yourself!" I hissed.

He nodded at me. "Now don't be worrying about that." He looked around. "So this is a German trench? Wide, eh?" He looked at me. "So what now, Corporal? Up and over again, or along?"

I could still hear the machine guns chattering overhead. "Along," I grunted, and led the way. The trench zigzagged. We came across two more bodies, both from our side, poor bastards who'd made it this far and then been killed; it seemed like more of an injustice, somehow, than getting killed in No Man's Land.

We came to the end of the trench, a ladder hitched over the east side. I climbed it halfway and peered over the edge.

"What do you see?" Gully asked.

"Nothin'."

"What about our boys? They've got to be *somewhere* . . ."

"I said bloody nothin', all right?"

Gully just shook his head. "Well, what about the other way?"

I turned around and gazed back toward our own lines. "There they all are! Bloody retreatin' again!"

"I didn't near the bugle," Gully said.

"Nor me. C'mon, let's get out of this trench before a German company pours in."

"I'm with you," he said, and we clambered up the west side and ran like blazes. We'd almost caught up with the last line of our retreating troops when Gully tackled me.

"What the fuck do ya think ya doin', ya mad Paddy?"

He grabbed my jaw and made me look up. Four soldiers were writhing on the ground not more than five yards from me, holes in their backs from a machine gun that had stitched them up. A moment later all four were still.

"Right, now," Gully said, grabbing the back of my jacket and hauling me up. We made the last fifteen yards in what seemed ten minutes, jumped feet-first into our trench. I landed on Colonel Haslop. Or what was left of him. Most of his face was all right, but there was just a black pit where his right eye used to be.

Someone grabbed my arm and spun me around. It was Captain Beith.

"I saw you make that trench, Corporal," he said. "Well done. And you too, Private Magginnen. I'll make sure you're both mentioned in dispatches."

"Um, thank you, sir," I said feebly.

"Get off the Colonel, would you?" Beith said. "Not good for the men to see that."

I scrambled off him.

When the captain was gone Gully and I could only exchange puzzled glances.

"What'd we do?" I asked.

Gully shrugged. "Whatever, darlin' Corporal, we're heroes now."

It was quiet for the next week. I don't know why. Sometimes it just happened that way. There were tides to the war that we could not understand. One day there would be five hours solid artillery barrage, and the next day nothing. Those were the good days, because it was possible to attend to matters of hygiene, like crushing lice. We discovered that if you took off your clothes and put them on an ant nest, the ants would kill all the lice for you, but even ants were getting hard to find in the trenches these days. One day there would be nothing left alive on the planet except us, the rats and the lice.

Frog asked Arthur about the ghouls.

"Nothin' more to tell."

"Why don't we see these vineyards you talked about? Why don't we see them taking bodies off the wire?"

No Man's Land

"It was you who talked about the bloody vineyards," said Arthur. "Anyways, they live unn'erground, see? They build these bunkers, deep down."

Benny guffawed. "They must be ritzy gardeners. Imagine growin' vines unn'erground!"

"I don't know they grow vines down there," Arthur said, almost indignantly. "Only tellin' you what I heard. Don't know how much is real meself."

"Well, what about the bodies, eh? Why don't we see 'em takin' the bodies?" Benny persisted.

Arthur shrugged. "Where's Barnacle, then?" he said to end the interrogation.

We all looked at each other, and we could read the same thought in each other's expressions. None of us had forgotten the morning Barnacle had been taken.

"I've seen something." It was Sergeant Prior; our expressions turned to surprise. "Months ago, when I was up the line, I went out into No Man's Land to recce. Saw something. Don't know if it was them ghouls you're talking about. But I saw something with my glasses, on the horizon at midnight with a big moon in the sky. Dragged a dead man down a hole. Too big to be a dog."

I shaved as I listened to the banter. Gully Magginnen was behind me, waiting to use my razor. "You're very quiet, Corporal," he said to me. "Not a believer, I take it."

"I'm with Benny," I said.

Gully shook his head. "I wouldn't be so sure, lad. Arthur's a complete gobshite, but the sarge ain't one for making things up."

"Where you came from every second ruin is supposed to be haunted. You're superstitious, born and bred." He only grunted. "Got your fag?" I asked him. I handed over my razor and he passed me a cigarette in exchange. It was already burning. I gave Gully an evil look.

"Don't waste it or I'll take it back." He laughed as he lathered his face.

I sucked on the cigarette and surprised myself by finding two minutes of happiness.

Michaelmas night was a terror. The Huns were pounding our positions, but they obviously hadn't updated their maps for a few weeks and most of the rounds overshot by more than fifty yards, although the Scots in the salient were getting hell.

We were dug in where the ammo used to be kept. We didn't move if we could help it, or if we couldn't help it we scurried like green beetles. We'd never experienced a barrage like that before.

Gully Magginnen and I were hunkered down in a pocket made of sandbags, playing poker for matchsticks. As the night went on we were driven deeper into our greatcoats, unable to sit up straight in the cacophony. Gully was a good poker player and every half hour he'd clean me out, then divvy up his winnings and start all over again.

"So when do you think the war will end?" he asked me between shells.

"It's never going to end."

"Everything ends."

"What about a circle?"

"Shut up and ante." He started whistling, although it wasn't a happy melody.

"What's that?" I asked.

"It's called 'The Foggy Dew.' It's an old song."

"What's it about?"

Gully smiled. "Home."

"Let's hear the words?"

"Not tonight, I'm thinking."

"Why did you join up?"

Gully smirked. "I didn't join. I was joined. After the Easter Uprising, one of the Black-and-Tans told me that my prospects would improve considerably in the Army."

"Why you?"

"Well, it turns out that my father knew a teacher who was a friend of the cobbler who mended Michael Collins's shoes."

"Who's Michael Collins when he's at home?"

"Don't worry your head about it. You putting up or shutting up?"

I put up. "Do *you* think the war will end?" I asked.

"Sure."

"You've got somethin' to look forward to, then."

"Not really. I can get shot here, or I can get shot back home. I don't suppose it makes a difference if the gun's fired by a German or an Englishman or someone from Londonderry."

"You don't want to go home?"

"I don't want to bleed at home, more's the point."

A round of shells seemed to march toward us, the ground shaking under their impact. The matchsticks wiggled.

"They're 150s," I said. "Hun's bringing in corps artillery. They're goin' to attack."

"You're sounding like Frog."

"They're comin'," I said with certainty. "An' we'll push 'em back, and then it's our turn again."

Gully grunted. "Maybe it *is* all a circle."

I licked my lips. "I don't want to end up in No Man's Land," I said quickly.

"You're starting to believe, aren't you?" He grinned without humor.

"I don't mean that. I mean I don't want to end up havin' you or Frog shootin' my fuckin' brains out. I want someone to come and get me, even if my intestines are trailin' out like barbed wire."

"I'll come for you," Gully said levelly.

"You would?"

Gully nodded.

"Then I'll come for you," I said.

"I already know that. Your deal."

I was right about the Hun. He came over an hour before dawn, running low to the ground like a ferret after a rabbit. Frog heard him first, started shooting at shapes in the dark. Within seconds everyone was shooting, not knowing why. Then the first Germans spilled into our trench, shooting and bayoneting. We lost Jo Jo Wicliffe and Bill Stubbins right away. I saw Benny stick one of them in the neck, then one of them stuck Benny in the gut and he squealed and fell over. I fired from the hip and Benny's attacker slumped to the ground. I rushed over to Benny and Gully covered me. Benny still had the bayonet in him, and before I could stop him he grabbed the German rifle and pulled it out. Blood gushed, he looked surprised at the amount of it and then his eyes rolled back into his head and he died. The German I shot moaned, tried to sit up. He looked sixteen and I had shot him in the groin. I detached the bayonet from my rifle and cut his throat before he knew what I was doing. Gully watched me but didn't say anything.

The attack sort of petered out at our end, although we heard later the Scots had been massacred and the salient lost. That afternoon, before we could remove all the dead, clouds built up over the front and it started to pour; at the same time the Hun artillery started firing on us again. It was eerie, the sound of the shells exploding around us amid the patter of rain, and the bright, phosphorescent explosions against the darkening sky. I was talking to Frog when we both heard the high-pitched whistle of a shell arcing toward us. I shut my mouth and we waited to see how close it would land. I was looking at Frog when I saw Arthur, standing ten yards away, simply disintegrate. I didn't hear any explosion. I blinked. Frog turned to me, a puzzled expression on his face, and I saw a sliver of white and bloody bone impaled in his head. He dropped. I just stood there, refusing to believe.

The next morning our artillery let loose a desultory barrage for fifteen minutes, then all the officers blew their whistles. We were up and over, checking the man on our right and on our left, quick step, rifles held across our chest, machine-gun fire stitching the ground in front of us, the *pot-pot* of single rounds skipping in the mud at our feet, the distant crump of artillery, the closer sounds of shrapnel rending limbs and bodies, knowing they have your range, breathing like you're in water to your neck, the sigh of a passing bullet, the wailing of the wounded already left behind, the metallic whang of someone's helmet being struck, and Gully calling out.

I stopped in my tracks, not wanting to look behind me. He called out again. I looked over my shoulder and saw him lying in a shallow lake of blood, his chest open to the sky, his cheeks broken, his limbs all a-tangle.

I knelt down next to him. I wanted to cry, but couldn't anymore. "Jesus, Gully, what have you gone an' done?"

He blinked at me but couldn't get his mouth to work. Part of his neck was missing and air was whistling through it. His right hand grabbed my arm so tightly it hurt, then let go as life let go of him.

We captured the Hun trench again. I was in it alone this time. No Gully, no Frog or Arthur or Benny. I heard Sergeant Prior's voice around a bend. There weren't enough of us to hold the line. The Hun would be back soon. I sat in a puddle of water, not caring. I was caught in a circle and there was no end for me. I waited until darkness, heard the familiar sound of artillery shells falling. I was flung down into my puddle by a wall of hot air and invisible fingers plucked at my clothes and my chest and face, feeling like sleet on a winter's night. All around me I heard the sound of a furious battle.

Then my eyes closed and I could not force them open again.

I woke.

Everything was quiet. There was no artillery, no rifle shots, no men clambering along the trench. The Hun must have pushed on, driving our forces back. What a disaster. We had fought six months for that hundred yards and the Hun had snatched it back in an afternoon.

Night was falling. I was still in the puddle, and knew if I didn't move I would freeze to death, but I couldn't even lift my hands. I was afraid a bullet had taken out my spine. I concentrated as hard as I could. Still my hands would not move.

It's shock! That's all, just shock! I told myself to get a grip. To think of Mother England. To just get up and goddamn move!

Not a flicker.

I was stuck at the bottom of the trench looking up at the sky as it blackened. The stars came out and I thought it wasn't such a bad way to die after all. As the stars wheeled overhead, a planet rose above the trench until it looked straight down on me. I'm no astronomer, but I fancied it was Mars.

At first the cold was terrible, but soon it brought a welcome numbness and I knew I would die presently. Unbidden, I thought of the comrades I would be joining. It must have been near midnight when the light of the stars began to fade in my eyes. I was sinking, and the slit of sky above made me think I was already in my grave.

Then I heard a shuffling sound. There was hissing and dragging and a ragged breathing, and it was coming closer.

A voice started singing quietly. I recognized the tune, but I had never heard the words before.

> *"Right proudly over Dublin town*
> *Hung they out a flag of war.*
> *'Tis better to die 'neath an Irish sky,*
> *Than at Suvla or Sud el Bar."*

A shadow peered over the rim of the trench. I tried to call out, but could not.

Closer now came the song. There was an odd tone to it, a breathy over-tone like a voice piped through a church organ.

"Their graves we'd keep where the Fenians sleep
'Neath the hills of the foggy dew."

An arm reached down into the trench and pulled me up into the starry night. He had a hole in his chest the size of a dinner plate. The ribs jutted out. His skull was misshapen. His left arm ended at the elbow. His breath rattled through the crater in his windpipe and wheezed out between his ribs.

He put his mealy face right next to mine.

"Hello, darlin' Corporal," Gully said. "Welcome to No Man's Land."

The Watcher at the Window

BY DONALD R. BURLESON

Charlotte was not sure she was happy to see her sister after all. Now that Doris wasn't just a voice on the telephone or a swatch of crabbed, inconsequential handwriting on a postcard ("Worked in my garden all week, the petunias aren't taking the heat very well")—now that they were no longer a safe three thousand miles apart—Charlotte was having second thoughts about their reunion here in Larkwood. But then what choice had she, really?

By the time they had walked halfway down Sycamore Lane, Father's house was swallowed up by a convex blanket of shrubbery, and the street showed only visages of unfamiliar housefronts, bedecked in Halloween trappings and gazing out at the passers-by like rows of blind half-forgotten faces, darkly festive, in a school yearbook. The neighborhood was only a vague, transmuted echo of her childhood memories; the years had altered almost everything.

"Yes, it's all changed," Doris said, as if privy to her thoughts.

They turned right onto Bolton Street and walked north between other bland rows of houses. This early in the morning no one else was about, and the autumn mists of dawn were only now receding like faint grey spiderwebs, and the town seemed cheerless, almost forlorn. Charlotte knew now, glancing sidelong at Doris, what it was that bothered her about seeing her sister again after all these years. Doris's face was too much like a mirror. Seeing the ponderous furrows of time that had settled there, Charlotte knew all too well that she, too, had grown old. Usually she could ignore her own reflection in the mirror, but not *this* mirror. Looking at Doris's gaunt and desiccated form, she thought of a line from William Butler Yeats—"Old clothes upon old sticks to scare a bird"—but she knew the words might just as well describe her own angular and time-ravaged frame.

They crossed Walnut Lane and continued north up Bolton toward Dedham Street, and Charlotte knew what occupied both their thoughts.

"You say it's all changed," she said. "Some things are the same. You see that house?" She indicated a cottage ensconced in bushes. Black-and-orange paper skulls grinned from the windows like strange morning wraiths. "I remember it. The Reverend Patterson used to live there."

Doris glanced at the house and snorted. "Someone's painted it brown," she said as they came to the intersection with Dedham Street. "Not the same at all. Besides, you couldn't care less about the Reverend Patterson's house. I know what's on your mind."

They turned onto Dedham Street and walked west, toward downtown Larkwood. Gradually the placid residential neighborhoods would give way, first to a laundry and antiques shops and a grocery store, and then to the increasingly commercial facades of the business district, such as it was. But before the laundry and the antiques shops and the grocer's, one would see a nondescript stretch of what might once have been outlying little business establishments of one sort or another, now only a depressing assortment of boarded-up windows and collapsed ambitions, sad little storefronts on whose dirty panes there remained only stuttering remnants of lettering to suggest in some remote fashion what these buildings once were. This area had been called Dedham Square, and Charlotte remembered when most of these bygone stores were open and thriving. Walking through the area now, she felt more than ever the oppressive hand of time.

But there was one building that was different. It was boarded up and empty now, of course, but it had been boarded up and empty back then, too, when she and Doris had been children here.

The Place, they had called it.

And here it was now, coming up on their right. The trees lining this part of Dedham Street had always been so thick that one couldn't see the Place until its ugly, unpainted front loomed directly overhead. Indeed, the ramshackle three-story wooden building leaned toward the avenue at so grotesque an angle that it seemed to be over you rather than beside you, and nearly formed an arch with a similar building (the old furniture store, Charlotte recalled) across the way, now long defunct.

The difference here was that while the gloomy edifice they called the Place was now just as abandoned and lifeless as its neighbors, it had been so even in the old days, and neither Charlotte nor Doris had ever known what sort of establishment it might once have been. One fancied, sometimes, that it had always been just as it was now—purposeless, empty.

But not quite empty?

The thought must have shown on her face, because Doris was regarding her with a knowing smirk that contained no trace of humor. "As I said, I know what's been on your mind," she remarked quietly, almost as though it were a reproach.

As they came closer, the emerging sun cast enough radiance from the east-southeast, behind them, to throw the old building's one remaining window into a confusion of reflected light, and it was probably only this effect that made it seem to Charlotte, for one breathless moment, that a bloated face peered at them from behind the pane. A Halloween face again? No, infinitely less wholesome somehow. The impression passed, with or without Doris's sharing it, she couldn't tell, and in any case they walked beyond the building and continued toward town in silence.

The limited attractions of the business district did little to uplift Charlotte's thoughts or to make Doris more talkative. As they dawdled over dishes of ice cream, Charlotte remembered more of the old days than she wished to. How distant, yet how unsettlingly clear in the memory, those times—the two sisters, all pigtails and skinned knees and buckteeth, walking past the Place, whispering, shuddering, their childish imaginations running wild.

But how much had been imagination? Even then, the ground-floor window had been scarcely less bleary, and one never knew whether or not it was a caprice of the light that made it seem as if a pale, corpulent face stared from behind the grimy glass. The Watcher, they had called him. Or her, or it. They could never see it too clearly, and on occasion not at all, yet more often than not its eerie contours, anticipated on long hushed walks approaching Dedham Square, were at least a suspected presence in the window, and both gawky girls would run past, terrified. Thrilled, too, in an odd way, but still terrified. No imaginable enticement would have moved them to pry their way past the dusty boards and enter the building, or even linger before its spectral window.

What had always been particularly repellent about the glimpsed face of the Watcher was its pasty, unhealthy color. Recalling it, Charlotte pushed her ice cream away, no longer having any appetite for it.

"Remarkable, isn't it?" Doris asked. Charlotte thought that she meant the chalky color of the ice cream, with its dreadful suggestiveness, but Doris only said, "That it took Father's death to bring us both back here at the same time."

On the walk back to the house, Charlotte thought: Yes, I moved fifteen hundred miles west, to California, and she moved fifteen hundred miles east, to Vermont, and decades later Death, the great average-maker, pulled us back to the middle, whether we wanted to come or not.

Charlotte cooked the dinner that night, with the uncomfortable reflection that Death had handed her a house, too, or half a house. They would sell it, of course, since neither owned it outright or wanted to live in it, and then they would no doubt revert to their bipolar existence on opposite ends of the country. Charlotte was rather looking forward to returning to her high-rise apartment in Santa Rosa.

Except for one thing.

"You know," she said over dinner, "there's a place in Santa Rosa where I walk sometimes, and there's an abandoned building where I think I see— someone watching me as I pass by."

Trying to imagine how Doris would react to this remark, she hadn't anticipated the expression that met her from across the table. Doris looked not contemptuous or skeptical, but a little frightened. "Go on," she said.

"Well," Charlotte said, "there isn't much more to tell. Sometimes when I walk by and look, it's there, and sometimes not. The face. When it's there, the disturbing thing about it is that color, a sickly kind of white."

"Like the underside of a toadstool," Doris supplied.

Charlotte, surprised, faltered a moment and then said, "Yes, something like that."

This time, as they walked west on Sycamore, Charlotte didn't glance back toward Father's receding house, nor ahead, even in her mind, toward Dedham Square. She just walked, with Doris as taciturn as ever, beside her. Charlotte was grateful for the silence. Her sister looked thoughtful, and Charlotte wasn't eager to hear her thoughts.

The Watcher at the Window

They walked north up Bolton Street again, past the same noncommittal rows of houses. Now and then a robed figure (some priest of the Darkness?—no, a common mortal in a house robe, and Charlotte had to get her mind in order) would appear briefly in a doorway to retrieve the morning paper, or in the shadows of some yard a stray cat, startled at the approach of strangers, would dart away into the bushes, gone. The two sisters crossed Walnut Lane, continued up to Dedham Street and turned west again, toward downtown.

Gradually the modest houses thinned out and the melancholy wooden facades of Dedham Square replaced them, frowning upon the quiet early-morning street with withered faces of decay more somber than any jack-o'-lantern's. And among these ponderous facades—that unsavory building. The Place.

Involuntarily, both women slowed their pace. Charlotte winced at the incongruity of this gesture. What good was it to approach the building more slowly, when what they most needed to do was hurry past and get it behind them?

"Don't look," Doris said.

Charlotte was startled. "What?"

Doris elbowed her in the arm. "I said, don't look at it."

But of course Charlotte had to look. This time the bleary windowpanes reflected not a confusion of morning sunlight but only the grey indeterminacy of an overcast October sky, and it was hard to say whether this made everything better or worse. It was better in that without the dazzle of bright light one could see more clearly through the dirt-streaked glass. But it was worse precisely because you *could* see.

And although Charlotte had only the most transient glance at the pasty-white, bloated face that seemed to nod and waver behind the pane, she wished indeed that she had not looked. She couldn't tell whether Doris had seen it too, and didn't want to ask; they made the remainder of their journey in silence.

Over lunch, finally, Charlotte asked her, "You said not to look at it. What did you mean? Not to look at the window, or not to look at what's behind it?"

Doris took a sip of coffee and dabbed at her mouth with a napkin before replying. "Who said there's anything behind it?"

"You didn't see anything?" Charlotte asked.

Doris sniffed contemptuously. "No."

Charlotte finished her own coffee in a gulp and wanted not to have to say it. "I wish I could believe you."

"Believe whatever you wish," Doris replied.

The day passed in dreary errands, and the evening passed at the house in silence. Finally Doris said, "All right."

Charlotte looked up from a magazine in which she had read the same sentence three times, too preoccupied to concentrate. "What? What's all right?"

Doris sighed and laid her own tattered magazine aside. "I did see it."

Charlotte scarcely knew whether to be relieved or horrified. In any case she wasn't entirely surprised. "What did you see?"

"Don't play games with me," Doris replied. "You know perfectly well. The face. Dear God, that face, too pale, and too large." Her words seemed to be tumbling out now, as if she were anxious to be rid of them. "Too white, and too—"

"Too what?" Charlotte urged, caught up in the words.

"Too much like the other," Doris said.

Both of them needed a few moments of silence to catch their breath. Finally Charlotte asked, "What other?"

Doris's face in the lamplight was sharp, severe, appallingly frightened. "The one near where I live."

This was too much for Charlotte. She let the words hang in the air and die away, and did not try to reply. Doris at length went on.

"I walk sometimes, in the evenings, in Brattleboro, when the weather is decent. There's a lonely kind of a road that I turn down, and it winds on and on, nearly out of the city, but before you get out into the country it leads through a cluster of old abandoned buildings, and in one of them—"

"My God," Charlotte whispered.

Doris got up and walked to a window and stood looking out into the night. "I've tried to tell myself it's just a trick of the light. Especially since the face isn't always there. But when it is . . ." Her voice trailed off, and no one spoke again that night.

"But why do you have to leave today?" Charlotte asked, hating herself for seeming to whine. "You were going to stay awhile longer."

"I just don't think I want to be here," Doris said simply. Somehow she sounded like the child Doris again, pigtails and scabby knees. But the face in the morning light was ancient.

"Well, I don't want to be here alone," Charlotte protested.

Doris put a hand on her hand, for the first time in uncountably many years. "Don't worry so much. Most of the paperwork is done. The rest we can manage through the mail. I just want to get away. I mean, I just want to get back."

Get away is what she means, Charlotte thought. But all she said was, "You know best."

Alone in the house, she reflected upon the different kinds of silence. When Doris had been here, across the room, silence was a well of uncertainty, of expectation, of knowledge that something, for better or worse, would eventually be said. Now, without her sister, silence was just silence: endless, unpromising, devoid even of the illusion of momentary comfort. She had to get out of the house, if only for an hour.

It had been late afternoon when Doris left, and by now the sun was down and the western sky was dying like an ember. The lengthening shadows made Bolton Street a tunnel of trees, woody sentries black against the gathering night, forbidding in the intervals between streetlights, where dusky outlines of hedges seemed to change their shapes and small creatures scurried, restless, unseen.

"Scared of cats and trees," Charlotte chided herself aloud, crossing Walnut Lane and continuing northward, but when she turned west onto Dedham Street, the shroud of night had really fallen, and even the wan procession of streetlamps stretching ahead of her seemed unable or unwilling to relieve the gloom. Maybe she would see a movie in town. But she knew that there was no need, knew that she could simply turn around and go back to the house. She went on, though, toward Dedham Square.

Toward the Place.

Pausing under a streetlamp goosenecked high in the air above her, she reflected: I don't have to go on *or* go back the way I came. I can turn down the next cross street and that will take me—

But that was how it was in Santa Rosa, not here. What could she have been thinking?

Walking on, past the last lonely houses before you reached the edge of Dedham Square, she thought: It's not bad enough I forget I'm in Larkwood,

I even think I confused it with Santa Rosa, where I've never even been. Heavens, what would Charlotte think?

And this troubled reflection stopped her cold beneath the next street-lamp. I *am* Charlotte, and I *live* in Santa Rosa. Why was I thinking like Doris? Surely the strain of the whole situation—Father's death, putting the house up for sale . . . but how could she stand here making excuses?

Reluctant to leave the glow of the lamp, she nevertheless felt oddly drawn onward by the darkness, even as the ruined shells of the nearer buildings in Dedham Square began to take form, shapes of darkness against the darker sky. The old furniture store across the street was innocent enough, though sprawling and eaten through with holes like a rotting pumpkin. But the building before her now—the Place—was another matter.

She stood in front of it, fidgeting. Furniture store? But no, there had always been a vacant lot across the street. In Brattleboro there had always been a lot of—

Charlotte had never been to Brattleboro, Vermont. This was Larkwood, Indiana. Across the street were the ruins of the old furniture store, pure and simple. But how had she known—

The nearest streetlamp here was some distance away but cast a familiar glow upon the familiar window. Was that a furtive movement at the glass, a withdrawn face? Perhaps not. In any event, before she knew what she was doing, she had stepped up to the building, pulled a board from across the ancient door, and pushed her way inside.

She stood absolutely still, not even breathing, and listened to the silence around her. This was crazy. There was no reason for her to be here, none at all. Yet here she was.

Outside, the wind came up momentarily and sent a fit of creaking through the dusty boards around her and above her. It probably wasn't even safe to be here; the place might come shuddering down around her at any time, burying her in dirty rubble. She sensed the decaying bulk of the building above her, and it was like being at the bottom of an ocean of rotten wood, gasping for breath. But the groaning timbers gradually grew quiet, settling, settling. She listened.

Nothing. Not a sound.

Or was there just the faintest impression, as if something shifted, unseen, unheard, felt only as a subtle alteration of pressure in the musty air?

Her eyes began to adjust to the darkness, but even so she could make out only the vaguest outlines of timeless clutter: a half-fallen-down table, perhaps, and some rotted boxes muffled in dust. Charlotte would really be surprised to see her now, standing here in the dark like a—

But she *was* Charlotte, wasn't she? Absurdly, she reached up and felt her face in the dark. She should know this face. She had certainly seen it enough times from the window. Right here in Santa Rosa.

No, what was this, what was she thinking? Before she could even wonder, a pallid and puffy face nearly as large as the dirty window out of which it had been looking turned slowly toward her. Was it she who screamed or that woman across the shadowy room, the one who had taken down a board from the door and come in? Or was it only an aberration of the light that made it seem as if someone had come in? But it was she who turned, she, Charlotte, who perhaps had never had a sister, and it was Doris, whoever that was, Doris who had perhaps never had a sister, and it was a thousand others, yet it was the Watcher, pale and lonely at a thousand obscure windows, windows like mirrors. Peering across a mirror-maze of lightless rooms, the wan-faced Watcher turned slowly in the murky dark.

It was insane to be the woman coming down the lane again and again and again, and the other walker and the other and the other, coming down a thousand quiet lanes in a thousand quiet towns, yes, surely it was madness to be all of them and the Watcher, too.

But then, how could one watch and watch and watch and *not* be mad?

Coming of Age

BY JOEL LANE

A violent death made waves, Rajan thought. The image of a shattered body, a torn mouth, hung around like a tattoo on the daylight. But the disappearance of an adult, or even a teenager, left no mark. The only images that haunted you were normal ones. There was a gap, a missing face, like a door that wouldn't shut. A violent death left a scar. But a disappearance wouldn't ever close. With time it became a mouth, a vortex into which your entire world gradually fell.

He had no specific memory of the last time he'd seen Ashok. Just one evening among many. He'd not even told the boy to take care—he was nearly eighteen, after all, and such reminders made him uptight. And being home by twelve was a given. But not this time. It was only after midnight that a typical evening had become *that night*. The coach of normality had become a pumpkin, with a candle flickering through carved teeth. By two, they'd phoned all the hospitals. Then the police. Not Ash's friends. Kavita was sure they'd ring if they knew where he was.

Over the bare weeks that followed, the August sun had scoured the inside of their house like bleach. The air was so bright that shadows became impenetrable, pieces of dead space. Somewhere in the shadows outside, Ash was hidden. The police had spoken to his friends, the school, the community center where he sometimes worked. Rajan thought they were doing what they could. But they had nothing to give.

Ash's possessions had yielded no clues. Even searching through the compacted chaos of his bedroom had felt like an admission that he wasn't coming back. The lost have no secrets. Not that much was uncovered. A packet of condoms, still wrapped. A single copy of *Mayfair*. Some letters from his former girlfriend, Tara, mentioning the fact that they'd slept together. Rajan didn't bother pretending to be shocked. What struck him most was that nothing was missing. You didn't leave home without ID or a passport. Unless you wanted to stop being yourself.

Even the boy's diary was no help. The police were very struck by the fact that in March, when he'd broken up with Tara, Ash had written: *I wish I was dead*. Rajan remembered him being quite down for a week, then developing an obsession with the maudlin albums of Pearl Jam—who even Rajan knew were truly lame. He was more bothered by a recent entry: *Think I might join the business*. The police assumed he meant the family business; but, as he explained to them, there wasn't one. He was a designer, and his brother worked in sales. Ash was hoping to make films.

Kavita thought he was dead. "He wouldn't just disappear. We're hearing nothing because . . . there's no one to speak. He's in a canal or an empty building, or under the ground. We should mourn him, not torment ourselves with a voice we'll never hear again." Rajan wasn't ready to accept that. He didn't think Kavita was either. But where was he supposed to look for his son? There was no other world for him to explore. No secret life. Only the life he knew, which was over. Burned like cellophane in the bright August sun.

Ash's friends had no idea where he was. They were looking for him too, all over Birmingham. He'd gone to the Arcadian Center cinema with two friends, had a drink with them afterwards, then gone to Snow Hill to catch the bus home. Maybe he'd decided to walk. It was only three miles. Something had happened. His friend Vijay remembered Ash had been quiet. "Not really down, just thoughtful. Staring into space, maybe looking for someone, I don't know." They'd been to see *Cruel Intentions*, which had featured an actress with whom Ash apparently had a slight obsession.

Vijay didn't know what *the business* might be either. "Films? TV? He used to talk about that sometimes . . . I don't think he was into anything . . . you know, dodgy. If he was, I'd tell you. Ash always seemed kind of innocent.

Sometimes he'd say *When I'm rich and successful*—but it was kind of a joke. He didn't talk about money." Rajan recognized that as a trait of his own.

Ash's picture appeared in the local papers and on *Midlands Today*. Rajan avoided looking at the photograph. He didn't want the living face to harden into a fixed image in his head. As the weeks went by and the searches began to tail off, it seemed less and less likely that what was found would be recognizable.

The muggy heat of late summer began to thin out. The terrifying stillness in the house had become something else, a gradual decay that at least made time real. Answering the phone was so painful they were discouraging friends and relatives from calling. And they made excuses to avoid letting people visit, because the house was in chaos. Neither of them could face cooking or housework. It was as if they needed to make their grief visible, but had to keep the result a secret. Kavita's acceptance of the situation was slowly unraveling, leaving her empty and silent. Rajan couldn't talk to her, or to himself. He'd never experienced despair like this. Not something inside you, but something you had to live inside.

The only relief came from walking. Night after night, he paced aimlessly around Handsworth and Hockley, looking for any trace or sign of something unusual that might explain how a boy could disappear. The whole process of searching was an elaborate kind of prayer. It reminded him of his own teenage years in Birmingham, when he'd tried to get out of the house every evening to avoid his parents' arguments. Of course, he'd been leaner and fitter in those days. Now, walking for miles made his legs ache and darkened his shirt with sweat. But there was the same feeling of wanting to believe that the city could give him what he needed.

The industrial part of Handsworth hadn't changed much in the last twenty years. There were still the same foundry and metal works, the same jigsaw of iron and concrete. The barbed wire had become razor wire. But along the Soho Road, the shops had changed beyond recognition. Even ten years before, they'd been mostly grocery shops selling cheap tins and stale vegetables. Every facade was whitewashed, and half of them were boarded up. Now, the street was a major shopping center for the Asian community: imported fabrics, clothes, videos and books were displayed alongside DVD players and mobile phones. The more bourgeois the customers became, the more they bought in the commodities of their parent culture.

Coming of Age

Kavita worked there, assistant manager of a clothes shop that became more fashionably retro every year. Rajan hoped that her career would help to get her through what was happening now. Complications with Ash's birth had meant that they couldn't have any more children. Perhaps they'd over-protected him, kept him from becoming streetwise. Or perhaps they hadn't protected him enough.

Near the top of Soho Hill, a new Sikh temple stood in a cloud of blue light. Its flawless white-and-gold structure drew Rajan's reluctant admiration. Beyond the crest of the hill was the shallow curve of the Hockley fly-over. There were usually kids underneath it, smoking or skateboarding. A few times, Rajan had shown them the photo of Ash he kept in his wallet. They always said they'd seen him, then described someone who worked in a local shop or was going out with a friend's sister. Was it stupidity or malice? Or did most teenagers really live in a world where what they didn't know couldn't exist?

Hockley was a patchwork that made no sense. Jewelry workshops, empty warehouses, Yuppie restaurants, beat-up housing estates, vandalized grave-yards. Rajan felt sure that something had happened to Ash here. Maybe he'd been involved in some kind of criminal deal. Maybe the film had turned him on and he'd gone looking for a prostitute. Or maybe—and this, in a way, was worse—he'd just been walking through and been jumped by a gang of skin-heads. Ever since their brief success in Tower Hamlets, the neo-fascists had been on the lookout for trouble. Any incident they could provoke, they'd claim as a vindication of their hatred. What had happened to the Dunkirk spirit they went on about? The root of the whole problem, Rajan thought, was that people couldn't stand to be reminded of their own failure.

It wasn't easy to assimilate into a culture so full of ghosts. The English couldn't adjust to the fact that they could no longer help themselves to whatever they felt like. Colonial rule had turned in on itself, like a cancer. Rajan remembered a recent TV program about the British regime in India. A retired soldier reminiscing about how his squadron had enticed a village girl into the barracks with promises of money. She'd been gang-raped by "about twenty" men, and in the process her neck had got broken. She'd been thrown out with the empty bottles the next morning. And the English wondered why there was anger.

Hockley was linked to the city center by Livery Street, a long straight road that always seemed to be in shadow. One side of it was a solid block of thin office buildings, at least a hundred years old. The other was a viaduct, through whose arches you could see white light reflected on the motionless surface of a canal. Near the end, close enough to hear the roar of traffic on the expressway, there was a nightclub called Subway City. Maybe something had happened there. But Rajan knew better than to hang around outside a nightclub asking questions. He wasn't suicidal yet.

The more he walked around these parts of North Birmingham at night, the harder it became to separate what he was seeing from memory. If there was a part of the city where Ash still lived, perhaps his own teenage self lived there too. In those days, he'd found the city frightening and his own place in it chilly. Yet in the happier moments—his first girlfriend, his first job, leaving home—he'd wanted to be young forever.

In September, the catalogue company Rajan worked for increased its productivity targets after a time and motion study. Rajan found himself working longer hours, often skipping breaks, just to keep up. Needless to say, the workforce got nothing from the increased profits. Kavita was putting in a lot of overtime as well, trying to recover herself through work. The time they spent together began to improve a little. They started making love again, more out of loneliness than anything else. It was only a matter of time, Rajan thought, before they split up.

One cloudy evening, he walked from the office in Aston to the jewelry quarter. The clock at the top of Vyse Street indicated midnight, but it was about seven. The graveyard was littered with Special Brew cans. Along Hockley Hill, several of the ground-floor shops had recently changed hands; the upper stories were the same as before, their elaborately carved windows framing wooden boards or darkness. Only the obsolete had staying power. The flyover was streaming with rush-hour traffic, all heading out of the city. In the shadows underneath, pigeons were tugging at shreds of naan. Three pale youngsters were standing by one of the concrete supports. They gazed coldly at Rajan as he approached them.

Two boys and a girl, all with bleached hair. He couldn't even see any color in their eyes. They looked about fifteen. "Excuse me," he asked. "Have you seen this person? Anytime in the last few weeks?" He held out the snapshot of Ash. The three kids looked at him with a kind of distant curiosity, as if he were something on a microscope slide.

One of the boys took the photo and passed it to the girl. She looked at it for a few seconds, then gave it back to Rajan. "I don't know his name," she said. "But I've seen him. He went to the business."

"What business? Where?"

"You'll find it." She turned away. The other two followed her.

"Wait," Rajan said. "You've got to tell me . . ." They'd gone into the underpass, which had no light. He stumbled after them. His feet splashed in a pool of rainwater. Their pale heads flickered like distant lights.

They *were* distant lights. He was standing in the open square under the middle part of the flyover. The grey stone above his head was singing. There were four other passages back out to the streets, each one flanked by stone panels with abstract carvings. No one was there.

Later, he tried to explain what had happened to Kavita. "They were completely white," he said. "I don't mean Anglo-Saxon. I mean they had no color at all. If you cut them, they'd probably bleed white. Like correction fluid." What had bothered him most was the way they'd just dismissed him. Their attitude of complete indifference. "If they know what *the business* means . . ."

"It's some teenage slang," Kavita said. "Probably just means going to school, or behaving like an adult. Kids like that live in a different world. You should take no notice." She reached across the table and touched Rajan's hand. "You're not doing yourself any good with these questions. How can it help?" He looked into her eyes and couldn't explain his need to believe.

It was a fortnight before he saw them again. He'd spent hours drifting around Hockley, through the park and the graveyards. The police had said "the business" might refer to crime, but that wouldn't help them much. Rajan wondered if they'd given up. He'd stood in the concrete square under the flyover, praying. It was no use. And then he saw three pale kids on the canal walkway, in the shadow of a bridge. They were staring into the dark water, which didn't reflect them or anything else.

Instead of calling, he ran down the metal steps to reach them. They looked at him and didn't move. He wanted to grab one of the boys and slam him against the bridge wall; but their blank stares made him wonder if he existed at all. They must be drugged, he realized. Even in shadow their faces had an unhealthy sheen, like mold. "Where is he?" Rajan asked. "You said he'd gone to the business. Where is it? I'll give you money . . ."

The girl smiled. Her teeth were dead white and very small. "Try looking some time." She reached into a pocket of her tight jeans and took out a card.

"It's here." She gave the card to Rajan; her finger touched the edge of his palm. The card was black, with white lettering: THE BUSINESS, then an address in Factory Road. That was only a mile away, he realized, off Soho Hill. Was it a club of some kind? When he looked up, the teenagers were under the next bridge, only just visible. He didn't pursue them.

Factory Road, as you would expect, ended in a factory. The only other buildings were thin terraced houses, some of them boarded up. The address on the card was number 74. He paused at the door, breathless. A thread of nausea crept into his mouth. It was one of the empty houses. Boards were nailed over the windows. On the first floor there was a small balcony, the kind where you'd stand a potted shrub or hang some washing. The railings in front of it were twisted to leave a gap, like the outline of a face.

There was nothing here. The card was a sick joke. Rajan slipped it back into his pocket. The edge of his right hand felt cold. So did the inside of his skull. The children were playing somewhere. In empty houses, on a different street map. He wanted to find a pub and drink until the pale brightness in his head went away. But he couldn't go home drunk. Alcohol was one of the few things on which Kavita had fairly traditional views.

On the bus home, Rajan thought he needed to go back to his faith. It would protect him against humiliations like this. Give his life a frame that wasn't this city. He'd drifted away from the Hindu religion as a teenager, trying to rebel against his parents. Hidden somewhere in that thought was a connection he couldn't make. Like a gap between curtains that he couldn't reach to look through.

The third of October would have been Ash's eighteenth birthday. It was a Friday. Too depressed to stay in the house, Kavita had gone to her sister's in Coventry for the weekend. Rajan decided to stay in and do some work. Then he decided to stay in and pray. Then he bought a half-bottle of whiskey and drank it, sitting alone in the dark. At some point, he heard Kavita's voice on the answerphone saying she hoped he was all right.

Later, he woke up and switched on the light. It was nearly 2 A.M. His glass had fallen onto the pale carpet, staining it gold. He didn't care. In his mind was the image of the house on Factory Road. It was the house where he'd been born. Not the same road, not the same city. But the same house.

His parents had come here from Gujerat in the fifties. They'd lived in Sheffield for nine years, then moved to Birmingham when Rajan was five and his brother Ajay was eight. That was when the problems had started: lack of money, lack of friends, his parents arguing bitterly over everything. By the time Rajan was sixteen, his parents weren't broke any more. But they still argued, because it had become a habit. And because their love had died.

Rajan picked up the slim briefcase he took to work and slipped a screwdriver, a hammer and a torch into it. As an afterthought, he added a small kitchen knife. If the police stopped him, he'd have a lot of explaining to do. His vision was blurred from alcohol and memory. He'd looked down through that gap in the railings and seen a world of stillness and peace. He turned out the lights and closed the front door behind him.

The sky was cloudy; the city's light hung like a translucent dome over the quiet streets. There was no one about in Factory Road, though the factory windows were all lit. A song from the late seventies echoed in Rajan's head: "Dreams of Children" by The Jam. It took him only a few minutes to prise away the board from the front window of number 74. The nails were rusty. Underneath, the glass was mostly gone. It was lucky he'd lost so much weight.

The room was full of rubble: boxes and broken furniture. His torch cast a fragile web of light. Near the door was a bookcase filled with rotting volumes of some encyclopedia. In the hallway, cobwebs and wallpaper hung from the ceiling like ruined lampshades. There was a small pram near the foot of the stairs, with a doll in it. A wreath of blond hair framed its waxy face. Its eyes were missing. Rajan touched its cheek, and his fingers sank into cold flesh. Not a doll. But not long dead. Where the fuck were they hiding?

The staircase had fallen through; it didn't look climbable. Then he remembered the cellar. His mother had kept jars of pickle and tins of condensed milk down there, as well as some old trunks from Gujerat that were never opened. He stumbled through the mess of cobwebbed paper and fabric to the door at the back of the stairs. The handle was coated with rust and grime, but it turned. A faint red light came from the room below, and a sound of metallic throbbing. Carefully, he began to walk down the steps.

The cellar was full of rusted machinery. Hulks of metal, held together with chains and bakelite-covered wires. Yet he could see wheels turning, pistons moving back and forth. A light came on behind a dusty pane of glass. Rajan's feet made no sound on the rotting floorboards. There was a narrow doorway in the far wall. He passed through.

Lit by a thin red light that had no apparent source, two teenagers were lying side by side on a filthy sofa: a boy and a girl. Their heads were shaved, and they were horribly thin. The boy was fucking the girl from behind. Their faces were expressionless. They didn't notice Rajan as he walked past them to the next doorway. It led into a hall or corridor, where a number of half-naked youngsters stood in alcoves. They were cooking up some fluid in spoons over gas burners, then injecting it with dirt-flecked syringes into their breasts or genitals. Water dripped from the ceiling, like the ticking of a clock.

The next room contained two baths. In one, a girl was using a kitchen grater on her buttocks and thighs. A trickle of water from the taps rinsed the blood from around her feet. In the other bath, a boy was slowly pulling a strip of flesh from the inside of his left arm. His face and body were half flayed, but Rajan recognized him. The boy looked up and stopped moving. The slow pulse of machinery came through the walls.

They stared at each other. Rajan felt sick with exhaustion. "So," he said. "What kind of time do you call this?"

There was no answer. Ashok stared at him until he backed off, then picked up a razor and resumed his work. Rajan touched the black wall. It was covered with a thin layer of disinfectant. His throat swelled, but what came out was only laughter. An empty laughter. But there was some relief in it.

Slowly, he walked back through the red-lit basement rooms to the steps. The shuddering of a hidden engine made his legs buckle, and he almost fell. The next thing he knew, he was back outside the house. He'd left his briefcase somewhere in the cellar. And he'd left the baby. It didn't seem to matter.

A van drove past. Daylight was filtering through the blue-grey clouds. The streetlamps were looking paler. At the end of the road, men in working clothes had gathered outside the factory for the start of the morning shift.

Picking Up Courtney

BY TIM WAGGONER

"On the q.t.—was I staring at you when the incident occurred?"

Brent looked at the old woman for a moment, trying to decide if he'd heard her right. He chose to play it safe and shook his head.

She smiled, relieved. "Good."

They stood on the sidewalk in front of Haven Falls Elementary. Cars zipped by only a few feet from where they were, as drivers ignored the SLOW: SCHOOL ZONE signs. For the thousandth time Brent wondered what genius had decided to build a school on one of the busiest streets in town.

"We bring her here to get her used to the noise."

The woman had an accent he couldn't place. He recognized it as European, but that didn't narrow it down much. She was alone, so Brent wasn't sure who the "we" she referred to might be, but the "her" was plain enough. The woman held a thin leash attached to the collar of a tiny tan dachshund. The animal's tail was between its legs and it shivered as if this were the dead of winter instead of early October. Its eyes were moist, and Brent thought the dog might start crying any second.

"She's afraid of loud sounds," the woman said. "Every day I come to get my granddaughter, and I bring Peanut. The cars, the children, they make plenty of noise, and we hope she'll become . . . inoculated? No, *acclimated*, yes, that's it."

The dog didn't seem to be doing much "acclimating" at the moment. The way it shivered, it looked like its tiny heart was close to bursting.

Brent glanced at his watch: 2:24. Six minutes until the bell rang. He wished they lived on the bus line. Dropping off their daughter for afternoon kindergarten and picking her up again every school day was getting to be a real drag. Not to mention the way it cut into his work.

"Each day she seems a bit better, I think."

The dog pressed against the woman's leg and started to whine. This was better? Better than what?

"I'm sure she'll do fine. It'll just take a little time is all." He didn't pay attention to his own words. He'd been a realtor for seven years, and in that time the small-talk portion of his brain had become so developed it operated on autopilot.

The woman grinned, displaying slightly crooked teeth that were yellow at the edges. "Yes, exactly so!"

Brent had never seen the woman or her dog before. He was usually five minutes late to pick up Courtney, sometimes ten. This was the first day he'd managed to get here early. He'd congratulated himself on being a Good Daddy, but now that he was stuck talking with Frau Non Sequitur and the Amazing Vibrating Wiener Dog, he regretted it.

Brent replayed the woman's strange question in his mind: *On the q.t.—was I staring at you when the incident occurred?* They'd been talking about last week's open house at the school. It had been crowded and hot as hell, with far too many glassy-eyed parents trying to cram themselves into closet-sized classrooms only to stare at enigmatic creations of construction paper and glue. It had been so stifling that Sandi, Courtney and he had ducked out early after making a token appearance in Ms. Watson's class. Had something happened after they left? Perhaps the old woman had fainted from the heat. Naturally she would've been embarrassed by such an incident, and confused as well. She might have seen him in the hall earlier and couldn't recall later whether or not he'd been there when she'd passed out.

Then again, maybe she suffered from Alzheimer's or something. Or she simply was a loon. It didn't matter. A few more minutes—three, to be precise—and Courtney would come running through the school's glass front doors, and he'd hustle her into their minivan and get the hell out of here.

The dachshund's whining grew louder as it pushed harder against the old woman's leg, as if it hoped it might be able to slip its molecules between its owner's and vanish into her flesh. Brent wondered if he made it more nervous, if he should excuse himself and walk away. But the little dog yapped then and nipped at the old woman's leg. Not hard enough to draw blood through her slacks, probably not even hard enough to make a dent in her skin. Still, the old woman scowled, her lips contracting into a tight ring of flesh that made him think of a puckered anus.

"Bad Peanut. Nasty Peanut." Her tone was calm but her eyes glittered with anger. She began wrapping the leash around her hand, taking up the slack until the black leather strand was taut.

Brent thought she would stop there, but she didn't. She continued winding the leash around her hand, pulling Peanut's head upward, baggy skin wrinkling around the collar. The dog's front paws lifted off the ground, dangling almost daintily before it rose onto its haunches, sitting the way dachshunds do when they beg. Brent thought she would finally stop there, but she kept wrapping, her fingers now starting to redden and swell.

Peanut rose onto its feet, then its tiptoes, and then there was space between the hind feet and the concrete sidewalk. Not much, maybe just enough to slide a child's construction paper drawing under, but it didn't matter how much space was between Peanut and the ground, did it? When you're at the end of a noose—and that's what the leash had become—a few inches is the same as a hundred feet.

Now Peanut hung slack, not struggling, oddly calm after her earlier display of terror. The only sign that she was strangling was the way her wet black eyes bulged out of their sockets. Dark streaks rolled from the corners of those eyes, and Brent realized that the dog was crying at last.

The bell rang then, snapping him out of his daze. He reached for the old woman's wrist, intending to make her drop the dog. But before he could close his fingers around her arm she opened her hand, releasing the coils she'd gathered, and Peanut fell back to the ground, back paws first, then front. She didn't gasp, didn't pant for air. But she started shivering again.

He looked up at the old woman. She smiled at him as if she hadn't just tried to strangle her dog.

"What the hell—" he started.

"Daddy!"

He turned at the sound of his daughter's voice, saw her running down the school's front walk toward him, so beautiful she shone like a star among the crowd of awkward, mussed-haired kids around her.

"Lovely child," the old woman said, then turned and walked off, heading away from the school. A girl with long black hair broke out of the pack of running, laughing children and jogged in her direction. She caught up with the old woman and fell in step beside her, but neither of them spoke. And, Brent noticed, the girl didn't reach down to give the dog a hello pat, didn't so much as acknowledge the animal's presence.

A tug on his sleeve. "Daddy, what's wrong? Aren't you glad to see me?" Courtney gave him the pout he had named her monkey-face. He knelt down and kissed his daughter on the cheek, grateful that she hadn't seen the old woman abusing her dog.

"Course I am, Pumpkin. You have a good day at school?"

"I sure did!"

He stood, held out his hand. She took it and they started toward the car.

"What did you do today?" he asked.

"I don't know. I don't remember."

It was her stock answer, one he usually teased her about, but today he said, "That's nice." He watched the old woman, her granddaughter and Peanut continue down the sidewalk, and again he heard the strange question she had asked, saw Peanut's tear-slick bulging eyes, and without realizing it he gripped his daughter's hand tighter.

The next morning, Brent told his wife he was getting backed up at work and asked if she could pick up Courtney after school. Sandi said she couldn't take off in the middle of the day, he knew that. She'd only started back to work full-time at the doctor's office a month and a half ago. She couldn't ask that yet.

They argued a little, but it didn't go far. Brent couldn't tell his wife that the real reason he wanted her to get Courtney was because he didn't want to see the old woman and her dog again. He knew he wouldn't be able to make her understand; hell, he didn't understand it himself.

That afternoon, Brent arrived at the school ten minutes early. He wanted to pick up Courtney and get the hell out of there before the old woman showed up and did something else disturbing—something his daughter might see this time. He parked at the curb and sat in his van, thinking about why the encounter with the old woman yesterday had so unsettled him.

He supposed it had something to do with the death of his uncle when Brent was nine. His uncle Larry—or "Red"—was like a father to him.

Picking Up Courtney

Moreso than his real father, a salesman who was always on the road. His dad never had time to play catch, teach him how to throw a football, take him fishing. But Uncle Red had time, and even when he didn't he still found a way. Brent had loved Red, practically to the point of worship. And then one day Red went to the doctor's for a checkup. The physician gave him a clean bill of health, and then Red went out into the reception area, sat down and waited for his name to be called so he could pay his bill. He never got up again. His heart gave out, the doctor said, and he died instantly, probably didn't feel a thing. As if that were any consolation.

Red had seemed so healthy, so full of life. His death struck Brent as so unfair, so damn absurd that he had himself a nine-year-old's version of an existential crisis. He questioned whether life had any meaning, if there was any design to the universe, or if existence was nothing more than raw, blind chance. Eventually he came to uneasy terms with his grief, and as he got older he began to believe that life *did* have meaning, even if people had to make that meaning for themselves.

But something about the old woman's crazy behavior had dredged up feelings he thought dead and buried long ago—feelings that life might be utterly random and without purpose, after all. And now here he was, hiding in his van like a frightened child.

He kept an eye out for the old woman—how could he not? But he didn't see her. Other parents got out of their cars, walked toward the school's main entrance with the steady, deliberate paces of adults who'd rather not be here but couldn't rationalize being anywhere else. He looked at the digital clock on the dashboard: 2:29. He turned off the engine, removed the key from the ignition and got out of the van. He stayed close to the vehicle for a moment, watching traffic, scowling at the drivers who sped by. Idiots. Didn't they know that in less than a minute the sidewalk was going to be full of kids? Didn't they care?

He walked around the van and started toward the entrance, glancing around for the old woman and Peanut without appearing to look. When he didn't see them he let out a relieved breath that he hadn't realized he'd been holding.

He reached the front doors, nodded to the other parents—mostly moms—standing outside. He didn't know any of them well enough to start a conversation, and he didn't feel like trying, especially after what had happened yesterday. He just wanted to get Courtney and take her back to day care.

There was a sign on one of the glass doors.

WE'D APPRECIATE IT IF PARENTS WOULD REMAIN OUT-SIDE UNTIL THE BELL. TEACHERS ARE CONDUCTING CLASS UNTIL 2:30 AND HAVING VISITORS IN THE HALL ARE DISTRACTING.

He frowned. He'd noticed the sign before but had never paid much attention to it. The grammar error annoyed him. He expected better from the school his daughter attended.

The bell rang. Several seconds passed and then the doors banged open. Kids wearing and carrying backpacks came flooding out, faces beaming with the tired joy of being free again. Courtney had her Barbie backpack slung over her shoulder at a sassy angle. She looked so grown-up. Brent had no trouble imagining that she would look much the same years from now, in college, sass and all.

She saw him, smiled. "Hi, Daddy!"

"Hi, Pumpkin." He reached out to tousle her hair, but she gave him a look that said *I'm not a baby* and he withdrew. *Only five years old,* he thought, *and already she doesn't want me touching her that way, in front of others.*

He started to ask her how class had gone (though he knew darn well how she'd answer), but before he could she dropped her backpack at his feet and ran off after a red-haired girl, calling, "Kristie! Kristie!"

The girl turned, grinned, shucked off her backpack, shouted "You're it!" and took off running across the school's front lawn.

Courtney followed close behind, both girls shrieking and giggling.

We don't have time for this, Brent thought. *I* don't have time. But he didn't want to tear Courtney away from her friend. He hesitated, unsure what to do. He reached up, scratched the dry skin at the side of his nose, an old nervous habit. Three minutes, he decided, no more. He checked his watch to mark the time.

He watched the girls play, sometimes following the rules of tag, other times abandoning the rules entirely just to run and make noise. He envied their ability to be so wholly alive in the moment.

Courtney, about to tag Kristie on the elbow, stopped and looked to her right. "Doggie!" she squealed, and started running, Kristie right behind.

Brent looked ahead of them and saw Peanut and the old woman.

They stood in roughly the same spot as yesterday, the dog shivering against her owner's leg. The old woman smiled as the girls came pounding across the grass toward her.

Brent started moving before the girls reached Peanut. He felt an urge to run but checked it. He didn't want to alarm the other parents or startle the old woman. It was a cliché—don't make any sudden moves—but that's exactly what his instincts told him now, so he walked across the lawn at a measured Goldilocks' pace: not too fast, not too slow, keeping his gaze firmly fixed on the old woman the entire time.

Courtney fell to her knees before Peanut, making the poor dog jump, and began rubbing its side.

"Good dog, you're a good dog, aren't you, you cutey-wooty-wooty!"

Kristie started petting the dog's other side, adding her own variations of baby-talk patter.

The old woman looked down at them, still smiling, but now there was something about her expression that made Brent's spine go cold and tingly. Nothing overt—it wasn't as if her eyes were wild, her teeth bared in a snarl, froth bubbling over her lips. There was just something *wrong* about it.

She said something to the girls, but Brent wasn't in earshot yet. Whatever it was—it might be any crazy thing, mightn't it? Another non sequitur, or perhaps a bark of profanity à la Tourette's syndrome. The girls were so caught up in their doggie love fest they either didn't hear or chose not to respond.

The old woman looked up and smiled as Brent approached.

He had no idea what to say to her, but Courtney saved him from improvising. "Daddy, I want a dog, can we have a dog, pleeeeeeeeeeease?"

"We'll see, Pumpkin." His reply was as automatic and unthinking as the outgoing message tape on an answering machine.

He found himself staring at the dachshund's neck, scrutinizing the hide around and beneath the collar. The skin looked fine, but then it was covered with fur, wasn't it?

"Peanut seems to like you girls," the woman said. "Maybe you could come over to my house sometime and help to give her some exercise, yes? Chase her in the backyard, throw the ball for her to fetch, put sharp little sticks into her behind. Wouldn't that be fun?"

Brent was shocked. He looked at the girls, but they didn't seem to pay any attention to the old woman, thank Christ.

"That's enough, now." He leaned down, took each girl by an arm and pulled them away.

"Aw, Dad-dee!"

"We need to get going, Sweetie, and I'm sure your friend does, too." He spoke to his daughter, but he kept his eyes on the old woman as they backed away. "And this nice lady has come to pick up her granddaughter, and we should let her go about her business." He kept backing away, towing the girls with him.

The old woman continued smiling. It was as if her face were made of wax and permanently molded into that expression.

"The mirror's cracked, you know."

"That's nice." He kept moving, kept hold of the girls, who were starting to squirm.

"It always has been," the old woman continued. "But now the cracks are spreading. Growing wider and deeper, yes? It's only a matter of time before the glass breaks."

"I really hadn't noticed. 'Bye, now."

He turned and led the girls back toward the school. Kristie's ride evidently hadn't arrived yet, and he couldn't bring himself to leave the girl alone with that crazy bitch. He decided that he and Courtney could wait inside with Kristie until her mom, dad or whoever came. Besides, he wanted to be near other people. Other people were safe. Other people were sane.

"Daddy!" Courtney whined. "You're hurting my arm!"

Brent didn't loosen his grip, afraid the girls would take off if he did. He kept his hold until they passed through the front doors and stood inside the lobby. He turned and peered through the glass, saw the woman looking at him, smiling her wrong smile. Her granddaughter now stood at her side, and there was something odd about her face: the skin was yellow-tinged, and the girl's expression was slack. Peanut squirmed as if in pain, and then Brent saw why. The old woman was grinding the dog's tail beneath her shoe.

A little after eleven that night Courtney woke up, complaining that her tummy hurt. They'd eaten fast-food that night and the greasy glop had made her constipated. Sandi marched straight for the medicine chest, only to find they were out of laxative. So Brent threw on his windbreaker, hopped into the minivan and headed for the grocery in search of gentle, soothing relief for his daughter.

While Bellwether wasn't huge—few towns were in southwestern Ohio—it was big enough to have a twenty-four-hour grocery. He parked as close as he could and crossed to the entrance, looking right, then left, keeping an eye out.

For what, he wasn't sure.

Once inside, he got a cart and steered it into the produce section. He was here for laxative, but Sandi figured why waste a grocery trip? She'd given him a list of a dozen must-have items that they couldn't get along without for another day. He got bananas, a bag of Gala apples and a single lemon—he had no idea why just one, but he put it in the cart.

As he made his way toward the bread rack, he passed a middle-aged woman whose face looked as if someone had grabbed the corners of her eyes from behind and pulled backward. It was like a picture that had been scanned into a computer, then stretched horizontally a few clicks. It couldn't be some sort of deformity, could it? Plastic surgery, maybe a botched face-lift?

The woman noticed Brent staring and scowled, an expression that made the distorted, taut flesh of her face bend and twist as if she were her own fun-house mirror.

Brent looked away and moved on.

In the dairy aisle, he saw a bearded man with a gauze bandage over his left eye. There was a wet patch in the middle of the bandage, and as Brent watched it widened, as if the eye—or whatever lay behind the bandage—was seeping something fierce. The gauze appeared to pulsate slightly, like the skin on top of a newborn's head where the skull hasn't grown together yet. The man opened his mouth to speak, but Brent hurried on before he could hear what the man had to say.

In the pharmacy section, he got a bottle of Philips Milk of Magnesia (cherry flavored) and put it into the cart along with the other groceries. He reached into his coat pocket, took out Sandi's list and double-checked to make sure he'd gotten everything. Without thinking, he reached up to scratch the dry skin on the side of his nose and was rewarded with a sharp pain.

"Damn it!"

He pulled his hand away, examined the finger, saw that it was dotted with blood.

Perfect. Just perfect.

With the finger pressed against his nose, he tried pushing his cart one-handed toward the front of the store where the restroom was. But the cart, though far from full, was too awkward to steer, and he said fuck it and left it where it was. He'd come back and get it after he'd tended to his scratch.

In the men's room he stepped up to the sink, tore a brown paper towel from the wall dispenser and pressed it to his nose. The paper was coarse and his scratch stung, but at least the towel absorbed the blood. He removed the towel, turned it around to a dry patch and pressed it once more against the cut, harder this time, hoping to force the blood to clot faster.

He looked at his reflection in the mirror over the sink and thought of the old woman's parting words today.

But the cracks are spreading. Wider and deeper, yes? It's only a matter of time before the glass breaks.

He half-expected to find a crack somewhere in the glass, but its surface was unmarred and surprisingly clean for a public restroom. Yet he couldn't shake the feeling that the old woman had tried to impart some manner of vital knowledge this afternoon.

He thought of Stretch-Face and Mr. Eye Patch. In a way, they were like the old woman: a glimpse at something that lay beyond the seemingly normal surface of the everyday and into whatever lay on the other side of the mirror.

Brent hoped they'd have to keep Courtney home from school the next day. At this point he would have been glad to take the time off from work and to hell with his sales percentage. Just so long as he didn't have to go near that school.

But come dawn the laxative had done its job and Courtney felt fine.

He dropped her off at day care, and then spent the rest of the morning chauffeuring a couple who wanted to look at some houses. Mostly they talked to each other, ignoring him. After a while he became aware of an odd, almost inaudible sound that seemed to accompany their voices when they spoke, like the hiss and crackle of radio static or the electronic noise of a modem trying to connect. He began to have a sense that this secondary sound might be their true voices and that they weren't really saying anything at all that he could hear, just exchanging bursts of white noise.

By the time he parted ways with the couple they still hadn't settled on a house, but he'd picked up a throbbing headache. He had worked through lunch without realizing it, and now he didn't have time to grab anything to eat, not if he wanted to be on time to pick up Courtney.

He drove to the school, doing five miles under the speed limit without realizing it. He pulled up to the curb, parked and sat gripping the wheel so tightly that his knuckles bulged white. He experienced an urge to put the key back in the ignition, turn it, put the van in gear and roar away from the curb, leaving Courtney behind. He'd pick a direction—it didn't matter which one—and keep driving until he ran out of gas. He reached up and rubbed the scab alongside his nose, trying to ignore the pounding in his head.

He wasn't going to abandon his daughter, of course. If he did he would be a Bad Daddy, and he couldn't bear that.

He got out of the van and closed the door. There was the normal *chunk!* of the door shutting, but beneath it was the sound of fingernails raking a chalkboard. Another crack, another glimpse?

Stop it, he told himself. *Just goddamn stop it.* An old lady says a couple weird things, abuses her shivery little mutt, and you end up doubting your own sanity. Hell, doubting the nature of reality itself. *That* was the insane part. He lived in a world of rules and structure, of mathematics, of laws, regulations, statutes, custom and convention. The alphabet had 26 letters; there were 365 days in a year; and 30 days hath September . . . September . . . and several other goddamned months. The mirror wasn't cracked because there wasn't any dumb-ass mirror in the first place. The world was the world and what you saw was what you got. If you wanted meaning you had to make your own, simple as that. But by God, once you made it, it was *real*.

Right now his meaning was Courtney, and he was here to pick her up.

He headed up the walkway to the front door of the school. He didn't see the old woman around, and he was more grateful for that than he liked to admit. There were no other parents standing outside today. It was a bit nippy, and he supposed the others had decided to wait in their cars.

He glanced at the faded printout he had noticed yesterday, and saw that it now read: INSTRUCTIONS FOR THE AUTOPSY AND POSTMORTEM EXAMINATION OF THE AVERAGE KINDERGARTENER. What followed were simple step-by-step instructions accompanied by appropriate full-color diagrams. Brent stared at the poster, willed it to return to normal, but it didn't. He looked away, shivering like Peanut.

The bell rang.

On one level it sounded the same as always, but on another it sounded like jackhammers biting into ancient, brittle bone. Along the curb, parents and caregivers got out to meet their little ones. At the same time, as if on cue, the school doors banged open and children poured forth.

He watched for Courtney, afraid to see her, afraid of what she might look like to him in his present state. But there she was, as beautiful and happy as always, eyes bright, smile wide.

She ran over and hugged him, and she felt so good, so normal that he hugged her back too hard. She made an *oof* sound and pulled back. She grinned, smacked him lightly on the back of his hand. She said, "You're it!" and ran off.

He called after her, shouted that he didn't want to play, not today, but she kept running across the lawn, crunching leaves, hair flying behind her.

He hesitated, unsure what to do. If he gave chase, she'd just run all the faster. But if he didn't go after her, she'd keep running and laughing until she grew tired of the game, and he wanted to get out of here right now, before—

The old woman came strolling up the walkway, Peanut plodding along at her side.

She held the dog's leash gently and the dachshund seemed in good spirits, was even wagging her tail a little, turning her head this way and that to look at all the children gabbing, playing and laughing as they slowly dispersed.

He wanted to run, wanted to hide.

Instead he started walking toward the old woman. He managed to keep from shaking, but his forehead was slick with sweat, and he could feel it trickling down his face. He met her in the middle of the walkway.

She smiled pleasantly and Peanut kept wagging her tail.

"Look, I don't know what hell is wrong with you, and I don't care. But I'd appreciate it if you'd stay the fuck away from me and especially from my daughter. You got that, you crazy bitch?"

He looked for Courtney, saw she'd hooked up with Kristie and that they were playing tag now, her slow-poke daddy forgotten for the moment.

The woman didn't reply; she just kept smiling. Her granddaughter walked up, backpack slung over one shoulder. The old woman looked down at her. "Ready to go, dear?"

The girl didn't respond. Her face was slack, her skin yellow-pale, eyes roiling circles of darkness. He had the impression he could poke his finger into the churning inkwells of her eye sockets if he wished.

Picking Up Courtney

"I think Peanut might like to run a little. Should we let her off the leash for some exercise?"

"Sure, Grammy, that'd be fun!"

The girl was normal now. Face animated, eyes a rich brown.

"Go ahead," the old woman said.

The girl unhooked the dachshund from the leash. For a second Peanut just stood there, not realizing she was free. Then she took off, tiny legs pumping as she flew across the grass. The granddaughter squealed and ran after the dog. Other kids noticed, shouted, laughed and took up the chase. Peanut wove between their legs, avoiding little hands desperate to grab hold of dog fur. Courtney had joined the pack, was at the head of it.

"Stop, Doggie! I want to pet you!" she pleaded.

She got close, reached out, her fingertips brushing fur, but Peanut put on a burst of speed, zigged left and Courtney followed, squealing with delight.

Then Peanut dashed between two parked cars and out into the street.

Brent shouted something. It might have been "No!" or "Look out!" but it just as easily might have been an inarticulate cry of horror. Tires squealed, there was a sickening, muffled *thump* and Peanut came trotting back between the parked cars and onto the sidewalk, looking pleased with herself.

Horns honking, kids screaming, parents running into the street. Traffic stopped, and drivers got out of their cars, faces frozen in shock.

Brent ran into the street, knelt beside the wet red thing that had been his daughter, cradled it in his arms.

The old woman was standing beside him.

"You lied to me, didn't you?" she said softly. "You *were* staring at me when the incident occurred."

In his mind Brent answered *yes*, but what came out of his mouth was the sound of shattering glass.

Watchmen

BY AARON STERNS

The illuminated advertisement on the front of the cigarette machine is a slivered beacon of blue sky and clouds among the smoke and strobe lights; a slice of heaven obscured by a couple deep in conversation: the guy all pained mouth and gesturing arms; the woman silent, staring. They are oblivious to the throng around as if enclosed in a vacuum. I stare at them from my post, trying to work out what they're saying—their voices drowned out by the brain-regressing bass pounding up through my feet—but an image of Lisa arguing with me kicks in and I have to flick my eyes away across the dance floor. I try to suppress a surge of anger.

The straining flux of dancing bodies moves in waves of artfully ripped faded clothing, bleached hair, and pale flesh made gaunt and alien-blue by the overhead fluoros. The sunken dance floor—the Pit—is huge, nearly thirty meters across, and it's hard to survey its entire length. I glance over at the other black-clad figures on their raised podiums: impassive dark statues almost lost in the belching haze of smoke machines and cigarette smoke, legs spread and hands clasped over their groins as if cupping themselves. They seem like ciphers to me, unsmiling names, protective of their cohesion. I'm still the interloper.

Two girls walk past below, staring up. One is breathtakingly beautiful: tight tan in red lycra, angry auburn hair and clear eyes. She smiles and I reflexively smile back, feeling instantly guilty. She pauses, tracing the neckline of her dress as if considering approaching my podium to stand at uncomfortable groin-height and flash her hungry smile up at me, then runs a finger down her perfect cleavage. Unsettled, I'm about to look away when she flicks down the right side of her top to reveal a dusky nipple. She teases it to quick stiffness, then disappears into the crowd, hungry eyes melting into the crush of bodies. Her friend follows.

The two-way almost slips from my sweaty hand as I try to track their passage toward the front of the club. I lose them among the squawking, impatient drinkers clamoring at the huge main bar for the attention of the bar girls. Disappointed, I glance up at the semicircular balcony and its darkened tiered couches overlooking the main bar, the figures standing at its edge separated from death only by a thin brass railing. But the massive scale of this cavern has lost its novelty value by now and my gaze drops.

An angry voice pierces the oppressive techno music and I search again through the disorienting sweeping lasers. The man by the cigarette machine throws his hands in the air and stalks off. The girl stares transfixed, tears on cheeks. Just broken up, presumably. I shake my head and start to look away.

The man whirls and punches his girlfriend. Hard.

She crumples to the ground. The guy looks at her without expression, then reaches down and grabs her by the back of the neck and the waistband, lifting her off the ground to swing her like a battering ram into the illuminated blue cigarette machine. The crack sounds even above the deafening techno bass. The machine short-circuits and spits flame.

I slam into him. We skid through the crowd, his nose smacking into someone's shin in a spray of blood. As he struggles I snap him in the nose again with the two-way, pinning him around onto his front so I can cradle his throat in the crook of my arm and lace the other arm behind his head. He tries to claw up at my arms, my eyes, but I put him out with a vicious tensing of my biceps, cutting off the circulation in his neck. I rest his dead weight on its side and bring the cracked and blood-flecked radio up to my mouth to call the others.

A group of middle-class yuppies ring me, too scared to help but perversely rooted in place by the bloody spectacle. I stare back from my crouch, wondering if the guy has friends here, if someone will launch from the crowd to kick at my face. I cannot see the girl past the gathering designer jeans but don't want to risk leaving him alone: sleeper-holds aren't debilitating enough; when they wake they wake instantly, mad and in control—and then splitting the crowd like huge black-clad figures of death, smooth-shaven and short-haired, barely contained, white badges floating ghostlike on their chests. They push the crowd back, striking one guy who won't move with an open hand to the face, sending him beneath their feet. A fury of movement around and then Lucs over me, omnipotent Lucs, always uncannily first on the scene, grabbing the unconscious boyfriend from me, eyes gleaming red in the searching light. Raph beside him, staring past me. I follow his gaze to the prone body of the girl; her head split like a melon, open and weeping, curled brains nestled within.

We take the boyfriend up the stage stairs, a warning procession past groping couples on low-slung seating, and shoulder through the milling dancers to a door reading STAFF ONLY. Lucs bursts through the swinging door using the boyfriend's head and dumps him on the corridor floor. The doors close after us like a dampening field. An overhead light glares above and my vision swims as I adjust from the dimness outside, getting a brief glimpse down a corridor extending away in progressive darkness. Raph barks something into his two-way.

Lucs in my face: "What happened?" Angry goatee and sharp slicked crew cut: I'm bigger, nearly six-four, but step back anyway.

"They were arguing—just a domestic—right near me, and he snapped her and . . . and before I could get to him he rammed her into the smoke machine. The sound . . . fuck—"

He grabs my shirt-front, silencing me: "This is what we do."

I shrug him off and nod, straightening my shirt, my number. "I know."

He looks down at the sprawled body; the guy waking now, eyes flitting open and straining at the light. A kick to the side of the head and he is out again. "Take his foot," and we drag him down the corridor and the stairs at the end, the soft thud of his skull on each concrete step keeping beat with the muted, somehow-threatening music through the walls next to us. He leaves a soft trail of blood. Raph walks ahead and unlocks the door at the bottom of the stairwell. I hear a car pulling up outside, then voices through the wood. A few steps from the bottom my boss pushes me away and reaches down to grasp the shuddering body, standing up with a hand on either side of the guy's head, a raggedy-doll in his grasp. Lucs holds my gaze and then snaps his wrists around, sending the guy's arms and legs flailing to flap against the huge chest. A moist crack sounds from the guy's neck. Lucs lets the body slide to the floor. I feel like I'm going to vomit.

Raph opens the door to waiting uniforms and a huge white van. Silent revolving lights on its roof spark blue and red eerily around the alley. One of the uniforms walks up, a cop: "This the fucker?" Lucs drags the body to the van's back doors and throws it inside. A soft thud. The back hadn't been empty. His partner closes the doors and they drive off, still without the siren, faces swiveling back at me as they turn onto the street.

Lucs waits in the doorway, badge stained with blood. I look at the empty street and the fading ghostly lights and then back at him, my head spinning. The reek of the alley is like a cocoon. Nausea floods my stomach.

On the way back to my post I stop at the staff toilets to scrub the blood off my face. I grip the sink and stare at the mess of flyers pasted above the mirror: among them are missing persons photos, a mix of male and female faces, mostly young. Someone has mockingly drawn mustaches on a few. The door opens behind me. Gabe. "We know you get this, Jakob. We wouldn't have let you in otherwise." He stares at me for a moment, then leaves. Eventually, the smell of stale urine and pervasive shit from the cubicles forces me out as well.

The dark figures across from me now seem ominous, always on the periphery of my vision as I scan the Pit. The feeling that they are all watching me, silent, unnerving, is greater than ever and my heart quickens. As much as I want to drop the two-way and rip off my badge and leave, I can't. The warning in Lucs's eyes as he broke the guy's neck is enough to stop that.

Old Max from the Colonial, where I used to do the door, had warned me the security at the Metropolis were "hard cunts"; a tight-knit, dangerous crew. When I was still at the Colonial I'd see them come in for a quiet drink, these huge guys dressed in black talking among themselves at the bar. I'd tense up, expecting them to cause trouble, but they never did anything, just stared at any patron stupid enough to come near. They were there the night I lost it, beat the fuck out of this asshole yuppie, some drunk suit who told me he didn't make three hundred thou a year to have a steroid meathead tell him what to do. He'd spat on me, threatened me with his lawyer. All the shit I'd put up with, all the abuse and violence and threats working as a bouncer, became too much. I'd stood over his bleeding body, feeling my chest constrict, the room beginning to spin. I'd failed. I'd fucked up my life. I'd be going to jail. I dropped to my knees, feeling the shock burn through me. Then this big guy beside me, one of the Metropolis guys—Mikhaels—picking me up and dragging me away. Two cops had run in and another of the Metropolis security had stopped them, explaining what happened. The cops had looked at me. Then one had nodded to Mikhaels, letting him quickly drag me out the back. After that I started working at the Metropolis. Lucs never mentioned what happened, just said he could use someone like me. I'd never seen them go this far until now. They must have been testing me the whole time, waiting until I'd proven myself enough to be accepted into the crew. Until they could trust me.

Dammit. There's always too much time in here to think: an endless stretching of seconds, minutes, hours into meaninglessness; aided by the curtains shut against the outside sky, encouraging timelessness and the rejection of reality. I used to let my mind drift so that I wouldn't worry about how long was left on the shift—imagining passages of the thesis and thinking of new themes and films I should be using, so when the close finally did come it would be a surprise and a reward for not giving in to the boredom, and I could go home and scrawl out my thoughts before collapsing into bed. But I can't retreat to that now: I gave up the thesis long ago. It stopped making sense to me after a while, after working the clubs so long. There didn't seem a point to anything anymore.

Fuck it. The guy deserved it. What scares me is it makes me think of her. Of Lisa and that fuck Jason. My hands shake. Sweat rises on my face and across my back. I should have fucking—

A drunk is dancing with a chair he has dragged onto the dance floor as if it's his partner. He clutches it in his arms and pirouettes, then throws it onto the ground and awkwardly leaps over the seat. The crowd around him seem to enjoy his absurd parody of some forties musical star—even the muscle-shirted Greek guy takes the hit in the shins good-humoredly—and I'm roundly booed as I jump off my podium and grab the chair, handing it to Mikhaels who has appeared from across the Pit to back me up. But I need the distraction of work. I push the drunk past the bar to the front door and he gibbers at me: "I was pretty swish out there though wasn't I?" infectious humor that catches me offguard. His eyes are dilated, oversexed on e's as well; he wants to touch me as I walk him out, feeling my shoulders through my shirt. I just shrug him off. He's harmless.

Then he catches a glimpse of Mikhaels behind me and starts pulling away, seeing something I don't, some revelation his drugged-out brain throws up. "Keep him away from me! Don't you see what he is?"

Mikhaels, following a few meters behind, stares back stonily, eyes drilling into the patron. The drunk gets more and more agitated and I tell him not to worry, just to walk out, but he seems oblivious to me and then tries to run as we enter the foyer, dodging to his left and around a group milling outside the toilets. Mikhaels is already blocking his way to slam him in the chest, and we drag the guy kicking and swearing out the front to dump him on the pavement. He rolls into a ball at Mikhaels's feet, wrapping his hands protectively around his head, and then there is a bark behind me: "That's enough, get back inside." I turn and Lucs stands glaring at us, two doormen behind like twin Cerberus statues at the gates of hell. There are people in line staring at us, elderly couples and families from surrounding cafés, theatergoers passing by. Too visible.

Mikhaels slinks beside me as we head back to our posts, his bleach-blond hair and powerlifter-traps like talismans splitting the crowd before him. He leans in as we reach my post: "These sheep don't understand anything else," then leaves me staring after him.

I continue my watching, unnerved and searching for order in the madness, in the frenetic, restless movement; for some shifting code, some meaning in the faces that coalesce into momentary distinction only to become unformed clay when I look away—brown eyes, blue eyes, blond hair, black hair, blue hair, in an interchangeable mélange. I search for joy, for revelation, for knowledge in the faces, for some reason why they come here to waste away their lives with drink and mindless primal movements. All I find is blankness, slack-eyed vapidness. I'm so sick of this.

A hole opens in the crowd and I wonder for a moment if the dancers are avoiding someone's vomit. I look closely at those ringing the gap to see if they have that coy disgusted fascination, like dogs trying to avoid their own feces in the backyard. Then I see the swinging arms and sudden surge of bodies across the space and even as I raise the two-way hear a voice, Gabe's perhaps, rattle in my hand: "*Security to dance floor. Security to dance floor,*" and I jump off to push roughly through the crowd, chest and shoulders hard and unforgiving, distantly savoring the passing looks of dumb shock. I emerge into chaos and grab two of the fighting patrons, tearing apart their clutch by pushing one away, grabbing the other around the neck. The guy I'm holding starts lashing out instead with his feet. "Settle down," I yell with a jabbed compression of his neck for emphasis and he subsides. I look around and Gabe, Mikhaels and Raph are also restraining fighters. We stand each with subdued patrons hanging in our arms searching for further threats, for something missed. I'm about to turn and haul off my captive when from nowhere comes a fist swung wild and hard to smash into my temple. I hear the disembodied thump rather than feel it—having had much worse before—and swivel to focus in on the terrified tanned face. I drop my forgotten captive and like a berserker lost in fury pummel the face. On the edge of vision I see the other security react as if under fire, choking out their quarry and launching into the crowd with random punches, staining the beer-soaked floor with spatters of blood.

And then I'm sitting on my attacker's chest, yelling at his dazed face: "Why the fuck did you do that? We were breaking it up!"

Spit splays into his mouth as he tries to speak, no air in his lungs. "Be—because you . . . hit me."

I grab his shirt: "Like fuck I did!" and bring his face up to mine.

He persists: "So—someone hit me."

I stare into his glazed, convincing eyes and then a hand lands on my shoulder; quick spin and armlock, bending the elbow back to breaking point, my fist cocked—and Lucs stares back at me, a hand raised instinctively to protect his face. I let him go.

He moves in close, goatee like a pointer: "Kill him."

I step back though it's hard to hear him above the music, above the screams of the crowd. "What?"

He surges in again: "Now, while there's still confusion, while there's justification." I push him away, openhanded against the hard solidity of his pecs. "Damn you," he says, slit-eyed, "stop fighting it."

I stand over the bleeding kid and, eyes still on Lucs, reach down to haul him up: "Get the fuck out of here." The kid looks at me in disbelief so I slap him across the cheek, bringing sudden clarity to his eyes. I look back at Lucs as he watches the patron disappear into the crowd. He glares at me and walks away, saying something to Mikhaels.

Mikhaels looks at me and heads toward the front doors, pushing past the doormen and disappearing outside. I wonder what the hell he is doing, leaving the club halfway through the night. I don't understand anything about this place anymore.

I watch as Gabe and Raph drag away the injured. But the patrons soon start dancing again, the music an unstoppable Pied Piper calling to their gyrating and fondling, to the slackening of the vague, drugged faces. Their shoes smear the forgotten blood into the polished floor.

I'm dismissed from my post at the Pit and sent upstairs. Danteis, who I'm relieving, passes me on the stairs with a nod, dwarfing me with his bulk. Heaven, the upstairs bar and club's wasteland, looks much easier to patrol than downstairs: a bar and small dance floor on one level, leading up to another small bar, some pool tables and a series of isolated grimy couches ringed around a balcony overlooking the Pit. I stand midway up the stairs that splits the levels and look out over the sweaty, milling drinkers by the larger bar.

I can't take in anything. I feel strange, panicky. The faces around me, the colors of the lights and bright yellow walls seem to warp and shift. I wonder if it's the cocktail of drugs I'm taking: uppers to get through the night; stanozolol to maintain my size, my intensity. I feel like I'm tripping.

A girl wearing only a black bra top and set of tiny shorts walking up the stairs toward me catches me glancing at her and stops briefly. "Three," she motions at the number on my chest. "Does that, like, stand for your IQ, or your inches?" She is gone before I can respond, before I can even take offense at her insult. She passes me later, smirking over her shoulder as she heads downstairs, tight, arrogant ass rolling beneath the black leather.

"You're not naive, Jakob." I jump at the voice in my ear; Lucs has sidled up beside me while I was looking at the girl. He stares out over the crowd, eyes reflective and distant, silent for a moment. I follow his gaze. "Look at these weak, pitiful people," he finally says quietly. "Most of them can't even string two words together; fill them with alcohol and they become zombies, mindless scum."

"And that justifies killing them?"

He turns to me, as if contemplating this for the first time. "This is the way it's always been. You know that. There's always been those like us."

"What the fuck are you talking about?"

"Think about it, Jakob. Think of how you feel about them. Remember that night at the Colonial."

He touches my shoulder. Sudden pain along my chest and arms, as if I'd done a heavy workout, the muscles burning. Just like I felt after beating the yuppie. Jesus.

I break his grip and back away, spooked, mouth groping for a reaction. I grab my chest but the pain has just as quickly receded.

Lucs stares at me as I back down the stairs. What the fuck was that? What's wrong with me? He watches me go.

I stumble downstairs, knocking patrons out of the way as if they aren't there. The radio bucks in my hand but I don't hear what's said. Lucs perhaps, telling the others. One of the doormen appears from the foyer near the front door and stands waiting for me. I double back, heading for the back doors. I traverse the edge of the dance floor, trying to keep out of sight of the other security perched like gargoyles on their posts.

I reach the stage unharmed and burst through the double doors into the muted corridor to rest panting against a damp wall, waiting for my smoke-stained eyes and nose and throat to clear. Blood pulses in my head, keeping complicit time with the music rumbling through the walls.

The one hanging light casts weird shifting sprays of illumination down the corridor. I touch my chest again, recalling that strange pain. I must be going insane, too many late nights, the shock of seeing someone killed. Maybe it's the drugs finally getting to me.

Yet Lucs's words nag at the back of my brain.

I force them from my mind. All that matters is getting out of here. I push away from the wall and head for the back door.

I round a corner. Too late I realize I'm not alone.

A figure is coming toward me, filling the narrow space. When I see the size of the guy I instinctively put one foot back, planting myself.

Pieters. He's big, bigger even than me, almost scraping the roof with his head. The white badge seems lost against his chest. I tense and wait for him. Then I glimpse over his shoulder another darkened figure bent over something on the ground, something framed by yellow—it is blond hair, it is a woman. Tight black shorts. Bra top.

There is blood on her neck.

As I stare at it my vision narrows, focusing solely on its dark stain.

I forget about Pieters, about the club, about the patron being killed.

Pulsing sounds in my ears, strong, blotting out everything else. Spit fills my mouth. I can smell the blood. It floods my senses. My head spins at the thought of tasting it.

I tear my gaze away to look at the hunched-over figure, but the shifting light edging past Pieters's head and shoulders and underneath his arms warps everything and it seems the figure's face is somehow stretched and lupine.

Watchmen

"Thought you were a patron," Pieters says, breaking through my concentration. "Just as well." He points at the blackening egg on my temple. "You got hit before."

Disarmed, I raise my hand to my head slowly and feel the lump. My refined senses dissipate, leaving me feeling washed-out and empty. I must be going insane. I look at the other security—it is Raph—but his face is normal. For a moment I had thought . . .

"You can't let that happen again," Pieters is saying. "They must fear us."

I stare at him, then look at the girl.

"She overstayed her welcome," Pieters says.

Raph hauls the black-shorts girl up underneath her arms and drags her to the back door. But there is blood on the wall behind, splattered like the blood on Raph's cheek. He waits for Pieters to go down the stairwell and open the door and, as I stand watching, the girl's head lolls to one side on a too-pliable neck and her mouth, split at the corners as if punctured by something, gapes open, drooling a line of spittle onto her top. Raph sees me looking at her face and stares back openly. He reads something in my eyes that satisfies him and he dismisses me, dragging the girl outside.

"You should get back to your post," Pieters says.

I hesitate, looking toward the back door. Instead I nod and head back into the club.

When I return upstairs Lucs is still on the stairs. I don't ask how he knew I'd return. He doesn't say anything for a while, then: "You okay?" I nod. He stares at me for a moment, then nods also. "I'll check back soon." He leaves.

I try to watch the crowd but I'm too fucked-up, trying to understand what just happened, what I saw in the corridor. In need of air I head up to the top bar to stand beneath the air-conditioning vent jutting from the roof, savoring its cool whisper over my sweating, fevered face.

I open my eyes and see Kelly standing at the bar, the one bar girl I actually like and would speak to on occasion. But looking now at her tanned shoulders and the tight lycra top hugging her breasts only makes me think of Lisa, remembering how she used to wake up when I got home, the jut of her breasts and shoulders above the bedcovers, how she'd listen to my purging stories, or masturbate me or have sex. Anything to soothe away the darkness. That had changed after so many long months of going out. She started complaining about the smell of cigarette smoke when I came in, or the shower waking her up. About my temper affecting the relationship. Or how I was spending too much time in the gym, only concerned with putting on size, matching the Metropolis guys. About me giving up my thesis, having no future. She started spending more time at work, often going away overnight for conferences. A couple of weeks ago I returned home to find all her stuff gone. She hadn't even left a note. And then I found out about Jason. Another PR consultant from her work, a smooth-shaven, expensive-suit prick she must've been fucking for months—she'd mentioned him once or twice but I didn't read anything into it, didn't want to seem jealous. I didn't know the bitch was about to leave me. After she left I eventually found her new apartment. I'd pass by on the way home from work, sometimes sitting outside for a while. Once I thought I'd seen Mikhaels standing outside, hands shoved deep into his pockets, staring up at her window. But it couldn't have been him. There was no reason for him to be there. I'd told him she and I had broken up, of course, but he wouldn't know where she'd moved. That made me realize how paranoid and fucked-up I was getting. I felt stupid, jealous. But I couldn't stop myself. Then one morning, about a week ago, this Jason guy walks out of her apartment, smoothing his suit. The shock was quickly overtaken with anger, burning rage. I couldn't believe the fury I was feeling. I wanted to rip him apart. It scared me. I didn't know how far I would go. So I drove away. I chickened out. And now I can't stop imagining what I could have done. Should have done.

I stare at Kelly and feel a rising anger and hatred. She smiles over at me but I turn away and descend past the vomit and beer-stained couches and stand at the balcony looking out over the huge gothic expanse with its sudden three-story drop to the Pit, crisscrossed and bisected by lasers and spotlights like prison-camp searchlights that pierce the hanging smoke. The dancers are a sea of sweaty, jerking bodies, a blind mass of conformity. I feel like jumping, smashing into them from above, shocking them out of their trances. Destroying their oblivion.

It would be so easy.

But I had the chance to run. And I couldn't.

Something distracts me. A frenzy of movement in the far-right corner couch, a couple in oblivious ecstasy, the girl with goth-black hair and raised skirt, her face slackened as she straddles a greasy guy, some mafioso scumbag. As I approach I see the slimy length of his penis jamming up inside her with every raise of her fleshy white cheeks.

I should tell them to zip up, walk them outside.

I wonder if Jason's cock looks like that.

I grab her shoulder and roughly pull her off him, baring her seeping cunt. She tries to break away and stumbles backward, hitting the brick wall. I let her fall. She lies spread-eagled, blood trickling down her face. I stare at it.

Everything shuts down.

Then I am grabbing her by the throat, leaning in. She smells like metal, copper.

Something on the edge of vision. The guy fumbling for something in his jacket. I swivel as he lunges at me and something wet slices my face, like a spray of cum, like he has opened my face with his cock.

I touch the blood on my cheek. The guy stares at me in shock, as if surprised he has cut me, virgin knife held before him like a talisman.

I tense and spring and he instinctively arcs the knife back to defend himself. He is too slow. I grab his wrist, then slam the heel of my other hand into the crook of his elbow. His arm jackknifes into his skull and he falls back onto the couch. There is a moment of silence before the girl slumped at my feet wakes up and starts screaming.

The guy sits completely still, arms hanging by his side; dripping, alien cock pointing up from his open zipper. The knife is buried to the hilt in his right eye. The socket leaks blood and a clear viscous fluid.

I stare at him, shaking my head in disbelief, in horror.

A figure by my side. Lucs, taking my arm. Behind him, Raph and Gabe close the area, moving in on the witnesses, silencing the girl. One of the patrons tries to run and Gabe chases him up the stairs, slamming him into the ground.

"You are ready now," Lucs says.

He leads me back past the upstairs bar and downstairs. I move in a daze. Patrons jump out of the way when they see the blood dripping down my face, and stare after us dumbfounded. We head for the stage doors. The club sinks away as the doors close behind. Down the barely lit corridor and toward the back door.

The outside air is cool on my face. I savor the stinging of the wound. It grounds me. I look upward, staring at the sky. There is a calmness and order to the spread of stars that I wish I could understand.

Movement in the darkness of the alley. Figures emerge from a doorway. Mikhaels holds a blond-haired girl by the throat, one hand over her mouth. She is dressed in blue silk pajamas and shivers in the night air.

I look at her face.

Oh God. It is Lisa. She stares at me with terror-filled eyes.

I move toward her and Lucs grabs me, his touch burning.

Danteis stands next to Mikhaels, dwarfing a struggling man dressed only in tracksuit pants—dragged out of bed also; thin but muscular, like a skinned rabbit, impossibly defined abs a downward V. So this is what she wanted. I feel the hatred hit.

Then in the darkness beside me I sense Lucs *changing*. He towers over me, back and shoulders thickening with cords of muscle. The hand grasping my arm lengthens, the fingers stretching into talons. I look up at his face. His jaw has distended, brow flattened out. Fathomless black eyes burn into mine.

"Become one of us, Jakob. Finish the Change." His voice is guttural, strained.

I want to recoil but the muscles on my arms and chest ripple in sympathy. I shudder as a wave of pain surges through me; like something opening out inside. My face itches as the wound closes over. It has already healed by the time I touch it.

I want to ask Lucs how he knew. Why he picked me. But as I look at him I realize it does not matter. It was inevitable.

He grins at me with pride, his face all teeth, and rasps in the old tongue: *"Tu ars la dievs."*

A primal memory surfaces. I understand him.

You are now a god.

I turn back to Mikhaels, to Lisa in his arms. The growl sounds deep in my throat. She tries to scream and I can smell her fear, imagine the taste of her blood.

This is the way it should begin for me. Ending the life I once had. I feel my eyes dilating, becoming black holes in my face. Jason pisses himself in fear; the stain blossoms across his track pants. Mikhaels and Danteis laugh.

Yet inexplicably a part of me senses I have started crying. Burning tears that score my face. I wish I could tell my girlfriend I'm sorry, that part of me will be forever destroyed by this. That I loved her.

But when I look at her weak, pleading eyes, like an animal at the slaughter, the realization eclipses everything.

She deserves this. They all do. They are only prey.

The Change takes me.

Gardens

BY MELANIE TEM

*big Christmas tree lights, red and blue and green and yellow and a few white,
and no other light in the living room; a Santa Claus on the front porch as tall as
me and fat when I put my arms around him sometimes we'd both topple*

"Remember that Santa Claus we always had on the front porch?" I'd
asked my mother once, never doubting she'd remember, thinking it might
give us a shared moment of affectionate nostalgia. "Daddy built him out of
wire? And you made a red suit with white fur?"

She'd looked at me blankly. "I never made a Santa Claus suit."

"Yes, you did," I'd persisted, a bit panicky. "He had a wide shiny black belt
around his middle, and black boots, and sometimes we wrapped up empty
boxes for his sack." She'd shaken her head imperiously and dropped her eyes
back to her knitting. Understanding from the squaring of her shoulders and
the grim set of her mouth that there would be no common ground here,
either, I'd let it go.

*lilies of the valley tiny and low-growing and all but hidden in the deep shade
where my mother planted them, their intense fragrance barely noticeable unless
I fall on my knees and then it lays me flat*

*violets free in the grass and my mother with the lawn mower bearing down,
I crawl frantically back and forth across the huge lawn and pick them to save
them but they die in the palms of my hands and by the next morning the grass*

is violet-sequined again and my mother is complaining that she'll have to mow again in a few days

    begonias delphiniums clematis spirea—magic growing in the mere names

"French Creek Drive," announced a green-and-white street sign exactly like those in the city where I lived now. If the road had had a name while I was growing up here, nobody'd known it. We'd always just given directions to our house: "A mile north of town on Route 19, first dirt road to the left past the goat's milk fudge sign, down toward the creek, the only house on the left-hand side. The one with all the gardens." Although the gift shop on the edge of the highway that had sold the goat's milk fudge had been converted to a house, it looked almost exactly the same, except the sign was gone. Just past it ought to be the first pink glimpse of the house I'd grown up in—there.

Jackie turned in at the row of mailboxes. Trees, bushes, vines, grass, weeds had grown so dense that if I'd been alone I'd have missed the turn. The road still dipped. Back then Route 19 was a major trucking route between Erie and Pittsburgh, and every time I went up to get the mail at least one semi would roar past, scaring me a little, its wake sending my hair across my eyes and taking my hoarded breath. Ours was the fourth mailbox from the end and shaped like a big loaf of bread. I remembered the dusty-metal feel of the box floor under my nails, how our long last name had had to be crowded to fit on the side, the perky angle and squeaky hinge of the little red metal flag that announced there was mail to go out or mail delivered, the shiver of pleasure when there was a letter addressed to me and of dread when my mother got one of her big envelopes with medical records, test results, research information, insurance statements—not about her except that they were about me. I wasn't allowed to open them, but sometimes she'd read to me from a sheaf of tri-folded white paper as if it were a bedtime story, and I'd feel very close to her.

This was not one of the flashbacks that regularly transported me out of an everyday conversation or activity or identity into some other dimension. I wasn't disoriented. I hadn't missed anything. This was a normal little memory, one I could share with my daughter. "I used to come up here every day in the summer to get the mail," I told her over my shoulder.

From the back seat, Abby pronounced, "Cool," with no pre-adolescent irony, and I was gratified. Reveling in the clear uncompromised strength of her voice, I managed to stop myself from reaching behind the seat to grasp some part of her, just to be sure she was okay.

"From your house to the mailbox was quite a walk," Jackie observed.

Gardens

By any objective measure, it wasn't very far, maybe a city block. Abby could run up there and back without a second thought; the image of her strong legs and steady breath brought tears to my eyes, both jealous and triumphant. "By the time I was in high school I couldn't do it anymore," I acknowledged.

"I'm surprised your mother let you do it in the first place. She was always so protective of you." We'd been friends for a long time. There was something in her tone. I waited. "I was always jealous of how close you were to your mother."

"We weren't close."

"She seemed devoted to you."

"She was devoted to my sickness."

"Well, you know, it couldn't have been easy for her, either," she said carefully.

Realizing I'd been flirting with telling her the secret I'd only lately begun to guess at myself, I retreated from the chasm. "I'm sure she had a hard life." My voice broke.

Jackie heard it and glanced at me. "You okay?" People asked me that question a lot, referring to my physical health. Jackie meant more than that. Throat constricted, I just nodded.

We drove slowly. The road had always been potholed and wide enough for only one car at a time, with a hubcap-deep ditch on either side. Adult scowls had followed cars traveling more than about five miles an hour—which had happened mostly when there were teenagers living in one of the houses at the end of the road from which they could get up a pretty good head of steam by the time they reached the highway.

That made me think about when the Rowland kids were teenagers, some years before my own adolescence. I remembered watching them dance to Elvis and Chubby Checker in their kitchen; sometimes Tom Rowland would scoop up one of us little girls and we'd bounce and whirl to the rock and roll. Tom Rowland had taught me how to do the Twist and applauded my attempts which would never get any less awkward. I had no idea what had become of Tom and his sisters, and was content to let them remain one-dimensional in my past.

Dandelions and goldenrod from the ditch bank between Rowlands' and my house, tea my mother brewed for me from the bouquets I complicitly brought her. "Drink it all, Nora, honey. Every last drop. It's good for you." "How come you don't drink tea, Mommy?" "Oh, it's for you. I made it for you. To help you get well." "Thank you, Mommy."

All along the road on the right, the outside of its long curve, were houses. Mrs. Sandbach used to live in the first one; it was still run-down, rather charmingly I'd always thought though my mother used to tsk. Then, past a green weedy field and a gravel driveway that went back farther than you could see, was the gray house with the screened porch. First the Flemings, with three daughters, and then the Worleys, with a bunch of kids somewhat amorphous in my memory, had lived there; when I'd felt well enough, we'd played canasta. At the very corner of the lot still stood the copse of three pine trees close together—or maybe three trunks of a single tree—leaning outward like a tall bouquet from roots that must by now be intertwined whether or not they'd started out that way. Concentrated clean fragrance and filtered sunlight, needles green plush under shoe soles, silky shafts and sharp tips when I filled my pockets for my mother.

Down in the steep shady ravine behind Flemings' house. A hot summer day, muggy, mosquitoes. The water isn't even ankle-deep, but we always use the bridge, which bows and has planks missing. I get dizzy. The stream makes hardly any noise. My bathing suit is getting too small for me; it binds at the crotch as I clamber up the bank, which is slippery with plants. Pine branches tickle my bare arms and knees, leaving invisible itchy trails.

At the top of the slope rises a set of monkey bars in a clearing with no house anywhere in sight. There's never anyone else here. A playground just for me, with no context. I shiver and grab on.

The bars are warm, the spans from one to the next awkward because I'm really too big for this. When I straddle the very top rung, there's a pleasure I don't yet recognize as vaguely sexual. The smell of rust is a taste in the back of my throat. Pale orange films my skin, just noticeable on top of my summer tan. "Brown as a berry," my mother would say, tracing her finger along my arm, but what berries are brown?

It's uncomfortable with the bar pressing into the backs of my thighs and my feet starting to fall asleep and nothing to lean my back against, but I like being up here. Birds trill at ear level and bugs buzz. I feel exposed and unreachable at the same time.

My mother is calling me. It's suppertime. I don't want to go home, but she calls again. I don't want to go home. When I lower myself and then jump down, I lose my balance and fall. Crying, I right myself. Hard little apples hurt the balls of my feet.

I'm late. She'll be mad. I fashion a pouch out of my towel and fill it with the squishiest of the apples, fecal brown with no red left at all, some with not just wormholes but the actual worms. What she makes out of them will taste bad and make me sick, but it'll be good for me.

My pink house on its treed and gardened acre was on our left now, the only house on the left-hand side. There used to be poplar trees all the way around where the road curved. All twenty or so had died the same year; learning in adulthood that poplars naturally have a short life span didn't lessen my horror and guilt when I thought of that arc of stumps, growing back but round instead of tall and feathery. Having a dead tree cut down from my yard thirty years later had caused me to say offhandedly to my mother, "Remember when all those poplars died when I was a kid?" Not only did she not recall that they'd died and been cut down and sent out new shoots, she would not even confirm that there'd been poplar trees in the first place. There weren't now.

"Remember the gardens?" I'd demanded recklessly. "People used to say our place looked like a little park—"

"Oh," she'd interrupted, "I remember the gardens, Nora." The fluttering in my chest was fear.

We passed the cottage that as far as I was concerned had always been abandoned although people spoke of its absent owner. Tufted grass and Queen Anne's lace and vines obscured it, including its roof, claiming its brown and gray as part of the natural landscape. My mother used to take me walking there. We'd pick things and bring them home.

"Do you want to stop?"

Separating the cottage from the Ewings' next door was a neat hedgerow. A willow tree hung low. "No," I finally answered Jackie. "Not yet. Let's go down to the end of the road."

She nodded, then suddenly stared left. "Look at that, Nora. They've put in a pool. The pool's practically as big as the house."

"My house doesn't have a pool," I objected, and laughed, and unwillingly looked.

White fence. Huge blue spruce trees in a row. Rocks like manatees. Moss. Seeing out my sickroom window my mother's bowed back as she scraped moss off a rock and deposited it shard after shard in a Kroger's bag

The house was very pink against the very green grass. The tubular structure of the pool stretched perpendicular to the house all the way across the wide side yard. Most of the time my mother had mowed the lawn; I remembered yellow shorts and a halter top, sometimes just a bra, which was sort of hard to believe now; I remembered her sweating. There was no fence now, and no spruce trees. The lawn had been reduced to a border for the pool. There were no rocks and, presumably, no moss.

gardens

"In the woods just on the other side of the fence was a tree that would eat you if you got too close," I recounted for Abby's benefit.

Jackie raised her eyebrows at me, and Abby squealed appreciatively.

"Right *there*." I stabbed a forefinger in the direction of Jackie's open window as we eased past the exact spot, or what I thought was the exact spot, hard to pinpoint without the fence and rocks. Both Abby and Jackie peered with me, but nothing remarkable showed itself. The trees just looked like trees, the bushes like bushes. I kept staring as long as I could, twisting to see out Abby's window and then the rear window.

"You never told me about the child-eating tree," Jackie remonstrated gently.

"You wouldn't have believed me."

Rows and rows of tomatoes, the sharp fragrance of leaves and stems but odorless blossoms, and squash vines with sticky orange flowers. Blueberries in a cup, each with a firm fringed topknot my tongue seeks first.

"This is the first time you've been back since your mother died, isn't it?" Jackie asked. It was the kind of query friends make of each other though they well know the literal answer—an invitation, an acknowledgment. I nodded, waiting to see what complex of emotion would reveal itself.

My mother had died almost exactly two years earlier, on a hot August dawn a thousand miles away. I'd been there during much of her dying, though at the precise moment of her death I'd been too sick myself to get out of bed and someone else, a hired stranger, had been taking care of her. Emerging on a tide of morphine from her only spell of real pain, a full morning's worth, she'd smiled at me and given me the "OK" sign with her thumb and forefinger, then lay down into her last coma. What was OK? Was she letting me know the pain had subsided? Was she signaling peace with death? Was she saying I'd taken good care of her, I'd done everything I could for her my whole life, I was a good daughter, things were OK between us?

Barely six weeks before that, she and I had sat in the oncologist's eleventh-floor office, not together, she on the examining table and I trembling on a sticky vinyl chair at her feet and out of her line of sight, watching through tall windows as storm clouds gathered over a long line of trees that made a false but convincing horizon. My mother, *my mother*, lay naked and swollen with a tumor under that blue paper gown. In a horrible irony, I was feeling fairly good that day, only slight nausea and vertigo, the headache only a suggestive throbbing in my temples. I wasn't sick enough to protect my mother. The oncologist spoke to her.

On a pretty morning just that previous June, the phone had rung while she was making lunch for us; it would not have been a companionable meal, but the best we could ever do. Her back to me, she said, "You get it," because we both were afraid to talk to the family doctor about the results of the tests, never mind that he'd assured us it was likely just a little constipation, not uncommon in people her age, easily treatable, nothing to worry about. I took the phone into the living room to listen; later I would wonder what she'd thought about during those minutes, while she went on dicing vegetables for the salad she would serve me but wouldn't eat herself, but even if I'd asked she wouldn't have said. The doctor offered kindly to tell her. I said I would. When I hung up, I didn't let myself sit there even for a second, but went to her where she stood at the counter, small and sturdy, back to me. I hesitated but I did put my arms around her. So she knew before I told her, although I said it quickly and clearly to get it over with, "It's cancer, Mom. You have cancer."

"I think I miss my mother," I said to Jackie, but that wasn't quite accurate. Jackie was my best friend; I hoped she'd know what I meant. I hoped she wouldn't.

"I miss Grandma," Abby echoed.

"No, you don't!" As I turned on her, I saw how she flinched, and how Jackie looked at me in alarm. "No, you don't miss her! You didn't know her well enough to miss her! I never let you spend time—" My vision blackened and for a moment I thought I would pass out. To steady myself, and to reassure her, I clutched Abby's hand. A good daughter, she let me hold on tight, though I knew I must be hurting her.

gardens
gardens

"Nora?"

With what I hoped was a gentle pat, I released my daughter's hand and righted myself in the seat and took as deep a breath as my compromised lungs would ever allow. "I need to walk around."

"I'll come with you." Abby was worried.

"No, honey, you go with Jackie."

"Mom, you can't be by yourself out here."

"Of course I can. I used to live here."

Jackie had turned around at the end of the road, beside the brown house that used to be and might still be the Rowlands', and we were passing the woods again. I waited anxiously for the pink house I'd grown up in to come into view, knowing I'd have to get past the pool first, and everything that was missing. "Are you sure you'll be all right?" Jackie asked.

"Well," I chuckled wryly, "no."

"I mean, you can walk well enough and everything?"

"I'll be fine." I turned to Abby again, this time smiling gently. "Really. I'll be fine. Just give me half an hour or so."

We were creeping toward the boundary of my side yard. From the soggy lower end, bordering the road, my mother had harvested colonies of mushrooms. There'd been an arbor outside the kitchen window; the purple grape skins had made my lips itch.

Back porch. Straw mat, pink roses around the edge. Sitting on the short step. Laying the flat of my hand against pink shingles; their dryness makes my fist clench with fingertips inside. Mother brings iced tea, sits in the big wicker chair to be sure I drink it all.

No car was parked in the driveway. The driveway was still gravel, nubby under my shoes and cane tip. I realized I was looking down for pretty pebbles. The tiny front porch had been totally rebuilt. I knocked. I'd thought it might feel odd to knock on my own front door, but this door wasn't mine. No one answered. I said in my head, nearly spoke aloud, the explanation and request I'd rehearsed: "I used to live here. I grew up here. Do you mind if I look around?"

It wasn't the house drawing me. It was the gardens. If anybody had answered the door, I'd have only asked permission to do what I did anyway, which was to go into the gardens. My throat seemed almost closed and my knees were weak. Leaning heavily on the cane, I veered off the driveway onto the flagstone path, maybe the same one I'd fallen on the first time I'd fainted; we'd spent all night in the emergency room, the doctors and nurses very attentive to both my mother and me, and I had a hard white scar on my knee from, I thought, that reddish ridged stone right there.

gardens

I was sweating and light-headed, awash with heat and humidity, with the sickness that had informed my life almost but not quite as long as I could remember, and with a new suspense. I stumbled. My cane caught the edge of a stone and flipped it. Things were growing under there. Although I couldn't actually hurry, my pulse raced and my limbs flailed as if I were running, and the landscape was streaming by.

blossoms enormous as babies and touching each other, overlapping and layering into one vast mat of placenta-colored, bloody emesis-colored, heart-colored growth, weedy, dry, in need of dead-heading, I never worked in my mother's gardens but now I am expected to

Paths crisscrossed. I couldn't see the road or the woods, and I was afraid if I looked behind me I wouldn't see the pink house. My lips and tongue were numb.

gardens

gardens

The fear of paralysis was old and cumulative, and now for long moments it came true. My legs would neither carry me anywhere nor support me standing still. I held on to the cane with both hands, not sure I was holding on at all. The muscles controlling my respiratory, circulatory, excretory systems were barely functioning.

If I turned left, I'd be among towering pigtailed corn and pumpkins with seeds and flesh and guts. Right would take me under the rose arbor hardly higher than my head whose hips and thorns made a ferociously purgative tonic. Straight ahead a living maze had grown up. Behind was the house where I couldn't live anymore.

In the hospital night, not dark nor quiet nor safe, she sits by my bed. When we are alone she touches me, caresses me, applies fiery poultices of her own making, spreads my lips and my legs with fat squirmy fingers, siphons off my bad blood

"Mama?"

feeds me tenderly with spoon and syringe

"Mama? What are you doing?"

feeds me poison she has planted and tended and harvested from her gardens. When the kind, puzzled nurses and the kind, baffled doctors come in, she is holding my hand and helplessly weeping. She never leaves my side.

With every panicked step my cane tip stuck, emitting a mean little sucking sound when it popped free, making my gait even more unsteady and my balance more precarious than usual, surely leaving holes. I imagined puncture wounds to take things out and put things in, tunnels for worms, airways and waterways, subterranean and subcutaneous and subconscious pocking only my mother and I would know was there.

And Abby.

Swaying dangerously, I lost my grip on the cane, and it was swallowed up by vegetation I didn't dare search. I crouched and bored my fingers into the ground for support. It gave and I collapsed, managed to raise myself enough to send thin pink sprinkles of vomit onto the tilled ground, which absorbed it like fertilizer.

When the retching stopped, I lay still. I could not stand up, couldn't even get to my knees. Where leaves and tendrils brushed, adhered, wound around me, my skin blistered. I found myself turning my head and obediently opening my mouth to receive familiar, poisonous fruit.

Somebody in the gardens

"*Mama?*"

"Mama?"

"Oh, Abby, no."

Abby was kneeling beside me. Her vigor and clarity penetrated my terrible miasma; I'd kept her at least from the kind of harm I knew best. She slid a firm hand under my neck and raised my head. "Here, Mama, swallow this."

I struggled, but of course she was stronger than I was and all I could manage was a feeble protest before thick warm liquid trickled into my mouth and down the back of my throat.

"Grandma taught me this," my daughter said soothingly. "It's a special plant she always had growing in her garden, I forget the name, but there's a bed of it way over there in the corner." She stroked my face, then took one hand away to squeeze juice and pulp from the stems and leaves in her lap. Her fingers came back, slimy and smelling poisonously green, and she crooned almost playfully, "Open up, Mama."

I gasped and choked. "Abby, no, it's poison—"

"Jackie will come and get us soon. She just dropped me off while she went to get gas. We'll get you to the hospital. Don't worry."

Weeping, she took my hand in hers. I knew then she would never leave my side.

gardens

Under the Bright and Hollow Sky

BY ANDREW J. WILSON

INTRODUCTION

Let me state from the outset that the source of the following material was weird; and when I say this, I don't just mean "strange" or "odd," but also imply the older sense of "fate" or "destiny." When you have read the fragmentary notes collected here, that remark will hardly seem surprising to you: the material is cryptic, esoteric and probably unique.

I was traveling home from a friend's house in Penicuik—a former mining town on the outskirts of Edinburgh—by LRT night bus. We had been drinking whiskey over the course of the evening, so I felt very tired indeed. I must have fallen asleep in the early hours of the morning because I suddenly found the driver standing in front of me, shaking me by the shoulder; we had arrived at the Waverley Station terminus. It was almost three o'clock in the morning by my watch. I apologized and stumbled toward the exit, only to be called back again. The driver pushed a tattered plastic carrier bag into my hands, telling me that I'd forgotten it.

I had certainly forgotten the Farmfoods shopping bag when I woke up late the next morning. I rediscovered it under my jacket that evening and recalled the incident on the night bus, only then realizing that the bag wasn't mine at all. It contained the following collection of fragments, stamped but unsent letters, and transcriptions.

The author of most of these pieces, one William Anderson, mentions me twice in the course of the notes, but I am unfamiliar with this name. To the best of my recollection, I cannot remember ever being questioned by anyone on the topics he discusses. The subject of his investigation is also a mystery to me; I have been unable to find any record of someone by the name of Cranston M. Alderton.

I have chosen to present these fragments in what I assume to be the most logical order. The material is unedited. If anyone can shed any light on their origin, I would be delighted to hear from them.

A.J.W.

WHATEVER HAPPENED
TO CRANSTON M. ALDERTON?
BY WILLIAM ANDERSON

Letter to Carol Anne

25 OCTOBER

Dear Carol Anne,

I'm not sure why I'm writing to you. It seems a ridiculous conceit since you said you never wanted to see me again. I suppose I hope to explain to you now what I couldn't articulate then. You wanted something I couldn't give you—commitment. I want to give you this apology instead. I'm going to keep you up-to-date with my progress, and in the end, I hope to have justified my choices.

I do love you, you know. I always did.

Ever since I first read Cranston M. Alderton's prose, I have wanted to write about the man. C.M.A. stole many nights of sleep from me, but gave me visions which made that all worthwhile. Sometimes I wonder how much of my own writing is infected with his ideas and style.

You never cared about that—you couldn't even be bothered to read his work. Now he seems to have stolen you from me, leaving me with only his pet nightmares for company in my bed.

Edinburgh is a God-forsaken place. The freezing wind howls around these crumbling tenements night and day, blowing over the beggars and drunks who swarm in the streets during the daylight, and battering at the rotten window frames of this attic when the sun has gone down. Glen told me that his flat was near the center of town, but despite the people and the buildings, it feels like the middle of nowhere. No one talks here—no one *does* anything. No wonder C.M.A. spent most of his life in this awful place: he didn't have to make up very much of his stories.

None of that matters—everything will soon fall into place again. The magazine has given me an advance to do the research here. The article will form the basis of a book, if I'm lucky, and an independent production company is interested in making a TV documentary about C.M.A. I will be commissioned to write the script if the project comes off. I might even get to present it . . .

Tomorrow I will start trawling the libraries and newspaper records. There are phone calls to make too. I don't have many leads, but I can make a start with what Glen has been able to dig up for me around town.

Maybe we can sit down together when I get back to Glasgow and I can talk about this with you. It's a strange kind of love letter, but it will tell you why I needed to follow my dreams.

It's now past midnight, and someone or something is screeching on the street outside. The sound is a dreadful, protracted wail, but I can't work out whether it is a squeal of pleasure or pain.

Do you miss me, Carol Anne? God knows, I need you now, my love.

Thinking of you.

Love,
William

Andrew J. Wilson

Unpublished Obituary from the Files of The Scotsman

Cranston M. Alderton, supernatural fiction writer
Born: 11 December, 1963, in Edinburgh
Died: INFORMATION NOT AVAILABLE

The death of Cranston M. Alderton brings to an end one of the strangest careers in Scottish literature. His surreal stories often verged on the nightmarish in their portrayal of an inimical and monstrous world in which characters could more accurately be described as victims. Nevertheless, the comments of his critics, which suggested that Alderton's work was merely sadistic fantasy, missed the crucial truth that a vast amount of his material was drawn from the peculiar circumstances of his own life. In fact, his *oeuvre* forms a sustained and complex elucidation of the consistent, if deeply pessimistic, philosophy of the man some commentators have referred to as "a twenty-first-century Poe."

Alderton was born in the Simpson Maternity Pavilion of the Edinburgh Royal Infirmary—or so he wrote in the skeletal biographical sketch published on the flyleaf of *Black Exits*. In fact, neither the hospital nor Register House has any record of his birth.

He received little or no formal education until his mid-teens, when he attended the local Rudolf Steiner school. This seems to indicate that his parents were free thinkers with liberal views on education, but so little is known about them that this lack of institutional schooling only serves to further reduce the meager documentation of Alderton's life.

What is known is that Mr. and Mrs. Alderton were killed in the disastrous Pan Am air crash in the Peruvian Andes. The remains of their bodies were positively identified by Cranston Alderton on the night of his sixteenth birthday.

He finished his schooling as a ward of his parents' solicitors and matriculated at the University of Aberdeen. After four years, during which he seems to have made little impression on his tutors or peers, Alderton gained a second-class honours degree in English Literature and Philosophy. His activities in the two years after his graduation remain undocumented, but he returned to Edinburgh in 1987 and joined a medical publisher as a production editor. His first work appeared in print soon afterwards.

Alderton was never a literary star, shining out of the best-seller stands and newspaper gossip columns rather he sucked readers towards his work like a black hole. His early stories, such as "The Psychopomp" and "MS Thrown from a Moving Train", and poems such as "Pseudonym", "Crocodile Tears" and "Taking the Doggerel for a Walk" appeared in small press publications—or fanzines—such as *Sky Pilot, Isolation* and *Cynghanedd*. It was his limited-edition chapbook, *The Crimes of Sleep*, which was to bring Alderton wider acclaim.

Larger independent publishers like the Gargoyle Press, Shock Rock, and of course Dunwich Tomes all signed contracts with him for books such as *Disjecti Membra Poetae*, his volume of verse, *Spoor of the Hydra*, a sequence of linked stories, and *The Dictionary of Palindromes*, one of the most obscure pieces of scholarship ever published. It is understood that Secker and Warburg even approached Alderton regarding the novel *Nystagmus*, but he rejected their overtures and is believed to have later destroyed the manuscript, although the fragments and extracts published in the little magazines still exist.

Alderton's writing was often described as contemporary gothic, but his measured, relentless prose eschewed the florid excesses of the genre. He often employed a near-documentary realism in his stories that underpinned their disturbing and dislocating imagery with foundations rooted in the cold realities of homelessness, genetics and personality disorder. His poetry is more opaque and elusive, and was best described by Alderton himself, who always referred to his verse as "dream trails."

He resigned from his job in early 1994 and allegedly dedicated himself to full-time writing, although the frequency of new material in print decreased during this period. He was rumoured to be working on a sequence of linked stories and novels which would both explicate and subsume his earlier work. According to the editors who knew him best, the working title for this mammoth exegesis was *The Devil's Crucible*. The subtext of the material, as always, was the proposition that humanity comprises the dead souls of a higher order of beings condemned to hell for incomprehensible sins, condemned to seldom—if ever—discover the truth.

The work was never to appear. Always reclusive, Alderton withdrew even further into the shadows of his impenetrable private life and broke contact with even his closest associates. He disappeared from his residence several months ago, for all intents and purposes vanishing from the face of the earth. He leaves no partner or children.

Contributed

Andrew J. Wilson

Letter to Carol Anne

Dear Carol Anne,

The discovery of an unpublished obituary in the files of *The Scotsman* was certainly a lucky break, giving me almost all the available details of Alderton's life. I must admit that I was shocked at first when I thought that I might be too late. Fortunately, it proves nothing since the newspapers write obituaries in advance. Whoever wrote the piece seemed to assume that C.M.A. was not long for this world, but I wonder if the anonymous journalist had the full picture. Perhaps C.M.A. simply wants to erase another part of his life? It's a good angle for my article. I had originally hoped to gain access to the man and conduct the first extensive interview with him, but it looks like this investigation is going to have to delve a little deeper into the mulch.

When I approached the various publishers of C.M.A.'s work at the beginning of this year, I was told that he was a solitary man who shunned publicity. Many, if not all, of his editors had never even met him. Some agreed to forward my requests for an interview, but I received no reply. Finally, I obtained two differing correspondence addresses from separate imprints, but again, my letters went unanswered. One envelope was returned eventually, marked "Not known at this address"; the other was finally recovered from a dead letter office.

Around this time, I re-contacted the publishers of C.M.A.'s most recent collection, *Black Exits*. No one had received any word from him for six months, and they were worried that he had become unwell. I persuaded George Breen of Dunwich Tomes to give me the post office box number to which he sent any royalty cheques. It was in Edinburgh, of course.

I sound confident, don't I, Carol Anne? The writing is going well and I think that it isn't going to take much work to turn my notes into an acceptable draft. I've managed to arrange several interviews over the next few days with people who knew C.M.A., or at least met him for one reason or another. With luck, the feelers I've put out may even put me on the trail of the man himself. He's out there, somewhere in this city. I can feel it in my guts.

Nevertheless, I'm reminded of the old Nietzsche lines:

> *He who fights with monsters might take*
> *care lest he thereby become a monster.*
> *And if you gaze for long into an abyss,*
> *the abyss gazes also into you.*

I keep coming across parts of the city which Alderton used in his work and have begun to mark out his "territory" on my *Edinburgh Streetfinder*. Sometimes passersby stop and stare at me, wondering what on earth I'm up to. I try not to return their looks because half of them also seem to have stepped out of one of C.M.A.'s stories.

Glen has explained to me that the howling sounds I have been hearing at night are made by foxes. Apparently, he thinks that these ghastly noises are mating calls. I wish that were some comfort, but someone rang me on my mobile phone last night and the same terrible shrieks screamed out for nearly a minute before the line went dead.

Love,
William

E-Mail Interview with Ken Macleod, Science Fiction-Writer, by William Anderson

William Anderson wrote:
I believe you met Cranston Alderton. What were your impressions of him?

The smell, initially. Many years ago, at the top of a ladder in a second-hand bookshop, I encountered a reek from rotting paper which sent me down the ladder and out the door. Alderton gave off a perfume-faint waft that brought this memory back, came to me late one evening in the Southsider. A dozen or so of Edinburgh's SF fans and writers were crowded around a couple of beer-slopped tables. The man perched on the end of the bench beside me hardly stood out in that company, some of whom carry eccentricity to the point of clinical insanity.

Younger than myself, with thinner hair, and skin as waxy as the cuffs of his old denim jacket, he was engaged in a serious discussion with one of our number, Judith. I half-listened in, paying more attention to her appalled countenance than to the man's mumbled rants. Eventually he turned sharply to me and said:

"So what do you make of that, MacLeod?"

Startled that he even knew my name, I replied:

"Well, I don't know, it's a very original and amusing idea, that we're the bedsores of higher beings . . ."

To my great surprise, he jumped up, clutching as he did so a frayed volume which may well have been the source of the smell, glared at Andrew Wilson and snarled, "Dead souls! Dead souls!" Then he stalked out into the night.

After he'd left, Andrew gave me a rueful look.

"Pity about that, Ken. You've just pissed off the best horror writer you could hope to meet."

"Um, well, sorry, but it wasn't deliberate."

I turned in relief to conversation with beautiful Judith, mad John and other Edinburgh SF usual suspects, and as I got up to catch the last train, Andrew thrust a bundle of small-press zines into my hands.

"Sorry, Andrew, Lovecraftian horror isn't my thing."

But he had that drug-pusher gleam in his eye. "Go on, just try one . . ."

The train ride to Dalmeny takes fifteen minutes, and the usual risk I run is sleeping past my stop. That night, a bleary glance at Alderton's writing jolted me sharply awake, and by the time I got off the train, my mind was buzzing. I almost ran home, and my wife actually worried that I'd run into some kind of trouble. I reassured her, poured myself a whisky and sat down, returning to the story as she watched a late pop-profile on MTV. As she went to bed, I glanced up from the zine and said I'd be along in five minutes.

She came downstairs three hours later, expecting to find me fallen asleep on the sofa. I had read all of Alderton's stories, and was staring at the curtain as though I'd just heard something move in the dark behind it.

Under the Bright and Hollow Sky

What did you make of Alderton's writing?

It's hard to say quite what I found so fascinating and disturbing about it. Unlike the pretentious, verbose, derivative diction of most of that kind of stuff, Alderton's writing was crisp and modern, almost hyper-realistic, and the scientific—or science-fictional—premises of his stories were eerily plausible. It added up to a world-view that was hellishly—and I use the term advisedly—compelling and nauseating.

How did you interpret that world-view?

Well, I've always thought of atheism as "a simple faith, but a great comfort" as the old Emperor says in Lois MacMaster Bujold's *Barryar*. But it's only so if we regard the universe in which we live as real, and one in which the only values are those created by us—that we decide what's good and bad, that in that sense, with all our insignificance we are as gods. It's what Nietzsche called "active nihilism", the idea that this world is one on which we can stamp our will.

Now what I saw in Alderton's work was some eerie consistencies—perhaps never quite made explicit, but obviously deliberately there—with some recent speculations about the future of artificial intelligence. I'm sure Charlie Stross could explain it a lot better than I could, but basically, the idea is that we can imagine entire solar systems turned into computing machinery in which virtual realities exist that could easily encompass simulations of every human being who ever lived.

Hans Moravec has speculated that the great minds to come may wish to give the odd passing thought to their human creators or ancestors, and those passing thoughts could be what I've just described. He points out that because there can be only one original, real world and—in the long future of the universe—countless simulations of it, the odds are overwhelming that we're living in one of them. As Charles Platt put it more pithily, "We're all dead and in Sim City already."

But suppose we are in the thought—or the pocket computer game—of a mind that's actively cruel, or actively experimenting? It becomes a sort of materialist Gnosticism or Manichaeism, the heresy that our world is an illusory creation of a dark Power. James Blish in *A Case of Conscience* has a Catholic Church whose orthodoxy—as is never pointed out in the book—is in fact a variant of this heresy, and that notion is no less disturbing than the idea that an atheistic view of the universe could be consistent with the possibility that we are at the mercy of an evil or indifferent creator. This notion haunts Alderton's stories and reveals his most apparently arbitrary plot-twists as very clever references to this literal *deus ex machina* in which, I think because of the many cruel twists to his own life, Alderton himself came to believe.

What do you think happened to him?

I don't know. Sorry, I've got to go now. There's something making a noise at the front door.

—Ken MacLeod

Letter to Carol Anne

27 OCTOBER

Dear Carol Anne,

Glen pulled a few strings and got the landlord to let me into C.M.A.'s flat in the Lawnmarket. It is on the top floor of a Victorian tenement just below the Castle. Apparently, C.M.A. had paid a year's rent in advance, so they haven't touched it.

At first, I didn't think that the place was all that remarkable. There are a lot of books, of course, and the walls are plastered with old prints and photographs of Edinburgh, but the rooms didn't have any particular personality stamped on them. The devil was in the detail, though.

I found a Cibachrome print of a stuffed giraffe wrapped in plastic! It was a startling image, but you know what writers are like. I assumed that the photograph had been taken at the Chambers Street Museum during a period of renovation. Then I turned the picture over and found that it had been labelled "Mother" in C.M.A.'s own handwriting.

Under the Bright and Hollow Sky

The bathroom also turned up a shock. The sides of the tub were peeling from the metal like flakes of leprous skin. I had no idea that enamel could actually do that. The whole thing resembled a fungus rather than a bath. I drew the landlord's attention to the damage and he became quite flustered, assuring me that he was unaware of what could have caused the decay. He withdrew, mumbling that he would deduct the cost of a replacement from Alderton's deposit.

Finally, I was struck by a framed print on the wall of the bedroom. At first I thought that it was simply a cheap reproduction of Andy Warhol's studies of an electric chair. Then I realized that, unlike the original, there was a person sitting in the execution device. The thin figure was strapped in and slouched over, but I couldn't tell if this was supposed to be before or after the current had been sent through Old Sparky. I have the nagging feeling that Alderton has had a photograph of himself inserted into the Warhol original. If so, this is the first image of the man that I have ever seen. The pale face stares out with wide eyes and a gaping mouth, looking like the Man in the Moon. When I took a few covering shots of the flat and its contents with my Instamatic, I made sure that I got several snaps of this possible self-portrait.

Just before I left, I scanned the bookcases and found a shelf devoted to C.M.A.'s own work. I sneaked a look at the books, hoping to find some personal annotations which might give me a clue to his thought processes. The books were filled with blank pages.

I think about you a lot, you know. I wonder what you're doing.

Love,
William

Tape-Recorded Interview with Mike Calder, Proprietor of the Transreal Fiction Bookshop, by William Anderson

W.A.: Did you sell a lot of Cranston Alderton's work?

M.C.: It ticked over. The people who bought it were big fans, and liked the expensive editions or the first printings. But generally, most customers went to the fantasy books beside him on the shelf . . . He was a minor author, but very popular with the people who did like him.

W.A.: Had you read him yourself?

M.C.: I've read one or two short stories. To be honest, he's not really to my taste.

W.A.: Did you ever meet the man?

M.C.: It's curious, but I'm not sure. I didn't really know what he looked like, but one time fairly recently this old bloke—he looked quite old anyway—came in and claimed that this was who he was. I didn't really believe him, but I've since seen photos of Alderton, and I think he did come in. He wanted to sign his books, but I wouldn't let him. That was a bit unfortunate, I suppose . . .

W.A.: How did he react to that?

M.C.: Like a trooper—with some colourful language! He was fairly harmless, but he was quite vocal about it and off he went. I never saw the person again.

W.A.: There have been rumours recently that Cranston Alderton is actually dead. How do you think that will affect his sales?

M.C.: In my shop, I don't think it will affect them very much because I'm no longer carrying that type of literature. In other shops, I suspect they'll plummet. If he's out of stock and there's no new stories coming, then generally the backlist doesn't sell.

W.A.: Thank you very much.

Under the Bright and Hollow Sky

Letter to Carol Anne

Dear Carol Anne,

Last night a fox ran past me on my way back to the flat. It had something clamped between its jaws. I suppose it had caught a rat, but whatever it had snatched seemed to have far too many legs. I'm finding it increasingly difficult to rely on my senses because I'm not sleeping very well at the moment. There are times when my vision shudders like film caught in the gate of a projector.

I have been trying to phone you, Carol Anne, but all I get is your answering machine. Have you been getting my messages? I desperately need to talk to someone who can ground me. We made a mistake splitting up, and I regret the things I said and did. I'd leave for Glasgow right now if I didn't have appointments tomorrow.

Glen and I fell out over a trivial incident involving a piece of mail addressed to me that was forwarded to this address. He told me that he was allowing me to stay for the duration of the research, not giving me permission to move in. I lost my temper and said that I had no intention of staying in this damn city for any longer than I had to. I also made it clear that I had given no one his address as my base of operations. All contacts have to call me on my mobile phone or use my e-mail address. He told me to finish the job and get out within the week. In the meantime, he was going on a business trip to London.

After he'd gone, I opened the envelope and found a photograph of the picture in C.M.A.'s flat. The image had been doctored again and I swear the figure in the electric chair has my face.

I spent the day pursuing some more fruitless leads and seriously thought about giving up and going home. Then I was accosted by a beggar. I gave him some spare change to make him go away, but the down-and-out followed me along the road, mumbling, "Xoanon, xoanon . . ."

"What's your problem?" I asked him.

"The 'X' is unknown, the 'O' is for zero, and anon is anonymous, anon—xoanon, xoanon!" he raved to my face.

The big beggar was stoop-shouldered and misshapen. His dirty black hair hung long and lank. He wore a shapeless donkey jacket, steel-toed workman's boots and a sailor's jumper. The man looked like the late Alex Harvey, after his death.

"I've given you some money, what more do you want?" I shouted.

He grinned slyly. "It's no what I want, it's what you want, son. Gimme your phone—go on, I'm no gonnae steal it."

I was desperate to get away from the smelly creature, so I pulled out my mobile and slipped it to him. What was I thinking of? Lack of sleep is scrambling my thought processes. The beggar stabbed in some numbers and began to mumble into the phone.

"Aye, aye, I've found him. Do you wannae talk to him now? All right. Bye."

He gave me back my mobile and told me, "He'll be in touch— he's got your number."

I began to realize that the down-and-out might have met C.M.A. after his disappearance, but when I asked him who he meant, he simply muttered, "Xoanon, xoanan," and shuffled away.

Despite my confused and exhausted state, I had the presence of mind to press REDIAL, but the last registered number was yours, which I'd tried to ring a few hours before.

I checked the *Concise Oxford Dictionary* later and discovered that there is such a word as "xoanon." It means a "primitive usu. wooden image of a deity supposed to have fallen from heaven". What the dictionary didn't make clear was whether it was the image or the deity that had fallen out of the sky.

I really don't know where I stand now.

A few moments after I wrote that last line, I looked out of the window and saw something big scuttling down the empty street. I could estimate its size because the beast had a dead fox clamped between its jaws. It looked like one of the beetles from C.M.A.'s story "I Remember Nothing."

Thinking of you.

Love,
William

Tape-Recorded Interview with Andrew J. Wilson, Science Fiction and Fantasy Reviewer for The Scotsman *by William Anderson*

W.A.: You seem to be somewhat the worse for drink—

A.J.W.: Who do you think you're talking to? You schedule an interview and then you're three hours late! Call yourself a professional? Now get the round in, you grave-robbing bastard.

W.A.: I'm trying to track down Cranston Alderton. I believe he was an associate of yours—

A.J.W.: Alderton was no friend of mine. I knew him briefly and we talked about writing, but he just sucked all the juice he could get out of everybody else . . . and he never bought his bloody round! You've never met him, have you?

W.A.: Not for want of trying . . .

A.J.W.: The man was cold, precise and exact in everything he did, even in the way he tried to cover up his disappearance—

W.A.: What? You mean he planned the entire thing?

A.J.W.: He didn't just plan it—he wrote it. I've seen the work, but I was never paid for editing it.

W.A.: Have you any idea how I can find him?

A.J.W.: No, I don't—and you'd do well to drop all this now! He's like Jack the Ripper—it's very interesting to read about the monster, but you wouldn't want to meet him. If you push this any further, you will find him—and you'll be sorry . . .

W.A.: You wrote the obituary, didn't you?

A.J.W.: Yes, I wrote it when I believed the bastard was safely dead. I thought, "We can lay him to rest and forget about him." But he isn't dead, is he? There's no body.

W.A.: I don't understand.

A.J.W.: Do you know the bookworm theory? Alderton swore by it and he was the one who came up with it. The egg is an idea planted in the writer's head, he called it a "xoanon". It hatches and produces a larva that takes the form of a text. This worms its way into the reader's head and forms a chrysalis, and when the time is right, a black and dreadful butterfly is born . . .

W.A.: What are you trying to tell me?

A.J.W.: That we're all trapped under the bright and hollow sky.

W.A.: I don't understand—

A.J.W.: It's a line from an Iggy Pop song—"The Passenger". That's who you are, the passenger, and Cranston Alderton's in the driving seat—and I'm not even going to get in the bloody car!

W.A.: You won't help me then?

A.J.W.: That's exactly what I'm trying to do, you idiot! If you're not going to listen, then I'm not going to waste my breath. Now get the hell away from me!

Letter to Carol Anne

29 OCTOBER

Dear Carol Anne,

I had a disturbing dream last night. It began after the end of my disastrous interview with an idiotic hack.

Under the Bright and Hollow Sky

Soon after I left the bar, I realized that I was being followed. I made a stupid mistake and cut into the side-streets of the Southside. The tall stone buildings funnelled me away from the light and the footsteps of three men echoed off the walls like slaps to the face.

I started to pick up speed and my pursuers began to run. Then I dodged into a small lane in an attempt to double back to more populated streets. I found that I was trapped in a blind alley with only a single, flickering lamp.

The men behind me stopped and blocked the entrance to the close. I turned slowly and saw their faces weakly illuminated in red by the blinking sodium light. Two of them were battered middle-aged men with faces swollen by too much cheap alcohol and too many brawls. The other one was younger and bigger in both height and girth.

I backed away and slammed into the crumbling stones of the wall behind me. My feet crunched in a drift of litter. The three men grinned vacuously. They knew I had nothing to defend myself with. I was easy meat for a mugging.

Then I felt a gentle breeze on my face and silvery strands drifted down into the space between us. The light was above me and I realized that I was the only one of us who could see them. The thugs began to march towards me, spreading out to prevent any escape.

The three men grunted as they walked into the gossamer threads. The bloated younger man yelled out as he tried to brush them away. The glittering strings had cut his hands open. Something black shifted on the wall above us and more of the sticky strands billowed down. The men started to scream as the threads wrapped round them and began to pull them off their feet. Slowly and carefully, they were lifted away from the ground and reeled in by the black mass clinging to the wall.

I picked a broken umbrella out of the rubbish at my feet and used it to work my way past the web as I inched along the opposite wall. The three men had fallen silent now and hung more than ten feet above me. Blood drizzled down onto the cobblestones.

When I got out of the dead-end lane, I ran back to the main street without looking back. I knew with dreadful certainty what had just happened: I had wandered into "The Weavers," a story by C.M.A., and I was damned if I was going to hang about for the end.

I woke up in the middle of the night and had to note this vision down, but as I've been writing, I've noticed that my clothes are covered in sticky threads which have cut the material to ribbons. I also realize that I cannot remember how I got home.

This can't have been real, can it?

Love,
William

Transcript of Telephone Conversation with an Unknown Caller
By William Anderson

W.A.: Hello, hello? Carol Anne, is that you?

U.C.: Glad you've turned up, William.

W.A.: Who is this?

U.C.: Saint Jack-in-the-Box the unrepentant, who else?

W.A.: What the fuck is going on? Who's speaking? I warn you, I'm taping this conversation—

U.C.: Calm down and listen to me . . . William Shakespeare, Mary Shelley, Gustav Meyrink—what's the connection?

W.A.: Are you serious?

U.C.: Deadly serious. Now answer the question, if you can.

W.A.: Well, Mary Shelley wrote *Frankenstein* . . . Meyrink's best known for *Der Golem* . . . I don't know, Shakespeare doesn't seem to fit . . .

U.C.: I'll give you a clue—*The Tempest*.

Under the Bright and Hollow Sky

W.A.: Caliban, Frankenstein's monster and the golem. We're talking about artificial creatures, aren't we?

U.C.: Yes. Homunculi made by man in his image. Things which walk and talk, but lack a mortal soul. I was wondering what you thought about such matters. People often confuse Dr Frankenstein and his monster. It's understandable, I suppose. The creature never had a name unless you imagine some kind of ghastly Germanic hybrid of all the titles of the dead men who contributed parts to its body . . .

W.A.: A kind of Frankenstein surname?

U.C.: Yes, that's the spirit! But such a title would be meaningless . . . Why would you name something that had no soul?

W.A.: Well, how do you prove it has no soul? *Cogito ergo sum*, after all.

U.C.: Descartes . . . I should have guessed that you'd still be a dualist in your philosophy, William. You may not have picked the best example. Descartes wasn't just a metaphysician he was also a vivisectionist. His neighbors used to object to the screams of the animals he tortured in his experiments—and this was in a century not renowned for its sentimentality . . . You see, William, I've been thinking about monsters, and I'm not sure that the creators weren't the real sources of evil after all.

W.A.: Look, who is this?

U.C.: I think a smart little fellow like yourself can hazard a guess—

W.A.: Alderton! Are you Cranston Alderton?

U.C.: We'll meet soon, William, and you can see for yourself.

W.A.: Where?

U.C.: In the House on Slaughter Avenue, where else?

Andrew J. Wilson

Letter to Carol Anne

Dear Carol Anne,

I'm coming back, my love. I still haven't been able to contact you and I'm getting worried—I even phoned your parents in Penicuik. God, I need to get out of this bloody city and this madness, but escape seems impossible. As C.M.A. wrote in "Voyage to the Bottom of a Life": "You might as well try to escape from the twentieth century or run away from this year. It can't be done on the spur of the moment. You have to wait until the right time. You'll get there eventually, you just have to be patient." I suppose I have to follow this through to the end.

And it ends tomorrow.

I've followed up the reference from the strange phone call. "The House on Slaughter Avenue" is a track by a local band called the Architects of Fear. They broke up years ago, but I found their only CD in an indie record shop bargain bin. Before I bought it, I checked the credits on the sleeve. They dedicate the song to C.M.A. I played it on Glen's stereo, and surprise, surprise, there's a reference to a house number and street. It's hard to make out because the recording is live, rough and very distorted, but I think I've deciphered it. I checked my *Streetfinder* and found the place. It's out in a council estate on the edge of town.

This is it then: I'll follow this one last lead and then get the hell out of here.

If nothing else, I've come to understand how stupid I've been. I should never have let you go, Carol Anne. I've been selfish and self-obsessed; worse still, I've been obsessed with Cranston Alderton, when I should have devoted myself to you. This nightmare has shown me that we only have each other to rely on.

C.M.A. is a closed book and maybe he should remain sealed forever. He may have disappeared to commit suicide, or he may have simply wanted to break from his troubled past and assume a new identity. In the end, I suppose that should be his business and no one else's. He had a brilliant mind, and that's a terrible thing to waste. I should learn from that.

I'm coming home soon, Carol Anne.

All my love,
William

Fragment of an Unpublished and Previously Unknown Short Story

WHATEVER HAPPENED TO
WILLIAM ANDERSON?
BY CRANSTON M. ALDERTON

The taxi driver refused to go any further into the abandoned housing estate. Anderson paid the cabby, but refused to tip. Then he began to trace his path through the crumbling tenements with his *Streetfinder*. He wanted to get out of the area before dark.

An unattended pram rolled down the shallow incline of a side street toward him. The black baby carriage was on fire, flames licking up the sides of the antiquated conveyance. Anderson staggered out of the way and caught a glimpse of what was inside. Something the size of a piglet was melting in the conflagration. The skin of its body blackened and peeled like plastic. The smell was a revolting mixture of the stingingly acrid and the sickly sweet. Anderson hoped to Christ it was a doll that was burning and walked on.

No one was visible on any of the streets. No lights shone from any of the cracked and shattered windows. There was no sound at all now, not even the bark of a stray dog or the cry of a seagull.

Anderson found the address with some trouble and much doubling back across the deserted neighbourhood. The house was no different from any of the adjoining council properties in the row. The buildings were all silent and dark. A few had blackened walls showing the traces of fires which had got out of hand. Most of the windows had been boarded up and those which hadn't gaped like jagged mouths lined with fangs of broken glass.

The front door gave easily under the pressure of Anderson's boot. He struck matches to light his way up the stinking stairwell, burning his fingers and care-

395

lessly dropping the used sticks on the piss-stained steps. Given the amount of rubbish littering the stairs, he was surprised he hadn't disturbed any rats, but there was no sign of life at all in the building, not even a spider's web.

There was a little light at the top of the stairs and Anderson realized that one of the doors to the flats was ajar. He paused and checked the number that he had discovered. This was the place.

The door opened silently and Anderson wondered if he should knock to announce his arrival. The flickering phosphorous glow coming from the sitting room put him off. He crept forward, close to the wall, but trying not to scrape his shoulder on the mouldy wallpaper.

Anderson's dry tongue rubbed like sandpaper over his palate and his nose itched with dust. His pulse throbbed loudly in his head as he sidled towards the end of his journey, a drumbeat driving him to the end of the line.

He edged slowly into the living room, his foot catching on a supermarket carrier bag.

A young woman lay prone on a rotting sofa in front of a television set. The box was the source of the light, but its screen had long since been smashed. A fire had been set in its innards and the plastic shell was warped and twisted.

Someone else was sitting in the shadows, typing at a word processor precariously balanced on a trestle-table beside the boarded-up windows. Anderson ignored the figure. He had stopped dead when he caught a glimpse of the woman's face.

"Carol Anne?" he whispered.

The woman didn't move, so he staggered towards the dirty sofa. He bent over Carol Anne and reached out to touch her. Her hands felt very hot, the skin dry and papery, and her eyes were closed. Anderson brushed the hair from the woman's face and her tresses crumbled in his hands, leaving a black smudge like printer toner on his fingers.

He pulled Carol Anne to her feet as gently as he could and then lifted her in his arms and backed away towards the door. The figure at the computer kept typing, but tapped the keys more slowly. Anderson carried Carol Anne outside into the hallway and reluctantly put her down on the cold stone. He made sure that she was propped up against the wall and then moved back into the flat to finish what he thought he had started.

"What have you done?" Anderson asked hoarsely.

The figure by the windows slowly swivelled its seat towards him. In the half-light, the man's face seemed pale and rounded, bloodless and scarred like the Man in the Moon.

"Hello, William. You managed to track me down, then?" he said, his gaping mouth struggling with the simple words. "Do you like what you've found?"

Anderson groped in his jacket pockets for something to defend himself with. His fingers brushed something hard. A knife? It felt sharp, but he knew he would never carry anything like that. It would have been out of character. His fingers closed round the thin object and he knew what it was a pen.

"What are you doing? What's going on here?" Anderson asked as he glanced back towards the door. It had shut silently behind him.

"Oh, come on, William!" the other man laughed. "You should know better than to ask something like that by now. Loose ends don't get tied up, and if you pick at them, they don't get better, they just unravel everything else. Life doesn't hold any answers—it's merely a meaningless joke at our expense. All you can do is keep your head down . . . and sometimes that doesn't even work, does it . . ."

"I asked what you've done, you bastard!"

"I've reaped my reward, William! I worked out the joke and so I get to play the joker . . ."

The writer used his mouse to click SAVE on his word processor and Anderson found himself brandishing his pen, clutching it like a dagger.

"Truly, the pen is mightier than the sword, isn't it, William?"

Anderson stabbed the writer through the eye. He staggered back as the other man fell off his chair. His limbs had taken on a life of their own, or someone else's life, certainly not his.

"What have you done?" Anderson asked again, unsure of whether he was talking to the other man or just himself.

The writer writhed on the filthy carpet and gurgled with something like glee. "I must be going now—my creation has destroyed me and so my work is done. Thank you for the darkness, William. I can feel the soft wings of oblivion finally taking me away from all this. Thank you, bless me and thank God—even Hell has its limits."

"What have you made me do?" Anderson whispered.

"You've finished me," the writer wheezed. "You've crossed the tees and dotted the eyes and written a big, black full stop. But remember, you're not the only monster I've created . . ."

The writer's face collapsed like a ball of crumpled paper and, in a moment, there was little left of him but a pile of seedy, malodorous clothes.

Anderson picked up the chair and sat down at the word processor, trying to focus on the text on the screen. He was at a loss for what to do for a moment, but he was sure that something would come to him.

Then the door opened behind him, and it did.

AFTERWORD

Yesterday, I received an unsigned, unstamped blank postcard. I paid the cost of the postage because of the peculiarity of the message typed on it. The words provide a fitting postscript to the preceding material, even though I have no way of proving that they or their unknown author have any connection with the above.

The three-word message is a Latin phrase that I believe Arthur Machen quoted in his work:

Omnia exeunt mysterium.

A.J.W.

The Dove Game

BY ISOBELLE CARMODY

for Danny

It was hot in Paris.

The minute Daniel stepped from the air-conditioned cool of Charles de Gaulle airport the sun dropped a hammer on his forehead. He stopped at the unexpectedness of it and a woman in a white dress detoured around him, thin arms and long neck a glowing pink. He had never imagined people sunburned in Paris. The heat seemed wrong here. Misplaced, as if he had somehow brought the aridity of the outback with him.

The travel agent had told him to board a Roissy Bus to Opéra stop in the city, and he took his place obediently at the end of a queue running back from the closed doors of the bus. The driver was visible reading his paper with his knees against the wheel. In front of Daniel, an older couple argued in another language. The woman's voice had an angry, stabbing quality and Daniel thought of the comfortable bickering of his own parents, which had always seemed to him like two old warped boards rubbing together whenever the wind blew from a certain direction.

The woman pointed savagely at a mound of luggage and Daniel wondered what there could be in all of those cases and bags. He carried only a half-empty canvas bag, but then again he would not be here for long. He thought of the travel agent who had arranged the trip.

"You want to be in Paris for one day?" Her voice tinged with disbelief. "Impossible." She typed rapidly and her face grew smooth as if the computer consumed her personality. "The soonest I can get you home is five days from the date you have nominated. The flights are all booked because of the World Cup game in Paris. Soccer," she added, seeing his blank expression. "Unless you can travel on another day?"

"I have to be there on July one," he reiterated, too baldly. Then he told her the district he needed to find and asked for the closest accommodation possible. He could have pointed out the street that was his destination because he had looked it up to make sure it existed, but she was already pecking at her computer.

"It must be an important meeting," she said crisply, having decided that he was a businessman despite the dusty jeans and faded flannel shirt. Her eyes flicked up to offer perfunctory curiosity as if it was part of her job to encourage travelers to talk about their plans so that they could be admired for their adventurousness; or maybe so that they could be reassured that they were doing the right thing.

"I am doing the right thing," Daniel said, and was startled to discover that he had spoken aloud.

"I'm sure." The woman smiled a red, wet-looking smile.

In the end, he had agreed to spend the extra days in Paris, but the decision had made him uneasy because it had been forced out of him. The travel agent had explained that countries wanted people to stay and spend money, hence various kinds of inducements and controls. Daniel had felt there was something under the little pat of facts and explanations. The bones of some harder truth.

He took the backseat of the bus because it looked as if his long legs would fit better there, but found himself pressed between a teacher from a Friends School in Baltimore and a German geneticist. He was amazed at how easily and quickly they told their business to one another and to him. He did not resist their questions.

"What is a jackaroo?" the geneticist asked with genuine interest.

"A sort of Australian cowboy," the American explained.

The geneticist admitted her regret that there had been no time to visit the outback. Ouwtbeck, she said. The American teacher had been on a short exchange to an Australian Quaker school in Tasmania, he said, but he had managed a quick trip to Uluru. He said the word as if it were a giant lolly he was sucking and Daniel almost smiled because tourists always said it that way, with slight self-importance.

"But the emptiness," the American murmured, shaking his head. "I can't imagine riding through it alone on a horse. All that red nothingness would scare me."

"Nothingness could be an interesting state to experience," the geneticist said, reminding Daniel of someone's nice aunt. He had a disorienting flashback to the campfire, Ti-tree talking fiercely about white doctors, his darkness limned in flame glow.

"Think they should do anything they can do," the old black man had muttered. "Maybe someday they find something that don't go back together after they open it up. What will grow in that black gap, eh?"

The teacher was asking why he had come to Paris and Daniel collected his wits and said that he had a meeting. "Not a business meeting," he added, to short-circuit the questions.

"Personal business," the geneticist said kindly, forcing the teacher to fall silent. But suddenly Dan wanted to hear it said aloud.

"I'm going to meet a woman in place of a man who died," he said. "She doesn't know."

"How sad," the geneticist exclaimed softly. "She will come to meet her friend and learn that he is dead?" Det, she said.

"A mission of mercy," the teacher approved. "You are a good friend."

No, Daniel almost said, but the bus lurched to a halt at a huge roundabout running with two wide streams of cars in opposite directions. It was as if someone had decided to tie a knot in a highway. Horns were sounding and brakes screamed and the noise was such that conversation was impossible. His two companions were gone by the time Daniel emerged and, contrarily, he felt abandoned. Passengers were streaming from their bus and from others into taxis. There were at least thirty lined up along the curb in front of the bus and he supposed the teacher and the geneticist had already been swallowed up and whisked away. It was like watching the wheels and cogs of a machine winding together and he felt momentarily helpless to exert any will against the inexorable efficiency of it.

On impulse, Daniel set off walking in long, loping strides, leaving the knot of traffic behind him. He was soon deep in a maze of streets of ancient buildings one and two stories high, where gargoyles leered with sly awareness at him over balconies, and impossibly muscled men and voluptuous women were wrapped around columns or holding up doorways.

He had a sudden sharply painful longing for the simplicity of the flat red landscape outside the bedroom window in his parents' home. That particular view of what some would call nothing, framed by limp, flowered curtains.

He crossed the street because there was a car parked on the footpath blocking his way, and realized he was panting like a dog. It was something to do with the way the heat was pressed between the stone buildings maybe. Compressed so that it was almost solid. In the outback, the heat was light, stretched thin, and you could ride through it slowly for hours without working up a sweat. He took out the map he had been given and unfolded it awkwardly. He didn't use maps back home.

Once when they had come up to the city so that his father could plead with the bank to give them more time to catch up the payments, his father had said sadly that cities were as confused as the people who lived in them, and you needed maps for dealing with them as well.

The hotel was a doorway with the name written above in fancy writing and a set of carpeted stairs. The bottom floor was a restaurant, and as he climbed the stairs the smell of strong coffee ambushed Daniel with a memory of his father, so vivid that for a moment he actually seemed to see the older man's hands on the rail instead of his own. Bigger, always bigger, soft-furred with golden hair that caught the sunlight, the huge scarred knuckles, and the missing index finger.

Daniel stopped, realizing that he was slightly dizzy. The feeling reminded him of having sunstroke as a kid. He still remembered how everything had sagged and tilted when he moved, the heaviness of the shadows and the silky feeling of the sickness. An older woman in a fitted green dress and a smooth bun examined him with shrewd eyes as he approached the reception desk.

Once he had filled out the papers and had proffered his passport, she pressed the lift button for him and explained that breakfast was to be eaten in the restaurant below. He had only to show his key to the waitress. The room when he reached it was tiny. He bumped his elbows on both walls going to the toilet and was forced to shower with the door open, struggling with a single anonymous lever that controlled heat, cold, and the force of the jet. At length he stretched out naked on the bed, the damp towel laid over his groin.

He had slept for long disjointed periods on the plane, yet his eyes felt gritty the way they did after a long day of riding in the sun, his body jumpy and tense from lack of exercise. He didn't remember when he had done so little, yet had felt so tired. He needed to walk, he decided.

He slept.

He was walking through the fields at dusk and he saw that there was a pool of light on the horizon where there ought to be nothing but more night.

"What's that, Dad?" he asked, and discovered from the sound of his voice that he was a boy again.

"Circus," his father said, squinting his eyes and peering toward the light. "Want to go, boy? Don't suppose it'll be anything special. A mangy lion with no teeth and a few clowns. A lot of rigged sideshow acts to draw your money. But we could take a look-see if you want." That slow, kind smile.

Dan felt an aching love for his father that burst the seams of the dream and he woke to find the room dark and stiflingly hot, the bedclothes wrapped about his limbs as if they were bandages. Disentangling himself, he padded over to open a window but it was as if he had merely opened the window into a larger room.

Leaning out into the still, hot night, he looked down into the street below and thought of the dead man's watch; the way its wide silver band incorporating the face had matched the overturned silver car and the silvery grey suit, which might have been sleek before the crash. The man had seemed as exotic as a metal spaceman, lying in the red dust. His eyes had been a light silvery grey too, when they opened.

"Help me," the man said. His accent was thick and heavy, but part of the heaviness was pain.

There were visible head injuries and Daniel knew it could be fatal to move him. "There's a property back about thirty klicks. The Watleys'. Tim'll radio the Flying Doctor."

The man made a strange rattling noise. Was he laughing? "I fear there is only one creature with wings that will come for me in time."

Daniel began to shake his head, but the man's blood was puddling in the red dust under him, darkening it to black. It looked as if his shadow was swelling under him. Daniel knelt but the man's nearest hand twitched in agitation, the silver watch throwing a knife of light into his eyes with accidental, painful precision.

"There is a woman," he rasped and Daniel half-turned in alarm to the crumpled car before he continued. "You must tell her what has happened."

"The police . . ." Daniel said.

"Ssst," the man hissed like a snake. "Will you help me?" The pale eyes held Daniel's with a strength that seemed hypnotic and he found himself nodding. "Tell her that I would have come, if I could. That she was right about me needing her. I have . . . have the ticket in my . . . wallet. You must go to Paris and meet her in my place."

How strange the word had sounded, spoken in the hot air, the end of it caught by the harsh flat arc of a kookaburra's laugh rising in the spare distance. "Paris?" Daniel said, relieved, because of course no one could expect him to go to Paris.

"I was to meet her on the first of July."

"But you must have a friend who could call her . . ." Daniel had protested. Again the rattling laugh, this time with a mocking note.

The light eyes were now fixed on his face. For a moment Daniel thought there was a radiance behind them. Something struggling to blaze out, but perhaps it was no more than a matter of contrasts and light; the white-hot light, and the tanned skin. Even so, he felt the touch of those eyes like fingers moving on his face.

When the man answered, the grain of the voice was stronger. Rougher, as if the smooth surface of it was being sanded away. "I do not have a telephone number nor any address for her. Only the date and the name of the café where we were to meet."

Daniel blinked, feeling as if a genie had appeared to grant three wishes. Only it was one wish, and he must grant it. "Maybe she won't come . . ."

"She will," the man said. He had begun to shudder slightly like a cat Daniel had once seen after it had been snake-bit. "We were to meet . . ." the man whispered, "in the café where I first saw her. Such an absurd . . . name for a café—The Smoking Dog—rue de Gris. July first at dusk. She said . . . it would be appropriate. I thought she was mad but now I know that she saw everything. Tell her that. The café has . . . had a view of the Sacré Coeur."

The Dove Game

Daniel had looked up the French words in a phonetic dictionary. Rue de Gris merely meant Grey Street, and Sacré Coeur meant sacred heart and probably meant Sacred Heart Cathedral. He had looked the street up on a map of Paris and found that there were seven different Grey Streets, but only one that would have a view of the cathedral.

Somewhere in the hotel, a baby began to cry.

As Daniel turned away from the window he heard men's voices in the street below, the words unintelligible. A hard blat of some other language that did not sound French. Arabic maybe? He took up the television control on the bedside console, pressed the mute button and channel-surfed. Usually he found it soothing to see people talking silently, gesticulating and laughing, cars driving silently along roads, washing machines being caressed. But tonight—today—for the first time, the images seemed weirdly significant, too filled with meanings he did not want to puzzle out.

He lay back and watched the play of light reflected on the roof instead, wondering again if the dead man and the woman he had promised to meet had been lovers. "Let sleeping dogs lie," his mother might have said. She had been a tough, stocky, practical little farmer's wife with a small beloved flock of hysterical silky chickens, and she had performed a staggering number of daily duties. Daniel had grown up with no idea that his mother was a domestic slave, though. She had been a woman with a sharp edge to her tongue and strong opinions that she did not hesitate to air. Discipline had been her provenance, too. She had wielded a willow switch with the same determined efficiency as she cleaned the rugs once a month; as if misbehavior could be beaten out like dust. Age had bent and narrowed his father, faded his blue eyes, but his mother became more and more solid without ever being fat. More densely energetic. Daniel fancied that in another life his father might have been a poet or a writer, but his mother could only ever have been a farmer's wife. Daniel had loved his father, and respected him, but it had always seemed a waste of time to bother wading through a lot of words written by someone he didn't know, when he could be roaming the hills rippling with dry grass like a golden sea, or swimming in the tea-colored water of the creek. It did not matter to him that he was barely average at school since he was to inherit and work the farm.

Of course it hadn't worked out that way. His father had overextended to buy some long-overdue farm equipment; then there was a bad year of droughts, and then a year of floods, and the bank foreclosed. They had gone under without a struggle and Daniel's mind stuttered to watching his mother crating her beloved silkies for sale. He had hated the unit in suburbia where they had shifted, but he knew that his parents needed his income to help pay the mortgage. He had gone to work loading in a trucking company; then, three months after they had moved into town, his father had a heart attack on the way to church, crashing the ute and killing himself and his wife both. She had been killed on impact, but his father had lingered for three days, though he had never become conscious.

Daniel had been glad it had happened so suddenly and that they had died together for their sakes. But even now, years later, memories kept jumping at him, forcing him to remember that his parents were gone and that he would never see them again. Never feel his father's gentleness and watch him tamp down the tobacco in his pipe; never see his mother's ferocious energy or taste her golden syrup dumplings. He had left the city, for the suburban unit had been sold to pay their debts, and so had begun his long drift from job to job, looking for some indefinable thing that would make him feel that same sense of rightness and belonging that he had felt on the old farm. The smell of eggs and bacon on dark winter mornings and the bitter aftertaste of strong sweet tea in the bunkhouse kitchens brought the home breakfasts back to him with such clarity that the present had sometimes seemed a thin, sour dream.

But if he was honest, it was his father he missed most. That quiet presence. His father had always known the best way to gentle people was to *be* gentle. To listen. You never got the feeling he was just waiting for you to finish so he could get on with what he wanted to say, or offer advice or an opinion. In fact, he said very little and seldom offered solutions or suggestions. Yet at one time or another practically every one of the neighbors had come to him for advice. People would invariably go away feeling less angry, less desperate. Daniel had consciously modeled himself on his father, wanting that quiet dignity. He had striven to be patient, gentle, courteous and honest. He was not and never would be his father, yet he believed that he had grown into a man his father would have respected.

How many times he had imagined telling his father about seeing the smoke and then the overturned silver Mercedes crumpled against the stand of eucalyptus? How many times had he described dragging the big foreigner in his supple steel dust suit from the wreck and the strange conversation that had followed? In his imaginings, as in life, his father never once interrupted his tale. Nor, when Daniel stopped, had he offered opinions or advice. Yet in the ambiance of his father's wisdom, Daniel had come to understand that he would go, even though it had meant flying farther than he had ever flown before.

Was it possible to return after coming so far? he suddenly wondered. The thought was like a kidney punch and he stumbled mentally backwards into a vivid memory of the way the dying man's eyes had grown more and more pale as he drifted in and out of delirium.

"It was so hard to trust anyone back then," he said. "You never knew who would repeat your words, nor how they might be used. You could never be high enough to feel safe. You had to be careful of every word. Yet she trusted me. Of all people, her. It was incredible. Unthinkable. She said I had offered her an ultimate truth. I do not think you could possibly imagine how rare truth was in that time. I swore that I would meet her, but I lied. She laughed and said I would come to her for the truth that she alone could offer." He bit down on a groan.

There had been something almost military in the stifling of the groan, Daniel thought. The man had been in terrible pain, the ambulance people had said after they came. Even if they had arrived in time, they could not have helped except to administer a mind-obliterating dose of morphine, they said. A little death to ease the bigger death looming.

It was the police, when he gave his report several days later, who had told him the man's name was Tibor Horvath, and that he was Hungarian and eighty-five. Daniel could hardly credit it. He would have taken the man for fifty at most. He had held a permanent residency visa for Australia for sixty years, and had not once left since his arrival. He had probably been a dissident, given the date of his arrival, one of the policewomen had observed. A political exile from his country, which had been under Russian occupation at the time.

Later that same night it had occurred to Daniel that if the man had made an appointment to meet the woman when they had been in Paris, the dates the police had given meant this agreement had been made more than sixty years ago. He thought of the dying man's final words, the eyes fastening on him with congealing clarity. "Tell her the knowledge that she was right tortures me."

The following week, when he had gone into town to sign his deposition, a policeman told him about the ticket found in the man's coat. The destination was Paris, and the departure date was two days before the date when the man had claimed he was to meet the woman.

That was when it had occurred to Daniel that the woman might be dead. He had assumed that she was the man's age, but if she had been older, say thirty, she would be almost ninety now.

Daniel had contacted the police to find out when and where the funeral would take place, wondering if anyone would attend who might offer a clue as to the woman's identity, and to whom he might confide the dead man's last wish. But no one came other than a policeman who was there for the same reason. Over a beer after, the policeman told him that the dead man had left money enough for his funeral. The remainder of his property was going to a charity that cared for children. It seemed that he had not worked at all, having come to Australia with a collection of antique family jewelry that he had sold, investing the money and living off the proceeds.

"It seems impossible that a man could have lived so long without making any sort of connections," Daniel had murmured.

"You would be surprised how many people live that way," the policeman responded.

Standing and watching the earth shoveled onto the coffin, Daniel pictured a woman coming to the café to sit and wait for a man who would never arrive. In the imagining, she was very frail. A female version of his father, emanating patience and gentleness. She was a woman who you could see would wait until the end of the day, hope slowly fading, until she was asked to leave.

Another thing that the dying man had muttered floated through his mind. "There is no greater intimacy than truth, boy. Remember that."

He woke to thick late-afternoon sunlight and showered again, thinking of Mick, the stocky Irish owner of the small boxing gym that Daniel had joined when he was fifteen. His father had not understood that the attraction of boxing was not the violence or the conquering of one man by another. Daniel had liked the gallantry of a sport where two men could drink and slap one another on the back between bouts. The sport was symbolized for him by Mick, with whom he had developed a relationship that had begun with respect and admiration and had become, though the word would never be spoken between them, love. Mick had been disappointed when Daniel decided not to go professional and it was love of Mick that had kept him sparring young newcomers. Trying to teach the aggressive young cocks the need to be smart fighters rather than street sluggers. But few of them had the deep-down gallantry that Daniel considered to be the secret of greatness.

After his parents had died, Mick tried to talk him into working for the gym, but Daniel refused and had started drifting. He hadn't seen much of Mick the last couple of years, but he had told the older man of his decision to go to Paris, and why, after asking him to stable his quarter horse.

"It's like . . . like I picked up a stone when that man died, Mick, and I have to find the place to put it down," he had said.

"It's a deep thing to watch a man die," Mick had murmured, a stern, distant look in his brown eyes. Daniel had remembered that once, earlier in Mick's career, one of his fighters had developed a blood clot in the ring. Mick still sent Christmas cards to the widow, though twenty years had passed.

"How will you know who she is?" Mick had asked in the car, having insisted on driving Daniel to the airport.

"She'll be alone and she'll be looking for someone."

"She might not be alone," Mick had said. "And everyone is looking for someone."

Walking through the streets, Daniel was again struck by the heat and by the ornate, battered age of the city. Many of the buildings had obviously been sand-blasted or repainted in recent times, and though more buildings were crumbling at the edges and gray with filth than refurbished, on every street there was at least one building undergoing a facelift, surrounded by a carapace of scaffolding and billowing plastic. He was startled when the asphalt suddenly gave way to smooth, oyster-grey cobbles like something out of a Grimm fairy tale, but he made no effort to orientate himself using the map. He was beginning to become aware of a flow along the streets, like a hidden current.

He turned a corner and collided with a couple kissing. They seemed oblivious to the impact. You didn't see kissing like that back home other than at the movies, Daniel thought. Not that he knew much about it. He had kissed exactly three women in his life, and one of them had been a whore who had taken pity on his embarrassed inadequacy. The other boys had not believed his tale, claiming that prostitutes did not kiss. Even now he did not know what to make of the fact that a prostitute had broken what seemed to be some sort of cardinal rule in kissing him, or what he had done to provoke it.

He passed through a square and there were a group of black men talking, dressed in expensive suits. They began laughing, flashing confident white teeth, and Daniel wondered what it would be like at home if the Aboriginals that drifted into town to drink and socialize in the park and in malls would dress in suits like that. There was something so crushed and battered about the old derelicts you saw drinking in the streets, no matter how aggressive or strident they would get about Native Title and the way it had split the Aboriginal community.

As Daniel walked, his mind flicking back and forward between life on his parent's farm and his current errand, as if it was trying to weave a tapestry connecting the two. It was only when he entered a street and saw the sun touching the tops of the buildings that he reached for his map. He traced out a path from where he was to Grey Street, near the Sacré Coeur Cathedral. He walked swiftly thinking that there was something primitive about arranging a meeting at dusk. Something that suggested a state where ordinary time and space did not apply. The roads had grown busier than before and people walked purposefully, their faces abstracted by end-of-day thoughts. Daniel found that no matter which way he walked or which side of the pavement he chose, he was moving against the flow of human traffic. He passed a rectangular pool of water where various mechanical devices were variously spitting, stirring, plowing or slashing the water.

"You see that one?" a man said in accented English. "I call it the jealousy machine. See how stupidly it threshes at the water; how ferocious its movement. Yet it goes nowhere."

The words provoked a memory of a fight Daniel had seen between two Aboriginal men in a camp far from towns and police. He had met them on walkabout during a boundary ride and had been invited to join them. The men had begun by talking but had ended up almost killing each other over a woman they both wanted. They had fought with a ferocity that Daniel had never witnessed between two white men. Not in the boxing ring nor out of it. There had been no sense of display nor of competition. They had fought almost silently and for nothing, since the woman had chosen another man.

The soles of his feet were burning by the time he turned into Rue de Gris. Two men standing on the opposite corner were watching him. Both wore their hair shaven so short that he could see their scalps shining pinkly through the black stubble. One had a swastika tattooed on his upper arm. He nodded, a half-smile curving narrow, soft-looking lips and Daniel's neck prickled. He had the sudden absurd notion that they had been watching for him.

It was the sun and lack of food making him imagine things, he told himself. A headache drilled into the top of his skull like a hot needle when he came to the end of the street and realized he must have walked right past the café. He retraced his steps and only then understood that there had been nothing to miss. The street was short and the only thing in it, aside from residences and apartments, was a small boutique with a hat draped in a swath of red cloth. When he reached the shop, he noticed there was also a small tobacconist on the other side of the road. He was about to turn away when his eyes fell on the sign above the tobacconist. THE SMOKING DOG.

"The name of this shop. The Smoking Dog. I thought it was a café..." Daniel told the owner. "I've come all the way from Australia."

The man's eyes slitted, but perhaps it was only that he had got some of the coiling, heavy-looking smoke from his cheroot in his eyes. "Then you've come a long way for nothing." The fact that he was English startled Daniel to silence, which seemed to prompt the man to elaborate. "There used to be a café here during the war. It was burned down by the Germans, and no one ever bothered to restore it. The place was a mess when I took it over. I bought it because the name seemed like a good omen."

"Burnt?" Daniel said softly.

"It was used by the resistance during the war, apparently. Locals say they were betrayed and the *Boche* took them all away, then burned the café out to make sure it couldn't be used again."

Daniel licked his lips. The policewoman back home had said that the dead man had probably been a political refugee. Was it possible he and the woman had been *resistance*? But how had they escaped the German raid of the café, and why plan to meet more than sixty years later? Unless the promise exchanged had been no more than a desperate reassurance for two people who expected to die.

"I was to meet a woman in the café this evening."

"You want a woman?" There was a mocking note in the man's voice.

"A particular woman. I have something I need to tell her," Daniel said.

"Forget about a woman who makes an appointment in a place that doesn't exist. Go back where you belong."

"I'm not sure where I belong anymore," Dan murmured and, though it was a simple enough comment to make, he felt a sudden dizziness at the depth of his words; the unexpected abyss of truth.

"You can see the café, if you want. The shop is only a frontage." The man stood up from his stool, becoming in an instant extraordinarily tall. He opened a door behind the counter and Daniel entered the darkness of an enormous warehouse-sized room whose walls retained striped sections of what once might have been a giant mural. There were round tables set in the floor and a few chairs stacked in the shadows, and he had a strange sense that he had stepped back in time, or at least into another dimension.

"The whole place was done out to look like a circus," the man said, relighting his black cheroot. The flame rocked back and forward in his eyes. "The name is supposed to have come from some famous sideshow act with a dog. Far as I can tell, it was the sort of place where people came and sat and smoked and talked poetry and waved their hands and burst into tears or danced on the tables. An emotional sort of place and good cover for secret meetings and the passing on of information and microfilms and all the rest of it. You can still smell the smoke from the fire. That's why I got it cheap."

The tobacconist turned back and as Daniel followed he heard, quite distinctly, a gasp or a cough. He looked around but there was no movement. The shadows hung like frozen smoke, darkening with every minute that passed.

The shop had also darkened in their brief absence and the owner reached for a panel of switches on the wall as Daniel dug out the receipt in his wallet and scrawled the address of his hotel on a desk blotter, and the name of the dead man. The woman would come in, or she wouldn't. The lights flickered on and the tobacconist touched the indentation of the words written on the soft, thick paper.

"I'll call back tomorrow," Daniel promised. He thanked the man and went out into the street. He had walked several blocks before he noticed a small boy shadowing him. Clad in scruffy, too-big clothes, his skin was the color of dark honey and his eyes fringed in lashes as long as those of a new-born calf.

"You want to go to the circus?" the boy asked, seeming unabashed. Cair-coos, he said.

"Circus?" he echoed, wondering if he had misheard.

The boy giggled. "I will show you the way."

"What kind of circus happens in the middle of a city?" Daniel asked.

"A very *zmall* cair-coos," the boy said, and they laughed together.

Daniel felt suddenly lighter. "All right then," he said.

The boy's pixie face lit up and he led the way to a lane of steep stone steps descending to a small square. There, to Daniel's amazement, was a circus tent. Lanterns were swaying around the rim, illuminating sections of the billowing cloth which blurred away into the growing night.

The boy ran lightly down the steps ahead of Daniel and vanished. Daniel might have turned back, but he heard music; long sobbing notes which seemed to be the essence of yearning and which roused in him an unexpected longing to be home, riding the red flat plains on Snowy, or up in the high country. He had the sudden unsettling thought that home, like his parents, was irrevocably lost to him.

"Shall I tell you your heart's desire?" The voice belonged to a Gypsy woman with a small baby in her arms. She was squatting in the doorway of a small tent which appeared to be an extension of the larger tent. His nonplussed silence seemed to irritate her. "But you have no time for that, have you? You have come to see her, of course. Another mooncalf lusting for the dove princess. She has nothing to offer you."

The Gypsy gave an angry shrug and suddenly bared a plump golden breast. The baby butted and struggled against its bindings, then began to suckle hard as Daniel moved away. He circled the tent until he came to a wide flap door pulled shut but hanging crookedly so as to leave a slit through which light leaked out into the darkness.

Daniel pushed through the flap into a curtained corridor. The tent folds were heavier than they looked and when the wind made them sway, a heavy musty smell puffed out of them. The music grew steadily louder as he passed through another flap into the main section of the tent. It was considerably smaller than it had looked from the outside, with only three concentric circles of bench seats behind the battered red bolsters that rimmed the spotlit central ring.

Daniel paid a hundred francs to a lean gypsy and then took an end seat, eyes snared by a high-wire artist in glittering red and gold spiraling down on a rope. She bowed and ran out through a slit in the tent as the audience applauded thinly. A man entered through another slit, clad in black, his hair slicked into a stiff black quill. A magician, his clothes and flamboyant gestures proclaimed. He bowed gracefully, then beckoned and a boy appeared wheeling a glittering gold casket as big as a fridge on wheels.

Cymbals clashed and another boy entered leading a small white goat. There was a burst of the tragic violin music and the gypsy magician began to speak. His words were French but it was clear from his movements that he was describing himself as an animal tamer of the most ferocious sorts of beasts. Then, very slowly and theatrically, he opened the mouth of the goat and pushed the top of his head gently against its teeth.

It ought to have been funny. That music and the seriousness of the dark-clad man allied to the eccentric performance. A plump woman nearest Daniel, chewing her nails, gave a bark of muffled laughter and an elderly couple that looked like tourists laughed, too, but uncertainly, as if they were anxious to do the right thing. A young man with a shaven head and ripped T-shirt laughed loudest, slapping his knee and rocking back and forward. Yet for some strange reason the performance brought tears to Daniel's eyes. It seemed to him in that second that he had been led to this place and this country in the same way as the goat had been led to the stage; to take part in some incomprehensible performance which he understood no more than the goat understood its part in this strange little circus.

The violin music swelled. Daniel's father had loved classical music, but he had said that most of it was like beauty prowling in a cage. He would have liked the strange wildness of this gypsy music.

The spotlight split and the music stopped abruptly. All that could be heard was the wind and the flapping of the tent walls and roof. Then a pale, strikingly lovely dark-haired woman stepped through the tent wall and into a circle of light, and Daniel's breath seemed to solidify and wedge in his throat. She wore nothing but a flesh-colored frame of a crinoline fastened at her waist through which her legs and bare feet could clearly be seen. Her nipples were a pale pink and very small.

A movement drew Daniel's gaze to the magician, who now held a knife with a broad, gleaming blade. Daniel saw the glitter of his eyes as he kissed the blade. Despite knowing it was part of the performance, he felt a hard jab of fear for the woman, whose hand rose slowly on the slender stalk of her arm. The gypsy violinist began to play a long, rising note.

The Dove Game

Suddenly the magician hurled the knife across the arena with enough force to make him grunt. Daniel's eyes followed the shining dart, but almost exactly halfway between the magician and the woman it exploded silently into feathers and light, and a bird completed the journey, fluttering to the woman's raised hand.

A white dove.

"A trick," Daniel murmured as he watched the woman bring the bird to her face and kiss its beak. Then she carried it down to the crinoline and it stepped neatly into one of the squares in the wide grid that caged her slim white legs.

She gestured to the man. A movement of the hands that was both an invitation and an offering, and he bowed and threw another knife. This time Daniel heard the whistle of the blade, or imagined he did, and the chill crept along his bones, though again sharp steel was transformed into feathers and beak, to land and be carried to sit beside the first dove. There was no kiss this time and the music had quickened. Another knife and then another was thrown. Daniel could not imagine how the trick worked but there seemed to him something deadly in this game of doves being played. The forehead of the magician gleamed with sweat, though in the tent it was cold enough that his breath formed a cloud when he exhaled. Yet as each bird swelled the dress, clothing her lower body, the woman became more and more ravishing and unreal-looking. It was as if she was becoming a dream or a legend before his eyes.

When the dress was a swaying bell of doves—how heavy it must be, though her face was serene and her expression distant—the birds began to land on her shoulders and upper body, leaving only the thin arms and the long throat.

Daniel noticed a streak of blood on her neck and another on her arm and realized that the doves landing on her shoulders and chest were tearing at her in their effort to gain purchase. One of the birds' claws must have cut her deeply for a seam of blood crawled down her arm and into her palm. Yet the woman's face was remote and her eyelids drooped slightly over her eyes as if she were half in a swoon.

Daniel felt sickened to see beauty coupled with pain in this way. The flight of doves had not faltered, and the defenselessness of the woman—her pallor and the way she offered it to the doves—seemed an invitation to pain. It was as if her beauty existed to serve only as an assistant to pain. The magician, his costume blotched darkly with patches of sweat now, threw another knife.

Daniel realized suddenly that the blood was part of the act, and felt a fool. Of course that must be it. But what did it mean, he wondered suddenly. The clothing of a woman in doves; the thin line of blood? Was he to see that even though knives became doves, the woman was still pierced? Was that it? Or was the meaning too foreign or complex for him to grasp? Something that he was simply unequipped to understand?

He found himself visualizing the two Aboriginal men engaged in their silent deadly fight. He had been transfixed by their beauty and the alienness of their culture, watching them. This performance seemed to him to contain the same violence, the same serenity, the same alien quality. He was repelled by the extremity of what he was seeing, but he could not leave.

As more birds flew to join the others, it became harder to see where each bird ended and another began, and the dress trembled and throbbed with a life that seemed separate from all of the lives that it strove to encompass. Daniel wondered what his father would say. But it was as if a thought from someone else's mind had drifted into his own. For the first time, his father's face seemed ghostly and insubstantial.

When there was no more room on her arms, the doves began to alight directly on her hair, consuming the darkness as they had consumed her arms. Another drop of blood slid along the side of her nose, curving in to the corner of her eye and then touching the edge of her lips. Her tongue flicked out to touch the blood and Daniel shuddered as if she had pushed her tongue onto his ear.

And still more birds landed.

It was going on too long, Daniel thought, realizing with a kind of dim horror that he was bored. Surely only a monster could be bored with something so finely balanced between beauty and freakishness as to dissolve the difference.

Outside the tent the wind was now howling, and the cloth billowed and heaved in convulsive shudders.

Then the music changed, falling steeply to a low, humming note. For one second she stood there, perfectly still, a woman in a living dress. The Dove Princess. Then another knife was thrown, which became three doves that rose and circled above the woman before suddenly closing their wings, hawklike, and plummeting toward the woman's upturned face. At the last moment they banked their wings and landed on her face.

Daniel gasped and started forward in his seat, seeing the claws nearing the wide-open eyes, but he did nothing to arrest the performance. He could not, for he must see what would come next. He was sickened by his own reactions and yet as he breathed too deeply and too fast, feeling as if each breath he took was clogged with old dust and feathers, he did not take his eyes from the woman-shaped mass of birds seething in the spotlight. Everything was in motion in those seconds—the tent, the air, the doves, his blood. The only fixed point was the black-clad magician; the eye in the storm.

He clapped his hands once and the doves rose up in a churning mass, swirling and widening at the top until they formed a shifting funnel, a white whirlwind. Then they exploded outward, and in their midst was nothing.

The woman had vanished as the knives had done.

For one brief moment there were only the falling of feathers, a pale benediction from the departing birds, and then the spotlights winked out, plunging the tent into near darkness. The performance had ended and there were only lanterns showing the way to the entrance. There had been no warning or space for applause, but people began to rise without the slightest protest or murmur of puzzlement. Daniel saw now that the men wore business suits as if they had come from work, while some of the women wore casual dresses of the kind they might wear about the home with coats over them. None of them looked as if they had dressed intending to come to see such a show. It was as if all of them had been summoned from everyday life to experience the dove game. Their faces were pale as if something had been drained from them, but Daniel felt that the churning forces of the performance had entered him and were beating their wings against his chest, clawing at his throat.

The boy that had led him to the tent stepped toward him from the shadows, as if on cue. "You saw her?" he asked with suppressed excitement.

"Why does she . . . ?" Daniel began, rising from his seat.

"That is what they always ask," the boy interrupted gleefully. "Maybe she will answer you. Come."

Daniel followed the boy again, discovering in movement that he ached the way he had after having ridden for days in the high country in winter, looking for lost stock. He stumbled twice, not because of the darkness but because the pale woman in her dove dress had imprinted her image against his retina so that whenever he blinked, that was what he saw.

The boy led the way into the tented corridor, but instead of passing along it as the other spectators did, he put his hand through a slit hidden in the folds in the wall of the corridor, his smile inviting Daniel into another corridor running parallel to the main tent. There was another flap ahead with reddish light showing at the edges.

The boy made an urgent pushing motion and Daniel found himself entering a small, circular room carpeted in overlapping mismatched mats. This tent was maroon and hung in thick, deep folds as if it were a larger tent erected in a too-small space. There were piles of cushions around a low table, and a half-drunk bottle of red wine glowed in the light of a lantern suspended from the cord of an old dressing gown. A plastic burger container beside the lantern was half-filled with cigarette butts and the air smelled of ash and some sort of chemical. There was a kerosene heater to one side of the flap, the source of the reddish light and the chemical-scented warmth. Suddenly a man stepped forward from the folds of the wall. It was the magician, whose black hair now hung loose and lank over his shoulders.

Belatedly it occurred to him that he had walked into some sort of trap. But the man said in guttural English, "You want to see the woman? Sit and we will discuss it." Daniel was startled to see how theatrical and foxy his features were in the reddish light, almost as if he had made himself up to look that way. His eyes, flecked with reddish brown, were expectant.

"No . . ." Daniel stopped, confused.

"It is the violence that attracts those who come here."

"Violence . . . you mean the claws?"

He looked momentarily irritated. "Wine?" He sat and Daniel nodded and sat too, awkwardly cross-legged. The man poured wine into two plastic cups which he had brought from beneath the table in a practiced gesture. "People always want to speak to her afterwards. They think that if they understand why she allows herself to be used, they will understand the essence of desire."

"Where is she?" The question burst from Daniel.

"She vanished," the fox-faced magician said. He offered a sly smile. "Didn't you see?"

"It was a trick."

"You don't think people can be obliterated by desire?" the magician asked. Suddenly his hand darted out and he caught Daniel's, turning it palm up with a quick, strong twist. "Here is a working hand and yet the hand of a child who knows nothing." He frowned and his mouth softened. "Nothing more than a child's pain, perhaps, which is far from nothing."

The Dove Game

Daniel pulled his hand free, wondering with sudden cynicism if he had been even more of a fool. "The blood wasn't real, was it?"

The magician's smile broadened. "Nothing is more real than blood. Where have you come from, my prince?"

Daniel felt his head jerk slightly. "I'm Australian."

"Ahh. So. A country of children, I think, full of light and thoughtlessness." His eyes now seemed to glitter. "Tell me why you have come here." He placed a suggestive emphasis on the word "you" that confused Daniel.

"I . . . I came to see a woman, but . . ."

"Our princess of doves will not meet you, no matter what the boy told you."

"I . . . no . . ." Daniel stammered.

The magician seemed not to have heard him. "No one ever guesses that she herself designed the game we play," he said. "They all want to save her. I am no more than her tool. We do her bidding, the doves, the boy, and even you. She trained the doves to tear at her."

"But that . . . It's monstrous . . ." Wine slopped over the brim of his untouched cup.

"Yes," the magician said mildly. "But that is what gives the game its power. She said it would be so. Those who come sense the truth of the game: that one sculpts one's own desire, one's own anguish, perhaps even one's own obliterations, though their wits insist otherwise."

"But . . . why does she do it?"

"The game of doves reminds her of a truth she experienced in the concentration camps. She says that the truth of pain allowed her to survive. Perhaps that"—he gestured vaguely—"is her way of surviving."

Daniel found his mouth was dry. "She . . . she was in the camps? But that was decades ago. She couldn't have been more than five."

"She is older than she looks. But she was a child then. Children were taken. And not just Jews. Gypsies also. The Chosen people prefer to forget that, of course. She bears the mark of the survivors. The tattoo of numbers on her wrist. She was actually taken from near here. We come here each year at this time for that reason, and she always sends the boy out for men. Like you." His eyes were suddenly darker, redder. "Her mind is gone, of course. There are brilliant shards left, but not much else. She says that one day a man will come, and she will show him the truth that he revealed to her."

Daniel fought a feeling of panic. He thought of the foreign man, dying on a remote outback road, and the pale woman in the dove dress who orchestrated her own pain, and wondered if it were possible that she was the woman he had been sent to meet. He seemed to hear the beating of wings and to feel the full living weight of the doves descend on him as the consuming shape of his own desire to understand.

"The boy who brought me here . . ." he gasped.

"A pretty little monkey whom our dove princess feeds and pets and sends running to do her errands. When we are here I think her madness worsens, and that is why she sends him for men, but she never meets with them. They watch the show and they come here, and when they leave there is money."

"I will give you money but I have to see her," Daniel said urgently.

"I told you," the magician said.

"You don't understand. I think I know the man she is looking for. There was an accident and he asked me to come. To meet her and explain."

"I suppose it was inevitable that eventually she would summon up a man whose madness matched her own," the magician said in a resigned voice. He rose in a fluid movement. "Go home, fool. The Dove Princess will not save you and you cannot rescue her."

"Please . . ." Daniel began, no longer sure of his motives. He wanted to see the woman to make sure that she was safe. That she existed, as well as to pass on a message that may or may not have been meant for her. But most of all he wanted to look into her eyes.

"No," the magician said urgently, but he was staring past Daniel, who felt a movement of air behind him. He tried to turn, but a cool hand descended on the back of his neck.

"Leave us," a woman spoke, her voice a low liquid flow. When the magician was gone, she said, "I have lived only to return the truth that was given to me."

And Daniel felt a knife at his neck, like the tip of a bird's claw.

Many things fluttered through his mind then. The sound of madness in the woman's voice like the beating of a bird trapped in a chimney; the way his father's breath had rattled as he died in hospital; the sound of the kookaburra's laugh in the dawn as the foreign man died; the way the desert air shimmered and transported images; the damp velvet touch of Snowy's muzzle against his palm. And then, at last, the sight of a woman wearing a dress of doves, a tear of blood on her face. Who lived for a truth that was only pain.

And he grew old with understanding that some suffering could be so great as to lift a person above life and ordinary experience into a kind of dark immortality. Such pity and longing filled him that Daniel felt his heart crushed under the weight of it. He felt that he was dying of compassion.

He turned toward the knife, not caring how it slid shallowly into his skin. She was older than she had looked on stage, but also more beautiful. Her eyes were dark and full of shadows and madness and her mouth hung slack though she still held the knife at his throat. He could feel the dribble of blood on his collarbone and the sting of the air and thought that she must have felt the same things when the doves clawed at her.

"He wasn't *resistance*, was he?" he whispered, noting how her hair, dark as a raven's wing, stirred at the touch of his breath. "He was one of them. A Nazi."

How white her face became. Like a skull. "I promised that he and I would face the final truth together, when he came," she rasped. "I waited for him . . ."

"He had no right to your mercy. I will face truth with you," Daniel said, and felt his body grow rigid with desire.

"You have not seen the truth of me that he saw," she spat.

"Yes," Daniel said, feeling that he was aging years, centuries with each breath. "In there tonight, you made me see it. There is nothing else."

"You are young," the woman breathed, but there was a kindling in her eyes. A flare of longing, of ultimate desire. "Can you understand that desire is pain?"

"Play the dove game with me," Daniel said, and it seemed to him that all his life had been leading him to this moment of exquisite pain, agonized desire.

"But you are not the one," the woman said, and with the movement of a striking bird she drew the knife across her throat. Then she laughed as the red mouth widened and her head fell back.

Daniel heard a high-pitched scream and knew it was his.

When Daniel woke he was in jail, having been found lying unconscious on the pavement. Two police came and heard his story. They told him he had been the victim of a scam. He had given the Gypsies all the information they needed to dupe him. They did not say he had been a fool, but it was in their faces. That his wallet had been taken was proof. There was no dead woman, they assured him when he insisted. No body. No permit had been issued for a small Gypsy circus anywhere in the city.

The day of his departure, Daniel went back to the square where the tent had been. There was no sign of it, of course. Only a drift of white feathers in a gutter that might have belonged to the hundreds of roosting pigeons in the building eaves around the square.

It was hot again and he sat down on the edge of a fountain and dipped one hand into the water. His temples pulsed with the heat. Two boys on roller blades sped by. A woman passed, dragging a screaming red-faced child, and then an ambulance clanged past, and then another. Or maybe they were fire trucks. Daniel tried to picture his mother and father and found their faces with difficulty. It seemed to him that they were drawing rapidly away from him, as if he and his parents had boarded two trains going in opposite directions. He felt as if he had begun his journey on the same train but had somehow left and entered another whose destination was unknown.

He thought about the man who had died, and wondered if he had been a Nazi soldier who had interrogated and tortured a child to the point where a sort of madness had fused their lives; or if, somewhere in this city, a woman was mourning the failure of her lover or friend to meet her after a long parting.

He had dreamed of the woman in the antiseptic night; dreamed that she had embraced him in her dove dress, so that he could not feel where her flesh began and the frantic dove trembling began, but when he entered her he had felt her touch as a cool hand, as claws, as a knife.

Had she cut her throat? Had he dreamed it? Had it been a trick? He shivered despite the heat, or perhaps because of it, and told himself that it was time to go to the airport to catch his plane home.

But he thought of the woman in her dove dress and it was as if that image was a monstrous, pale egg that had been planted inside him, and now he must wait for it to hatch.

Tiger Moth

BY GRAHAM JOYCE

Lenny suspected that other lawyers were passing him mad clients. He was known around town for his soft shell, and neither the competition nor his own firm were above abusing his good nature. Not that he hadn't passed over a funny-farm client or a litigious bore himself. That was in the mix, everybody did it if the file got too long or if they were getting through too many cans of air freshener after taking an affidavit. But fair is fair and bad law had to be spread around evenly.

Lenny was a matrimonial solicitor in the Norfolk seaside town of Hunstanton. He occupied an office cluttered with files, framed photographs and obsolete law books belonging to a senior partner who himself occupied a minimalist, dust-free suite across the hall. Plucking up his gold-nibbed fountain pen, a theatrical prop he kept to impress the likes of his present client, Lenny put the question. "Mrs. Grapes, why do you think the man you are living with is not your husband?"

"I already told you. He was very thin when we got married. Slim as a cigarette. I don't know what happened to my real husband. I don't know where this man came from." Mrs. Grapes dabbed her eyes with the tissue Lenny had given her.

"And when did this fatness occur?"

Mrs. Grapes blinked at the question. In truth, Lenny did too. He couldn't remember when in the last dozen years of legal practice he had phrased such a bad question. The fact is he wasn't paying proper attention. He was trying to remember which of his legal "friends" had steered him the case.

Mrs. Grapes, herself thin to the point of a disturbingly translucent skin, shifted on her bony haunches and tried to frame a reply.

"Mrs. Grapes," Lenny said, making it easier for her, "are you absolutely certain that this man is not your husband?"

"I told you already. I married a thin man, not this huge fat person. I want a divorce."

Lenny looked at the door, the window, the small ventilator panel in the upper corner of the room: all the usual means of egress. As Mrs. Grapes outlined her suspicions further, he fought a noisy internal dialogue about how he might tactfully get her out of the room, legally and with kindness.

Whenever Lenny found himself in a legal gray area, a point at which the meaning of the law might have to be massaged to fit, he had a give-away habit of shaping his mouth into an O before speaking. "Mrs. Grapes, if this man is masquerading as your husband, then it's a criminal matter not a civil one."

"Oh?"

"That's correct, Mrs. Grapes. I have to advise you on a point of law that you can't divorce this man because you never married him."

"Oh?"

Lenny got out of his seat and came round the table. "Indeed. You can't go around divorcing people you never married in the first place. And you do after all seem certain he's not the man you married. Mrs. Grapes, what you need is the police. Who will be vigorous in their efforts to help you."

He was already gently raising Mrs. Grapes by her elbow out of her chair and leading her to the anteroom to his office. There the secretary Lenny shared with the firm's senior partner tried to slip a gardening magazine onto her knees. She was known as "the redoubtable Susan," an epithet that baffled Lenny. "Susan, could you look after my client? Mrs. Grapes, my secretary here will give you the number of the police station."

"I will," Susan said, "but I'm very stressed."

Mrs. Grapes, impressed that her case warranted immediate police attention rather than the lumbering machinery of the law, seemed grateful and happy to leave. Lenny closed his office door, sank back in his seat and pulled off his tie.

Moments later Susan walked in without knocking and dumped a pile of new files on his desk. "What's this?" he asked.

"Mr. Falconer is hard-pressed and wanted you to take these extra cases on. You're lucky I brought them. I shouldn't be carrying all of these things, what with my back."

"No, Susan."

After she had left, Lenny made a call.

"Simon, is that job in Nottingham still available?"

Simon had studied law with Lenny at Nottingham Trent University. Lenny was best man at his wedding. Simon's wife Elizabeth was always trying to fix Lenny up romantically. Beautiful, kind Elizabeth, on whom Lenny secretly doted, didn't think a thirty-five-year-old man should still be living with his mother and told him so, often. "I spoke to George only yesterday. Said he's very keen to see you."

"Know what? I've been in this town too long."

"They dump on you, Lenny. What happened now?"

"Nothing. Just don't let Elizabeth see your fat rolls."

After talking to Simon, Lenny put a call through to the Nottingham legal firm of Chortleman & Brace, to arrange an informal lunch date for the following day. Then he asked the redoubtable Susan to rearrange all his morning appointments.

Susan made an unnecessary venting noise. "I will but I'm very stressed." Susan shopped at the same stores as Lenny's mother. She wore long kilts and lacy blouses, and kept a tiny tissue tucked inside her sleeve. Susan hauled herself out of her typing chair and made her kilt swing aggressively as she stepped over to the filing cabinet. The cabinet drawer was rattled open and banged shut. The relevant files thwacked her desk. "Very stressed."

"Yes," said Lenny, "I can see that."

Mrs. Grapes was Lenny's last client of the day. He gathered up the burden of the new files to take home and slipped out of the back door, trying to be discreet as he shuffled across the car park to his Saab. He sat behind the wheel for a moment wondering how he might break the news to his mother that he was considering a job in Nottingham.

"Well, you know best," his mother said.

She'd just served up a familiar dinner of steamed haddock, mashed potatoes and peas. Lenny looked through the steam rising from the fish, saw his mother compress her lips, and regretted blurting out his news. His stomach squeezed. He knew he wouldn't be able to eat one forkful of the meal before him. The worst of all possible responses was to hear his mother say that he, Lenny, knew best. When Lenny knew best, his mother often set her features and said not a single word for several days.

"It's just a preliminary discussion. An exploration. They probably won't even offer me the job."

His mother said nothing to that, hacking at her fish as if it were tough steak.

Lenny and his mother had relocated to the coastal town of Hunstanton shortly after his father had died of an unexpected aneurysm when Lenny was nine years old. His mother couldn't face the old house. It reminded her too much of the husband she'd lost. In fact she hadn't coped too well with the new life either, and Lenny soon became the man of the house, with an emotionally dependent mother. Lenny had missed the opportunity to escape through studying for a law degree. He made the fatal mistake of moving back in with his mother when he was offered a job in his home town. Several years on, Mrs. Pearce still baked and iced cupcakes and sprinkled them with hundreds-and-thousands every Sunday afternoon. Lenny's favorites, she said. She made his cocoa every night at nine-thirty in the evening. Lenny's routine. She washed and pressed all of his clothes for him, and she even pressed his socks. Lenny's preference.

When Lenny had first mentioned the idea of Nottingham, his mother had laid down the fish slice and said, "But think of the commuting time! You'd have to drive right around The Wash and then across the country. All of those winding roads!"

"Well, I'd stay in Nottingham," Lenny had said. Then, too late and unable to save himself, as he saw her stiffen he'd added, "Except for weekends."

Lenny pushed his food around on his plate before retiring to his room. Not fond of the lace frills and cotton flounces and ubiquitous glass ornaments favored by his mother, he often beat a retreat to the sanctuary of his bedroom. There he lay on his bed, hands folded behind his head, staring up at the model airplanes suspended from the ceiling by invisible lengths of cotton.

But Lenny knew best. And while even the sweetest but somewhat possessive mother might say, *Right then, wash and press your own stinky socks, buster, and your shirt and trousers too,* Lenny's mother rose in the morning, still marbled in silence, and laid out his shirt and tie, polished his shoes till they gleamed and brushed down his best dark suit.

Tiger Moth

"It's not an interview, Mum, it's a chat. My jacket will be more comfortable."

"You know best, Leonard." She hung the suit back in his wardrobe, took down the jacket and began to brush it for lint with stiff, downward strokes. Then she held it for him to slip into.

"I'll be back mid-afternoon, Mum."

"As you wish."

Mrs. Pearce opened the door for her son but failed to offer her cheek for the ritual peck. He kissed her anyway and hurried to his Saab. Lenny glanced back before he drove away. His mother, motionless, watched from the window.

His mother was entirely correct about the drive to Nottingham. It was necessary to hug the coastal rode to King's Lynn, through the flat reclaimed land around The Wash before cutting across fen land on the way over to Nottingham. It was a winding drive alongside grassy dikes and irrigation ditches, past muddy reed beds and canals teeming with eels under the open sky of Lincolnshire; a wind-blasted land reeking of brine. It was a land much beloved by Lenny, but which had one day mysteriously become his prison.

At a service station he stopped to fill up the tank, loitering, already early for his appointment. In the washroom he looked hard at his gentle, slightly pudgy features, wondering if he could slim himself down to a completely different person, one who might replace a woman's husband or a mother's son. His hand strayed to the red-and-yellow metal badge pinned to his lapel. He considered removing it, wondering if it made him look childish. But he left it. The badge was, after all, talismanic. It was a badge of a De Havilland Tiger Moth biplane. He'd found it in the grass shortly after he'd moved to the area with his mother almost twenty-five years earlier, on what had been a momentous day.

It was shortly after his father had died and the first time he and his mother had ventured out of their new home together. He'd had to beg her to take him out of a house rattling with his father's ghost, even though his father had never lived there. His mother had trailed the ghost all the way to Hunstanton. She never let a day go by without referring to his father or without making him the standard by which Lenny should measure his life.

Then Lenny hit upon the expedient of saying, "Dad would have liked it." He was learning to fight ghosts with ghosts. So his mother, dragging chains she'd made for herself, had made a brief, nervous drive to the beach. There she sat in a deck chair, knees pressed together, sweltering in a woolen cardigan. She'd made Lenny swear he wouldn't stray too far from the beach, already exhibiting a terror of being left alone out-of-doors, even for an hour.

But Lenny had of course strayed behind the beach and over the dunes to the coastal road. On the other side of the road was a steep grassy dike, and on the dike two boys were beating tremendous fun out of a giant cardboard box. The boys carried the box to the crest of the dike, climbed inside it and then powered themselves down the slope. In a pitch of raucous laughter they were spilled into the dry gully at the foot of the dike before dragging the box back up the gradient and repeating the ride. The boys, both about his own age, made it seem the most uproarious fun a boy could have in the world, and in watching them Lenny felt the deep sting of loneliness.

He ventured across the road.

With another ride imminent, one of the boys shouted from the top of the hill, "There's another Willard, Willard."

"Aye, Willard," said the smaller of the boys. "Looks to me like a Willard, Willard."

"Come aboard, Willard!" shouted the first boy. He beckoned Lenny on.

Lenny looked behind him for someone who might be called Willard. The dunes were utterly deserted and the road was clear. The sun baked down and seemed to move a notch in the sky, as if operated on a ratchet. Lenny squinted back at the boys, whose white shirts flared in the brilliant sunlight.

"Yes, you, Willard!" said the first boy. "Come aboard! We're about to let her rip!'

"Look sharp, Willard," said his companion. "You don't want to miss this!"

Lenny glanced behind him again, stupidly. There was no one there. The two boys were indeed talking to him, gazing down at him, expectant, as if his decision to join them were momentous. Lenny began climbing the steep grassy bank.

"Hurrah, Willard's joining us!"

"Good chap, Willard, climb aboard, plenty of room!"

Lenny panted at the top of the slope. "My name isn't Willard."

The first boy, older with sleek black hair and liquid dark eyes, shouted, "He says his name isn't Willard, Willard."

"Of course it's Willard, Willard." His pal had a wild tousle of brown hair and a face full of freckles. "Jump in, Willard. There's a chap."

Lenny got in anyway. It was a squeeze, but he saw that he could slide his legs around the boy in front.

"Willard's maiden flight!" yelled the dark-haired boy. "Fuel levels?"

"Check," his friend returned.

"Altimeter?"

"Check."

"Confubulator?"

"Check."

"Chokes away!"

They pushed off. The box slipped easily down the slope, propelled by the weight of the three boys. It gathered speed as it went, then as it hit the gully at the bottom it pitched the three boys right out of the box into a clattering, giggling heap.

"All okay, Willard Two?" shouted the slightly older boy.

"Okay," replied the freckled lad.

"Okay, Willard Three?" He stared hard at Lenny.

"Okay."

"Good! Then once more to the breach!"

Everything about the boys' behavior and speech was puzzling, but was compensated for by the scale of hysterical fun afforded by the brief ride in the cardboard box. Even if their phrases belonged to a forgotten time, the warmth and friendly overtures exhibited by the boys was startling in contrast to the usual surliness and hostility common to most boys of that age.

"The new Willard is a good egg, Willard."

"Jolly good egg, Willard."

"My name's not Willard, it's Lenny."

The older boy stopped in his tracks. He set down the box, put an arm round Lenny's shoulder and spoke confidentially. "Look, it's a crashing bore isn't it, when you come on holiday, to learn another chap's name. Far easier if everyone is called Willard. I'm Willard One, my brother is Willard Two, you're Willard Three. Right, Willard?"

Lenny met the boy's swimming dark eyes full on. "Understood, Willard."

"The new Willard catches on fast, Willard."

"Three cheers for the new Willard!"

And after cheers, the cardboard box runs went on and on, and if the baking sun slipped a farther notch in the sky none of the boys noticed. The box runs went on until disaster struck, when Willard One noticed the loss of a pin-badge.

"It must have come off in the grass."

"What's it look like?" Lenny asked.

"It's a biplane. We're going to be fighter pilots when we're grown up. Isn't that right, Willard?"

"Right, Willard."

Lenny wasn't sure what a biplane was but didn't like to ask. As for fighter pilots, his only notion of a career was that his mother had told him he was going to be a doctor or a lawyer. In any event, together the three of them combed the grass without success. And in that time the shadow of the dike crept longer.

Willard One seemed especially depressed at losing his pin-badge, but hunting for it was a lost cause. The search was interrupted when there came the sound of an engine in the sky, approaching from seaward. The three boys looked up. It was an old-fashioned biplane flying low, chugging over their heads, its engine popping, low enough to see the pilot in his leathers.

"It's a De Havilland!" shouted Willard One, as if astonished. "What a stroke of luck!"

"A Tiger Moth!" shrieked Willard Two, barely able to contain his excitement.

Lenny, to whom these words meant nothing, shielded his eyes from the sun and looked up at the double-winged craft soaring overhead.

"But that must be a sign!" shouted Willard Two to his brother. "Don't you see? You just lost a Tiger Moth pin-badge, and then one flies right overhead! It's a sign!"

"By God you're right, Willard!" He turned and watched the biplane chug away from them, trailing clouds of vapor. "We have to follow it!"

The boys ran up over the dike and set off in pursuit of the biplane. "Come on, Willard Three!" one of them called without looking back.

Lenny followed an instinct to scramble up the dike after the boys. He saw them chasing across the flat, reedy land as the plane banked and flew off in the direction of the sun. But Lenny faltered, remembering his mother sitting on the beach. He hesitated on the crest of the dike as the biplane disappeared across the horizon. Lenny heard the boys calling as they ran, saw them scramble up a second dike until they too disappeared behind it.

Lenny waited in an ecstasy of indecision. Too late he decided to go after the boys, but when he reached the crest of the second dike he'd lost sight of them. They were nowhere in the vista before him.

He trudged back to the place where the cardboard box lay abandoned. The sun had become like a burnished coin in the sky and the shadows were long.

Tiger Moth

Lenny tried taking a solo ride down the dike, but now the cardboard box was somehow discharged of all its joy. He felt as though he had missed an opportunity among the lords of life; that he'd allowed his mother to chain him back; that he should have gone when they called, wherever they went and whatever the consequences. Moreover the boys had taken with them the wings of the afternoon and Lenny was left to stand in the cool, creeping shadow of the dike.

But as he put down the box, Lenny found in the grass the lost pin-badge. He kept it as a souvenir, in the hope he might one day encounter the boys again. This souvenir of the afternoon almost compensated for the reception with which his mother greeted him when he returned to the beach.

She turned on him a white-cold fury. "Where have you been?"

"Playing."

"Playing? And didn't it occur to you that I would be sickened and worried senseless while you were playing? And what with your father only dead a few weeks? Didn't it occur to you that I might think you yourself were dead? Didn't it? Didn't it occur to you that I was left here alone? Haven't you anything but selfishness in your heart, Leonard? And your father dead just a few weeks and me alone on the beach! Your father would be ashamed of you. Ashamed. He would never, ever, ever leave me alone like that. Never."

"I'm sorry."

But she'd said her piece. And with that she turned on him a silence that had persisted for several days, and it was a punishment that had lasted Lenny a lifetime. It was a pattern repeated when he'd tried to bring girlfriends into his life, or when he'd tried to take a holiday without her. The ghost of his dead father, ashamed at his nine-year-old son's selfishness, never had to be invoked again.

The informal interview went well for Lenny. Chortleman of Chortleman & Brace had retired and George Brace was shaking loose a few cobwebs. He made it easy for Lenny.

"What fees are you earning over there, Lenny?"

Lenny told him. Brace blinked. "Substantial caseload?"

Lenny described a caseload that some might call backbreaking. Brace blinked again.

"And what are they paying you?"

Lenny told him. Brace blinked a third time and said, "Hell, Lenny, we'll knock that into a cocked hat."

"Serious?"

"I'm sorry to say this but they're laughing at you. We can up that figure by twenty-five percent, plus we've got health and pension plans we stitched in ourselves. I'll be straight: we need you to run matrimonial. Divorce is booming and yet marriage is still fashionable. Everyone's a winner. Plus summer holidays will be over soon and the caseloads rocket after all that togetherness, you know that. We want you, Lenny. Say yes."

"Gosh. I really don't know. I'd have to uproot. It's a lot of fuss."

"Generous relocation package. Full secretarial support. Everything, Lenny."

Lenny promised he'd give it serious thought, and George Brace drove him out to The Millwheel for lunch, where they parked amid the Jags and the Mercs. Over roast duckling and asparagus tips Lenny told George about Mrs. Grapes, whose thin husband had been usurped by a fat husband, and George laughed all over the place.

"That's a funny story," George said.

"Sad, too."

"Yes," George agreed. "Sad too."

Lenny took his time over the drive home. He told himself he wanted to suck in the country air but really he was avoiding having to face his mother. He wanted this job like a bird wants the air but he knew he wouldn't take it. It wasn't the first informal interview he'd been to over the years. He just wouldn't be able to look his mother in the eye and tell her that he was leaving her.

As he drove through the waterlands around the fens the sun began to dip, dispatching shadows from the canals and the dikes. He opened his car window to inhale some of the odor of the baked earth and the muddy silt commingled and he decided it was a good smell. Then as he took the coastal road toward Hunstanton he looked across at a steep dike and what he saw made him stop the car and get out.

Two lads cavorted with a cardboard box on the crest of the dike, with the sun dipping behind them. Silhouetted, they played in the exact spot where he'd encountered those other boys almost a quarter-century earlier. Lenny couldn't repress a laugh of recognition.

He made his way over as they came shooting down the dike in the cardboard box, spilling into the gully in gales of laughter. But when he drew up close, the smile disappeared from his lips. One of the lads had sleek black hair and liquid brown eyes. The other had a tousled brown mop and a face full of freckles. They were sprawled now in the shadow of the dike, suddenly aware of him.

"Boys," Lenny said. "Boys." He was standing in strong sunlight, beyond the reach of the dike shadow. He had to shield his eyes from the low sun.

"What?" one of them asked. "What is it?"

But Lenny couldn't speak. It was too absurd. What could he say? He continued to peer at them from beneath the flat visor of his hand. The boys stepped out of the shadow and into the light. Yet even though he was now but a few steps from them, and though they stood in the full glare of the sun, the boys' features remained disguised in half-silhouette. They were the color of grey slate. A wave of revulsion passed through him.

Then the expression on the boys' faces changed. They looked at him in an ugly manner, suspicious, as if they thought he meant to harm them in some way.

"Look, Willard," said the younger of the two. "He's got your pin-badge."

The older boy got to his feet, his face still dark, squinting at the badge on Lenny's lapel. "You're right, Willard. How come he's got my badge?"

"Willard!" Lenny shouted, fumbling with the pin-badge, trying to remove it so as to hand it back. "That's it! I remember! Willard!"

"He must be a thief, Willard," said the younger boy. "He must have stolen it!"

"No no no!" Lenny protested. "I found it! Right here in the grass! I never stole it!"

The older boy eyed the badge proffered by Lenny. Then he turned and began scrambling up the dike. "Let's get out of here, Willard!"

The second boy followed up the dike. "That's right, Willard. We don't want to hang around among thieves."

Lenny raced after them. "Wait! I didn't steal it! I want to return it. I've had it all this time!" But his shoes slipped on the grassy bank and his knee collided with the turf and twisted. As he got to his feet, Lenny looked back at the road. A car had slowed down to see what he was doing. He knew he must look ridiculous, a grown man scrambling after two boys.

But he went anyway, and when he got to the top of the gradient he could see the boys already disappearing over the second dike. He followed and, just as before, by the time he'd climbed the second dike the boys were nowhere to be seen in the flat, marshy expanse before him. The sun dipped behind trees and the landscape was plunged into shadow, and the temperature dropped palpably. And though Lenny's heart was bursting to follow the boys, some other instinct, some life-preserving reflex told him that he mustn't. But as he gazed across the shadowy marshland, with the yellow sun winking behind the charcoal sketch of trees in the distant wood, he heard a piercing birdlike cry of sorrow.

Back in his car, Lenny sat behind the wheel for some time. An hour passed before, with trembling fingers, he refixed the pin-badge to his lapel, started the ignition and drove home.

"You're later than I expected," his mother said.

"Yes, it went on."

"I thought something had happened to you on the road. I was worried."

"No. I'm fine and dandy."

She served up dinner. It was cottage pie, carrots, and peas, steam billowing upward as she removed it from the hot oven. "I managed to keep this warm. And I've made some gravy."

He peered through the thin cloud coming off the dish, wondering how many dinners of steamed fish and cottage pie he would be made to consume. "Lovely, Mother. It looks lovely."

He ate without pleasure, and after he was done he put his knife and fork together neatly on his plate and said in a quiet, firm voice, "I got offered a job in Nottingham. A very good job. I've decided to take it."

She stood up without a word and made to take his plate away, but Lenny said, "No, Mum, you sit down while I tell you about this. You sit down."

She sat and compressed her lips while he looked her in the eye and told her all about the benefits of the job, about Chortleman & Brace, about his plans and about how often he planned to visit her after he'd made the move.

"You know best," was all she would say.

"Yes," Lenny said. "I do. I really do."

Later he went and lay down on his bed, with his hands behind his head, gazing up at the model airplanes suspended from the ceiling. He knew that the boys had given him a second chance to follow them. Not into the shade, nor into the mudflats stolen from the sea, not into a land of silhouette, no, none of those dark valleys. But somewhere for himself where he might make his own way.

He thought of his future in Nottingham. He thought of the pin-badge; and of the Tiger Moth biplane; and of where the cavorting boys play forever on the crest of the grassy dike and in its creeping shadow.

ABOUT THE AUTHORS

RUSSELL BLACKFORD is a full-time writer and critic based in Melbourne, Australia. His main interests are in philosophy, popular science and fantastic literature (including fantasy, science fiction and horror). Since 1980, he has published many stories, articles and reviews in magazines, journals, anthologies and reference works in Australia, Europe and the U.S. His books include a sword and sorcery novel, *The Tempting of the Witch King*, and the definitive study of Australian science fiction, *Strange Constellations* (co-written with Van Ikin and Sean McMullen). His short fiction has won the Ditmar Award and the Aurealis Award. He has won the William Atheling, Jr. Award for Criticism and Review on three occasions.

RAY BRADBURY is one of the most celebrated authors of our time. His more than thirty books include *Dark Carnival, The Martian Chronicles, The Illustrated Man, The Golden Apples of the Sun, Fahrenheit 451, Dandelion Wine, The October Country, Something Wicked This Way Comes, Long After Midnight, The Halloween Tree, A Medicine for Melancholy, R Is for Rocket, S Is for Space, Quicker Than the Eye, Zen in the Art of Writing, From the Dust Returned*, and the mystery novels *Death Is a Lonely Business, Let's Kill Constance* and *A Graveyard for Lunatics*. The winner of multiple awards in science fiction and fantasy, Bradbury received the National Book Foundation's Medal for Distinguished Contribution to American Letters in 2000.

SIMON BROWN has been writing for thirty years. His short stories have appeared in magazines, anthologies and e-zines in Australia and in the U.S. His latest novel, *Sovereign*, the last book of the *Keys of Power* trilogy, was published in Australia in June 2002. Simon lives with his wife Alison and their two children—Edlyn and Fynn—in Mollymook, New South Wales.

SCOTT EMERSON BULL is a writer plying his dark trade amid the unlikely rural charms of Carroll County, Maryland. His first published story, "Champion of Lost Causes" (*Terminal Fright*, Winter '95) received an honorable mention in *The Year's Best Fantasy and Horror*. Other stories have appeared in the magazines *Gathering Darkness, The Grimoire, Outer Darkness, Nocturnal Mutterings, White Knuckles* and *redsine.com*.

DONALD R. BURLESON's short fiction has appeared in magazines such as *Twilight Zone and The Magazine of Fantasy & Science Fiction*, and in many anthologies. He is the author of the short story collections *Lemon Drops and Other Horrors, Four Shadowings* and *Beyond the Lamplight*. His novel *Flute Song* was shortlisted for the Bram Stoker Award in 1997. Other novels include *Arroyo* and *A Roswell Christmas Carol*. His nonfiction works include *H. P. Lovecraft: A Critical Study, Lovecraft: Disturbing the Universe* and *The Golden Age of UFOs*. Burleson and his wife Mollie live in Roswell, New Mexico, where he is the director of a computer lab at Eastern New Mexico University and a licensed field investigator and research consultant for the Mutual UFO Network.

ISOBELLE CARMODY began her first novel, *Obernewtyn*, in high school and has been writing ever since. She completed a Bachelor of Arts and a journalism cadetship while she finished the novel. Her award-winning *Obernewtyn Chronicles* have established her at the forefront of fantasy writing for young people. She won Book of the Year for her urban fantasy *The Gathering* and received considerable critical acclaim for this and for her collection of short stories, *Green Monkey Dreams*. The title story of that collection won the 1996 Aurealis Award for the best young adult short story. Her novel *Darkfall*, the first in the trilogy *Legendsong*, was shortlisted for the

Aurealis Award for Best Fantasy novel in 1997. In the same year her novel *Greyland* won the Aurealis for Best Fantasy novel in the young adult category. She has also won the 3M Talking Book of the Year Award and the Children's Book of the Year Award for Older Readers. She is currently working on a quartet of very long short stories to be titled *Metro Winds*, which is definitely not for children. She divides her time between Prague in Eastern Europe and her home on the Great Ocean Road in Victoria, Australia.

PETER CROWTHER is an author, editor, critic/essayist, and now, with the acclaimed PS imprint, publisher. He has produced fifteen anthologies, almost a hundred short stories (two of which have been adapted for British TV), plus a handful of limited edition chapbooks, and *Escardy Gap*, written in collaboration with James Lovegrove. *Darkness, Darkness: Forever Twilight Book One*, the first in a projected cycle of SF/horror short novels, has been published by Cemetery Dance Publications. Peter is currently working on the second installment, plus a mainstream novel, a couple of anthologies, several publishing projects and a TV miniseries.

STEPHEN DEDMAN is the author of the novels *The Art of Arrow Cutting* (a Bram Stoker Award nominee), *Foreign Bodies* and *Shadows Bite*. His short stories have appeared in an eclectic range of magazines and anthologies, and thirteen of the best have been collected in *The Lady of Situations*. Stephen lives in Western Australia with his wife and a finite number of cats.

ROBERT DEVEREAUX's short fiction has appeared in *MetaHorror, Weird Tales, Crank!, Love in Vein* and *The Museum of Horrors*. "A Slow Red Whisper of Sand," his extended treatment of vampires human and not-so-human, was shortlisted for the World Fantasy Award. His novels include *Deadweight, Walking Wounded, Santa Steps Out* and *Caliban*. Since 1993, Robert has lived in northern Colorado.

SARA DOUGLASS was born in rural South Australia in 1957. Since then she has chased sheep (she still has the scars), tried her hand at being a Methodist Lady (at which she failed), nursing (which she abandoned), academia (which she abandoned even faster), and finally settled for a life of cultivating her own garden, which she funds with her writing. An internationally bestselling author, her books include the *Axis* trilogy (*BattleAxe, Enchanter,*

Starman), the *Wayfarer Redemption* trilogy (*Sinner, Pilgrim, Crusader*), and the *Crucible* trilogy (*The Nameless Day, The Wounded Hawk, The Crippled Angel*). *Hades' Daughter* is book one of *The Troy Game*.

TERRY DOWLING was born in Sydney in 1947. He completed a BA (Honors) in English Literature and Archaeology and an MA (Honors) in English Literature at Sydney University. He is a professional communications instructor, a freelance journalist, and a musician and songwriter with eight years of appearances on the ABC's popular *Mr. Squiggle and Friends.* The winner of eleven Ditmar Awards, three Aurealis Awards, two Readercon Awards and the Prix Wolkenstein for his fiction, Dowling is a reviewer for *The Australian* and coeditor of *Mortal Fire* and *The Essential Ellison.* He is author of eight books, his most recent being *Antique Futures: The Best of Terry Dowling* and *Blackwater Days.*

GARY FRY was born in 1971 and still lives in his native Bradford, England. He is currently a part-time lecturer and full-time Ph.D. student in psychology (at the University of Huddersfield), and it is his interest in contemporary aspects of this field that informs much of his writing. He regards fiction as suitable a vehicle for his philosophical deliberations—which are existential-phenomenological—as his academic research. Among his literary influences he counts Ramsey Campbell, Stephen King, Roald Dahl, Ruth Rendell, Julian Barnes, Alan Ayckbourn and John Cleese. For some time now, he has been wrestling with Maurice Merleau-Ponty and Martin Heidegger—he doesn't expect to win; two against one is unfair. He is also writing a dark suspense novel entitled *I Witness.* He likes dogs, wine and curry. "Both And" is his first professional sale.

GEORGE CLAYTON JOHNSON is the coauthor of the novels *Ocean's Eleven* and *Logan's Run,* and wrote some of the most memorable episodes of the original *Twilight Zone* series, such as "Nothing in the Dark," "A Penny for Your Thoughts," "A Game of Pool," "Kick the Can," and "The Four of Us Are Dying," as well as scripts for *Kung Fu* and other television shows, including the premier episode of *Star Trek.* His short stories have appeared in *100 Great Fantasy Short Shorts, Author's Choice, Cutting Edge, Masters of Darkness* and *MetaHorror,* and in his own collection, *All of Us Are Dying and Other Stories.*

About the Authors

GRAHAM JOYCE was born in Coventry and is recovering. He actually claims to like the place. He is the author of a book's worth of short stories and several novels, most recently *The Tooth Fairy, Indigo* and *Smoking Poppy*. Four of the novels have won the British Fantasy Award. He lives in Leicester with his wife and two kids.

FRUMA KLASS has published short stories in *Synergy 3*, edited by George Zebrowski, *Writers of the Future Vol. XII* and *Six from PARSEC*. Her husband, Philip Klass, is well known to readers of science fiction as William Tenn, one of the seminal writers in the field.

JOEL LANE lives in Birmingham, England. His tales of the supernatural have appeared in *Darklands, Little Deaths, White of the Moon, Dark Terrors 4* and *5, The Museum of Horrors, The Ex Files, Hideous Progeny, The Third Alternative* and elsewhere. He is the author of a collection of short stories, *The Earth Wire* (Egerton Press); a collection of poems, *The Edge of the Screen* (Arc); and a novel set in the world of post-punk rock music, *From Blue to Black* (Serpent's Tail). Forthcoming books include a second novel, *The Blue Mask* (Serpent's Tail), and an anthology of subterranean horror stories, *Beneath the Ground* (Alchemy Press).

CHRIS LAWSON is a medical doctor with an interest in biotechnology, genetics and information technology. His short fiction has appeared in *Dreaming Down-Under*, as well as *Asimov's Science Fiction, Centaurus, Eidolon*, and both the Dozois and the Hartwell Year's Best anthologies. His work has been translated into French and Czech and optioned for feature film adaptation. "No Man's Land" is his first professional collaboration.

ROSALEEN LOVE has published two short-story collections with The Women's Press (UK): *The Total Devotion Machine* (1989) and *Evolution Annie* (1993). Her work has been included in mainstream as well as science fiction anthologies in Australia, Britain and the U.S., including *Heroines, Millennium, The Art of the Story, Coast to Coast, The Women's Press Book of New Myth and Magic, Alien Shores, Intimate Armageddons, Metaworlds, She's Fantastical, Women of Wonder, Women of Other Worlds, Dreaming Down-Under* and *Earth Is but a Star*. She is always at work on a novel, but all her novels magically transform themselves into short stories at the stroke of midnight. Her most recent book is *Reefscape, Reflections on the Great Barrier Reef*.

STEVE NAGY lives in Ann Arbor, Michigan, with his wife and two daughters. He studied journalism at Kent State University, and worked as a reporter and copyeditor for several newspapers in the Midwest. He currently works as a computer phone support technician at a software company that serves the newspaper and magazine industry. "The Hanged Man of Oz" is his first professional sale.

ADAM L. G. NEVILL was born in Birmingham, England, in 1969, and divided his formative years between Britain and New Zealand. His macabre imagination was nurtured by a father who read him the stories of M. R. James before bedtime. Educated at University College Worcester and the University of St. Andrews, where he studied creative writing, he is also the author of five erotic novels (most with a supernatural flavor). They are published by Nexus under his pen name, Lindsay Gordon. Currently he lives in London, where he writes and works in P.R.

KIM NEWMAN is a novelist, critic and broadcaster. His books include *The Night Mayor, Nightmare Movies, Anno Dracula, The Quorum, Life's Lottery*, and *Apocalypse Movies*. He is working on a novel called *An English Ghost Story*, and various less reputable projects.

MIKE O'DRISCOLL is an Irishman living in South Wales. He is fifteen years into his exile. He writes short stories, some of which have appeared in *The Third Alternative, Interzone, Crime Wave, Albedo One* and a number of anthologies. He writes a regular column on horror for the Alien Online Web site at: *www.thealienonline.net*.

TONY RICHARDS is the author of two novels, *The Harvest Bride* (nominated for a Stoker Award) and *Night Feast*, and has recently completed a third and its sequel. His stories have appeared in such markets as *The Magazine of Fantasy and Science Fiction*, the *Pan Books of Horror*, the Fontana ghost books and *Alfred Hitchcock's Mystery Magazine*. Widely traveled, he often uses the places he has been as locations for his work. He lives in London with his wife.

About the Authors

MICHAEL MARSHALL SMITH is a novelist and screenwriter. His novel *Only Forward* won the Philip K. Dick and August Derleth Awards; *Spares* was optioned by Stephen Spielberg's Dream Works SKG and translated in seventeen countries around the world; and *One of Us* is under option by Warner Brothers. His short stories have appeared in anthologies and magazines around the world, and a collection of his short fiction, *What You Make It* was published in 1999. A fourth novel, *The Straw Men*, appeared in 2002. He lives in North London with his wife Paula and two cats.

AARON STERNS's first published story, "The Third Rail," appeared in *Dreaming Down-Under* and was shortlisted for the 1998 Aurealis Award for Best Horror Short Story. A former editor of *The Journal of the Australian Horror Writers*, Sterns has also presented academic papers on *American Psycho* and *Crash* at the International Conference on the Fantastic in the Arts (as part of PhD work on postmodern horror), written nonfiction articles for *Bloodsongs: The Australian Horror Magazine* and other publications, and is the Australian correspondent for *Hellnotes: The Insider's Guide to the Horror Field*. Sterns is currently working on a number of screenplays and a novel. His story "Watchmen," which was written for this anthology, has been optioned for film. He lives in Melbourne, Australia.

MELANIE TEM has written the novels *Prodigal* (recipient of the Bram Stoker Award), *Blood Moon, Wilding, Revenant, Desmodus, The Tides, Black River* and, in collaboration with Nancy Holder, *Making Love* and *Witch-Light*. In collaboration with Steve Rasnic Tem, she has written the novel *Daughters*, the multimedia project *Imagination Box*, and the chapbook *The Man on the Ceiling*, which won the 2001 Bram Stoker, International Horror Guild and World Fantasy Awards. She is a recipient of the 1991 British Fantasy Icarus Award for Best Newcomer and a 2001–2002 associateship from the Rocky Mountain Women's Institute. She is writing and will direct a full-length play. Also a social worker, she lives in Denver with her husband, writer and editor Steve Rasnic Tem. They have four children and three granddaughters.

STEVE RASNIC TEM's latest short story collection is *The Far Side of the Lake* from Ashtree Press. He is a past winner of the British Fantasy, World Fantasy, Bram Stoker and International Horror Guild Awards. In 2001

About the Authors

Wormhole Books published his novella *In These Final Days of Sales* in hard- and softcover. His most recent novel is the experimental fantasy *The Book of Days* from Subterranean Press.

THOMAS TESSIER is the modest and elusive author of several highly acclaimed novels of terror and suspense, including *The Nightwalker, Phantom, Finishing Touches, The Rapture* and *Father Panic's Opera Macabre*. His novel *Fog Heart* and his collection *Ghost Music and Other Tales* received International Horror Guild Awards. His short stories have appeared in many anthologies. A former editor at Millington Books in London, he now resides in Watertown, Connecticut.

LISA TUTTLE has been writing professionally for thirty years now. She began as a short-story writer, and always loved ghost stories the best, but in recent years, sadly, hasn't been able to write as much in this genre as she would like. In the past few years she has written a number of books for children, and most recently a nonfiction handbook, *Writing Fantasy and Science Fiction* (A&C Black, 2001). She is currently happily in the thick of a new novel, working title *The Mysteries*, and at home on the west coast of Scotland.

TIM WAGGONER is the author of two novels, *Dying for It* and *The Harmony Society*, as well as the short story collection *All Too Surreal*. He has published over sixty short stories in the fantasy and horror genres, and his articles on writing have appeared in *Writer's Digest, Writers' Journal, New Writer's Magazine, Ohio Writer* and *Speculations*. He teaches creative writing at Sinclair Community College in Dayton, Ohio. His homepage is located at www.sff.net/people/Tim.Waggoner.

JANEEN WEBB has won a World Fantasy Award (for *Dreaming Down-Under*), as well as both the Aurealis and Ditmar Awards for her short fiction. She is currently writing *The Sinbad Chronicles*, a series of novels for young readers. Book 1, *Sailing to Atlantis*, was released in Australia in 2001; Book 2, *The Silken Road to Samarkand*, is scheduled for late 2003. Janeen is Reader in Literature at Australian Catholic University, Melbourne.

CHERRY WILDER was born and educated in New Zealand, to which she had recently returned after long periods spent in Australia and West Ger-

About the Authors

many. The author of many short stories, her nine novels include the *Torin* trilogy (*The Luck of Brin's Five, The Neasrest Fire, The Tapestry Warriors*), *The Rulers of Hylor* trilogy (*A Princess of the Chameln, Yorath the Wolf, The Summer's King*), the *Rhomary* series (*Second Nature* and *Signs of Life*), and the horror novel *Cruel Designs*. Some of her stories have been collected in *Dealers in Light and Darkness*. Cherry Wilder passed away in March 2002. She will be missed.

ANDREW J. WILSON was born in Aberdeen in 1963. After studying English Literature and Philosophy at the University of Edinburgh, he went into publishing and currently works as a freelance editor and writer. He is the science fiction, fantasy and horror reviewer for *The Scotsman*. Wilson has published short stories in magazines and anthologies in Britain and the United States, including *Year's Best Horror Stories, Fear, Farpoint, REM* and *Scottish Book Collector*, and he has also read his work on BBC Radio Scotland. *The Terminal Zone*, his play examining the life and work of Rod Serling, will be published in *Great Plays of Horror and Dark Fantasy*. Wilson is currently working on more than one novel-length project.

GAHAN WILSON's cartoons can be mostly seen in *Playboy* and *The New Yorker*, but they have also appeared in publications as diverse as *Punch, Paris Match, The New York Times, Newsweek, The National Lampoon* during its glory years, and *Gourmet*. His cartoons have been gathered up into something like twenty collections. He has written a number of short stories for magazines and anthologies, some of which were recently brought out in the collection *The Cleft and Other Odd Tales*. He has published a variety of children's books including the *Harry the Fat Bear Spy* series and two peculiar mystery novels (*Eddy Deco's Last Caper* and *Everybody's Favorite Duck*). He has recently extended his activities into film and television, and among those so far accomplished are an animated short for 20th Century Fox called "Gahan Wilson's Diner" and a special for the Showtime channel called "Gahan Wilson's The Kid."

ABOUT THE EDITORS

RAMSEY CAMPBELL

The *Oxford Companion to English Literature* describes Ramsey Campbell as "Britain's most respected living horror writer." He has been given more awards than any other writer in the field, including the Grand Master Award of the World Horror Convention and the Lifetime Achievement Award of the Horror Writers Association. Among his novels are *The Face That Must Die, Incarnate, Midnight Sun, The Count of Eleven, Silent Children* and *The Darkest Part of the Woods*. His collections include *Waking Nightmares, Alone with the Horrors* and *Ghosts and Grisly Things*, and his nonfiction is collected as *Ramsey Campbell, Probably*. His novels *The Nameless* and *Pact of the Fathers* have been filmed in Spain.

Ramsey Campbell lives on Merseyside with his wife Jenny and reviews films and DVDs weekly for BBC Radio Merseyside. His pleasures include classical music, good food and wine, and whatever's in that pipe. His Web site is at www.ramsey-campbell.com.

JACK DANN

Jack Dann has written or edited over sixty books, including the international bestseller *The Memory Cathedral*, published in over ten languages and number one on *The Age* bestseller list. *The San Francisco Chronicle* called it "A grand accomplishment"; *Kirkus Reviews* thought it was "An impressive accomplishment"; and *True Review* said "Read this important novel, be challenged by it; you literally haven't seen anything like it." His novel *The Silent* has been compared to Mark Twain's Huckleberry Finn; *Library Journal* chose it as one of their "Hot Picks" and wrote: "This is narrative storytelling at its best—so highly charged emotionally as to constitute a kind of poetry from hell. Most emphatically recommended."

Dann's work has also been compared to Jorge Luis Borges, Roald Dahl, Lewis Carroll, Castaneda, J. G. Ballard and Philip K. Dick. He is a recipient of the Nebula Award, the World Fantasy Award, the Australian Aurealis Award (twice), the Ditmar Award (twice) and the Premios Gilgames de Narrativa Fantastica Award. He has also been honored by the Mark Twain Society (Esteemed Knight). *Bad Medicine* (retitled *Counting Coup* in the U.S.) has been described by *The Courier Mail* as "perhaps the best road novel since the *Easy Rider* days." His latest book is the retrospective short story collection *Jubilee*, which *The West Australian* called "a celebration of the talent of a remarkable storyteller." He is also the coeditor of the groundbreaking anthology of Australian stories, *Dreaming Down-Under*, which won the World Fantasy Award in 1999.

Jack Dann lives in Melbourne, Australia, and "commutes" back and forth to Los Angeles and New York. His Web site is at www.eidolon.net/jack_dann.

DENNIS ETCHISON

Dennis Etchison has been called "the most original living horror writer in America" and "the finest writer of psychological horror this genre has produced." His stories have appeared in numerous periodicals and anthologies since 1961. Some of the best known are included in his collections: *The Dark Country, Red Dreams, The Blood Kiss, The Death Artist, Talking in the Dark* (a retrospective volume marking the fortieth anniversary of his first professional short story) and Fine Cuts. The title story of the first volume won the World Fantasy Award in 1982 (tied with Stephen King), as well as the British Fantasy Award that same year—the first time one writer received both major awards for a single work. He is also a novelist (*The Fog, Darkside, Shadowman, California Gothic, Double Edge*) and editor (*Cutting Edge, Masters of*

Darkness I–III, MetaHorror, The Museum of Horrors) and has received two additional British Fantasy and World Fantasy Awards (1993). Other novels include the bestsellers *Halloween II, Halloween III,* and *Videodrome,* all written under the pseudonym "Jack Martin."

Etchison also writes magazine articles, film reviews and scripts, including screenplays for John Carpenter and Dario Argento. He served as staff writer for the HBO television series *The Hitchhiker,* adapted the original *Twilight Zone* TV series for radio and was president of the Horror Writers Association (HWA) from 1992 to 1994. His latest books include *Got to Kill Them All and Other Stories* (CD Publications).